# UNKNOWN COUNTRY

*Also by Audrey Slaughter*

PRIVATE VIEW
BLOOMING

Audrey Slaughter

# UNKNOWN COUNTRY

**Doubleday**

LONDON · NEW YORK · TORONTO · SYDNEY · AUCKLAND

TRANSWORLD PUBLISHERS LTD
61–63 Uxbridge Road, London W5 5SA

TRANSWORLD PUBLISHERS (AUSTRALIA) PTY LTD
15–25 Helles Avenue, Moorebank, NSW 2170

TRANSWORLD PUBLISHERS (NZ) LTD
3 William Pickering Drive, Albany, Auckland

Published 1994 by Doubleday
a division of Transworld Publishers Ltd

All of the characters in this book
are fictitious, and any resemblance
to actual persons, living or dead,
is purely coincidental

A catalogue record for this book is available from the British Library

ISBN 0385 405073

Printed in Great Britain by Biddles Ltd, Guildford and King's Lynn.

For Charles Wintour
Michael and Sally
with love

# Chapter One

Inside the slightly lopsided front door of the cottage Douglas dropped the suitcases, sniffed pleasurably and heaved a sigh of contentment. 'It was a wonderful hol, darling, but it's even more wonderful to be home.' He kissed her. 'I've never been happier.' He picked up their cases again and as he started to take them upstairs said over his shoulder, 'Why does a cuppa seem so inviting after all that delicious food and wine? I always miss it.'

'I can take a hint,' Jill turned towards the kitchen.

She found him ten minutes later kneeling awkwardly beside their bed, a suitcase still in either hand, his head half turned into the duvet. The windows hadn't been opened whilst they were away and the bedroom had a dry airlessness. She stared at Douglas, at his buckled body and the way his right elbow stuck out making a rigid triangle, the hand convulsed on the handle of her blue suitcase.

Her mind, always so quick, refused to take in the implication of the scene and for a minute disbelief suspended emotion. Then a sudden shocking anger got the better of her. He couldn't do this to her! It was a joke. She wanted to shake him violently, tell him he had a misplaced sense of humour, but she couldn't go near. Her breath seemed trapped inside her chest and there was a curious singing in her ears. She put out her hand and felt the solidity of the bedroom door and gripped its hard edge, welcoming the pain as the sharp angle cut into her palm. She sank to her knees beside the still figure. She'd read somewhere that you should hold a mirror up to the nose and mouth to see if there was any breath. She scrambled clumsily to her feet again to snatch a mirror from the dressing table. Not the slightest mist clouded the cold glass surface. She felt for his wrist, but because her own hand was trembling she couldn't tell if there was a pulse.

'Douglas please, please Douglas, wake up!' Her own involuntary scream frightened her and she ran out of the room.

A reflex mechanism took over so that even with the icy hands she could punch out Roger Mander's number. 'He must come at once!' she screamed at the indifferent receptionist who attempted to tell her Dr Mander was busy. 'My husband is dead. He must do something.' Jill's mouth was trembling uncontrollably and she started to sob.

She ran upstairs again. She'd made a mistake. She must have. But she stopped just inside the door, staring at the horror of the still figure, wrapping her arms round her body in an attempt to stop the shivering.

He'd been so fit and well on holiday. She was the one who'd been ill. That's why they'd taken a whole month, so that she could recover from a bad bout of flu. He'd outpaced her swimming. And it was he who had always suggested the long climbs up steep hills to obscure monasteries or tiny hidden villages. He was the one who'd hired the *velos* and raced her all the way. This couldn't be real.

She thought if she stared long enough at the small mole on the side of Roger's face she wouldn't hear him telling her the truth. She wasn't ready. She concentrated on the way the mole moved slightly as he talked, didn't he realize the hairs in his nostrils needed clipping, that the shirt button under his tie was missing?

'You've got to make him better.' Her voice had the mulish obstinacy of a disobedient child.

'I'm sorry, Jill. You know there's nothing I can do. Look, I'm going to make you a cup of tea.'

'I was just making Douglas one,' she said mechanically. The shivering took over again as she let herself be led to the kitchen, her teeth rattling.

Roger guided her to a chair and got a coat from the hall cupboard. He looked anguished, unexpectedly helpless, as if he could think of nothing of comfort.

The coat was an old one of Douglas's and Jill clutched it about her, overcome by the human whiff of his sweat, willing it to contain the warm strength of her husband's familiar body. She looked at the two cups she'd put on the tray a lifetime ago and watched Roger empty the pot of stewed tea she'd made, his hand clumsy, as he peered in the fridge for milk.

8

'The jug's already there, on the tray.' She stared at him as if he was stupid. 'Mrs B ordered the milk. She knew when we'd be back. He wanted tea. I'd put everything ready. I called to him but he didn't come down.' Her voice was dreamy as if she was in some other world, half asleep. 'I thought he hadn't heard so I went up.' Her lips stiffened into silence.

'He didn't suffer, Jill. It was very quick.'

She fixed sightless, uncomprehending eyes on Roger Mander's face. 'He was so well,' she whispered.

The ridiculous coffin dominated the small church, hard and stiff. It mesmerized Jill. How could such a large, animated man be tidied away so swiftly? How did they turn him into such a neat, anonymous parcel? She couldn't reconcile the ugly wooden shape with the man she knew. The chill church and the scent of chrysanthemums gave her a sense of unreality, as though she were watching an old-fashioned film. She felt the unfamiliarity of Diane's arm press uncomfortably through hers, the fingers clutching on the soft part above her elbow as Tom Feathers, Douglas's literary agent, spoke from the pulpit. He recorded his affection and regard for Douglas, recalling his work, saying how Douglas would have chosen to die like this, at the height of his powers and enveloped by the happiness he had found with Jill. What an absurd thing to say, she wanted to cry out. There was so much else they had wanted to do together. How could he possibly have wanted to die just then!

She didn't really know Douglas's daughter. Diane had been cold and hostile when they'd first met, then dutiful at their wedding, and cool and offhand on the few occasions the three of them had had dinner together since. She had never come down to the cottage. Jill glanced at the beautiful face. It was impassive, closed-off and Jill couldn't tell what she was feeling. She was grateful for the girl's seeming calm and unemotional presence in the austere chapel. It gave her a standard to reach for when all her instincts told her to throw herself on the floor and howl.

People, mostly mutual friends from London, came up to her afterwards to say kind things, awkward and embarrassed at the sight of her pale face and blank eyes. They too obviously longed to get away from the hush of muted voices and leave behind their own stilted behaviour. There was nothing natural about a sudden death, particularly the death of a man they had known for his geniality, and a readiness to break into laughter.

'Nice part of the world this,' Tom Feathers looked down at Jill, his eyes kind and sympathetic. 'Frank Huxtable, you know the drama critic of *The World*, has a place somewhere near here . . . have you met him?'

'No.'

'Douglas knew him quite well. I think they were both young journalists on something like the *Daily Mail* or the *Daily Express* once. I'd have thought Douglas would have looked him up when you moved here.'

'We've been so busy on the cottage . . .' Her voice trailed away bleakly. We didn't want anyone else, she thought. We were happy just being together.

'I'll give him a ring when I get back to town, tell him you're here. I don't suppose you know many locals?'

'Hardly any.' She and Douglas had treasured the late joy of unexpected love. There had been a hunger about their relationship, a feverish greed. It had taken them so long to find this sense of peace, this confident assumption that each wanted nothing more than to be with the other, that they hadn't wanted to waste time in empty socializing.

'Well it's a bit remote from your sort of world isn't it? I don't suppose there's much fashion down here.' Tom gave a short uncomfortable laugh.

She stared at him, trying to speak, her mind filled with the obscenity of the last hour. How could he mention her work in this context? It seemed so long ago, so trivial in comparison. She felt a hundred years old, unutterably weary. She clenched her cold hands. Poor man. He was doing his best.

'Thank you for the things you said about Douglas.' Her own voice sounded far away and she heard Diane take charge.

'I'm Diane, Douglas's daughter,' the girl said evenly to Tom. 'You were very kind. Won't you come back for some tea, a drink?'

'Thanks, if you don't mind I won't. We're frantic – just back from the Book Fair. You know how it is.' He cleared his throat, relieved at Diane's appearance. 'Douglas was one of the best,' he looked away, his eyes unexpectedly gleaming with tears. 'I shall miss him.' He clamped his lips together, trying to control the trembling of his chin and squeezed Jill's arm. 'Come and stay with Gem and me, get back to your London life for a day or two. A change will do you good.'

Jill gazed at him uncomprehendingly as Diane, smiling politely, answered for her, 'She can't make plans just yet.'

'Of course. Too soon. Stupid of me.' Tom Feathers touched Jill's shoulder and turned to go. 'Take care now,' he smiled slightly and left, relief showing in the quickness of his step as he got into his car.

Gus, the Mortimers' jobbing gardener, was standing awkwardly next to Mrs B, their daily, both unfamiliar in sober Sunday best clothes.

'Won't you come and have a cup of tea?' Jill asked them, parroting Diane's words. They looked embarrassed and she didn't press them. She didn't really want anyone to come back. She struggled to thank Gus and Mrs B for attending.

'You'm mind now, tek care of yoursen.' The thin strands of his hair stuck up as Gus pulled off his cap.

Jill moved on to Roger and Miriam, virtually the only other folk she knew in the village. How would she manage without Douglas? A sob rose in her throat and she panicked, wanting to get away before she made a scene. She was grateful for someone bundling her into a car, for Diane's silent support. It would soon be over. Once she was away from the crowd, she could cope.

But a few people accompanied them to the cottage after all, a ghoulish reluctance to lose the vicarious experience of grief. Jill dreaded getting out of the car; the effort to be polite, appear normal, was crushing her. To hell with stiff upper lips! She wanted to rant and rage. It was all so unfair. She gazed with resentment at a man who said he'd done the script of Douglas's first film. He was clearly older than Douglas, why should *he* be alive and well? She turned away from a woman who said she'd been at Oxford with Douglas, and who seemed anxious to reminisce. Jill disliked her for knowing him before she had. She wanted to snatch back the wasted years before they'd met. The frustration tumulted inside her, but her face remained a pale mask. Her own voice sounded unfamiliar, a stranger's voice, as she forced herself to respond to the half-finished sentences, jollying tones. She was conscious of Diane following her around, controlled and polite, stepping in when needed.

'You'll go back to London now of course,' Diane said later, standing outside the cottage, as she prepared to leave.

'I suppose so.' Jill's response was automatic, listless. What could she do here, alone?

The few faces which regularly cropped up in the small shops flanking the one village street, she greeted with polite smiles or nods of recognition, but neither she nor Douglas had tried to break into the community. In London they'd known almost too many people, so that sometimes the social pace had been too hectic especially as they each worked so hard. That was another reason why Douglas had urged the move. 'I've got to the stage where I want a quieter life.' But he had smiled to show he didn't really believe he was getting older.

As Diane backed her narrow hips through the low door of a black sports car, and swung her legs gracefully under the steering wheel, she wound down the window. 'Tom was right,' she said abruptly. 'Daddy was at last a happy man.' She pressed her lips together as if she had said too much and looked straight ahead as she turned the ignition key.

Jill stared helplessly at her young profile, unable to speak, feeling the press of tears. She wanted to say, *Stay. Don't leave me alone.* But she forced a little smile.

'I'll give you a ring,' Diane said again, diffidence puncturing her sophistication.

'Please.' Jill wished she knew her stepdaughter better. 'I couldn't have got through today without you.' She put her hand through the open window to squeeze Diane's slender shoulder.

The girl had said little, shown no emotion, but she'd behaved impecccably. Was she close to her mother wondered Jill? She'd given a short, sarcastic laugh on the phone when asked if her mother would wish to come to the funeral. 'That's the last thing she'd do!'

# Chapter Two

The next day felt unreal. Jill wandered round the empty cottage, trying to force it to respond, to turn again into the home the two of them had made together. But it seemed inert, indifferent, no longer impregnated by Douglas's loud, joyful bark of a laugh, his habit of singing old Fifties hits when he was pottering, or yelling from bedroom or bathroom for his socks or mislaid sweater. Even his study, his first old typewriter kept sentimentally side by side with the gleaming state-of-the-art computer, looked characterless − although nothing had been moved. Jill looked curiously at the name on the book jackets: Douglas Mortimer. Fear clutched her. She couldn't visualize him: not as the enthusiastic lively man she'd married just over three years ago. The only image she could conjure up was that horrific crumpled figure, clutching the suitcases, collapsed against the bed. Where was he? And what was she doing here without him?

She rushed downstairs, sobbing, frantically scrabbling through the cupboard for Douglas's coat. She pulled it across her shoulders and blundered out of the cottage. He must be about somewhere. It was all just a hideous dream! She started to run down the lane, stumbling over the ruts, crying and calling, oblivious of the silence and the soft drizzle that had started. She rushed across the narrow stone bridge over the river and ran heedlessly up the steep hill that was overhung with trees, unconscious of where she was heading until a stitch in her side forced her to stop. Her breath was coming with heaving sobs and she leant against a tree trunk, her feet tangled in long wet grass, to recover. She put her arms into the sleeves of Douglas's coat and started to move again.

It was only four o'clock but it was already getting dark and the drizzle had turned to a steady rain. The trees waved their threatening black arms at her, shutting out what little grey daylight was left. Once someone went by on a bicycle and called out to her but she didn't respond. She was unaware of her surroundings, driven only by the need to find Douglas, for him to tell her she'd been dreaming, for the sound of his laugh.

She walked and walked, ignoring the pain in her chest, slipping and stumbling blindly until she met her match in the prickly branches of an overgrown hawthorn hedge. Her hair caught painfully in the sharp twigs, and she cried out in terror and rage, jerking her head sharply to free it. But then she slipped on the wet grass of a steep ditch and lurched headlong into its depths. Winded for a few moments, she tried to pull herself together and scramble out but the side was deceptively deep and she sank back defeated, brooding in the dark and wet as the significance of yesterday came back. It was no good. Douglas was dead. He wouldn't be back. Tiredness made her shut her eyes and lean back against the muddy wall of the ditch. What did it matter? She'd just lie here and let Nature take its course. How long did it take to die she wondered? Her knee was throbbing but she felt almost a comforting sense of irresponsibility: there was nothing she could do about it. There was only a little water in the ditch, choked with grass and weeds, but she felt it seeping through her woollen skirt.

She must have stayed like that for twenty minutes or more, sunk in oblivion. It was the excited yapping of a mean-faced little terrier that roused her. She was no country woman but she knew terriers were hunters. And whilst she didn't mind slipping into damp unconsciousness, she didn't want to be mauled to death. She tried to sit up, to shout at the sharp nose that had appeared at eye level amidst a frenzied yapping.

'What the hell are you doing down there?' It was a country voice, male, and a lamp shone in her eyes blinding her. 'Sit Trigger! Quiet.' The terrier obediently sat, his eyes gazing eagerly at her in the lamplight when not glancing appealingly at his master to cancel the frustrating instruction.

A large hand grasped hers. 'Can you walk?'

Jill nodded sheepishly, blinking in the glare of the beam. 'I fell in,' she said unnecessarily.

'Come on out now. Pull on me. My Lord, you're wet through! How long have you been there?'

Jill shrugged. 'I don't know. I hurt my knee, and I seemed to drift off.'

'Are you sure you can walk? Nothing broken? You'd better come along to the missus and dry off. You need something hot to drink, you're shivering. God bless my soul, what a night to be out . . .' He slipped his arm under hers and half supported her along the wet rutted lane. 'Where were you heading for? There's not much up here. Only the farm and my cottage. I'm the dairyman.'

'Just walking.' She was shuddering, her wet skirt clung to her thighs, her knee hurt, and she felt foolish and embarrassed.

The man's wife jumped up from her chair by an old-fashioned kitchen range, dropping her knitting at the sight of Jill's dripping hair and blotched face. She cast a half-reluctant look at the television set and turned to her husband. 'You gave me a fright, George. Whatever's up?'

'Look what I found in the ditch downside,' came the reply. His eyes snapped with curiosity. 'Tek her up to dry off. I'll mek some tea.'

'I'm sorry,' Jill mumbled upstairs, as she rubbed her hair and accepted a large, hideously patterned jumper and a voluminous skirt. 'I got lost. And then I tripped or something.' She bunched the skirt to her waist with her own belt.

'Where d'you come from then?'

'Compton Hill, just outside Sherville.' Jill couldn't meet the woman's eyes.

'Goodness gracious pet, that's more'n nine miles away. How ever did you walk all this way in the rain? Whatever for?'

'I don't know. I couldn't stop I . . .' Jill suddenly sat on the bed and put her face in her hands.

'There, there, don't worry. You've had a fright I dare say. D'you know the Baxters? They live on Compton Hill, Treetops, she married my cousin.'

'That's further up. I don't know them no, but I've noticed the cottage. We're right at the bottom of the hill. The last cottage before the bridge.'

'I know the one.' She nodded. 'It was empty for some time. Shall I phone your husband?'

'He's not there. He's not coming back.' Jill shook her head, unable to say more, tears seeping through her fingers.

'Oh, I see.' Her changed tone made it clear she believed Jill's husband had left her. 'Don't you worry, pet. George will tek you back. He knows the way. I'll tek your things down to dry off a bit whilst you have a nice cuppa. Then you'll feel better.'

She bustled off and Jill heard her subdued tones explaining things to her husband. She peered at her reddened eyes in the poor light of the small bedroom mirror and tried to pull herself together. How could someone as unflappable as she had always been lose control in front of perfect strangers? She felt ashamed and tried to pat and push her hair into some semblance of order.

Diffidently she made herself go down and face George and his kindly wife again. The steaming mug of strong tea was so hot it made her eyes water, but she sipped it, feeling the liquid slide down her throat, penetrating the sodden chill inside. She was grateful that they had left the television switched on, an excuse not to look at her, embarrass her.

'If you could call a taxi I won't disturb you any longer,' Jill said politely.

'Taxi? Ha! You won't get a taxi come up here this time o'night. It's after nine. I'll run you back. I knows the cottage. Coupla old ladies used to live there, kept goats din't they?'

'I believe so. Thank you for the tea, and for rescuing me. D'you think my things are dry now?'

'You wear what you've got on, pet, and I'll get George to drop your'n when he next comes your way. He often drives into Sherville. And get a doctor to look at that knee – I see upstairs it was swelling already.'

'I expect it's only a bruise. The ground was soft with rain.'

Once back in her own cottage, Jill paused as she took a couple of paracetamol. How many made a fatal dose she half wondered? But she was too cold and shivery, despite the central heating, to do anything as positive as counting out tablets; she was tired, her bones ached and her head felt muzzy. She dragged another blanket from the cupboard and miserably climbed into bed, wincing as she put pressure on her knee. If she could just sleep and not wake up, how easy it would be!

# Chapter Three

Roger Mander had treated Jill for the virulent attack of flu she'd had in the summer. He'd been thrilled to discover Douglas was Douglas Mortimer, almost as abashed as a small boy meeting his hero. He'd read all Douglas's books and had seen the three films made from them. He'd called several times; more, Jill teased, to yarn with Douglas than check on her progress. The two men usually ended up having a drink together. And then when Jill was back on her feet, Roger had asked them to dinner. Jill had liked his wife Miriam instantly, her broad rather plain face enlivened by a sweet smile and a sharp pair of small brown questioning eyes. She had reminded Jill of a robin by the way she quizzically tilted her head and by her neat, quick movements. She was a midwife and Jill could imagine her inspiring local mothers to fresh efforts as they heaved away in childbirth.

They had fallen into an easy informal habit of having dinner together from time to time, though once Miriam had also invited another couple: Faith and Humphrey Cruze. Afterwards Jill and Douglas had laughed at the Cruzes' gushing; the sharp eyes of Faith appraising and pricing Jill's clothes once she knew she'd been a fashion buyer, and the way both had struggled to hide how impressed they were by Douglas's fame and similarly, to conceal the fact that they hadn't read any of his books.

'They're all right,' Miriam had said the next day. 'Not exactly my cup of tea but no harm in them. I thought that once you got on to Faith's social circuit, you'd meet people round here; I'm not up to the sort of considered entertaining she does. She actually has a hostess book in which she faithfully records her dinner parties and what she serves – sorbet between courses and flower petals in the finger bowls sort of thing – so you can see I'm not in her class.'

'Douglas and I don't want to meet too many people,' Jill had replied. 'One of the reasons we moved here was to get away from a busy social life.'

'Ah,' Miriam had said. 'That's something difficult to do in a village. Besides, now Faith knows Douglas is famous she'll regard him as a catch – you won't escape!' And it was true. Faith had telephoned regularly, asking them to dinner, cooing as if Jill was her best friend, clutching her with glad cries whenever they bumped into each other in the village. But after suffering a couple of excruciatingly formal evenings, Jill had managed to be firm, explaining Douglas's need to be quiet when he was in the middle of a book. 'Soon, when it's finished, we'd love to come again,' she'd lied.

Jill woke late next morning, and lay there in the fuzzy warmth, detached and half dozing. Her head ached and her knee sent a sear of pain through her when she stretched out her leg. Her eyes lighted on the beautifully wrapped parcel from the French shop where she'd bought some hand-blown candle-holders. They were unopened, just as she'd dumped them after that terrible return from holiday. She winced as she remembered how pleased Douglas had been when it was she who'd been eager to return to the cottage, the car loaded with beautiful things she'd bought for it on their travels. He'd laughed at her extravagance, encouraged her spending, glad of this sign that she seemed to be reconciled to living in the country.

She, a dyed-in-the-wool urbanite, had never lived anywhere but a convenient London flat, and foreign hotels, as she'd whizzed to and from the fashion collections. She'd resisted Douglas's pleadings for them to move from his lovely house in St Leonard's Terrace to the country. 'What would I *do* there? I have to be in London for my job.'

'Give it up,' Douglas had urged. 'We don't need the money. I miss you when you're away.'

'I can't! Fred's would go to pieces.'

Jill had built up Fred's from an anonymous little dress shop in the Fulham Road full of cheap, fussy separates, and frocks that were sequinned to within an inch of their lives. She'd created a cornucopia of elegant boutiques sprouting inter-national designer labels like a *Who's Who* of fashion. She had added a special range of their own, under the label 'Freda', integrated and stylish, so that well-heeled women shopped at Fred's first. Fred Rosomon, who had bribed her from Bostons, the store where she'd been an eager young fashion buyer, shrewdly put her under contract as they expanded into the hardware shop next door, the radio and television rental firm and even a neighbouring butcher's. On her tenth year with Fred's, with everything going so well, he'd made her a director.

At the start of those years, Jill's first husband had given up trying to compete with her job and he'd left her for a chatty little blond secretary running to fat. Jill had felt nothing but relief at the time. She could concentrate on the work she loved instead of feeling guilty about a husband she didn't. Respect for her unerring fashion eye had grown, and there was little surprise in the trade when Jill had been asked to dress the film *White Meadows*.

She'd been introduced to Douglas in the producer's office and had been attracted to him instantly. He'd asked her to dinner on the pretext that he wanted Jill to understand the main character of his book and how important it was to bring out her personality with her clothes. 'Like Annie Hall,' he'd smiled.

She couldn't believe that at thirty-nine she could fall in love, virtually for the first time. She'd long ago realized that her earlier marriage had been built on transient sexual attraction and a desire to leave the dull comfort of her parents' house. Even more unbelievable was the fact that Douglas felt the same way about her. 'I knew as soon as I saw you that if I didn't grab you there and then I would regret it for the rest of my life,' he had told her a little later. Not only did Douglas seem the most enchanting man in the world but he was free. His own marriage was in the process of being wound up by mutual consent. His wife, a dedicated culture-vulture and self-styled intellectual looked down on the bestselling novels he wrote. Constant criticism and sarcasm at home had at first produced in him a polite indifference; and then, as she openly and publicly derided his 'facile popularity', an angry hostility. Three years ago, as soon as Douglas's divorce was final, he and Jill had married.

Jill had been amused at the way Douglas gradually stepped up his let's-get-out-of-town campaign. Copies of *Country Life* appeared on the coffee table, opened at alluring country homes, elegant and spacious or cosily thatched and creeper-covered, against a backdrop of perpetual blue skies. The city where he too had always lived and worked now openly irritated him. 'There's no grace here any more,' he would sigh heavily, returning home from a visit to his agent or publisher. 'Why are people always eating in public – the tube tonight seemed like a mobile works canteen.' Or he'd moan about taxi drivers. 'They never say a pleasant word. They used to be such chatty and amusing characters. The one I had this evening was deliberately unhelpful. The city is getting to them. His radio was blaring away whether I liked it or not.' And, 'Have you seen the filth in the streets?' he'd demand, glaring. 'Bins overflowing with rubbish outside those terrible fast-food places!'

His simulated gloom went on until Jill struck a compromise. Why not find somewhere just for weekends where they could recharge? Morosely, he'd agreed, cheering only when they'd both fallen in love with the cottage, so unlike the immaculate coffee-table illustrations. It had been empty for eight years, the windows dirty and broken, the plastered walls cracked and stained. It was built straight on to the earth, and the floor in what must have been the living room was flagged and thick with moss.

'Rather pretty actually,' Jill had laughed, pointing out the natural carpet. The garden was so rampant with elder, chest-high tangles of bramble and fierce thickets of nettles, that they'd had to take the estate agent's word for it that there was indeed a river flowing along the bottom.

'Stretches the imagination a bit to describe it as "flowing",' Jill had laughed when, after several backbreaking weekends, Douglas had hacked a rough path to the riverbed where some sluggish water struggled to ooze past the choke of fallen trees and thick reeds. 'But look at our view!' he'd shouted, trium-phantly. 'Just get this bank cleared and we can have a little summerhouse down here, sit and watch the sunset. Perhaps there are trout – or ducks.'

Jill had been seduced at the prospect of converting the cottage, knocking the tiny rooms into one, re-siting the steep staircase covered with worn linoleum that opened straight out of a cupboard in the living room. The aspect was good, the basic structure had survived nearly three hundred years of weathering and was sound, there were distinct possibilities. And it had seemed like fun at first, as they harried their solicitor to rush the sale through, fought the local authority for planning permission to build an extension. But they hadn't realized how much hindrance and hard work was entailed, *too* much work on top of a demanding week in town.

They'd stayed in a pub in the village two miles away to begin with, whilst they attempted to clear the garden, brief a firm of builders, and look for sources of old stone so that the extension would fit in gracefully. They'd driven miles touring demolition yards to find the oak planks Jill wanted for the new floors, buoyed up by triumph when they found an oak staircase complete with curved balusters that only needed two risers removed to fit. But there were disappointments and delays too. Jill battled with the builders to remove broken flagstones and use the best ones to renovate the kitchen floor. 'They think I'm mad,' she told Douglas. 'The foreman thinks I should have nice washable vinyl tiles.'

During the week they had to bully the builders by telephone. Each weekend was an exercise in frustration as empty Coke cans and cigarette packets revealed a builder's presence but not much progress. The stove stood miserably unconnected in the middle of the kitchen floor, pipes gaped from rough holes in the walls.

Overtired, depressed by yet another setback in the progress, they'd had a row. 'If you'd give up your silly job we could get things moving,' Douglas had burst out. 'What difference does it make to life if fashion styles change? It's so trivial.'

'Hah! You didn't think that when you wanted me to dress *White Meadows*!'

They'd had a circuitous argument about the importance of fashion and driven home in glum silence.

Then, on a day when Fred's seemed pointlessly frenetic, Rosomon was gloomy about last season's sales figures and a magazine had lost the Norma Kamali suit they'd borrowed for a shoot, Jill made up her mind. Why spend hours in arid little showrooms trying to pick the sales winners from a proliferating list of new designers, why spend all her days striving to make each year's turnover a record? She could make the cottage so attractive if she only had time to pore over fabrics and paint samples, go to auctions and antique shops. She was nearly forty-two, Douglas was sixty-one; wasn't it more sensible to enjoy time together? They'd met far too late, why waste any more life racing about and bickering over where to live?

'All right! You win,' she'd told Douglas. 'I'll tell Rosomon I'm taking a six-month sabbatical and we'll see how it goes. But if I feel like a displaced town mouse, we go back to weekending only. Fair?'

'Fair,' Douglas assented.

And Jill hadn't missed Fred's, at least not once she'd plunged into home decorating, haunting furniture sales. Douglas was right: things had moved quickly once they were on the spot. The derelict little cottage warmed to life. A farm a few miles away was bulldozing the remains of an old stone barn to make way for a new corrugated iron silo, and they'd paid the bemused man £300 for the stone to build an L-shaped extension to the cottage. 'We can pave the ground between the two walls and eat here in the summer. That new bit cuts off the wind. It'll be a sun-trap!' Jill had exulted.

Douglas discovered an enthusiasm for gardening. 'Sign of age,' he'd say cheerfully as he trudged outside in his gumboots. Before the end of the six months, Jill told Fred Rosomon she wasn't coming back, deaf to all his desperate blandishments.

She donned a dressing gown and walked painfully downstairs to the kitchen. What was she to do with herself? She fiddled with things in the larder as she waited for the kettle to boil, filing jars and tins into some sort of order . . . tomatoes and artichoke hearts; beans and lentils; rice and pasta. But who would eat it all?

She eyed the condolence letters she'd shoved on the dining-room table. Some were from people who didn't know Douglas but were eager to tell her how much his books had meant to them. Some were from friends of his before she'd known him. She knew they meant to comfort her but all they did was underline that he was no longer there. The kettle shrilled and she took a tray of tea up to her room and got into bed again. What was there to get up for?

It was Mrs B who made her get up. Mrs B who on Wednesdays always came in the afternoon because she helped run the Women's Institute market in the morning. 'There's George Morrish downstairs with a plastic bag of your clothes. Said you left them to dry. Whatever have you been up to? Says you have some of his wife's.' Her sharp eyes darted around the bedroom. 'Are these hers? I'll wrap them up.'

'No, no. I must have them cleaned. I must thank him. Ouch!' She tried to stand on the leg with the swollen knee. 'Hand me my camel skirt Mrs B, please, and a sweater. Hurry, I mustn't keep him waiting.'

Jill hobbled downstairs, anxious to show that she wasn't the same madwoman who'd been picked out of a ditch last night.

'You're all right? Haven't caught cold then?' the concerned, kindly face gazed at her. 'Mildred was sure you would. Soaked through, you was.' George Morrish turned to Mrs B as she followed Jill into the kitchen. 'Just below our cottage, in a ditch. Trigger thought she was a badger,' he guffawed.

Jill hastily protested that she was fine and then darted into the larder where Douglas kept his racks of wine on the cool floor. 'A small thank you for all your kindness,' she said, thrusting two bottles into his arms. 'I'll bring your wife's clothes back as soon as I've had them cleaned.'

When he'd gone she caught up the letters as a shield from Mrs B's probing gaze. 'I'm OK,' she snapped irritably. 'Why don't you go home – there's hardly anything for you to do.' She turned away sharply, guilty at the look of hurt surprise on Mrs B's face, and then pained by her shrug of silent understanding.

# Chapter Four

As the days dragged on it was odd how she felt constantly tired when she had so little to do. When she'd worked, she'd been used to dovetailing a myriad of jobs into a mental timetable, slicing through a long day, surmounting problems of late delivery or shortage of stock, constantly harassed by importuning manufacturers. At the end of it all she hadn't felt tired, but energized, stimulated, ready for an evening with friends, or the theatre or cinema.

Part of the problem was that things which had seemed worthwhile for two were an unnecessary chore for one. What was the use of lighting a fire? She spent hours huddled in a chair by the oil-fired stove in the kitchen, an un-read book in her lap, staring into space. One day she'd ventured into the village for a few groceries, but as she waited her turn whilst the shop assistant gossiped, she remembered how amused Douglas had been by the village shops. 'Your Mr Rosomon should stay here for a week or two,' he'd chuckled as the litany of explanations for not being efficiently stocked rolled out in the gentle West Country voices. 'No, no cream today. See it's Monday.' 'No, no ham. Comes in late on Thursdays the ham does. We have it cooked for us by Gerry's wife Nancy. Try after lunch.'

'But I want it for lunch.' Jill, who regarded not having an item in stock as the sin of a missed sale, had been filled with disbelief. Now as she heard the familiar excuses, she felt so emotional that she had to blunder out of the shop.

Outside the tears came, blinding her as she searched vainly for a handkerchief. Through the blur she saw Miriam Mander coming towards her and hurriedly crossed the road. She couldn't meet anyone in this state.

But Miriam crossed determinedly too. 'I'm not having that,' she said firmly, taking Jill's arm. 'You can't cut me.'

'Oh, Miriam,' Jill put her head on her shoulder and gave in

to tears, oblivious of the stares of passers-by. But, finally, she had to pull away and return home alone.

Roger Mander had already given her some anti-depressants; they'd made her feel like a zombie, yet they hadn't dulled the hurt. After three or four days she had flushed them away. She tried to concentrate. She'd always been reckoned a good organizer, able to keep tabs on the designers going up and those fading, controlling and motivating the enlarging staff, re-arranging the expanded premises. Now she found it impossible to decide what to do. They'd sold the town house. Douglas had said that they would get a small flat when they'd sorted out the cottage. She should find a flat, she told herself, go back to her own world, but the thought of estate agents and their impudently inaccurate descriptions of desirable properties de-pressed her. Inertia wrapped her in a grey blanket of indecision. She sat childishly willing Douglas to come back. Her life couldn't end like this! It was a nightmare.

The worst part was how, in the silent cottage, Douglas remained a shadowy person she couldn't recall. How could he disappear so thoroughly? She tried to remember the sound of his voice, his laugh, the way he looked at her when he was pulling her leg, but it was impossible to bring him into sharp focus. The void he had left was real, constantly yawning at her feet, but the pain of not being able to visualize him upset her the most.

Sitting at the kitchen table alone, trying to force down a boiled egg, contrasted awfully with the chattering mealtimes they'd had. Both of them had liked to cook, and it had been a kind of competition to see who could produce the most culinary surprises. In France they'd searched for interesting little restaurants, analysing what made the various dishes so attractive. She could remember all that, but she couldn't remember *him*.

I'll have to tell Mrs B to go, she thought suddenly. A daily was hardly necessary, there was no-one to untidy the cottage. Anyway she didn't feel up to the trials of strength she had with Mrs B. Jill had tried to stop her changing the sheets, shouted at her when she'd removed Douglas's gardening clothes and boots from the untidy cupboard in the kitchen lobby, clung on to her own grubby clothes. She didn't want her washing and ironing, sterilizing the place with vacuum cleaner and duster, eradicating the last little vestige of Douglas. It was Douglas who had called her 'Mrs B', unable to say 'Mrs Buggles' or 'Gert' without laughing, and afraid of giving the garrulous woman offence.

Mrs B chattered away to Jill, trying to brace up the thin woman with the huge brown eyes that followed her without seeing around the room. She was worried about her. 'If she don't buck up, she'll go into a decline like your Lucy when she lost the baby,' she'd told her husband.

Jill tried to let the inconsequential and repetitive chat wash over her.

'You put that nice yellow jumper on and I'll wash that one,' Mrs B looked meaningly at the soiled navy sweater Jill had worn every day she'd bothered to dress. 'And I'll take those trousers with me, Thursday's the day for the cleaners.'

Jill had protested testily but Mrs B had just rummaged in her wardrobe until she found another pair and handed them to her.

'You're impertinent, you know that?' Jill had shouted. 'I don't need to dress. There's no-one to notice any more.'

Mrs B had given a philosophical shrug and left the bedroom. Best to leave them alone when they were like that. When Jill dragged herself down at about two o'clock, determined to drink herself into a giddy oblivion, the kitchen table was bright with the plates she and Douglas had bought from a young potter, a girl living on the other side of the village. There was a fresh loaf, some cheese and a salad in the wooden bowl. Remorseful, Jill had fallen on the food ravenously, glad that she hadn't managed to give Mrs B notice after all.

On Thursdays Gus came. She watched bleakly as he swept the fallen leaves, raking them into neat piles, picking them up between two small planks of wood and stuffing them into rubbish bags. She almost wished she could be packed away like that, she felt as desiccated as those leaves. Why should it be any different for humans? Why did they have to go on, cluttering up the world, when something as monstrous as losing the one person you had ever loved took away any joy in living?

She wandered out into the garden and stood near Gus. He had cut back the exuberant summer growth, tidied the garden for hibernation. 'I was going to bring you a load of muck from the farm,' he said awkwardly, spotting her silent figure. 'But I don't s'pose you'll be needing it now . . . you'm going back to Lunnon now I bin thinking.'

'I don't know,' Jill answered slowly, words coming with difficulty. 'I haven't any plans. Please bring the muck. What's it for?'

'For the veg, see. I had thought of putting in a row or two of runner beans next spring – good sunny spot this is. Have you seen the peach tree is looking perkier? Who'd have thought it could've gone on growing under all that rubbish, miracle ent it! Made a good job of pruning it Mr Mortimer did, and it gets the warmth on that wall. I thought I'd give en a mulch.'

'It's all a mystery to me, Gus. I'm not much of a gardener. You must do as you think best.'

'Aye, I see that. You'll learn. Teks time. I'm afraid that rose Mr Mortimer planted is looking a little poorly. It'll have to go.'

'Oh no!' her cry was involuntary, piteous. 'He loved that one. He found it in a book, a striped old-fashioned one. It took him ages to track it down. You mustn't pull that up.' Her voice was frantic and Gus bent to the leaves to hide his embarrassment.

'*Variegata di Bologna* – that's its name! I remember. What's wrong with it? It looks perfect to me.' She knew she sounded hysterical, but it was Douglas's rose. It mustn't be destroyed like him. For a moment she was able to recall his face as he'd tracked down the nursery that stocked it.

'Well,' Gus shrugged. 'Wait till next year then, see if it can pull itself together but I have my doubts. You can't waste space on the no-hopers.'

*Next year* . . . the prospect of next year without Douglas overwhelmed her. She stared in horror at Gus. 'I think I hear the telephone.' She rushed in, scared that her easy tears would disconcert Gus.

She was ashamed of her vulnerability, she who had been regarded as the cool, archetypal career woman. There'd been little room for emotion in her job. She should get back to work,

27

try to think of these last years as a blissful dream. Her heart was pounding as she leaned her forehead against the kitchen wall. Then the telephone did ring.

'I'm coming down for the weekend.' It was Carla, one of her closest friends, a friendship that dated from her days with Bostons when they'd both been junior buyers. Carla had been in Japan when Douglas died. 'Don't tell me its inconvenient because I'm already packed.'

'I'm not much company right now. It's depressingly autumnal down here and the weather's cold.'

'Oh . . .' Carla's voice faltered for a moment. 'Well, I suppose there's a fire? I mean, you do have electricity don't you?'

Jill could hear the trepidation in her friend's voice. Like herself before her remarriage, Carla had a cat-like addiction to warm rooms and the kind of conveniences an expensive block of flats provided. Jill found her gloom lightened a degree or two. 'Surprisingly enough, yes – even running water.'

'Then I'm coming.'

'There's nothing to do. I know no-one. You'll be bored stiff.'

'I want to see *you*. Don't put me off, I'll be offended.'

'Please, Carla, I'm in no fit state for company.'

'I'm not company, I'm a friend. Anyway, I'm coming.' Carla cut her off.

Despite her initial reluctance, the prospect of seeing Carla began to seem inviting. Someone from her own world to help her over another empty weekend. A spurt of energy had her checking out the spare room, filling a pottery jug with rosehips and sprays of blackberries. What a good idea it had been to turn the big space under the eaves into this extra odd-shaped bathroom. It was comic with its sloping ceiling and ingeniously fitted plumbing but it was comfortable. They'd torn out the plasterboard hiding the rafters, insulated the roof and added a dormer window. Now with its cream carpet, Victorian bath complete with brass taps, and a converted washstand housing a tiny basin, it looked charming. She put a single rosebud that had bravely tried to flower in defiance of the season in a vase on the pink Lloyd Loom table and turned up the thermostat, pleased at the thought that Carla's primitive ideas of a life in the country would need revising. Douglas had liked Carla. 'She's got a hell of a mind, that one,' he'd said, amused by Carla's scornful political views. Jill had felt so happy, so proud that evening, introducing Douglas to her friends. As she made sure there were enough coathangers in the cupboard, the memory of it pierced her.

# Chapter Five

'So, what are your plans?' Carla sounded brisk and efficient over breakfast on Saturday, in contrast to the tired woman who'd climbed stiffly out of a car similar to Diane's last night. Then, she'd sunk gratefully into a sofa and had supper on a tray by the comforting blaze of the logs. She'd woken refreshed and was now, Jill surmised, ready to take her in hand.

The autumn sun flooded through the kitchen windows and for the first time since Douglas's death, Jill didn't feel the oppressive chill that sent her huddling for cardigans or blankets. 'I don't really know . . .' Jill carefully buttered a piece of toast.

'The sensible thing is to go back to Fred's.' Carla was definite.

'I suppose you're right. I was thinking much the same thing. But – Douglas loved this place. It seems disloyal somehow to leave it.' Speaking his name out loud made her feel exposed. She hoped Carla wasn't going to nag, she didn't feel robust enough to cope.

'You don't really fit down here, do you?'

'No, I know but . . .'

'Well, you could keep it for weekends – you have someone to clean and do the garden don't you? I can't see you weeding and planting.' Carla's voice had the clipped reasonableness of someone used to dealing with unco-operative staff or temperamental designers.

Jill felt a twist of resentment. She *had* planted; true, rather mistakenly in many cases but that was because she lacked the experience to know how large some things would grow. Secretly she'd been thrilled at the magical way some minute black foxglove seeds had transformed themselves into a small forest of regal spikes of cream, yellow and pink. She'd dragged Douglas to see her showpiece, ghostly in the dusk of the summer evening.

'That's another inspired touch, darling, a dramatic contrast,' he'd joked, pointing to a pathetic clump of white alyssum she'd unwittingly planted behind some rampant lavatera, not realizing alyssum were so small or lavatera so tall.

'You wait till next year,' she'd retorted.

She couldn't expect Carla to understand; she didn't even have a windowbox.

'I suppose the fact is we've put so much into this place that . . . well it's funny, but now I feel in a way *bound* to it. It's like adopting a rather withdrawn child nobody wants and watching her respond to love and care . . .' she paused, embarrassed. 'I never thought that about my flat. I never really *lived* there. I was as much at home in the local wine bar.' She looked up defiantly. 'If – if I left it would be as if Douglas had never existed.' The cottage seemed to surge into focus suddenly, exuding a protective warmth she hadn't felt since Douglas died. She was fearful of the vigour in Carla's voice; she didn't want to be urged and persuaded along a 'sensible' course. This was her home, the one she and Douglas had made together.

After a minute Carla ventured, 'You're not hard up are you?'

Jill shook her head. She couldn't speak. She wanted to rush to the hall cupboard and put on Douglas's old overcoat again.

'But lovey, you must do something. What goes on in the village?'

'Oh, nothing much.' Jill hated that 'lovey', the change to a soothing tone as if she were some invalid who had to be humoured. 'Everything seems centred on the church. I'm not religious.'

'What's that got to do with it? Few churchgoers are! In my limited experience it seems church is basically a social centre. A kind of weekly cocktail party where instead of making small talk you merely put on a concerned face when the vicar says the roof needs repairing.'

'That's shocking.'

'Well, stand for the parish council. You'd make a good politician. Look how artful you were when you wanted your own way with Rosomon.'

'That's different. I'm not a local. I don't know the burning issues.'

'Become a magistrate then.'

'I have too little respect for the law. I'd want the rogues who could tell a good story to get off.'

'Oh, you're just being defeatist!' Carla got up impatiently and clattered her coffee cup into the sink. 'Open a dress shop. Shake up the local matrons – show them what style's all about.'

'Fashion is virtually meaningless here. It's cardigan country. Some of the young girls in the village took to Azzedine Alaia knock-offs last summer, and you should see what stretchy short frocks look like on robust country figures built like shire horses.' She was beginning to enjoy thwarting all Carla's suggestions.

'There must be something. You can't spend your day tidying an immaculate cottage. Look at it now.' She glanced round the attractive kitchen at the dresser crammed with an idiosyncratic collection of pottery, mugs crowding jugs and teapots, their only common unity clear, bright colours. 'When I first saw the photograph you sent me I thought you'd gone off your trolley. It looked uninhabitable.'

'It was.' They both laughed.

'Well – you could do up more old properties or . . .'

'No!' The word came out explosively as Jill scraped her chair back on the flagged floor. 'Please stop. You're bullying me.'

There was silence, Carla had her back turned, washing up the coffee cups with unnecessary thoroughness. Eventually she said in a careful, conversational tone, 'Is the village far?'

'Two or three miles. We walked there once, but it's not so much fun on the way back with shopping. We sat on a gate and thumbed a lift.' Jill smiled as she remembered that the loud engine noise coming up the hill hadn't been a van, as they'd imagined, but a tractor. They'd stood on the back of the treacherously rocking machine laughing their heads off as the noisy animal lurched into a field and deposited them a couple of hundred yards from the cottage.

'There are one or two quite decent antique shops,' she answered Carla's question. 'And a surprisingly good delicatessen.' Making an effort to sound normal, she continued, 'Salisbury Cathedral is worth a trip. They have a copy of the Magna Carta there – it's under an hour. I could drive you there this afternoon.'

Carla looked unenthused.

'Well, let's see how you feel after lunch,' Jill added hastily. This visit was a mistake. She should have made some excuse. Carla had too much energy, she would take over and wheedle her, strip off the inadequate plaster she had pasted over her wound and force her into some unwelcome action. Jill had forgotten what it was like to be sharp, pragmatic, manipulative. She realized how the pace of her life had changed. She and Douglas used to garden, or tramp about the secret leafy lanes or watch the countryside from one of the many hills around. She contemplated Carla's pale suede suit and coffee-coloured boots. Had she, too, once looked as out of place as that?

'I thought we'd lunch at the pub . . . I haven't been since . . . since Douglas died.'

The pub was the one they'd stayed at in the early days, when they'd tried to renovate the cottage during weekends. It was comfortable and shabby, they'd played darts under the amused eyes of the locals, drunk a metallic red wine that seized up the inside of their mouths, and tucked into hefty plates of steak-and-kidney pie, happy as mongrels. Jill was glad that the lounge bar was full and John, the landlord, too busy to make a fuss of her; it was the kindness and sympathy people showed that undermined her. She felt her face stiffen as he noticed her, but she produced a smile of thanks as he quickly wiped a table near the fire for them.

When they'd settled with their drinks and were studying the blackboard menu, Carla seized on a local free magazine someone had left behind. 'Events . . .' she chortled, repeating a headline, 'Car-boot sale . . . coffee morning in aid of arthritis research . . . annual church jumble sale. Ye gods! What a dizzying social round.'

Jill glanced round quickly. 'Hush.'

'Barn dance for the PTA . . . shall we go? Oh, that's next week. Sponsored walk to raise cash for a scanner for the hospital – no thanks, my feet can only walk from the front door to a waiting car. Here we are – art exhibition Saturday at two p.m. Tom Houlderton. "A talented artist of rustic life, whose dreamy watercolours are inspired by the rivers and wind-tossed forests of the Dorset countryside." Can't say fairer than that. Let's go.'

33

'I don't feel like it.'

'We'd only have to wander around quietly – looking at dreamy watercolours, seeing if they really rate as nightmares.'

'You'll poke fun.'

'I shall behave beautifully.'

'It will be awful.'

'More my cup of tea than a cathedral.'

The exhibition, in the small hall of the village school, was surprisingly crowded. A slight dark-haired, dark-eyed young man with a nervous twitch in his cheek stood near the door talking distractedly to a large man in gingery Harris tweeds, and greeting people as they came in. A tall, too thin girl with huge brown eyes and a mournful expression gave Jill a badly duplicated list of the exhibits. 'Do please help yourself to a glass of wine,' she said without enthusiasm, gesturing to a wet tray of glasses. 'The exhibits are numbered and the prices are in the catalogue.' She repeated the words unconvincingly to Carla with the same lack of expression. Carla obediently picked up a glass, sipped, and quickly put it down again.

'The art has got to be better than the wine or they're in trouble,' she murmured to Jill.

They walked along the exhibits, surprised at their quality. Tom Houlderton had a delicate touch; there was a mysticism about the landscapes which, despite her lethargy, Jill found appealing. She recognized the local hills in the soft shades of grey and mauve he'd used as the sun sloped off behind them; he'd caught the pearly quality of misty morning sunlight lying over the fields and woods. 'Look,' she turned to Carla. 'That must be very close to the cottage. I can see that odd-shaped clump of trees on the hill from my bedroom window. Douglas always said it reminded him of a Mohican.'

'I see what he means, a sort of punk rocker's hairstyle, that bald hill and the line of trees running up it. It's charming though.' Carla studied it critically. 'That sort of thing is usually so sentimental, but he's made the hills and trees look timeless, as though people would be intruders.'

'They are of course. The hills must have come first, and some

34

of the trees are pretty old – before the tax-evaders started planting those dreary pine forests everywhere.'

'I must have dropped my catalogue – I'll get another, see what it's called.' Carla strolled back to the pair at the door. Jill drifted on round the walls, looking at the people chatting. One or two smiled vaguely at her, shifted as if to include her in their gossiping group, but she looked away, not ready for their good intentions.

'Jill, *dear*. I'm so glad to see you. How are you?' It was Faith Cruze, covering up with loud gushing emphasis her embarrassment at bumping into a woman who had committed the social offence of becoming a widow. 'We haven't seen you since . . . since . . .'

'Since Douglas died?' Jill offered stolidly. They had come to the funeral, Faith swathed in black as if she'd been a close relative.

'Er yes, well no. I was thinking since you both came to dinner before Douglas got embroiled in his new book. He was in such good form then. Who would have thought . . .' her voice trailed away and she looked over Jill's shoulder. 'There's Arabella, I promised to have a coffee morning for her Victim Support scheme. I must talk to her before she leaves.' She turned back hastily. 'You should come and see us, Jill dear – there's no excuse now is there? *You* haven't a book to finish have you? Time is your own,' she smiled roguishly. 'Only don't come at weekends – we usually have people then. Don't forget.' She started back as Jill's face whitened. 'Must go . . .'

Jill stepped forward, bending over the shorter woman until her eyes were two or three inches from Faith's, then she jabbed her forefinger in the air. 'I can see right through your empty little head,' she said through clenched teeth. 'D'you know that? Keep your silly face out of my way.' Jill stood breathing heavily, staring at her, and as Faith recovered herself and attempted to speak Jill shook a finger at her. 'Not one word . . . don't you dare utter one word.'

Faith's expression was a comic mix of fright, bemusement and a struggle for dignity. She brushed her sleeve, her mouth trembling. 'She's mad,' she said to someone nearby who had witnessed the scene. 'Quite out of her mind,' and then, as she

35

put a safe distance between herself and Jill, she said loudly, 'She should see a doctor, poor thing, or a psychiatrist.'

Jill felt physically sick. She closed her eyes and leant against the wall. She wanted to go home. She shouldn't have let Carla invite herself down; she'd never have come here otherwise.

Carla reappeared. 'What's up? What was all that commotion about?'

'Let's go home.' Jill felt unable to breathe. She was oblivious to the stares and murmurings around her. Carla glanced quickly round, took her arm and guided her outside the school.

Jill sat on the grubby steps and put her head between her knees. 'I could happily have killed her,' she muttered.

Carla could hardly hear, but stroked Jill's hair and her back, murmuring soothingly. Eventually Jill stood up and Carla shepherded her towards the school gate just as the Manders were turning in.

'Hullo,' Roger said to Jill through his opened car window. 'I didn't know you were an art connoisseur. Buy anything?' His voice changed. 'What's the matter?'

'She's feeling a bit faint – it's hot in there,' said Carla untruthfully. 'We're going home. I'm a friend staying with her this weekend.'

'I'll follow you. I think I should look at her. We'll just go and register an appearance in there,' he jerked his head towards the school hall. 'Be with you in half an hour.'

'I don't need you,' Jill called childishly, but allowed Carla to push her into the passenger seat, sitting numbly as Carla attempted to start the unfamiliar car.

36

# Chapter Six

'Now, tell me what happened?' Roger held Jill's wrist, checking her pulse three quarters of an hour later. 'I gather there was a scene. When I went into poor Tom's exhibition, people were gathered in knots talking about you and not looking at his pictures.'

'I'm sorry.' Jill leant back against the pillows. Carla had insisted she lie down. 'It was that awful woman.' She told him what Faith had said, tasting bile as she repeated her words.

'She's an insensitive fool,' Roger commented. 'Not worth upsetting yourself for. How have you been these last few days?'

'All right. How am I supposed to be?'

'Didn't the pills help?'

'No. I felt worse.'

'You mustn't take it too hard. Life has to go on. Douglas wouldn't want you to be miserable,' he said quietly.

Jill's vision swam and she dashed her hand angrily across her eyes.

'Jill dear, there is nothing I can say, or do to make anything easier for you. You've got to face it alone, draw strength from your own resources, gradually make a sort of life for yourself.'

'How? I don't know what to do. That's what's so awful.' Her voice held fear. 'I just can't think. I can't even see Douglas in my mind's eye, only his body that dreadful day. It upsets me that I can't remember his features – as if I hadn't loved him enough.'

'Just take each day as it comes. Try to take up some interest.'

'Like a piece of knitting,' she said sarcastically.

'Yes, if you like, a piece of knitting – doesn't that grow a row at a time until you've made a jumper?' He smiled gently at her. 'You've got to knit yourself together again, make a new garment.'

'I never expected to hear you dish out the platitudes.' She

couldn't help her voice sounding scornful. He couldn't appreciate her emptiness, her fear of the future. Her heart was thumping and she felt constricted inside.

Roger took her hand. 'Hold on, Jill. You'll be all right.' He bent to his bag and took out some pills. 'This one will make you sleep now. I think you need to rest and you won't with all that going on inside. And these,' he gave her a little sachet of four foil-wrapped pills, 'they're different from the last lot. They may suit you better. Take one in the morning and another after lunch. I'll give you a ring tomorrow to see how you are. Don't be hard on yourself. Grief is natural. Don't be ashamed of giving in to it. To hell with stiff upper lips.'

Jill came down shamefaced the next morning to find Carla had already laid a breakfast tray for her.

'I was going to bring you your breakfast in bed,' Carla sounded disappointed. 'Only it's taken me ages trying to find where you keep things.'

'It's OK, I'm not an invalid. And I'm sorry about the outburst. I was just so angry. I could have choked that stupid woman! Makes me realize how crimes of passion are committed!'

'I don't think you'd have succeeded, her hide's too thick. I gave your nice doctor a drink, I hope you don't mind. And I had one – well, several, myself. You went out like a light. I came in a few times to see you, but you didn't stir.'

'I'm sorry. Did you have anything to eat?'

'Sure. Your fridge was stuffed with goodies. And I watched the box. I had a good time.' She reassured Jill and they read the Sunday papers as they ate toast and coffee, both shuddering at the idea of eggs.

'That Tom Houlderton told me he runs a painting class,' Carla said from behind the shelter of *The Sunday Times*. 'Why don't you go to that?'

'Oh for crissake! You're indefatigable. You were like this yesterday morning. I can't paint.'

'Well, you can try . . . you'd meet people.'

'Like the charming Faith Cruze,' Jill sneered. 'Why can't you bear to see me idle?'

38

'Not idle – going to waste,' Carla said firmly.

'You're a menace,' Jill said irritably.

They'd been close friends for so long. Carla had shared a lot of her freewheeling, independent days, both intoxicated by the challenge of their respective jobs, a mutual desire to succeed, an intense interest in their heated world of fashion. They'd picked each other up after the end of unsatisfactory affairs, combined buying trips with a few days of relaxation in Milan or Rome, New York or Tokyo. They'd had so much in common. Now Jill wanted to hurt Carla, puncture the self-confidence and assurance with which she dispensed advice.

'I don't know why you wanted to come down,' she scowled. 'You're not dressed for the country. There's nothing to do but walk and you can hardly do that in those,' she gestured scornfully at Carla's suede boots.

'I came to see you. I thought I could cheer you up.'

'I've lost a husband, not a pet cat.' Jill felt a certain satisfaction at Carla's wounded expression. She was reaching for the coffee pot when the telephone rang. It was Roger.

'How are you? Did you sleep?' When Jill reassured him, he said Miriam wanted them both to come to lunch.

'I don't think I—' Jill started to say, and then thought why not? It was too wearying to go on fencing with Carla. 'Thanks. That would be nice,' she said flatly.

She drove Carla to the Manders', taking a circuitous route so that she could show her the countryside. A weak sun struggled with the shreds of low wispy cloud clinging to the hills, but Jill drove to the top of Bulbarrow Hill where the whole of the Blackmore Vale spread out below. Here the sun picked out the unreal viridian green of a field, punctuated by the tiny black and white rectangles of cows standing as motionless as toy farm animals.

'I can see it grows on you,' Carla said after an unusually long silence for her. 'But I think I'd miss the old concrete high-rise in a day or two.'

'You've no soul,' grinned Jill, pleased that she had been impressed. 'C'mon, Roger will be mixing the martinis.'

'Now that's the sort of view I do like,' Carla smiled back apologetically. 'A cocktail shaker and a tray of chilled glasses. He sounds an ideal doctor.'

Ten minutes later they were lounging back on a collapsed old sofa, glasses in hand as Miriam performed what she called her 'loaves-and-fishes' act at the stove. Jill took pleasure in watching Carla fastidiously picking dog's hairs off the unsuitably chic black suit she was wearing.

'What's Tom Houlderton like?' Carla asked Roger. 'Can he really make a living from those paintings?'

'No. He teaches at a couple of schools round here and runs a weekly art class in his barn. You could join his class,' he turned to Jill. 'He needs more people. One old lady has died and the Wilsons have moved away.'

'Not a word out of you,' Jill warned Carla. She looked up at Roger. 'Carla has been going on like an occupational therapist ever since she arrived.'

'Good for her.' Miriam plonked a huge bowl of pasta on the table. 'You must do something.'

Determined to forestall that track, Jill asked, 'What about his wife? Was she the one handing out the catalogues? Does she paint too?'

'Claudine? No. She's made a career out of infertility,' Miriam laughed. 'She's dying to get pregnant and treats us all to a detailed report on monthly cycles and sperm counts. Usually in Watson's.' She spooned meat sauce out and gestured them all to the table. 'You know what Watson's is like – more of a social centre than a delicatessen but it's hard to concentrate on a choice between trout or mackerel pâté when Claudine is describing her latest visit to the clinic.'

'She's bored,' Roger said. 'She needs a job but she's got no ambition.'

'Neither have you,' Miriam said comfortably.

'I've achieved mine. I only ever wanted to be a country GP.'

Jill watched enviously as they exchanged smiles, her own loneliness heavy on her shoulders.

'*My* ambition,' said Carla, 'is to open a beautifully co-ordinated accessories shop. Only elegant shoes – nothing too practical; the newest bag shapes, good belts, a few original jewellery designers and scarves, masses of scarves . . .' She was oblivious of the Manders' tolerant amusement. Jill felt a pang of envy. Carla was so confident, so busy; she had purpose.

On Sunday evening when it was time for Carla to go, Jill hugged her. 'You were good to put up with me. What a rotten weekend you've had!'

'Idiot. What are friends for? Anyway, I miss you,' she said sadly, swinging an expensive grip into the back of her car. 'Come and help me with my accessories shop. We'd be an invincible team.'

'Still at it? Don't you ever give up?' As she spoke, she thought of the rush and tear of Fred's when the new stock came in: the excitement of unpacking; the fun of the preview she gave the sales staff so that they could sell a whole look properly; the newest way of wearing a scarf or piece of jewellery. It had been her world for so long, much longer than her short time with Douglas. And she had been good; she knew that. Much better at predicting women's fashion than at pretending to be a gardener.

'Well, at least come up and stay for a night or two,' insisted Carla. 'We could have some of the old gang round or go to the theatre. Fred would like to see you – I think he's a bit depressed. I had a chat with him at Vivienne Westwood's show recently. Give him a ring. You can't . . .'

Jill knew she was going to say something like, *You can't moulder here.* So she cut in quickly, 'That would be nice. I'll be in touch.'

# Chapter Seven

Carla's visit had been unsettling. Jill got up on Monday earlier than she had since the funeral. She felt driven, a latent surge of energy making her feel restless, yet there still wasn't really anything to do. Carla and Roger together had succeeded in making her realize that she was drifting aimlessly through the days like some displaced person. Except that I *am* a displaced person, Jill thought. She had no rôle. Douglas had uprooted her, an unwilling transplant at first, but warmed by love, encouraged by the satisfaction of discovering how to turn a barren heap of stone and tile into a home, she'd begun to put down tentative new roots.

She remembered the triumph she'd felt when she'd insisted to an army of baffled, reluctant workmen that a hideous tiled fireplace should be torn out of the small breakfast room, and the wall smoothly plastered. Instead, behind the tiling, they'd found a pretty iron range, still capable of warming the room and of keeping an old-fashioned kettle singing on the hob. But what was any of it without Douglas?

'I don't belong here, now.' She spoke out loud. 'I don't know how to function.' Pulling on a thick knitted coat and boots, she stomped into the garden. It had been raining for the last two days, and she squelched across the rough grass to the river. It was surprisingly full, rushing along with a vigour and urgency she hadn't seen before. Gus and Douglas must have cleared more of the bed than she'd realized. A slight movement on the opposite bank attracted her and she saw a duck eyeing her with anticipation. There were ducks then! Douglas would have been so thrilled. She hurried back for some bread, and was surprised to see Tom Houlderton rounding the path at the side of the cottage.

'I'm sorry,' he smiled as she came up. 'I tried the front door, but there was no reply. So many people round here only use the back . . . I thought you might be in the garden.'

'It's hardly gardening weather.' She waited for him to mention the scene with Faith Cruze. Had she really disrupted his exhibition? Why was he here? She looked at him apprehensively.

'I brought you your picture. The school need their gallery back on Mondays,' he smiled. 'If you don't like the frame I can change it.'

'My picture?' she repeated stupidly.

'Yes, the one your friend bought. Didn't she tell you? She said you could see the view from your bedroom window. She said it was her "thank you" for the weekend.'

She watched unhappily as he unwrapped the parcel. Some weekend Carla had had! His hands lingered over the task as if reluctant to produce the contents. Jill spoke to break the tension, 'It must be awful to put so much of yourself into a painting and then see it go away. Like being robbed.'

He smiled. 'I don't mind when people really like a work . . . but I feel upset if people who don't care buy something as if it were half a pound of butter. Then I don't want to let it go.'

'I really like it,' Jill assured him. 'I pointed it out to Carla – I didn't realize she was buying it for me. How lovely! She didn't say a word.'

'Do you know where you're going to hang it?'

'How can I? I didn't know about it. I haven't had time to think.' She wondered if she ought to apologize for her outburst. Perhaps he hadn't noticed.

'It needs to be where there's a good light, at the right eye level I think. Can I have a look?'

Tom followed her through the kitchen to the sitting room, looking around him with frank interest. 'I'd hardly recognize the place. I used to come here to fish as a boy. The old ladies used to give me an apple or a biscuit and ask to look at my jamjar of tiddlers. I remember it as being very dark, and a rather overwhelming smell of goats.' He laughed.

'I know,' Jill agreed. 'When we found it, it was covered in jungle – even in here. The wisteria and a wild rose were poking through a broken window and there was actually a buddleia growing out of a crack by the hearth. It was still rather pungent.'

'It's lovely now. It looks so natural, as though it's just grown like this. So many people do up old cottages and they look uncomfortable, like an elderly lady sporting an unwise face-lift and a short skirt.'

'I know what you mean. We enjoyed working on it. But my husband died suddenly, before he could really relish the improvements.' She was surprised at the almost conversational way she had said 'my husband died'.

'I know.' He looked slightly apologetic. 'News travels fast in a village. Gertie Buggles works for you, doesn't she?' he said as if in explanation. 'I'm very sorry. And I'm sorry you were upset on Saturday. I heard about it, though I wasn't aware of anything at the time – too nervous I suppose. That Cruze woman is a tactless fool. You mustn't take any notice of her. Shall I put the picture up? Have you a drill?' Jill led him to the small outhouse and let him ferret for the things he wanted.

As he stood on a stool to mark a spot for the picture he said, 'You're staying on?'

'For the time being.'

'You could join my painting class,' he said smiling. 'Or . . .' as she vigorously shook her head, 'the Drama Group are short of numbers. But,' he stopped speaking as he drilled a hole, 'whatever you do, don't let Arabella Montgomery-Fitch hear you say you have time on your hands . . . she'll rope you on to one of her fund-raising committees like a flash. Have you met her?'

Jill shook her head and he went on, 'She's the wife of the local MP – Sir Harold – and believes she runs the neighbourhood. She's not a bad sort underneath I suppose, and I realize that it's people like her battling away raising money for this and that who keep the country going, but she goes at it like a bulldozer which puts people's backs up. At least if you were involved with one of her projects you'd get to know the locals.'

Why is everyone so anxious for me to meet people, as if it were some kind of panacea, Jill thought irritably.

'I prefer her to her husband,' Tom went on. 'He's the squire, straight from Central Casting. His father made a packet after the last war in property . . . a kind of Rachman Mark Two, only car parks instead of flats. He went in for a lot of strong-arm stuff to "persuade" people to give up their bomb sites for car parks, and he was skilled at greasing the right palms in the planning committees. So, hey presto, a great many over-priced car parks sprang up in the wartime gaps between London's buildings. I'm sorry, I'm gossiping,' he broke off.

Jill shook her head. 'Go on.'

'Oh well, he sold out, bought this estate down here and set about turning young Harold into the perfect country gent – shooting, hunting . . .' he wrinkled his nose in distaste. 'Lots of entertaining.'

'How do you know all this? I mean, about the Rachmanish father?'

'There are no secrets in a village. Besides, my wife's father was Montgomery-Fitch's accountant. Only he was just plain Fitch and lived in Potters Bar then. The Montgomery was added when Harold married Arabella. Then, thanks to the old man's money, he was knighted a few years ago – services to politics I think they called it. Everybody knows everybody's business here – or think they do. You'll find that out.' He climbed down from the steps, looking with satisfaction at the picture. 'There, that's done. If you tire of it you can always move it to a dark corner.'

He carried the steps back to the outhouse.

When Tom Houlderton had left, Jill switched on the light to relieve the gloomy wet morning and kicked the logs into flame. She picked up a book and tried to read. The loneliness was worse in the daytime. The silence seemed almost physical, another presence. She switched on the radio and the silence retreated temporarily. She punched the button to escape from Radio Three's overly enthusiastic illustrated talk on contemporary Chinese music; Radio Four had a righteous consumer programme looking into the merits of package holidays, and Jill couldn't stomach the relentless joviality of the local station – jangling pop music interspersed with birthday greetings to listeners and halting inarticulate phone-ins.

She switched off, and the silence crowded in again, mocking her, defiant. Oh, this was ridiculous! What did she do before Douglas? She'd spent evenings alone then. She was turning into a wimp, the sort of helpless female she'd always despised. She jumped as the phone rang.

'Jill Mortimer? Hullo . . . I'm Frank Huxtable. Douglas and I were friends . . .'

'Yes, I know.'

'I was in New York covering the opening of *Shadowlands* when Doug . . . when I heard the sad news. I'm so sorry. He was a great chap. We shared a lot of good times on the *Daily Mail*. I did write, but I think to the London address . . . I didn't know your country one until I heard from Tom Feathers.'

'Your letter was forwarded. It was very sweet of you. I should have replied but there've been so many letters. I haven't managed . . .' She sounded inadequate.

'Well, Douglas was very popular. He had a great following too for his novels. I don't know how he managed to write so many and keep them so fresh. I envied him his talent. I just sit through lousy plays, wasting my life.' Hurriedly, conscious of his lack of tact, he asked her to come over for dinner on Saturday. 'I know it's early days but it's just us – Clement and I, and perhaps Fiona . . . d'you know her, Fiona Trentbridge?'

'I know *of* her – I saw her in *Sailing*. She was very good.'

'Yes, pity about the play. Well, she may come down if some man doesn't whisk her off first. She's very relaxed, you'll like her.'

'Thank you – but I don't think I can. I'm not much good socially at the moment.'

'My dear, you don't have to sparkle with us. And I very much want to meet you. Douglas was good to me, and he told me about a year ago how happy you'd made him. I'm glad of that.'

Jill couldn't speak.

'Douglas always promised we'd all get together,' Frank continued, 'but we hadn't been able to fix it – we all lead such silly busy lives, so much of it quite unnecessary I'm sure. You'd make me very happy if I could talk to you a bit about Douglas . . .'

To talk about Douglas. She suddenly very much wanted to do that, if only to try and brush in his features on the blurred image she had. She was still deeply grieved by her inability to picture him clearly. Perhaps it was because she couldn't talk

46

about him to anyone who'd really known him, had kept him locked in her desolate mind, that she'd lost his reality.

'Thank you,' Jill said in almost a whisper. 'I'd like to come.'

'Hooray. I'll be up in Scarborough with Mr Ayckbourn tomorrow, but I'll get Clement to write telling you how to find us. We're about six or seven miles your side of Bath; only the last bit is complicated, but Clement will put it all down. About seven-thirty for eight?'

Jill replaced the receiver. She picked up a book and began to read. The silence now was peaceful, even friendly.

# Chapter Eight

Jill vaguely noticed a small poster about the Drama Group that Tom Houlderton had mentioned on the glass-fronted cupboard of the freezer in the delicatessen, and then another in the window of the hairdresser's, next to a silver cup and a yellowing newspaper cutting showing the proprietor accepting it as a reward for the sort of hairstyle only another hairdresser could love. She paused to read it.

Sherville Drama Group.
New season's production about to start. Casting shortly.
Wanted actors, actresses, volunteers to help with scenery,
costumes, make-up, publicity, box office, prompting. Call
Miles Lambert 0453 324 519.

'Oh, hullo Jill.' It was Miriam, pink-faced from the old-fashioned hairdryer hood, just leaving the salon. 'I did like your friend Carla despite the fact she made me feel an absolute frump. What are you studying so carefully?' She looked over Jill's shoulder. 'Ah, the Drama Group. Thinking of treading the boards?'

'Not in the least. I was just wondering how much of a group is the Drama Group if they want so many new members?'

'Ah that's the point. It's been pretty much a closed shop up to now. The same old dears in the same old party pieces. Then young Miles Lambert and a few of his friends came in and agitated to do modern plays – previously there was nothing later than an overworked *Pride and Prejudice*. Unfortunately most of the old hands weren't up to it. It was a disaster. Worst part was that the *Wessex Weekly*, who'd never bothered to send anyone before, reviewed it. Well, damned it really. Some of the performers were so ridiculed that feelings were hurt, general umbrage was taken and there was an abrupt exodus.'

'And that was the end of the group?'

'Oh, some of them are still around. Not many. Ed Posner, of course, he's one of those stolid characters seemingly unaware of atmospheres and temperament, and naturally Arabella. She adores Miles. I suppose I'll have to help, the village needs a drama group to keep a community spirit going.'

'Sounds as though it did precisely the reverse.'

'Don't mock – people do get upset. It'll blow over. Anyway I can prompt or look after props, or something else requiring neither skill nor talent . . . come with me.'

'I can't.'

'You can,' Miriam said firmly.

'I can't act.'

'There are other jobs – look at the list.' Miriam tapped her finger on the notice. 'What about costumes – isn't that up your street?'

'I was a fashion buyer,' Jill said reluctantly. 'Not at all the same thing.'

'Well, look they need someone. You'd be an absolute gift. Don't say no.'

As she said her goodbyes and then finished her shopping, Jill caught herself wondering why not? She had to do something to get through the looming winter. She didn't want to end up huddling under the bedclothes or knocking back a bottle of wine to pass the time. Perhaps after Christmas, she'd find the energy to start looking for a flat in London, pick up the threads again.

Miriam must have acted immediately because that afternoon just as Jill was about to go down to the river, armed with bread, to see if the duck had reappeared, the phone rang and a lively voice announced itself as Miles Lambert.

'Miriam tells me you'd like to join the Drama Group,' he said. 'That would be nice. May I come to see you, to discuss how you can help?'

'I'm afraid Miriam is guilty of exaggeration. I didn't say anything of the kind.'

'Look I'm *desperate*. You don't know how hard it is to get any enthusiasm going. I really need new people. You're from London?'

'Yes.'

'Well, then!' he said triumphantly, as if that settled it. 'You *must* join. Let me come round and talk to you about it.'

'Now?'

'Please. There's so much to do if we're to put on a production in March.'

'Come if you like, but I don't see how I can be of use.' She knew she sounded offhand, uninviting.

'I'll be right over.'

Jill put the phone down, worried at the prospect of the visit. She wandered down to the river with her bread. There was no sign of the duck. Disappointed she threw the bread on to the opposite bank. It was a dull duck anyway. Brown and drab. She'd rather fancied the look of plump white feathers and yellow beaks on the grassy bank. When she strolled desultorily back to the house, stopping to pull at a few determined dandelions as she went, she found a tall, fresh-faced young man standing by the back door. He'd propped a bicycle against the wall and was looking round with impatient jerks of his head.

His expression cleared when he saw Jill. 'Hullo – I rang the front door. I was afraid you'd forgotten.'

'Already? You phoned less than ten minutes ago.' Jill put out her hand. 'I take it you're Miles Lambert?'

He smiled apologetically and engulfed her hand in a painful grip. 'I'm sorry. It's just that I'm so anxious to get on – there's so much to do and at the moment very few people to do it.'

'So I heard. How did you come to lose so many people?' She led the way inside and offered him a chair. He frowned. 'It took me ages to persuade the group to put on something written since 1950, but I couldn't move them on casting. John Begard has always played the lead and he had to be Guildenstern with about as much idea of irony as . . .'

'*Rosencrantz and Guildenstern Are Dead* is a bit ambitious for a village drama group isn't it?'

'It was only the Edinburgh Fringe version . . . but Begard wouldn't take direction, and as for Joe Allsop.' He looked exasperatedly at Jill. 'He's the chemist – have you met him? He played Rosencrantz as if dosed on a heavy prescription of

Mogadon. Half the time the cast didn't all turn up for rehearsals . . . it was the pits.'

He leaned forward eagerly in his seat. 'Are you sure you can't act? We need someone young and attractive.' He looked at her appraisingly.

Jill couldn't help smiling at his cheek. 'No, I can't act. I'm really no use, you're wasting your time.'

'Oh, there are masses of jobs. Can you paint scenery, prompt, be a wardrobe mistress.'

His gaze was so beseeching she felt warmed, wanted. 'I know about clothes – I was a fashion buyer for a London shop until eighteen months ago. I could help with the costumes, I suppose.'

By the time she watched Miles Lambert cycle energetically up the steep hill, Jill had agreed to turn up at the first reading the following Wednesday, design costumes, do the make-up and generally lend a hand. She closed the door, inwardly saluting the easy charm that had so successfully manipulated her.

# Chapter Nine

Frank Huxtable's house was a small Georgian jewel. It was about six miles from Bath, slipping off the main road, first down through a steep valley and up through wooden slopes to a flattened bit of hillside, where an old wall encircled the entire garden.

'Lovely isn't it?' Frank said. 'Clement found it all by himself. I had this excited call right in the middle of writing my review of *Norman Conquests* – can you imagine? – to say he'd put down a deposit. Of course, sixteen years ago it was comparatively cheap but we both beggared ourselves, absolutely beggared ourselves to buy it.' He pressed a switch and ushered Jill to the French windows. 'See? So theatrical isn't it . . . Clement fixed that too. He can turn his hand to anything.'

Jill gazed out at the garden, lit by silvery concealed lighting so that the evergreen shrubs threw sharp, dense shadows contrasting with the delicate filigree tracery of the bare branches of the deciduous trees.

'I've never seen anything so beautiful,' she breathed, entranced. 'I expect Natalia Maakarova to glide across any minute.'

'And in spring the grass is carpeted, positively *carpeted* with tiny bulbs – aconites, snowdrops, anemone blanda, miniature narcissi, primroses, cyclamen . . . it's like a spilled jewel box. Never tire of it,' Frank beamed. 'Now come to the fire. Clement will be in in a minute – he's putting the last touches to our meal. A drink?' He raised a sherry decanter and waved a graceful white hand to an array of bottles. 'Whisky! Hum . . . you must have caught that from Douglas. He could put it away at times; mostly, I may say, when Frances got him down. I'm sorry my dear, I'm talking too much.'

'No it's comforting. There are so few people who mention him by name . . . I begin to wonder if he ever existed. It's such a strange feeling.'

Frank sat next to her on the sofa. 'Talk about him as much as you like. I was very fond of him. He used to look after me on the *Mail*. I wasn't up to the newsroom's so-called sense of humour – they made me the butt of every gay joke going. Dreadful time it would've been,' he shuddered delicately, 'if it hadn't been for Douglas.'

'What did you do on the *Mail*? Douglas told me he used to be a reporter.'

'Yes, but for a very short time. I went there because they offered me a great deal of money to write about what they call *showbiz* – ugly word isn't it? I'd contributed to the *Spectator* at Cambridge, little pieces but I'm happy to say they were noticed.' He flicked at the sleeve of his blue velvet jacket. 'And when I came down I was offered a job on the *New Statesman* which was quite important in those days, but I'm not really interested in politics and the pay was so poor that I jumped at what seemed a princely sum from the *Mail*. Fortunately for my sanity *The World* were kind enough to ask me to be their drama critic not long afterwards and – ah Fiona, darling, you've changed, you shouldn't have!' He leapt to his feet and put his arm round the shoulders of a tall, slender blonde with turquoise eyes and full, pouting lips. She was wearing a cream silk shirt and a long Stewart tartan kilt.

'Gerrorf, you old queen,' she scolded. 'This shirt costs a fortune to clean. Course I changed. Couldn't wait to get out of that bloody mini dress. It feels like a corset. Who'd think we dumped whalebone in 1890 only to take up with elastic bandages in 1990. I ask you! Hullo.' She smiled at Jill, her eyes wrinkling attractively whilst dimples dented her cheeks. 'You're Jill, I assume. I didn't hear you arrive . . . I dozed off in the bath.'

'Hullo,' Jill warmed to her at once. 'I agree about the short tight stretchy fashions. No wonder the shops are doing so badly . . . ravishing on two per cent of the female population who are as slender as you, but ridiculous on the rest.'

'Jill was fashion director for Fred's,' Frank said to Fiona. 'Where you spend all your men friends' cash.'

'And a great deal of my own,' Fiona returned imperturbably. 'I swear if my taxi's in a traffic jam it always seems to get stuck outside Fred's, and then there's no hope for me or my bank balance.'

'You leap out?' Frank glinted at her through his blue spectacles.

'Of course! As dear Mrs Thatcher once said, "There's no alternative." Am I not to be given a drink?'

'Whisky, like Jill? Sherry, gin, vodka, what would you like, dear heart?'

'Champagne?'

'Done.' He clapped his hands. 'The butler's off-duty tonight, so it is I who must slip to the cellar.'

'He's a fool,' Fiona said to Jill. 'But one of the nicest men I know. Pity he's gay – what a waste! Although I don't know, there's something very restful about a man who doesn't leap on you every five minutes.'

'I haven't met him before. He was one of my,' she paused at the pain of saying it, 'one of my late husband's friends.'

Fiona, even if she noticed the huskily uttered 'late', didn't react but carried on talking. 'Frank and I have been friends for years. He wrote a very perceptive review of a play I was in – he didn't mention me, I'm not telling you to roll out past glories – but the playwright was very young and ready to slit his throat thanks to the sadist of a director. And the set was diabolical. However, Frank spotted the hidden merits of the play and his piece was so encouraging that the grateful playwright put off suicide. I wrote and told Frank what his review had meant, and how nice it was that there was a critic who wasn't merely showing off his own erudition and superiority. He replied thanking me for thanking him,' she waved her hand backwards and forwards, 'and he came backstage to see me in something else later. I was pretty struggling then . . . so it was nice that he bothered. My stock went up with the management no end.'

Frank returned with a bottle of champagne and a short smiling man wearing black needlecords and a green shirt under an embroidered waistcoat that failed to disguise a corpulent stomach. 'Sweeties, our masterchef is joining us for drinks. It's the only way I can keep servants these days . . . let them feel part of the family.'

Clement aimed a good-humoured swipe at Frank's head as he walked up to Jill. 'How are you now? You have had a rough time.'

He spoke in such a gentle voice, taking both her hands, that Jill felt a lump rise in her throat. 'What a smart waistcoat,' was all she could remark.

Clement preened. 'I made it myself from a remnant of *haute couture* silk.'

'Yes, and it needs letting out,' Fiona said bluntly. 'Your cooking's too good for your waistline, you old fart.'

Frank sighed deeply. 'I've tried and tried to teach her. Fart is not a nice word for a young lady.'

'Balls!'

'Neither, dear heart, is balls – at least, not the kind I think you mean.'

The three of them were good companions. Jill was a new audience for their outrageous stories of well-known thesps and she was entranced by the unselfconscious way Frank talked about Douglas's exploits on the *Mail*. He didn't tread carefully and apologetically around her feelings, which made her feel as if she was coming out of some long convalescence.

She hadn't known Douglas as anything but a successful writer and it intrigued her to hear how, as a young journalist, he'd bluffed to hide his ignorance of how to set about getting his stories. How, when he was bored, he used to parody the human interest articles the editor believed were of vital concern to the readers.

'He picked it up quickly enough – and wrote well, even then, so he lasted. Until his first book was accepted and then he took a chance to see if he could make it as a writer. Of course he wasn't married to Frances then so he could manage on a pittance. I used to feed him from time to time – I think he lived on Bovril and bread.'

'You didn't cook for him?' Clement broke in, horrified. 'Frank's the world's worst cook,' he told Jill.

'Of course not,' Frank said disdainfully. 'I took him to the Savoy on my expense account.'

\*   \*   \*

The meal was miraculous. Clement had once been a top chef. 'Keep my hand in with a few parties,' he twinkled at Jill's praise.

'*A few parties*,' Fiona scoffed. 'He's the one called in for all those smart society affairs. I don't know why you're not as well known as Anton Mosimann.'

'The hostesses with the leastesses try to keep him a deadly secret in case a rival pinches dear Clement and his chocolate truffled soufflé appears on *her* table. It's all so competitive, so tiring. One,' he mouthed the words, 'will only let him deliver his frangipane after dark at the tradesman's entrance.' He clapped his hand to his mouth and looked round in mock alarm.

'Best time to have it,' gurgled Fiona.

Eventually Jill struggled up from the depths of an armchair, reluctant to leave the warmth and undemanding friendliness. 'I'm sure Fred's would give you a discount if they knew who you were,' she said as she said goodbye to Fiona. 'You're a credit to their clothes. Would you like me to ask Rosomon?'

'How kind, would you really?' Fiona enthused. 'If you'd like to come, I'll send you tickets to the play I'm rehearsing now. I think it's a runner. Come backstage and see me.'

'I'd love to. I've got to make an effort and get up to town soon. I've been rather cowardly, stayed in my burrow!'

Jill threw a wrap round her shoulders and kissed Frank's cheek. 'You've been very kind. Will you and Clement come to Sherville? The kitchen staff aren't up to your standard, but I'll get something instant from Marks and Spencer.' She smiled at Clement's shocked face.

'There there, she doesn't mean it Escoffier,' Fiona drawled. 'Come on, I want a game of Scrabble.'

Frank walked her to the car. 'You won't get lost? Shall I pilot you to the main road. No? All right, take care. And Jill . . .' he poked his head into the car window. 'Douglas picked the right one at last . . . I'm positive you made him very happy. Good night my dear.'

She drove home feeling less lonely and rather cherished. It was some time before the familiar shape of the cottage loomed towards her in the dark. She'd left the porch light on and with its softened silhouette the house looked welcoming and friendly.

Her mind shied away from the emptiness within. Perhaps she should get a dog for company. Or a cat. But then what would she do with them if she went back to town? She let herself in, grateful that the food and wine were making her too sleepy to ponder that point.

# Chapter Ten

The village hall smelt of old clothes, a damp mouldiness, and that sharp, distinctive woody scent of chrysanthemums, left over from the recent horticultural society's autumn show. Jill shivered, the chrysanthemum smell reminded her of the funeral. She was glad she had taken Miriam's advice and worn warm clothes. There were already twenty-five or thirty people there, so either someone had been an effective press-gang or Miles had been energetic on his bicycle. Some were giggling and gossiping together. Others, on their own, were staring fixedly at a faded reproduction of a portrait of the Queen above the stage to hide their shyness, sitting in the two semi-circles of chairs, with careful gaps between themselves and the next person as is the English wont.

'I'm not the only newcomer then,' she murmured to Miriam.

'No. I said you wouldn't be.'

Miriam gave a bright-eyed nod to a number of people and sat down next to a middle-aged woman whose solid figure sprawled, legs apart, on the hard chair. Her rust-coloured hair showed half an inch of new grey growth, and her hooded grey eyes gave her a look of cynical knowingness.

'Hullo Molly, you didn't desert then?' Miriam greeted her.

'No, of course *I* didn't. The *Wessex* was quite right,' Molly Ferness said equably. 'We were pretty dreadful. If you can't take a bit of criticism you shouldn't prance about on a stage anyway. Besides, I was all for doing something modern – those bloody period wigs were a nightmare. Some people have very fragile egos.'

Molly lit a cigarette as a tall, well-built woman with greying hair and a decided nose stopped fondling a small black dog with unfriendly eyes to call out: 'Ah Miriam, so glad you made it. I was worried the Lampson baby would turn up – such an inconvenient family as a rule. You must encourage Elsie to go to the Family Planning Clinic – three children under six and another imminent – what a burden on the State!'

'Quite a burden for poor Elsie, too,' Miriam replied. 'Except she seems to enjoy them. At any rate they're a healthy, jolly family. I admire them.'

'Yes, well, I think she should stop now. Enough is enough. I . . .'

'Arabella,' Miriam cut in, 'this is a friend of mine who's offered to help with costumes, Mrs Jill Mortimer – Lady Montgomery-Fitch.'

'How do you do,' Arabella nodded at Jill, her gaze sharp. She looked at a clipboard on an empty chair beside her. 'Ah, yes . . . Mrs Mortimer. Miles tells me you were a dressmaker?'

Jill found it hard to keep a straight face as she heard Miriam smother a giggle. 'Roughly, yes.'

'Splendid.' Arabella walked importantly to a half-open door at the left of the hall and pushed it wider. 'Have you finished Miles, dear, I think we're nearly all here?' She shook her head fondly. 'Poor boy, he's been working all afternoon photostating the play for us to read. He's written it himself,' she said impressively.

Miles came hurriedly into the hall, smiling boyishly. 'Hooray,' he cheered. 'Now we can get started. Miriam you, of course, know everyone. Jill – may I call you Jill? – has offered to help with costumes. Next to you is Molly Ferness, our only real pro.'

'Variety, Miles, not drama,' Molly smoothed her skirt complacently.

'Sandra Teller,' Miles put his hand on the shoulder of a young woman with a ripe beauty and too much make-up. Then he checked himself. 'Oh look, it will take too long to introduce everybody, I think we'll soon get to know each other as we get down to business.'

Jill marvelled at the self-confident way Miles swept a smile around the chairs, producing shy answering smiles from the newcomers.

'There's just one thing, I may not be able to come every week,' Sandra put in, hooking her arm over the back of the chair so that the bosom in her cerise wool sweater was clearly outlined. 'I can't give up my entire social life.'

The smile disappeared from Miles's face. 'Listen everybody,' he looked sternly round the two half circles of chairs. 'If we want to be taken seriously we must be professional, make a commitment. We don't want the *Wessex Weekly* down here ridiculing us *again*. This time I want to show them what we can do.'

'Quite right, Miles!' Arabella broke in, looking frostily at Sandra. 'For my part, I'm ready to do my utmost to put Sherville on the Arts map of Dorset.' She paused as if expecting a round of applause, just as the door opened and Tom Houlderton came in with a slip of a girl whose large eyes, straight light brown hair and a rather curious assortment of clothes made her look like an underfed waif.

'Look here, you can't turn up late like this, keeping everybody waiting . . .' Arabella began fiercely.

'Sorry,' Tom seemed unperturbed. 'I arranged to pick April up, but my car wouldn't start. I think rain got in the engine. It's too old to stand out in this weather.'

'Like me,' Molly rasped a chuckle, the cigarette still in her mouth.

'April?' boomed Arabella. 'April who? There isn't any April on my list.' The girl flushed and looked awkwardly at Tom.

'April McIntosh,' Tom explained. 'I've just persuaded her to join.'

'Where do you live?' Arabella ignored Tom.

'Frimpton, on the main road.'

'Her dad runs the garage Arabella, you know where the river goes under the road.'

'I see. Well, I'm not sure we can have just anyone joining,' Arabella said severely. 'It's meant to be Sherville Drama Group. Frimpton is in Wiltshire.'

'Oh Arabella, come off it!' a clipped middle-class voice cut in. 'Tom doesn't live in Sherville, come to that. I thought you were advertising for new members. *Especially*,' she looked meaningly at Arabella, 'young ones.' Thin, elegant in a good skirt and sweater, the speaker's face wore an expression of exasperated boredom.

'This is meant to be a *community* affair, Tania,' Arabella said severely. 'We can't have all and sundry joining.' While the young

60

girl looked down at the floor, Miles led Arabella over to a chair, whispering to her. Her expression mellowed and she said almost coquettishly, 'Oh all right. Just this once we'll make an exception.'

Another figure edged nervously into the room: a young man, who nodded at Miles and groped his way to a seat at the least conspicuous end of the semi-circles.

'Hi Pete,' Miles's grin widened into a genuinely friendly one. 'OK guys, let's get on. You all have homes to go to.' He gave a pile of pages out to the first row. 'Take one yourself and pass them along will you? If there aren't enough perhaps you'd share. I was afraid to do any more in case that old photostat machine in the back blew up – it got as hot as hell. No wonder Bellweather's donated it. It'll set the place on fire one of these days.'

Miles stood in front of the two rows of expectant faces. 'Look here, I don't want to sound conceited but this is a play I wrote myself – we put it on in my last term at Cambridge and it went down very well. But if you all hate it, and think it wrong for the village, just sing out. Personally, much as I admire dear old Oscar, I can't raise much enthusiasm for yet another rerun of *The Importance of Being Ernest*.' He looked appealingly at the audience. 'I would so much like to do something up to date, that reflects how we think and feel today.'

There were a few half-hearted nods and yeses, but a tall, thin woman said crossly that the professional theatre didn't think that way about Shakespeare and look how many times Ibsen was performed. Another chap asked with the air of a concerned front bencher in the House of Commons if they could kindly be told what Miles's play was about.

Miles ignored the lack of enthusiasm. 'We'll read it now, see how it goes. Perhaps you, Edward, would take the first man; Tania, the first woman, and so on along the row. And then in a few minutes the next lot take over, OK?'

'Er, well, Miles, I made it clear I wasn't going to act,' Peter Smith said blushing fiercely. 'I'll help with a bit of carpentry, fix things up for sets but I can't act.'

Miles flashed his smile. 'That's all right Pete – this isn't a casting, we're just reading it through so we can get the feel of it, say whether we think the play's a good idea.'

Jill, too, had been nerving herself to protest. She hadn't bargained for this, but as the row in front stumbled and stammered through the lines she relaxed. What did it matter? Surely she was capable of reading aloud? Despite herself she became absorbed in the play, impressed by Molly's reading of the part of a bitchy department manager in the small factory where the play was set. She was surprisingly good, her voice taking on the cold enunciation of someone putting down an upstart, in contrast to Miriam who read the part of a trouble-some trades union member as if she was reciting a recipe. Jill had a few short speeches as a pert secretary which she managed to read without disgrace, if with little conviction.

At the end of the reading, when they swapped the parts around, they all sat up and smiled in relief at each other. The atmosphere was warmer, more friendly.

'Well? What do you think?' Miles, for the first time sounded anxious.

'Let's have some coffee and discuss it,' interrupted Tania Fellowes, the woman who had put down Lady Arabella. 'Did anyone put the urn on?'

There was a general clatter as some stood and others bustled knowingly to another door at the right of the hall.

'I thought it was brilliant,' Arabella said decisively. '*The Glass Ceiling* – such a good title. How did you think of it, Miles?' She smiled fondly at him, holding her spoilt little dog under her arm.

'Ah, you don't read the right papers, Arabella – it's not original. The glass ceiling is the invisible but effective male block to a woman's progress.'

And what could a young man inexperienced in the world of work know about it? Jill wondered.

'Ah, er Mrs Mortimer, is that right?' Someone bore down on her. 'Miriam pointed you out. I'm Edward Posner, the hon treasurer. I'm afraid I have to relieve you of a tenner. It's our subscription.'

'Yes, well I'm not sure if I do want to join, er . . .'

'You can't be in it if you're not a member' he said officiously, as if she was privileged to be there instead of having been coaxed and bullied. 'You can give me a cheque if you haven't the ready. I won't ask you for a bank card, ha ha.' He took it for granted she wanted to join.

As she meekly wrote the cheque, she wondered why she hadn't the strength of mind to say no. It was no use getting involved with something like this. In all probability she wouldn't be here next March but she handed over the cheque and shyly drifted towards the knot of people who'd gathered round the door of the kitchen as a couple of women emerged with trays of tea and plates of bright pink and yellow iced biscuits.

'Have an Assorted?' Tania thrust a plate of biscuits at Jill. 'You're new to the village, aren't you?'

Jill refused the biscuits and nodded to the statement. 'Fairly. I've been here almost two years now.'

'And so far escaped the Sunday sherry circuit? How did you manage that?'

'We've been renovating an old cottage that had been empty for years.'

'Ah! I know now. You live at the bottom of Compton Hill, by the river. Josh, my builder, was telling me about it. You're the reason I couldn't get my conservatory done two summers ago.' She smiled. 'He told me he was too busy with a "major" job.'

'It certainly was major – I didn't think we'd ever be rid of his cement mixer in the front garden.'

'Are you happy there?'

Jill looked desperately at her, willing someone else to claim her attention before she had to answer such a dreadful question. It was silly. She had to face up to this sort of thing.

'I'm afraid my husband died just over six weeks ago. It hasn't been possible to enjoy it,' she said bravely. She swallowed, managing to ask if Tania had been a member of the Drama Group for long.

The older woman's eyes were kind and she picked up the change of subject. 'Yes. I wasn't in *Rosencrantz* fortunately – I went to Australia last winter to visit my son and his family, so I was spared the row. My name's Tania Fellowes. Short for

63

Titania, would you believe, but at least it's better than Titty which is what my husband used to call me. I'm a widow, too,' she added more quietly. 'For the last nine years. You get used to it, work out a sort of life.'

Jill didn't trust herself to speak, glad that Molly Ferness joined them at that point and she didn't have to.

'I thought the script was quite good, didn't you?' A woman with fine features crumpled by age also drifted over. 'But perhaps a bit sophisticated for a village audience. D'you think it's too risky? There aren't many ambitious career women around here are there? I don't think the village will get the point. Still there are some good lines.'

'And there's the love element, Pauline,' Tania said. 'That's universal. And the divide between the factory and office staff, just like at Websters.' Websters was a local business manufacturing agricultural machinery components housed in a hideous factory outside Shaftesbury.

'I'm just worried about the number of characters – ten. Can we afford that many? Nice for those who want to act, of course, but a bit hard on the exchequer.'

Jill forced herself to join in. 'I thought it really clever. The language rang true. Miles made some really strong political points I thought. How does he do it?'

'His mother.' Pauline said succinctly. 'Her husband ran off just after Miles's young sister was born. She had to work her tail off keeping them all, she even charred.' She paused to sip her tea. 'Yet she managed to get herself a Ph.D in geology. She's very attractive. Miles idolizes her. But she still has a hard time. She works for an oil company now in research or something brainy, but Miles told me that they treat her as a glorified secretary. I should think most of his play's based on her.'

Changing the subject, Molly nodded her head towards the handsome Pauline. 'This is Pauline Rogers, my sister though no-one ever believes it. Pauline takes after Mother and unfortunately I was landed with Dad's looks.' Both women went into peals of laughter. 'Ah, but I got Dad's green fingers,' Pauline added. 'We run a nursery . . .'

'Plants not babies,' Molly put in. They both shrieked again.

'Come and see it. We're good on evergreen shrubs,' Pauline

added. 'My husband said we had to have a speciality, that evergreens give a garden structure. He's right of course, but he doesn't do a thing in the garden himself.'

I can't cope with this, Jill thought in sudden panic. Pauline talking so contentedly about 'my husband' gave her a fierce longing for Douglas's warm body, his jokes and companionship. She couldn't imagine ever laughing so freely as these sisters again. She looked round wildly for some escape.

'Come on, our young boss is looking at his watch. Back to our seats.' It was Miriam, holding her arm and guiding her to the second row of the chairs. 'I've been chatting to Peter Smith, he's desperately shy. A very good tree surgeon though, just started on his own. He tells me he's just bought one of those machines that demolish tree stumps – I must get him to come over. We've one that must go, its decayed roots have produced a startling crop of honey fungus all over the lawn. Peter was telling me it was edible, delicious in fact, I must say I haven't the nerve to sample it . . .'

Miriam's calm, matter-of-fact voice and the hand steering her to a chair, helped Jill to recover herself. She sat down and, as Molly lit yet another cigarette, leant across Miriam and asked her if she could beg one.

'Of course – sorry. I would've offered before, but I'm usually the only one to smoke and I can't tell you how many black looks come my way.' She handed Jill a cigarette and lit it for her. 'Nothing like a fellow outcast to cheer me up.'

Jill drew heavily on the unfamiliar cigarette, praying she wouldn't choke, her eyes watering. She must get a grip on herself.

'Now ladies and gentlemen,' it was Miles again. 'Let's get on. Hands up if you'd like to have a shot with *The Glass Ceiling*.'

Most hands went up, Sandra ostentatiously waving both hands.

'Thanks Sandra, one will do,' he gave her a winning smile.

The tall, thin woman who'd spoken before muttered, 'How about *Arms and the Man*?'

Faint exasperation showed on Miles's handsome face for a moment, but he hung on to his smile as Arabella called loudly,

'I think the show of hands was quite decisive, Miles.' She glanced fiercely round the group, daring anyone to disagree. 'We have a lot to do.'

Cajoling, bullying, dictating, flirting, Miles had everyone hanging on his words, convinced that each of them was crucial to the success of the Drama Group. Jill found herself enjoying his performance. It reminded her of her own manipulation of Fred Rosoman in the early days when he'd jibbed at the more avant garde designers she wanted to stock. He'd nearly fainted as price ceilings went up. 'They'll never pay three hundred for a sleeveless dress Jilly, love! There's not a metre of fabric in it. It's too plain. Get the manufacturer to embroider the bodice,' he'd pleaded. At first he'd accompanied her to the Collections, moaning audibly when afterwards she placed their orders totally ignoring the numbers he'd marked in the catalogue. 'It won't sell. I tell yer we'll be marking it down before a fortnight's out.' Yet in the end, inspired by the climbing sales, Fred had borrowed from banks, bluffed with estate agents, bullied manufacturers to give him credit so that he could expand, backing her flair. She felt a pang of nostalgia for that busy, focused life. Why had she given it up? She looked down at her hands clasped idly in her lap and caught an echo of Carla saying, 'I don't want you going to waste.'

The play was about a brilliant young woman engineer who believed that conscientious hard work would overcome male prejudice and female jealousy in the chauvinistic engineering company where she worked. The lead part went to April, the young girl who'd come in with Tom, much to the disgruntlement of Sandra. Arabella, too, tried to veto the choice, hustling Miles aside to hiss, 'Not that skinny newcomer from Frimpton! She'll be a disaster. She looks insignificant, her voice is uneducated and her father is a petrol pump attendant.'

Jill glanced across at April to see if she could hear but she seemed to be deeply immersed in the script.

'Really, Arabella!' Miriam, overhearing, expostulated. 'That's so snobbish.'

'Some of us care about standards,' Arabella returned with heavy dignity. 'If that's snobbish . . .'

'I thought April was very good in all the parts she read,' Miles said firmly. 'There's no-one else to touch her. Tom took me to see her in a play at one of the schools where he teaches and *I* asked him to persuade her to come.'

'There's Celia,' persisted Arabella. 'She went to Sherborne, such a nice girl. She doesn't have that dreadful Wiltshire burr in her voice.'

'A slight local accent is not only right for the part, but attractive.' Miles put his arm round Arabella's shoulders and led her back to her chair again. 'Celia is far too upper class for the rôle. The female lead is a determined young woman, Arabella, who in spite of a comparatively under-privileged background and the attitude of her male colleagues, is going to win through. A bit like a grocer's daughter ending up as Prime Minister,' he added mischievously. 'And of course I'd like you to be the trade unionist.'

'The trade unionist!' Arabella's scandalized voice boomed like Lady Bracknell's. 'My husband's a Conservative MP, Miles! You must be joking.'

'Your voice has such authority Arabella – this woman wields terrific influence over the work force. A Brenda Dean in the making,' he said smoothly.

And much to Jill's surprise, the large Arabella subsided, smiling coyly, muttering, 'Oh all right then, if that's what you want.'

Sandra was more difficult. 'Now Sandra, do you look like an engineer?' Miles asked her, hands on hips and surveying her figure with amusement. 'The lead is not glamorous. She's disastrously naive and she wears very drab clothes. One can hardly say that about you. No, I very much want you to be Bella, the secretary; she's absolutely vital to the action,' he added quickly as Sandra's expression remained mulish. 'And she has to be very, very sexy.' He bent to put his arm round her shoulders and whispered something, after which Sandra settled back reluctantly, lifting her shoulders and tossing her head, clearly not entirely convinced.

Beyond a request from Edward Posner, who was to play the factory boss, to rewrite some of the lines because, 'As a company chairman of many years standing, I think you haven't quite got the voice of authority in this part, Lambert,' the cast were surprisingly meek.

Jill, having watched Miles's placatory arm round two very different, difficult women was aware how sure he was of his charm. Along with Miriam, Peter and three others, she was asked to be on 'The Production Committee'. Miriam assumed charge and they were all allocated various jobs, arranging to have another meeting shortly to discuss how they were going to achieve sets, lighting, props and costumes when money was in short supply.

It was after ten before Miriam dropped Jill at the cottage. 'Good of you to help,' she commented as Jill got out.

'Between you and that determined creature Miles, did I have any choice?' Jill asked.

'Not much,' Miriam's grin was almost audible in the dark. 'Can't let you go to waste. Blast!' she exclaimed as her car phone shrilled. 'Oh no. How long? All right, keep calm, I'll be with you in twenty minutes. It's the Lampson baby,' she explained as she put the receiver back. 'Contractions every two minutes. Just as I was longing for bed! Oh well,' she reversed the car in the dark lane. 'Can't be helped, but I'd hoped she'd hang on till morning. See you.'

Jill stepped gingerly down the path in the damp darkness, envying Miriam. She was so needed, so necessary. And when she got home from delivering the baby, she could climb into bed and tuck herself round the warm, comfortable back of Roger. She stumbled along the path, cursing that she hadn't got into the country habit of always taking a torch with her and that she'd forgotten to leave the porch light on. Just as she was fumbling the key into the lock, something rushed out of the porch, brushing her legs as it passed. She screamed, in a frenzy to get inside, calling helplessly for Douglas, until her grappling hands found the lock again and she let herself in.

Sobbing, she flooded the hall with light and fought to calm down. How could she be so silly! It was probably some wild animal foraging for food, as startled as she was. She poured herself a large whisky and huddled on the sofa in the cold room, feeling bereft and foolish. The fire had long since died but she couldn't bring herself to go up the stairs to the empty bedroom. She'd leave tomorrow. Go and stay in a hotel somewhere. All she had to do was pack a few clothes and go. There was nothing to keep her here.

# Chapter Eleven

It was about five o'clock when she awoke on the sofa, cold and stiff with a blinding headache and a desperation to go to the bathroom. She climbed the stairs, pins and needles in her left leg causing her to stumble. She sat on the lavatory feeling ashamed and ill. It was little more than six weeks since Douglas had died and yet already she'd degenerated into a whingeing, pathetic heap unable to keep her nerve in the dark, drinking too much, shrinking from people, afraid of a badger or a fox.

She undressed, intending to climb into the soft womb of the bed, her refuge in these last nightmarish weeks, but an unexpected surge of energy made her change her mind and run a bath. She recognized the excited, butterfly feeling she used to have at the start of the buying season, or when the discovery of a new designer proved to be a winner. Once when the first recession of the mid-seventies had led to sales drooping, she'd had everything sober and classic taken out of the windows and ordered them to be refilled with gold, terracotta and sunny yellow stock against a glittering gold paper background. The display had looked so cheerful that it had drawn customers like a magnet.

As she remembered that resourceful woman, Jill grimaced at herself in the bathroom mirror: she had lost weight; her hair needed cutting; her skin looked sallow. If Douglas had seen her for the first time looking like this, he wouldn't have inveigled her to dinner. He'd told her that what attracted him to her at first was the energy crackling out of her. 'No wonder your hair is so curly,' he'd joked, pulling a dark strand and letting it bounce back into a corkscrew. 'You practically spark. Your teeth, your eyes, your touch – they're electric. I ought to approach you with rubber gloves.'

She dipped her head backwards into the water and let the

hair drip down her shoulders. She'd wash it, do her nails, pull herself together. Douglas had had no time for helpless women. He would hate this droopy ninny.

Deliberately she switched her thoughts to the play. That female lead, she *shouldn't* be drab, as Miles had said. He'd described her as clever and determined. Anyone with a brain would know how to make the best of themselves or where to seek help if they acknowledged their own taste was suspect. She'd wear sharp, modern outfits. Some of the other characters, though, could go over the top in tartiness; and Arabella, as the humourless stickler for union rules with an inflated sense of her own importance, she would wear no-nonsense, stiffly tailored business suits emulating men. Jill smiled: she would copy Margaret Thatcher's early style of solid suits and bow-tied necks.

She washed her hair and, wrapping it in a towel, looked at her clothes in a heap on a bedroom chair. Distaste filled her for the creased and sloppy mix, and picking them up with a fastidious hand she bundled them together and stuffed them into a plastic rubbish bag. Mrs B could dispose of them; she would not be wearing them again.

'Has the Drama Group got any money, any resources?' Jill's voice had echoes of its old crisp, businesslike ring as she rang Miles, determined to plunge straight into her new job.

'I doubt there's anything here,' Tania told her three or four phone calls later when Jill discovered she stored the group's stock of costumes. 'But why don't you come and have a look? Have some tea with me. The clothes are all quite clean, but I don't think there's anything later than circa 1950.'

Jill arranged to go over that afternoon. She was suddenly impatient, anxious to be busy, grabbing at the chance to haul herself from inertia. She sat down to read her copy of the play again, making notes on a pad as she did so. Absorbed, she was startled by the telephone ringing.

'Jill? It's Diane. How are you?'

Taken aback, Jill stammered that she was fine, thank you. Her stepdaughter had never phoned when Douglas was alive. It was he who'd made efforts to keep in touch, taking her to lunch from time to time, asking her, without success, to spend a weekend with them.

'I was wondering whether I could come down for the weekend?'

Jill couldn't believe her ears. 'What! Down here? Of course, that would be lovely . . . do you mean this weekend?' She managed to hide her confusion.

'Yes. If that's OK? I thought I'd drive down Friday afternoon, so that I arrive before it gets too dark in case I miss the signposts; you don't have streetlamps do you?'

'No – nothing like that.'

'Doesn't matter – it's not as if it's my first time, and I'm used to finding my way to strange locations.' Diane worked in a large, fashionable estate agents in Mayfair. 'Between three and four then?'

'How lovely. I shall look forward to it.' Jill's voice was high with the effort of seeming welcoming. She put the phone down feeling uneasy. How would the two of them get on without the tactful buffer of Douglas between them? When Diane had left after the funeral, Jill had assumed that that was the last she'd see of her. Why would she want to spend a weekend with a stepmother she barely knew, probably resented and certainly didn't have any affection for?

Perhaps I'm the only one she can talk to about her father, thought Jill. Frances apparently never mentioned Douglas's name after their divorce. She recalled the difficult times when Douglas and herself had attempted to talk across the silent and unresponsive Diane over a restaurant table. Even the smart place they'd chosen, a favourite of actors and writers, had failed to evince any enthusiasm. Douglas had sighed wearily afterwards and thanked Jill for her forbearance. 'She's spoilt I'm afraid. My fault. She was the only pleasure in my marriage, and she quickly learnt to play off Frances and me. I don't think either of us gave her the kind of love and proper attention children need. We were too wrapped up in our own battles, and when things got bitter, I stayed away a lot. I suppose I made up for it by indulging her.'

Surely Diane wasn't worried about her? No, she didn't care enough. But why was she coming then? Jill hurried to check on the room Carla had slept in. It was perfect. Poor Mrs B was frustrated at the small amount of work there was to do and kept every inch of the cottage spotless. The thought of Diane and herself alone together for a weekend was unnerving. What would they talk about? Diane had always been monosyllabic with her, and apart from the supportive comfort she'd given Jill by putting her arm through hers at the funeral, she'd never previously made any effort to ingratiate herself or get to know her. Or I her, for that matter, Jill thought. She'd always found Diane an intrusion, a reminder of Douglas's life with another woman.

I'll have to ask someone to dinner, she decided, dreading the prospect of her stepdaughter's visit. But who? Tom and his wife, Claudine? She barely knew them but they were the only young people she'd come across. Perhaps Miles? No, Miles was too overwhelming and single-minded. Diane wouldn't want to hear the minutiae of the Drama Group. Would this be a good opportunity to ask Frank and Clement . . . would they all get on?

Pondering such things, Jill drove to Tania's. Her house was at the top of the village street, the front latticed with a gnarled leafless wisteria, two wooden tubs either side of the front door full of lilac autumn crocus. 'I don't have much of a garden now so I lavish attention on the tubs and indoor plants,' Tania smiled as Jill exclaimed over them. 'Though you don't need green fingers for those – just shove the bulbs in. Are you a gardener?'

' 'Fraid not,' Jill admitted. 'I've never had one before – I used to live in a block of flats before I remarried.'

'It's a great time-waster. We used to have three acres and I seemed to spend most of the day pottering in the garden, even though we had a full-time chap. Nigel's idea of gardening was sitting on his lawn-mower and careering about the grass as if he were drag racing.' She smiled and led the way into a sunny sitting room looking out upon a tiny conservatory leading to a patio. 'That's the extent of my efforts now,' she gestured towards some attractive pots on the paved ground. 'I get frustrated sometimes.'

'You're welcome to get rid of that on my garden,' Jill offered. 'I'm a total ignoramus. But I can see it's addictive. I was so thrilled when the seeds we sowed last year actually flowered that I began to get ambitious.'

'There's a horticultural society in the village you know.'

'Mmmm. I'm not sure of my plans . . .' Jill was vague. 'I'm not even sure I should have got involved with the Drama Group.'

Tania filled the teapot and handed Jill a cup. 'Don't decide anything too quickly. It isn't long since you lost your husband, is it?'

Jill swallowed. 'No.' It was a strange phrase, smacking of carelessness. Perhaps she had been. Perhaps she had not looked after Douglas sufficiently well; she should have watched his diet, monitored his drinking, made him rest more.

'I couldn't bear my house after Nigel died. I sold it much too hastily and moved here. It was probably a practical thing to do but I miss it. I had to get rid of a lot of much-loved furniture which I regret now; frankly I miss the space. This is too small to have people to stay – it means that I don't see my children or friends as much as I like.'

'How did you get through, how did you survive?' Jill's voice was low. 'The future seems so grey.'

'You just *do* survive. You can't help it however much, at first, you wish otherwise. After the first shock, I used to give myself little treats, something to look forward to, avoiding the painful present. A new book that I wouldn't start until the weekend. Going to stay with a dear friend. Writing long letters to my son and grandchildren in Australia. Trying to sound cheerful and positive to them somehow made me feel better, count my blessings. Oh, lots of things – deliberately making plans so that I could wrench my mind away from feeling sorry for myself.'

'It's not easy,' Jill said in a small voice.

'Of course it isn't. One of the things I found hard was learning to cope with the business side of life: income tax; getting the boiler to work; silly things like knowing who to contact when the drain blocked; even, I'm ashamed to say, how much money I would need to live on. Nigel used to take care of everything. I can't believe now how blithely ignorant I was. It was his idea of looking after me I suppose, but when he died so suddenly I hadn't a clue.' She stared into space for a moment and then seemed to pull herself together. 'And other women.'

'Other women?'

'They regard a woman alone as a danger to their own status. I once went to a society meeting in a friend's house. It was fairly innocuous, the local history society and the first time I'd had any company but the children for six months. Then when my host offered to drive me home afterwards, his wife called out "I shall be timing you. I know exactly how long it takes to get to Tania's house." Everyone stared at me as if I were Carmen or someone. Women like her virtually shut me off from dinner parties and mixed company, as if I was some infectious disease.'

Jill could hear Faith Cruze's remark: 'Don't come at weekends – we have people then.'

Tania smiled and shrugged. 'It seems I only counted when I was half of a couple . . . it was quite a sobering lesson. Come upstairs and look at the clothes; you may find something,' she said more briskly, and gave a gentle squeeze to Jill's shoulder. 'And keep busy.'

It didn't take Jill's experienced eye more than a moment to realize there wasn't much scope among the Drama Group's stock for the kind of costumes she'd subconsciously been planning. 'Oh dear,' she said. 'Mr Posner tells me the kitty's almost broke yet there's not much here for a modern play . . .'

'Nothing new about that,' Tania said cheerfully. 'Just means we have to comb through the area's jumble sales – there seems to be a clutch of them every week in some village or other, and we can always organize one of our own. Makes a bit of money and there's generally something you can use or adapt. Lizzie Boston is a clever little dressmaker – she can turn anything into anything.'

'A *jumble sale*! It doesn't sound very likely.' Jill's nose wrinkled in distaste.

'Ah, that's because you're not an experienced scavenger! Leave it to me. I'll see when the village hall is next free and book it for a jumbly. Nothing I like more than a good old rummage.'

# Chapter Twelve

Jill had felt cheered by the pragmatism and humour of Tania Fellowes. And she was someone who had coped with widowhood, so perhaps there was hope for Jill herself. But Tania had had a long married life *and* children. We had only three years, she mourned. She had to make herself telephone Frank and Clement.

'How are you?' Clement had answered and asked warmly, as if he really cared and, 'What a nice surprise! We'd love to come. Shall I bring something?'

'Your frangipane? No, I shall try cooking for a change, but you must lower your standards.'

Claudine Houlderton, when she spoke to her, did not at first know who Jill was, and then, when Jill told her about the picture she said, 'Ooh of course, you're the one who had a row with Mrs Cruze . . . I'm sorry, yes oh dear! I'm always putting my foot in it. I mean I *do* remember you.'

'Well, are you free?' Jill ignored the stutterings.

'Gosh, you don't dress up do you?' Claudine's voice was still childish and anxious. 'I haven't anything smart to wear.'

Jill reassured her.

'Oh great. So many people round here get all done up, and Tom hasn't got a dinner jacket.'

'Dinner jackets in the country!'

'God, yes! Everybody is powdered, lipsticked and squeezed into court shoes and glamorous silk jobs. That's why we don't get asked out much. The farm's so muddy I spend my days in jeans and wellies. I don't have much else except my wedding dress.'

'Come in jeans if you like, but perhaps just change out of the gumboots.'

'Oh, good!' Claudine missed the teasing. 'Then we'll come. Anyway it'll save us a meal,' she added ingenuously.

But when Jill saw Diane she wondered whether the dinner party was a mistake. Since she'd last seen her, her stepdaughter had lost weight. Her skin had lost the creamy sheen of good pearls and was chalky white; she looked heavy eyed, her face was gaunt, and after the initial polite greeting she hardly spoke. When Jill showed her proudly to the pretty bedroom with its comic bathroom she merely said, 'The cottage is bigger than one would guess from the outside.'

Jill yearned to put her arms round her, comfort her, tell her that they shared their grief, but there was a chill reserve about Diane. When Jill attempted to hug and kiss her on her arrival, she'd turned her cheek and unwillingly given a polite social buss.

'I thought we'd have soup and an omelette by the fire,' Jill attempted to sound cheerful. 'There's a good play on after the news, Alan Bennett. I like him, don't you?'

Diane shrugged and lit another cigarette, her fifth. 'I can take him or leave him.'

'Well, we don't have to watch. I can record it for another time. There's so little that's worthwhile on the box that I hoard anything halfway decent. And we're supposed to have the best television in the world! Makes me wonder what the rest is like.'

'I don't watch TV,' Diane returned indifferently. 'Anyway, I'd rather have an early night.'

'Fine, we'll eat about half past seven, that suit you? How's the property market? Still in the doldrums?'

'So-so.'

'What exactly do you do?'

'I'm working in the furnished lettings department at the moment.'

'Is that interesting? I mean seeing the inside of other people's homes, how they furnish. Do you think decor reflects personality?'

Another shrug. 'I've no idea. I just get sick of showing smart alecs round desirable flats and having them leer at me in the bedroom.'

'You don't go alone do you?'

'Of course.'

'But isn't that asking for trouble? An attractive young woman like you and a strange man . . . think of Suzy Lamplugh, that estate agent who disappeared.'

Diane gave a derisive laugh. 'I can look after myself.'

But can you? thought Jill, looking at her surreptitiously. You look pretty rough to me.

'Come and help me in the kitchen. Would you like a cheese or mushroom omelette? You'll find the soup in a blue jug in the fridge.'

Jill ignored Diane's lack of enthusiasm as she reluctantly poured the soup into a saucepan. She was puzzled as to why she'd wanted to come since she didn't seem very pleased to be here. She determined to make another effort, but the weekend already seemed doomed. 'The cutlery's in that drawer there. Have you seen any new plays, been to any concerts?'

'No. I mostly go to clubs. I did see *The Song is Sung*, much against my will. I was dragged there by a friend.'

'Oh – what was it like? I met Fiona Trentbridge two or three weeks ago. She was telling me she was about to open in it.'

'She was very glamorous, and the play was all right, if you like heart-rending stories about talented emigrés forced to wash up in restaurants, but I thought the ending weak. Anyway I'm not keen on the theatre.'

'I read Frank Huxtable's review of it and the *Mail*'s . . . both were very warm. You must have met Frank – he was an old friend of your father's.'

'Before my time,' Diane said carelessly. 'He goes back to when Daddy was a reporter, I wasn't even born.'

'He's been very kind. He admired Douglas. In fact he and his friend Clement are coming to dinner tomorrow.'

'Oh no! Are you being social already?'

'I asked them because I thought people to dinner would amuse you. I'm not much company.'

'I wouldn't have come if I'd known you were going in for junketing. I never know what to talk about to old people.'

'Frank's roughly your father's age. Anyway, they're not all *old*, as you kindly put it. There's a young local couple coming too. The chap, Tom Houlderton, who painted that picture in the sitting room. Did you notice it?'

'Can't say I did.'

78

Gracious, is the whole weekend going to be such hard work? Jill thought. She was appalled at the amount of alcohol Diane put away. She'd poured herself two very large gin and tonics before supper, and drank two thirds of the bottle of white wine, yet she'd barely touched her omelette. Then Jill thought wryly of her own lonely drinking; she could hardly talk. Perhaps this was the way some people reacted to grief, wasn't that why it was called 'drowning your sorrows'? It hadn't drowned hers, merely made her headachey.

She was relieved when Diane stood up and said abruptly, 'I think I'll go to bed now.'

'All right, if you're tired. I'll wait for the ten o'clock news. You have everything you want? Good, then sleep well. Good night.'

'Good night.' There was an explosive 'Shit!' as Diane stumbled at the curve on the narrow stairs.

# Chapter Thirteen

In spite of Saturday being a beautifully sunny day, unseasonably warm, Diane didn't surface in the morning. Jill had gone hopefully to the river with her daily offering. The bread always disappeared but there had been no further sign of the duck. Gus had looked disapproving when he saw her throw out the bread. 'Bring rats that will,' he said. 'You don't want none of 'em 'ere.' She told him about the duck, but he'd sniffed, 'Mess up the grass, ducks do.'

She pottered in the kitchen with preparations for the dinner party, wondering whether to take Diane breakfast in bed but thought better of it.

When, at one o'clock, Diane finally wandered into the kitchen, smoking, she looked very little better for the long sleep. She went first to the sideboard and helped herself to a gin. 'Do you usually get up so early at the weekend?' she asked Jill, but she wasn't quite so offhand as the previous evening.

During lunch she even asked about the dinner guests. 'So what am I supposed to say to Frank Huxtable? I don't read *The World*. Did he come to the . . . the funeral.'

Jill caught the slight stumble over the word 'funeral'. She does care, she thought. She was overcome by the thought that Diane was all that was left of Douglas. If only we'd met years ago, she thought, perhaps we'd have had children. It was a desolate thought and for a moment she bitterly resented Douglas's earlier marriage. She'd missed so much of his life, his struggles to write, his triumphs, the excitement when the first film was made. It made her feel deprived, but she wrenched her mind away from that track. It only meant another wallow in self-pity.

When Frank and Clement arrived, Diane was charm personified. Jill was stunned at the change in her as she asked Frank about the time he'd worked with Douglas; told Clement she'd heard that Anton Mosimann regarded him as a serious rival; actually listened with apparent sympathy to Claudine's plan to try to have a test-tube baby if the current hormone-boosting injections didn't work.

'Spare me,' shuddered Frank.

'He's delicate,' Clement explained to an offended Claudine. 'He has to have a tranquillizer if I put a plaster on a cut finger. Now *I'm* fascinated, tell me, how does the baby get into the test tube, and more importantly, how does it get *out*?'

'So you're saddled with the costumes,' Tom grinned at Jill. 'At least you don't have to rustle up eighteenth-century ball-gowns from some rather faded curtains and a stained Nottingham lace tablecloth like Geraldine Sinclair did. And one year we had a Mrs Malaprop with sixty-two-inch hips.'

'I sympathize,' Jill grimaced. 'I bet you never have dealings with theatre companies that have to hold raffles and a jumble sale to quarry for cash and costumes?' she said to Frank.

'Jill, dear, I don't like the turn of this conversation. Do you mean you're involving yourself in *amateur dramatics*! This could be the end of a beautiful friendship. I've had to judge, for my sins, far too many unprofessional productions when some misguided industrialist has offered prizes for up-and-coming actors or playwrights. It's too cruel to critics. How would you like to have to deliver a serious judgement on would-be Oliviers with bandy legs and a nasal drawl, or umpteen Maggie Smiths where the only resemblance is dyed red hair? Oh dear!' He affected to be quite overcome.

Jill patted his hand. 'There there, no-one's asking you to see it.'

She refilled his glass as Tom laughed at his theatricals and told him, 'Our lot were slaughtered by a critic from the *Wessex Weekly* last year. It was nearly the end of the Drama Group.'

'Then their critic is braver than I am. I'll take on Trevor Nunn, David Hare, Vanessa Redgrave – even John Osborne but when it comes to am drams, I run a mile. Two miles,' he added.

When they'd all gone, Diane helped Jill clear the table and stack the dishwasher. It was their first companionable moment. 'He's a bit of a flirt, that young man,' Diane said unexpectedly.

'Tom?'

'He kept pressing his thigh against mine during dinner, and it wasn't accidental. And he's asked me to his studio tomorrow afternoon, made a point of saying Claudine was going to see her sister.'

Jill turned in astonishment. 'I didn't hear that.'

'It was after the meal, he made some pretext of showing me that picture of his you have, asking if I knew the spot – you were all sitting round the fire.'

'Good heavens, I'd no idea! Are you going?'

'Of course not. I've enough problems.' She stood drying a wine glass so rigidly that she twisted the bowl off the stem. 'Oh I'm sorry. *Sorry*.'

To Jill's horror she began to cry. 'Don't worry about it, it's nothing. I've plenty more.'

But when the girl just stood in the middle of the floor sobbing, Jill took the broken glass and tea towel from her, and put her arms round her.

'Come on, there's something more than a broken glass behind this. Whatever's the matter? I've been worried about you ever since you arrived.'

But Diane drew another shuddering breath and broke away from the embrace. 'There's nothing wrong. I'm just tired.' She started to wrap the broken glass in paper towels.

'Diane, look you can tell me if something's worrying you. I'm quite worldly. Is it a man?'

'It's nothing, I tell you.' She reached for her packet of cigarettes on the kitchen table and inhaled deeply. 'Don't worry.'

'I *am* worried. Douglas loved you very much. I'm sure he'd have wanted to help you in any way he could.'

'Then why did he have to go and die on me?' she gave a fierce puff of her cigarette. 'First you took him and then he *dies*. I lost him twice over.'

'You never lost him through me. He spoke of you all the time. His only regret was that we didn't seem to click. He wanted us to be friends.'

82

'He only had eyes for you. I was shouldered out.'

She's jealous, thought Jill for the first time, looking at Diane's face struggling for composure, her mascara smudged, nose pink, eyes apprehensive.

'We loved each other, sure,' Jill said quietly. 'I think we were both surprised that at our age we could fall in love like a couple of teenagers.' She gave a half laugh, and picked up the saucepan she'd been attempting to clean of the remains of a blackberry sauce before Diane's outburst. 'But I was as well as, not instead of, you. He had enough love for both of us.'

They were both silent for a moment.

'Why did you want to come down?' Jill's change of tone made Diane blink.

'I told you. I was tired. I wanted to get away from . . . from London.'

'You said you had enough problems . . . what are they?' Jill, surfacing from the constant preoccupation with her own feelings, was relentless.

Diane's expression was mulish for a moment and then her face seemed to break up, her lips trembled as she turned her back. 'I've been having an affair with a married man if you must know. Is that so unusual?' The words came out in a sudden rush. 'But – but now he's disappeared.'

'Married men often do when they get too entangled.' Jill kept her voice noncommittal.

'No, you don't understand. *I* gave *him* the push. I think he may kill himself.' She looked over her shoulder into Jill's face to register her degree of shock, but it was expressionless.

'What makes you think that?'

'He said he would. When I told him that it was over for me, he made a big scene. He couldn't believe I hadn't meant it when I . . . when I . . .'

'When you let him believe you were fond of him?'

Diane nodded. 'I told him it had just been a bit of fun, and he went mad.'

Jill could well imagine Diane's cool off-hand treatment of a man she was trying to ditch.

'He shook me so hard I thought my head would come off. Then he sprang it on me that he'd just told his wife about us, told her he was leaving her for me. I didn't know he'd done that!' She gave a little sob and bent her head. 'I thought he was bluffing, trying to make me change my mind. When I said that it made no difference, we were still finished, he said he'd kill me and then himself and rushed out of the flat. I was terrified. His eyes looked awful and his skin was a dirty white. I don't think he's normal.'

'Most people behave strangely when they have a shock.'

Diane looked up again and shook her head. 'No, he's moody. He used to gamble like crazy, or do stupid dares. He'd act like a raucous schoolboy one minute, and then be sunk into depression and refuse to talk the next. He just got too much to take. Look, can I have another drink?'

'If you must. It doesn't help.'

'It bloody well does.' Diane gulped at the drink. 'He hasn't been in the office for the past week either.'

'So he works at Rutlands, too?'

Diane nodded.

Jill ushered her into the sitting room and stood with her back to the fire. 'When did all this happen?'

'About ten days ago. Christ, I've broken up with enough men before without any trouble. I just keep imagining his body somewhere . . . and his wife phones me at all hours, screaming at me. She says her three-year-old can't sleep and she's four months pregnant. She won't give me any peace.'

Jill was taken aback at the way she talked of the wife, as if she were a mere inconvenience, not someone whose life she'd wrecked. But she was anxious not to alienate Diane, so she simply said, 'If he'd done anything terrible, he'd have been found by now. People have broken love affairs every day of the week. They might feel like suicide, but that's usually as far as it goes. He's probably gone somewhere to lick his wounds, to get over you.'

'I keep thinking he's behind me, jumping out on me from a doorway or – or climbing into the flat. He said he'd kill me, too.'

In spite of herself Jill felt a twinge of fear. The papers were always full of terrible stories. But she downplayed her reply.

'You've been seeing too many thrillers. Everyday life isn't

that melodramatic. He probably said those stupid things to get back at you for hurting him. He'd just smashed up his family life for you. No wonder he felt murderous.' She kept her tone reasonable, even.

'I told him I was sorry.'

'That must have made it a lot better!' Jill couldn't help the sarcasm.

Diane twitched away. 'I knew you wouldn't understand. If I'd told Daddy he would have helped me. I could always talk to him. Until *you* came.'

'Don't be childish.' Jill's voice was curt. 'You just don't want anyone to tell you you've behaved badly. I don't think even your father would have been amused by this little escapade.'

There was silence.

Jill put her hand on Diane's shoulder. 'Look I'm sorry it's such a mess. Stay here for a few days until it blows over.'

Diane shrugged off her hand petulantly. 'And have sanctimonious lectures from you all the time? No thanks. I can look after myself. If you don't mind I'll go to bed now. I'll leave in the morning.'

She stalked out of the room and Jill heard another 'Shit!' as she caught her foot in the same twist of the narrow staircase.

Jill looked ruefully at Tom Houlderton's picture. Douglas would not think much of her handling of his daughter. There was no doubt he had adored Diane. I should have been more tactful, she thought. But Diane was bloody irresponsible. She shut up the wood-burning stove for the night and went to bed.

# Chapter Fourteen

To Jill's surprise, Diane came down early the next day. Jill waited for her to dump a suitcase on the floor and announce she was off, but instead she said a cold 'Good morning' and sat at the breakfast table, reaching for the coffee pot. The atmosphere was strained, with them both being carefully polite to each other until their chilly 'Would you like some more coffee?' and 'No thanks. Can I pass you the butter?' struck Jill as so comic that she burst into giggles.

'This is all too much of an effort,' she said laughing openly. 'OK, I sounded like a pious old judge last night – I'm sorry. And you did a good imitation of a hard-hearted bitch. Let's call it quits shall we and start again?'

Diane's frozen expression wobbled and broke into a smile. 'I'm sorry too. It's been so awful. Of course, I know Daddy would have been furious with me. And I know I'm selfish, but I am also really really scared.'

'Well, let's be practical. We can let the police know of the threats just for your peace of mind . . .'

'The police!' She looked alarmed.

'They'll take the threats seriously, I'm sure. They'll check up on him, let him know they're protecting you.'

'I don't want any cops poking their noses in! I just thought I could stay here for a few days until he calms down.'

'You can, of course. But what about your job? Could you arrange some holiday?'

'If you must know I've just been given the sack.'

'Oh no! Why?'

'I suppose I wasn't much good. They need more hard-nosed sales people – the property market is contracting. There isn't much scope. I was thinking of leaving anyway.'

'What will you do?'

Diane shrugged. 'I'll survive.'

Jill wondered if she assumed another man would soon be picking up her bills. She considered whether it would do any good if she talked to the pregnant wife? What was there to say: my stepdaughter is very sorry for the trouble she's caused, she has no further interest in your husband and now please will you forgive her and forget all this unpleasantness?

Diane leaned back and looked at Jill coolly, drawing deeply on her cigarette. 'I suppose you think I'm an absolute pig.'

Jill bit back the sharp words she first thought of and asked obliquely if Diane's mother knew.

'Christ, no! She'd simply tell me I'd brought it all on myself and to get on with it. I thought of this place because it's so cut off, though how you could let Dad bang you up somewhere so remote as this I can't think.'

'There's a train to Waterloo or you can drive to London in a couple of hours.' Jill was defensive.

'Convenient for popping into Harrods, I suppose.'

Jill smiled and handed Diane a tea towel. 'Here, it's not worth putting these in the dishwasher.'

After lunch Jill forced a reluctant Diane to go for a walk. She was pleased when Diane involuntarily exclaimed at the beauty of the autumn afternoon, the sun still strong enough to turn the trees into spectacular colour. They leaned against a gate and there wasn't a sound except for the soft rustle of the leaves as they left the twigs to join the thick damp carpet made by their companions.

'It's so quiet.' There was a touch of awe in Diane's voice. And walking back, more relaxed, she started to talk about her parents. It was as if, in the anonymous open country, Diane could ditch her inhibitions.

Jill wondered if Diane realized the appalling picture she was painting of an only child caught in the crossfire of two hostile parents, but then she hadn't known anything else. To some extent, it explained her withdrawal, her desire to enter only into easy, undemanding relationships.

What sort of mother would I have made, Jill asked herself. She had never had any maternal yearnings. Her first marriage was so brief; in less than a year she'd realized that she and David had little in common in either outlook or interests. He was an attractive man and sex had kept the illusion of happiness going for some while, but when he'd suggested they start a family she had been unwilling. Unnerved at her own reaction, she had tried to picture herself and David in the future with a brace of children, but she'd felt suffocated at the prospect.

It was then that she'd faced the fact that their marriage was empty, pointless. And yet she hadn't ended it. Something to do with a reluctance to admit to failure, to shock and upset her conventional parents, had made her channel her frustration into her job. Longer hours, frequent buying trips abroad, a constant shelving of plans for the two of them, had turned the normally good-tempered David into a testy and irritable creature prone to criticism. He had gradually become distant, until one evening he had come home after her, a surprising thing in itself, and told her he had found someone else.

Initially Jill's pride had been hurt, but relief had quickly superseded any other emotion. Her parents, predictably anxious and worried, had counselled her to have another try. 'You can't break up a marriage over a little difficulty,' her father had said. 'You have to work at it, smooth the rough edges, make allowances for each other.'

'It isn't a little difficulty, Dad. It's fundamental. There's nothing to patch up. We don't love each other; I'm afraid I never did.'

'Then why did you marry David in the first place?' he'd demanded, turning away in embarrassment when she had said succinctly, 'Sex'.

Perhaps she and David, too, would have used children as a scoreboard for their marital disharmony, spoiling them with material blandishments to make up for their own guilt? After the divorce she'd been profoundly relieved that there had been no kids, yet when she married Douglas she surprised herself by a sudden longing to have his child.

'It's possible,' she had said. 'Lots of women over forty have their first child these days.'

But he had shaken his head. 'You're young enough Jill, but I'm not. It's not fair to a child to be fathered by someone old enough to be their grandfather. Besides, you're all I want.'

Jill now had an urge to make up to Diane for her unhappy childhood, to have Diane love her. She was part of Douglas, her mother had let her down, why shouldn't she turn to Jill?

She pulled herself up, shocked at her own thoughts. How could she think of taking over a grown young woman, someone else's daughter? Had grief made her really crazy?

'Did you ever think of going to university?' she babbled, unnerved by her unexpected longing.

'Mum desperately wanted me to be brainy, to go off and shine at Oxbridge. Unfortunately the fact that she wished it was enough to make me determine not to.'

'That's a pretty negative reason.'

'I am negative.'

Jill ignored the truculence. 'What are you good at?'

'Nothing.'

'That's nonsense.'

'It's true. Most things seem to need years of training. Life's too short.'

'Well, actually it's pretty long if you're bored stiff. Come on, the light goes quickly at this time of year. I reckon we've taken enough exercise to justify crumpets for tea, don't you?'

The evening was more relaxed. They settled in the sofas either side of the log fire with the Sunday papers, reading items out to each other. Sometimes Diane broke in with a 'What if . . .' speculating about the dreaded Peter's actions and his possible whereabouts. For the first time since Douglas's death Jill felt comfortable, at home. She looked across at the beautiful girl gracefully curled up on the sofa, and didn't want her to go.

# Chapter Fifteen

On Monday morning, to Jill's astonishment, Diane again joined her for breakfast. 'Heavens – it's only eight o'clock! Couldn't you sleep?'

Diane looked uncomfortable. 'I feel gruesome. I didn't mean to unload everything on to you. I just felt too terrified to stay in the flat on my own, and I didn't know where else to go. You must think me a pill.' She was staring fixedly at Jill.

'Don't be silly – it's nice to have you here. I have to go to the village for some odds and ends,' Jill said hurriedly, troubled again by the rush of feeling for Diane. 'Do you want to come?'

'I think I'd rather stay here.' She was fidgeting, ill at ease. Jill thought she was embarrassed at her attempt at an apology, or regretting telling her so much. 'Make yourself some coffee. I won't be long.'

In the village she bumped into Tania.

'Ah! Just the person I wanted to see,' Tania beamed. 'I was going to phone you as soon as I got back. I've booked the village hall for Saturday week – can you believe it, they had a cancellation!'

Jill looked mystified.

'The jumble sale,' Tania reminded her. 'We have to work fast. I've made a list for you, and got the others at it too. You work through that and get them to cough up their junk.' She was taking Jill's help for granted.

'Oh, I couldn't do that,' Jill protested. 'I wouldn't know how to begin.'

'Just knock at the door, smile and ask for their help. They won't eat you. People are kind, gives them a chance for a clear-out.' She tucked a handwritten list under Jill's arms. 'Here's your patch. Don't lose a moment.' She waved and trotted busily up the hill leaving Jill, appalled, looking after her.

'Mrs Mortimer!' Arabella, clutching her pug, and accompanied by a thin young man, was the next person to bear down on her. 'I've just been told your husband was the writer Douglas Mortimer, is that right?' Jill nodded. 'Then you must come to one of my Sundays – my husband, Sir Harold, was a devotee, wasn't he James? What a pity your husband died, Harold would so liked to have met him.'

The young man looked agonizedly at Jill, his eyes pleading forgiveness for his companion's lack of tact.

'Have you met my son James? Mrs Mortimer is helping with the costumes, James. I only wish you would get yourself interested, too.'

James shook Jill's hand and mumbled something.

'The younger generation, never do anything worthwhile do they?' Arabella's eyes swept irritably over her son. 'Don't slouch, James. He left Eton last year and has done nothing since except get under my feet. Won't go to university . . .'

'I wasn't offered a place, Mother,' James's voice was firm and unexpectedly attractive. 'I didn't get good enough grades.'

'Good gracious, that doesn't matter with the right families. These things can always be arranged. You mustn't be so accepting. D'you know,' she turned again to Jill. 'He says he'd rather go to a polytechnic than university.'

'Mother, I don't think we should keep Mrs Mortimer, she must be busy and I need to get some silken tofu from the deli,' he nodded politely to Jill and turned towards Watson's.

Arabella shook her head at Jill. 'If only he were more like dear Miles. *And* he's vegetarian! Now Sunday, mind, twelve o'clock, d'you know Stourbridge Court? It's just behind the church, anyone will tell you the way.'

'I'm afraid I can't come,' Jill found her voice.

'Can't come?' Arabella boomed in surprise, taken aback. 'Of course you must come!'

'I'm sorry, I have other things to do.' Jill turned away sharply. Awful woman! She was shaking with anger. *What a pity your husband died.* How unreasonable of Douglas when Sir Harold would so like to talk to him! She felt the same murderous passion that Faith Cruze had generated.

She hurried up the hill to the funny little post office-cum-supermarket for some stamps, and to dump her washing. The post office was agent for the only laundry and dry cleaners in the area. Molly Ferness was standing by the old-fashioned grille. How odd that suddenly the village street was bristling with people whose names she now knew; she had probably seen them all before, but they had not impinged on her consciousness. Now they had turned into personalities.

'You look white,' Molly turned from the counter, hastily hiding her pension book. 'Are you feeling all right?' She held open the door festooned with postcard advertisements.

'Oh, it's just rage. I haven't had time to calm down.'

'Come and have a coffee – there's a coffee "leeownge" on the side of the hardware shop.' She raised her eyebrows enquiringly.

'That would be nice,' Jill said dubiously. 'I didn't know we boasted a coffee shop.'

'Opened last week, probably closes next; the venture of the manager's entrepreneurial new wife. But Sherville's a very close-fisted little place. People don't spend money freely. Eating out would be considered louche if they knew what louche meant. Sometimes I hate it and wish I was out on the road again.' They walked slowly up the hill, and entered the coffee bar together.

'You miss the theatre?' asked Jill.

'Terribly. Every night about six I get these awful withdrawal symptoms. I imagine everyone in their dressing rooms, doing their make-up, gossiping . . . some of the orchestra tuning up . . . there's nothing to beat it.'

'What happened?'

'Television I suppose. There's no work for someone like me – a bit of patter, a song or two . . .' her eyes glazed as she stared at some inner vision. 'What made you so angry just now?'

'Not what, *who*.' Jill smiled wryly. 'Oh, it doesn't matter. I expect I was unduly sensitive.'

'Then it must have been Arabella,' Molly said definitely. 'I saw her steaming down the streeet like a galleon in full sail with her unfortunate son beside her. She always leaves casualties.'

'In here James, Mrs Truscott has just opened this dear little coffee shop, just what Sherville needs.' Arabella seemed to fill the small room, with her son trailing behind her. 'Ah there you are, Mrs Mortimer; Molly,' she inclined her head icily to include

Molly in a slight greeting. 'I'm glad I caught you up. If you can't manage next Sunday, how about tomorrow? I always have the people who run my Riding for the Disabled in for a drink after the committee meeting, and one or two neighbours. You can manage that, I'm sure.'

'I'm afraid not. I have my stepdaughter staying with me . . .' Jill cursed herself for giving a reason.

Arabella beamed. 'Then bring her . . . no problem. At six then. Come James,' she swept out again, ignoring the sharp rattle of cups from Mrs Truscott.

Jill looked ruefully at Molly. 'I've never known a more impossible woman! She must have pursued me here.'

'You can't say "no" to Arabella. She makes life such a misery if you do. At least they're generous with the drinks,' Molly said wistfully. 'Champagne all the time. You'd think it was tap water the way they pour it. She used to invite me when she wanted me to put on a pantomime for the hospital – once it was over I was dropped.' She sipped her coffee reflectively. 'Of course I did get drunk at her first-night party and tried to make her do the Twist with me.' She laughed so infectiously at the memory that Jill had to smile. 'Give her her due, she's energetic at raising money, sits on practically every committee you can think of. She gets through twice as much as most people. If she weren't such a disgusting snob and about as sensitive as a rhinoceros she'd be quite nice really.' Then she burst into another school-girl peal of laughter. 'Poor Arabella, it can't be much fun being married to Harold. It was she who pushed and pulled him into Parliament. Her father-in-law admired her enormously. She should have been the MP and left Harold down here to chase girls . . . though she's too much like Mrs Thatcher. I don't suppose Parliament could stand two of them.'

She changed the subject. 'When are you coming to see our nursery? Well, it's mostly Pauline's but since I seem to be forever "resting" she's given me an unskilled job. Now's the right time to plant shrubs, as long as there isn't a frost.'

'I'd love to,' Jill said, 'but I haven't a clue about plants. I wouldn't know what to choose.'

'Pauline will help. She's marvellous . . .'

By the time they left the tiny coffee shop, Jill had arranged to go to the nursery that afternoon. Douglas, delighting in gardening for the first time in his life, had made great plans. He'd wanted the east side of the cottage to have more trees and shrubs, to make a glade, 'And masses of bulbs underneath,' he'd said. 'It will attract your birds.' He'd given her a pair of lightweight binoculars and a field guide because she'd become entranced with the wild birds she could see from the kitchen window.

The invitation to the nursery somehow kindled a compulsion to continue his plans. It will be something he wanted, she thought. Even if I go back to London his little glade will go on growing there every year. Her face softened and smiled in recall. She had felt soaringly happy and really alive in those short years with Douglas.

Back home, Jill went up to Douglas's study, wanting to find him, to feel his presence, and was taken aback to see Diane curled in his armchair reading. 'What are you doing in *here*?' she demanded, dismay throttling her at the sight of Diane so much at home in Douglas's silent shrine. She stood almost menacingly over the girl, until she saw Diane huddle back into the chair, her eyes fearful.

Then the familiar expression of disdain came back to mask Diane's features. 'He was *my* father before he was your husband,' she retorted. 'I wanted to see his room, something that was just him and not the two of you.'

Compunction, and the sight of the dried tears on Diane's cheeks made Jill stumble an apology. 'I'm sorry. It's just that you gave me a turn. I can't bear anyone to come in here. I won't even let Mrs B clean it.'

Diane's expression relaxed a little, too, but there was a certain wariness as she said, 'I've been reading *To Jericho and Back* again.' She held out the book. 'Daddy could write, couldn't he? I'd forgotten how well. I suppose Mum was always criticizing him so much that I came to look down on his work.'

Jill softened again. '*To Jericho and Back* was his favourite. That's why he left you the royalties.'

'The solicitor didn't make it clear – are they just from the book or do I get any more whenever the film is shown again?'

The question wounded Jill in its materialism, and she answered coldly. 'I've no idea. I suppose so.'

'I'll have to find out. The fact is, I'm broke. And now I haven't a job.'

'Broke? But you'll have thirty thousand soon, when Douglas's estate is settled. You're worrying unnecessarily.'

Diane held the book to her face so that only her apprehensive eyes showed over the top.

'I'm afraid not. I – I lost a lot of money gambling. Peter used to take me to casinos. He gets a high from betting. I suppose I got caught up in the fever. At the time I thought it was rather cool. I'm behind with the mortgage on my flat. And I still owe for some of the redecorations. I got carried away when I was doing it up and it cost a bomb.'

'What did you decorate with – gold leaf?'

Diane sighed oblivious of the sarcasm. 'You've no idea – the curtains for my bedroom cost twenty-five pounds a metre. I had to have a complete new bathroom – the old one was dire.'

Jill's eyes were steely as she looked at Diane. 'So let's have it straight. How much do you owe?'

'Thirty-six thousand.'

'Christ!' Jill sank on to the windowseat. How could a slip of a girl of nineteen spend that much money? Douglas's word 'spoilt' was an understatement. 'What would you have done if you didn't have the legacy?'

'Daddy would still be here. He'd have helped me. He always did.'

There was no answer to that. Jill wondered to what extent Douglas had helped her before. Surely £36,000 was a lot even for a successful author?

'Have you told your mother about all this?'

'Of course not.' The reply was scornful but her face was piteous. '*Why* did Daddy have to die, when I need him so.' Her eyes welled and big drops plopped on to the page.

Jill's throat contracted and she knelt down and put her arms round Diane. The girl was openly blubbing. 'You have got yourself into a mess,' she said gently.

'I know. My life is ruined,' Diane sobbed in agreement.

Jill smiled slightly as she blotted Diane's eyes with a tissue.

'Not quite, but you've made a good start.' She pulled her up from the chair, and shepherded her out of the room with its urgent memories again conscious of the childlike way Diane leant against her arm, allowing herself to be propelled along.

Downstairs in the kitchen, her mind busy with the extent of Diane's confession, Jill made coffee. She handed Diane a newspaper she had picked up in the village. 'There, read about Somalia and count your blessings.' She smiled at the huddled figure. 'We'll work something out. I've said I'd go to a nursery garden this afternoon. Care to join me? Your father wanted to plant a glade, with masses of bulbs underneath the trees at the side of the cottage. Apparently now is the time of year to do it.'

'No thanks. I can't imagine Daddy a gardener. You certainly influenced him.' Resentment once more iced her words.

'Not I. I know nothing about gardening. It's just something he'd always wanted to do apparently. I found it curious too.'

'I suppose he stopped writing down here? It's not exactly stimulating. He used to travel a lot, always bringing me presents from the country where he'd researched the background to a new book. Then it stopped when he met you. You kept him pegged down here.'

'You mustn't blame me for everything,' Jill said lightly. 'I took a great deal of persuading to move down here. Douglas loved it, particularly his study. He wrote every day, beginning before breakfast. He liked going out into the garden in the early morning – but I expect you know that.' She broke off abruptly.

'I hardly saw him at home. He used to work from a little office he rented somewhere.' Diane's voice was sulky.

'His last book was almost finished. I suppose it's somewhere in the word processor. I'll have to ask Tom Feathers about it. He and Douglas kept in constant touch.' With difficulty, Jill kept her tone conversational. She was going to make it impossible for Diane to have another row.

'Daddy must have left you a very rich woman. Twenty-three books and three films.'

'Twenty-two – you have one of them remember and they were by no means all bestsellers.' She tried to smile, angry at Diane's words but making allowances for her. She must be at her wit's end. On top of her father's death there was this unhinged man and a large debt. Jill wondered if she had been told everything now.

# Chapter Sixteen

Jill picked up the phone several times to ring Lady Montgomery-Fitch to say she would not be going to her drinks party, but each time she put the phone down before dialling. She was going to have to see the wretched woman at rehearsals, bump into her in the village street, was it worth the discomfort of antagonizing her? Wouldn't she just cause unnecessary friction in the Drama Group by refusing? She'd have one drink, be unfailingly polite, and leave. It was much the best course.

In the afternoon she went to the nursery to find that choosing plants, as directed by Pauline, was not simply a matter of picking something that looked pretty.

'Where are they to go, sun, shade? What's it for – a screen, to make a shape, for flowers?' Pauline bewildered her with questions, made her visualize the height and breadth of the shrubs and decide whether it mattered that they shed their leaves in winter. And even if she decided on, say, a sorbus, which variety? There were masses of different ones, each with a redeeming characteristic or a drawback.

'I didn't know there was so much to it. No wonder I've made so many mistakes,' Jill said.

'We all do. It surprises me that so many people think you can garden naturally, as if you absorb knowledge by some kind of mysterious osmosis. I've spent my whole life here and I'm still learning.' She wrote out an invoice for Jill. 'I've given you a ten per cent discount,' she smiled. 'As a new customer.'

'Help, I've been extravagant!' Jill exclaimed at the daunting total.

'No more than two or three cases of decent wine would set you back – and these will last much longer,' Pauline assented cheerfully. 'I'll get Sam to load your car, and if you like, I'll help you place them. You have old Gus to garden don't you?

He's reliable, though he prefers vegetables to anything more decorative.'

Jill returned excited at the thought of the glade becoming reality, clutching a book Pauline had lent her. She hadn't realized colour and shape mattered as much in a garden as in a house, or in fashion. Pauline had said it was essential to visit other gardens. 'See as many as you can. Some will give you ideas – others will show what *not* to do, just as important.'

To Jill's surprise, Diane seemed quite keen to go to the Montgomery-Fitches. 'May as well. There's nothing much else to do. She sounds unbelievable.'

Stourbridge Court was at the end of a long drive, comparatively modern and as pretentious as a Hampstead Garden suburb. The front of the house was floodlit and ubiquitous carriage lamps shone brassily either side of the wide front door. Lawns, punctuated by beds of gloomy rhododendrons, loomed out of the dark as they drove up.

It was James who opened the door, abashed at seeing Diane. 'Oh, er, hullo. I'm James,' he stammered, and received a cool nod from Diane in return.

Arabella bustled up wearing the sort of violently patterned cocktail frock that Jill had banished from Fred's when she'd joined in 1970.

'Ah Mrs Mortimer, so glad you could come . . . do you know everyone here.' She pattered busily about, introducing Jill and Diane to an assortment of retired army types and county women who apparently made up the committee, ordering James to bring them drinks.

'I'm afraid my husband isn't here yet – he's often late. I expect there was a division. Even Harold has to obey the Whips you know.'

Jill was left to talk to a robust woman in an unfortunate knitted dress as Diane accepted a glass of champagne and took a sip whilst looking at James over the rim, so that he blushed and cleared his throat.

'James, go and refill Griselda's glass,' Arabella said sharply, and took Diane's elbow. 'Tell me, are you staying permanently with Mrs Mortimer?' she asked her.

'No, I live in London,' Diane replied.

'How *do* you stand it?' Arabella exclaimed. 'Sometimes when I go there I feel as if I'm in the middle of Calcutta. Last time, I swear, I hardly saw a white face.'

'I've hardly seen one here,' returned Diane, looking pointedly at Arabella's ruddy and weather-beaten complexion. 'Everyone looks so healthy. What party does your husband belong to?'

Arabella stood still in shock. 'Could there be any doubt? My dear child!'

Diane wrinkled her brow. 'I thought there were three parties,' she said innocently.

Arabella's mouth opened, but a suitable crushing comment eluded her. Instead she was distracted by the sight of her husband and Miles in the doorway.

'Miles!' she shrieked delightedly and, leaving Diane, rushed over.

'Hullo, Bella,' her husband greeted her indifferently. 'Lambert was on the train and I persuaded him to come along.'

Arabella's face was beaming as she scolded Miles. 'You naughty boy, you didn't tell me you were going to London. I might have had a little errand for you.' She caught his hand and took him to the drinks tray, leaving her husband to fend for himself.

'D'you ride?' an elderly gentleman sporting a deaf aid shouted at Diane.

'No, I'm afraid not.'

'Should y'know. Shakes up the liver. I'm eighty-eight and I ride out every day, rain or shine. My liver's dandy despite punishing it with this,' he held up his glass, which was whisky, not champagne. 'Can't stand that fizzy stuff,' he said in disgust indicating Diane's glass.

James loomed at Diane's shoulder. 'Colonel, Mrs Wayneflete is leaving. She says do you want a lift?'

'Course I do; she knows that.' He downed his whisky. 'Can't drive now, arthritis. So damned early to leave. Worst of having to rely on others, no will of one's own. All right, I'm coming,' he bawled across to a woman almost as old as himself, who was standing impatiently in the doorway of the drawing room, her coat already on.

'Are they safe?' Diane asked James, as they watched the elderly pair, both with bowed shoulders and unsteady feet, totter through the hall.

He laughed. 'She drives a motor as if it were a carriage and pair,' he said. 'She can barely see over the steering wheel, but she hasn't had an accident so far. Of course, I haven't counted how many she's caused.'

'Is Miles your brother?' Diane queried, gazing to where Miles was talking animatedly to Arabella.

James turned away from the sight. 'No,' he said shortly. 'I think my mother wishes he were. Much more her sort of son than me.'

Diane tilted up her face to look at him. 'What's wrong with you?'

Jill had been collected and ushered into Sir Harold's presence. He looked a little surprised to hear from Arabella how much he had enjoyed Douglas Mortimer's books. 'Don't have much time for reading,' he said heartily, as though it were a virtue. 'You must be lonely in that cottage. So cut off. I rode past it not long ago and hardly recognized it. The two old ladies, coupla witches, who lived there wouldn't let anyone near the place. I must say you improve the scenery,' he added jovially. 'Not enough pretty women in Sherville.' He leered at Jill and took her half-empty glass. 'Let me top you up.'

'Thank you, no, I was just leaving,' Jill said coldly.

'Oh, stay and have a bite with us. You're widowed aren't you? Nothing to go home for then is there? You're one of my new constituents, I have to get to know you. That's as good an excuse as any, what?' He barked a loud laugh.

Jill gave him a look of pure hatred, repelled by his words as well as the way he stood too close to her, thrusting his face into hers. 'I have to go. I must collect my stepdaughter.' She looked round the large room, and saw Diane with both James and Miles in tow. Miles was talking animatedly, whilst James looked on stolidly. Diane had a faintly amused, indulgent expression, as if a puppy was playing at her feet.

'Your stepdaughter is doin' all right,' Sir Harold said meaningly. 'Another lovely woman. Too young for me, I like them more mature,' he leered at her again. 'But I hope James gets stuck in there. He's so slow that boy, look at him letting young Lambert have all the innings.' He drained his glass in disgust as Jill pointedly turned her back and walked across the room to Diane.

'God, what a crowd,' Diane exclaimed in the darkness of the car going home. 'That woman! I thought she'd have a stroke when I asked her what party her husband belonged to.' She went off into giggles. 'The boy's nice.'

'Miles?'

'No, James. But he hasn't a shred of self-confidence. His mother has done a pretty good hatchet job on him.'

'Helped by his beastly father,' added Jill. 'I came near to throttling him I was so angry. I can't believe how many murderous impulses I've had lately.'

'Oh dear, Daddy has a lot to answer for bringing a Londoner like you to this neck of the woods. What on earth can you do down here? You won't stay, of course.'

'I don't suppose so,' Jill answered slowly. 'I shall stay until the play's put on. I was dragged along to that Drama Group, but now I've made a commitment there.'

'Well, they must have managed before you came.'

'With difficulty, apparently. There's hardly any cash in the kitty but I'm going to get Fred Rosomon to cough up some clothes – he must have some old stock I can take off his hands. I thought I'd have the lead in some really snappy clothes, the sort Moschino does, and . . .'

She hadn't realized how much she was thinking out loud until Diane interrupted, resentfully: 'You're enjoying this aren't you?'

Jill pressed on the accelerator to take the hill. 'It's something to fill in time, something to do,' she replied evenly. 'I can't make plans. Not yet. I haven't healed enough. I can't face the future. I need this just to help me move from one day to the next.'

Diane was silent. Then she said abruptly, 'I haven't healed either. It's not only your loss.'

'I know that.' Jill put a hand on her knee. 'We've both got to get through this period. We must help each other.'

A slight sob escaped Diane. 'I'm so bloody selfish. But I just don't know what to do with myself.' Her voice was a wail.

Jill drove carefully into the garage beside the cottage and switched off the engine. The dark, after the headlights, was intense.

'You haven't thought about it, that's why,' she said quietly. Turning in the dark to the girl beside her, half-bewildered child, half-confident vamp, she commented, 'I always thought I'd be a fashion designer, then when I worked as a Saturday girl at Biba, I realized what fun a shop was. I was in my element when I got the job at Fred's. It didn't seem like work. I loved it. You must find something you enjoy.'

'I've told you, I'm no good at anything.'

'Rubbish. There's bound to be something that uses your energies, that really interests you. Come on, let's get inside. It's cold – there'll be a frost tonight.'

'You're beginning to sound like a country woman,' Diane grumbled. 'Any minute now you'll be pickling beetroot or some such disgusting activity.'

# Chapter Seventeen

Diane left at the end of the week, promising Jill she would keep in touch. She looked a little less wan, but was still nervy and fidgety, ready to snap if anyone made a careless remark. Both Miles and James had telephoned to ask her out. Offhand, she'd reluctantly agreed to go for a walk with James, and had a meal in a pub in another village with Miles. She'd returned exhausted from her walk, a slight colour in her cheeks, and out of breath. 'That guy is so fit, I practically had to run to keep up with him! He's a nutter. I was treated to a lecture on the healing properties of plants, the life and times of hedgehogs, and the name of every bally bird in sight. They all looked alike to me.'

When Jill asked about her date with Miles she was vague. 'It was all right.'

After Diane's outburst about her financial situation, they'd had one serious discussion when Jill made Diane sit down with her and go through her expenses. Her flat was large and in a smart area.

'Do you have to live in Notting Hill Gate?' Jill asked. 'And why three bedrooms?'

'I hate seedy places – besides, I got this at under the market price. It came in through the office. It was a bargain.'

'Maybe, but your mortgage is horrendous. I think you should either sell the flat or sublet to a couple of nice girls. There are two bathrooms after all.'

'I didn't realize you were so beady-eyed about money,' Diane said tartly.

'I've had to be,' Jill retorted. 'I didn't have an indulgent father to bail me out every time I made a mistake.' Diane said nothing but her lip pushed out in a pout.

Jill thought of the bedsit in Battersea she had lived in as a nineteen-year-old, sharing a kitchen and bathroom with three other young women. Douglas had not been interested in luxuries either, Diane couldn't have got her lavish ideas from him. Jill was puzzled by her swings of mood. One minute she would be friendly, even comparatively warm, and then some time later, fidgety, nervous, unable to sit still. She'd try to needle Jill with spiteful remarks but when Jill didn't rise to the bait, she'd flounce off to her room. Later, she'd come back, benign, good-tempered, anxious to help prepare a meal, seemingly unaware that she had been anything but angelic.

Alone again, Jill returned to her costumes. She was determined that that side of the production should be professional. Tania had phoned to ask how she'd got on collecting jumble and she had lied, saying she was just about to start. The prospect of knocking on the doors of complete strangers and asking for their throw-outs unnerved her.

She had to force herself up the hill. At the first cottage she was daunted by the fierce dog which bounded up. Jill shrank back, and attempted to assure it she was a friend. Fortunately a woman came round the side of the cottage, and at her authoritative 'Quiet!' the dog subsided into a tail-wagging softie.

'Of course pet, but there's not much,' the woman said pleasantly when Jill explained her errand. 'The church was round only a month ago for their jumble. Call back tomorrow and I'll sort something out for you. Where'd you say you come from? Oh, the Bates cottage, I know it. Fancy anyone taking on that old ruin I says to my Ernest, but it looks much tidier now. You had to have the roof done I see.'

'Yes, and the wiring and the flooring and the woodwork and the damp course,' Jill smiled. 'It's taken the best part of two years.'

Encouraged by that reception, she toiled on up the hill and received a very disgruntled greeting from the next house. 'I was listening to *Woman's Hour*,' the woman said accusingly. 'No, I haven't any jumble and if I had I wouldn't give it to the Drama Group. Just an excuse to show off I call it.' She shut the door firmly in the middle of Jill's apology for troubling her.

But most of the neighbours were welcoming and pleasant, as Tania had said they would be, anxious to chat, curious about

Jill. Any illusions she'd had that she was a stranger were soon dispelled. It was clear they knew of her as the newcomer who'd taken over the Bates' wreck of a cottage, whose husband had died a short time ago. The village was much too small for such an event to go unremarked and unnoticed. She was touched by one or two offers of help. 'Bit cut off in that place down there, aren't you? Have you got candles and plenty of wood? We sometimes get electricity cuts in the winter. You call, mind, if you're in trouble.'

When the day of the jumble sale arrived, Jill's heart sank at the piles of rumpled clothes in the middle of the hall; the broken lamps and battered kettles that were produced, ancient radios and old books, chipped cups, and glass objects which seemed to have no purpose either useful or decorative. Tania was in her element directing four or five helpers: 'Anything too disgusting, Mrs Chambers, stuff in the sacks for the ragman . . . put women's clothes on this rail and the men's over there. Children's – they always go well, over here, they look so much more appealing hanging up.'

She looked bright-eyed at Jill. 'Some lovely green velvet curtains over there from Lady Maplethorpe, and there's almost a half tea service from Brigadier Oliver – Minton, no less – that should fetch a lot. At least twelve pounds wouldn't you say Nancy?' she turned to a woman scanning the offerings next to her. 'Nancy's good at pricing – done all the jumbles here for fifteen years.'

'You do get to know what people will pay,' Nancy said sagely. 'It's not what it's worth it's what they're prepared to fork out.' She sniffed at the pretty teacups. 'People prefer mugs these days, still, start at twelve quid anyhow, you can always come down before the end. A dealer will snap them up in the first five minutes if they're any good.'

Jill looked through some of the clothes. Some would dye, perhaps . . . and there was the perfect suit for Arabella, she picked it up excitedly. Alexon too, hadn't Mrs Thatcher worn Alexon? She began to collect bits and pieces – anything that looked clean and had some body in the fabric. A bias-cut crepe dress – that might convert to something suitably tarty. And that raincoat! She snapped it up feverishly, the doors would open shortly and she must comb through all this lot.

'That's mine, thank you,' One of the helpers snatched back the raincoat and glared at Jill. 'Can't put anything down a minute in this place.'

Jill apologized. 'I thought it was jumble.'

'Oh you did, did you?' She gave Jill a disgusted look. 'It's almost brand new.' She rolled the coat up and put it defensively under her chair. Jill apologized again.

Tania swooped up. 'We're opening the doors any minute – are you ready Mrs Billough?'

'When I've made my belongings safe,' she muttered grimly. '*She* nearly pinched my mac.' Tania laughed.

'Oh, poor Mrs Billough – something like that always happens doesn't it? Remember when we had music and George sold the loud-speakers the vicar had lent us? I had a terrible job finding out who'd bought them and persuading them to give them back. The fuss the vicar made – puce with fury when he heard we'd sold them for a fiver – that was the last time we had music.' She laughed again and Mrs Billough reluctantly softened her scowl. 'I've got Mrs Briggs coming to relieve you at three o'clock and there's tea and cakes for the helpers in the back room.' She moved on round the other stalls, checking everyone was ready for the opening.

Jill was astonished by the rush when the doors did open at 2 p.m. prompt. Women surged in, the light of battle in their eyes, reminding her of sale time in the big stores. There were about half a dozen who headed the rush, who sorted through the stalls with miraculous speed. 'Professionals,' murmured Tania. 'They run market stalls of their own and unerringly pick the bargains.'

Bemused, Jill watched the hunters as she sold tea and cakes from her stand just under the hall's platform.

'Can I treat you to a rock cake?' It was Miles smiling at her. 'I've just bought a dozen 78s for twenty pence the lot. There's "Begin the beguine" and "Down Mexico Way" and "I'm heading for the last round-up". Delicious! My cottage has no running water or electricity, but came complete with a wind-up gramophone. Now I have something to play on it.'

At 4.30 it was all over. A few sad-looking leftovers were being folded up and stuffed in plastic sacks. 'We'll offer that lot to Hilda Fortescue,' Tania said, as the takings were being counted. 'Her village has a jumbly coming up for their recreation ground, she'll be glad of this little lot to start her off. The rest can go to the totter.' She smiled across at Jill, who was perched on the edge of her table and sipping a cup of stewed lukewarm tea. 'Fun, wasn't it? One woman bought a tweed coat for thirty pence and found a fifty pence piece in the pocket.' She laughed. 'And we've made sixty-seven pounds, plus over twenty from the raffle for that basket of fruit. Raffles always do well.'

Jill shook her head. Fred Rosomon should have been here.

# Chapter Eighteen

'You coming back then?' Fred Rosomon's throaty voice was hopeful. 'Work is the thing you need now, my girl. You was always a worker. You don't belong in the country. Whadda they wear down there, smocks?'

Fred's family had been in what he called 'the garment trade' ever since his father had come to England in the Thirties and set up as a tailor with a second-hand sewing machine in London's East End.

'Fred, I'm really ringing to ask you to have lunch with me – I want to ask you a favour.'

'You do me a favour me girl and come back. Fred's just isn't the same any more. That Christine has no sense. She bought twenty sarong skirts in the *same* colour. I ask you Jilly, twenty tomato-red skirts!'

'Oh come on, Fred – you used to tell me I didn't know what I was doing.'

'Ah yes, that's diff'rent. That was only at the beginning. When I saw you knew what you was about I left you alone, dint I?'

'How about lunch then, tomorrow week? You can tell me all your troubles.'

Fred was always happy when someone took him to lunch. He read out every item on the menu with relish, together with the price. 'I ought to be in the restaurant trade, Jill. Look at those prices. What a mark-up! How much does a pound of sprouts cost, eh? Here they charge three pounds for a portion, about four sprouts I expect.'

When he'd eaten his way through the most expensive dishes, garnished so much it was more a disguise than a trimming, he shot Jill a canny look. 'So you want to come back eh? What will I do with that Christine? She won't go back to being your assistant after being Merchandise Director of Fred's, will she? It's a big job now, prestijus.'

'Fred, you must understand. I can't make plans. Not yet. I wouldn't be any good. Until I get my head together, I can't concentrate. I'm out of touch.' She put her hand over Fred's thin, yellow one. 'I want you to give me some of your old stock.'

'What! You settin' up on your own then?' His eyes narrowed suspiciously as she explained about the play. 'Don't seem much fun in that. An amacher production. A lot of village idiots prancin' around in old stock. Now I believe you when you say you're off your rocker.'

Jill smiled at him. 'It's something to pass the time, helps take my mind off . . . off . . . things.' She looked at him sadly. She was fond of Rosomon. They'd been through a lot together, taken risks, experienced triumph, faced, in the early days, the threat of bankruptcy.

'That's what I'm saying. You come back. You'd soon pick up the threads. I'll sort out that Christine – Jack Cohen said he was looking for someone, course it's a bit downmarket from Fred's and out at Belsize Park . . .'

'No Fred. I've made a commitment to this Drama Group. Dressing a play three months off is about all I can cope with. I thought you might have some suitable things – the group has no money. Could I come back and have a look through the stock room?'

'I suppose so. There's a lot of unsolds hanging around. That Christine won't listen to me but who's the loser, eh? Me. A lot of her stuff didn't even go in the sale and I marked it down forty per cent . . .'

'Then I'll be doing you a favour,' Jill grinned. Fred was always petrified of losing money. 'Oh – and by the way, I met Fiona Trentbridge, the actress recently. I think it would be a good business move to offer her a discount at Fred's. She has a lovely figure and is in *The Song is Sung* at the moment. She's always being interviewed. Good publicity for you.'

'Jilly, you crease me. You buys me a lunch and then before I've finished me coffee you asks me to give you me valuable stock and let some dolly have me clothes at cut price. It'd have been cheaper to take *you* to lunch.' He shook his head at her, his expression pure melancholy and then it brightened as a thought struck him.

'I suppose this Fiona woman isn't looking for a boyfriend is she? I'm a lonely man you know, Jilly.' He stared hopefully at her. Jill remembered his pick-ups, a stream of disasters, young girls on the make, often models from the catwalks, or a young designer whose clothes he would suddenly discover were pure genius.

'I doubt it, Fred. She seems to have a string of men after her, and no wonder. I'm going to her matinée tomorrow. I'm staying overnight at Brown's. I've got to see my solicitor, and Douglas's agent and, if I can contact her, my stepdaughter.'

She walked back to Fred's with Rosomon, hearing his grumbles about the business climate, the way fashion magazines always picked the worst sellers to feature and then expected him to back the editorials with stock. 'You used to guide the fashion editors, Jilly. You made contact with them in Paris, or had lunch with them here; but with that Christine they just rings up and tells her they're putting in a Lacroix or someone unwearable and she agrees to stock it.'

'Editorial mentions in good magazines are valuable, Fred.'

'I know that, but you have to control them, not let *them* say what's in or out. They've no idea!'

Jill was concerned to see Fred's seemed to have declined. There were so few customers that the staff were standing around with little to do. The displays looked tired. Her fingers itched to remove an insignificant necklace from a half mannequin wearing a Donna Karan top and a stunning hat tilted at the wrong angle.

Later, at the hotel she fell into an armchair exhausted. She'd done a very satisfactory deal with Rosomon, but it had taken most of the afternoon. She was appalled at the amount of sales stock he had. 'That Christine' had certainly made some expensive mistakes. Poor Fred. No wonder he was so down in the mouth. It was her fault. Christine had been her assistant and Jill had assured Rosomon that she would be competent enough to take her place. Now there seemed to be no clear direction in the shops. Jill had been careful as each expansion had been made to keep a separate character in each one; there'd been the classics, like the Jean Muirs; the weekend clothes, relaxed and fun; the frankly young and sexy Azzedine Alaia; the glamorous evening clothes. All the staff were aware of the current stock throughout the departments so that a sale was never lost if Jill could help it. She'd used colour strongly, and changed the displays every seven days. It was important to keep a feeling of excitement going. She felt deeply disappointed at the way Fred's had slipped.

She was having dinner that evening with Tom and Gemma Feathers. He'd been insistent when she'd telephoned about Douglas's last book. 'We're longing to see you. Come to the flat. You'll stay the night of course.' But Jill had thought it would be a strain to keep up a social act for so long and made some excuse about early appointments.

Both were warmly welcoming. 'You've lost weight. You haven't been looking after yourself,' Tom accused her.

'Oh, I do. But it seems too much trouble to cook for one. I nibble a lot; I'll soon be quite fat.'

Tom talked about Douglas's last book of which he had ten chapters and a synopsis. 'We had a few, er, discussions about it at the publisher's,' he said judiciously. 'It's very different from his other books. It's got a rural background. I don't know how his fans are going to take it – they're used to exotic locations. A critic once said a Mortimer novel was as good as a travel guide.'

Jill recalled Diane's words: *He used to travel a lot . . . Then it stopped when he met you. You kept him pegged down here.* Had she wrecked Douglas as a writer?

'Isn't it any good?' She desperately wanted his last novel to be his best, to have distilled into it some of his happiness and contentment with her.

'*I* like it,' Tom said heartily. 'It's just that it's uncharacteristically romantic; Douglas has always been a writer of action-packed adventure. The great British public like roughly the same book in different covers. It's what they come to expect from a writer.' He shrugged. 'Douglas has been a popular author for a long time. I don't think there's anything to worry about. But do you know if he finished it?'

'I think so. He was working solidly before we went away, but he didn't actually say.' She felt ill informed. Surely Douglas would have given a whoop of joy at having finished the book?

She tried to remember the one before. He'd come down from the study and opened a bottle of champagne. 'Another useful cheque on the way towards all those expensive improvements you're making,' he'd said. He'd finished that one just as they'd got planning permission to extend the cottage. But this one? Jill felt disturbed. She realized now that Douglas hadn't discussed the book much with her. Whenever she'd asked about it he'd just said, 'Oh it's going along. Just have to keep at it.' He'd changed the subject. And she hadn't known him long enough to know how much or how little he liked to discuss his work in progress.

'Well, have a look on his word processor. It must be in there somewhere. I'll get my secretary to give you the file code. He always put it on the top of the manuscript.'

'I'm not knowledgeable about word processors, but I'll see what I can do. What if it's not finished?'

'Oh, he was bound to be so far along that there would only be a little tinkering to do. I have the synopsis. We could get another writer to polish up the ending if it needs it, don't you worry. You haven't read any of it then?' He looked at her intently.

Jill shifted uncomfortably. 'No.'

'Ah, then you'll be surprised when it comes out, I think.'

'Oh, don't go on talking shop,' Gemma broke in. 'Tell me about the cottage. Are you going to sell it?'

'I haven't made any plans,' Jill's tone was cool.

'Of course not,' Tom shot a warning look at Gemma. 'Much too soon. How's that beautiful daughter? I thought she was very supportive at the funeral.'

'She's just lost her job with an estate agency. She's at a loose end. And broke. In fact, I wanted to ask you about *To Jericho and Back*. Douglas left Diane the royalties on it. Could she live on them?'

'My dear girl! It's been out some time. She'd have enough to buy herself a new frock now and then.'

'Is that all? She'll be so disappointed.'

Tom clicked his fingers. 'I've an idea. I wonder if I could talk the publishers into bringing out a new edition – a boxed set of Douglas's books.' His enthusiasm grew. 'It could be rushed out to capitalize on his death. Would Diane write a preface to it, a kind of short memoir about her father . . . ?' he broke off. 'I'm sorry. That was insensitive.'

Jill smiled faintly. 'You forget I am – was,' she corrected herself, 'a businesswoman. Anything that would help boost the royalties would find favour with Diane right now.'

'Can she write?'

'I've no idea. But she must buck up and do something. I think she's going to waste.' She mentally winced at her use of the words. Wasn't that what Carla and Miriam had said about herself?

'Well, the genes are there – Frances used to review for the TLS at one time, quite good if a touch lofty. This daughter may be able to string words together. I remember Douglas once showed me an essay she'd written when she was still at school. He was tickled pink by it, I can't remember what it was about, except that she had an attractive descriptive touch. Would you like me to talk to her, see if there's anything I can do?'

'Would you? I don't like her being at a loose end.'

'You sound more like her mother than a stepmother,' Gemma said. 'Are you close?'

'Not really,' Jill admitted reluctantly. 'She's been staying with me for a few days that's all.'


She woke early and stretched in the hotel bed. It was nice to have a full day ahead again. She was going to see her solicitor, have her hair cut, a check-up with her dentist, then Fiona's matinée, and a train back about seven. She was tempted to call Diane, suggest a quick lunch, but it was too early and she had to be at the solicitor's by nine. She'd drop by her flat after the dentist. She'd picked up a beautiful sweater at Fred's, a deep violet. She smiled, visualizing Diane's surprise and pleasure when she gave it to her. The kid had had a hard time.

But when Jill rang the bell of the eccentrically built house where Diane had her flat there was no reply. Disappointment engulfed her. It had been foolish to come on the off-chance like this yet she had wanted to see the girl, mentally picturing her opening the tissue-wrapped sweater that Jill knew would suit her. I'm being ridiculous, Jill told herself. She's not my daughter. She was just turning away when the door opened.

An unkempt-looking man stood staring at her. 'You want something?'

'No,' Jill answered coldly, 'I was calling on someone in Flat Three, but she's out.'

'Oh, Di,' he said familiarly. 'She don't like visitors. You can leave a message with me. I'm in Flat One. Her friend.' Behind him Jill caught a glimpse of the hall of the block. It looked dusty, scruffy with bits and pieces of battered furniture scattered about and a black plastic bag spilling rubbish. What on earth was Diane doing here? The man was still staring, smoking a stained roll-up cigarette in a repellent, slack-mouthed way.

'Thank you, I'll go up and leave a message myself.'

'You can't come in,' he half closed the door behind him and towered disagreeably over her. 'Only householders are allowed in – how do I know Di wants to see you. Besides she's out. I saw her go.'

Jill knew he wasn't telling the truth, but she couldn't force her way in, and there'd been no reply to Diane's buzzer. 'Very well,' she said coldly. 'I'll telephone.'

'What did you say your name was?' he demanded. He was still standing in the doorway, but Jill felt a change of atmosphere from suspicion to menace.

'I didn't,' she said flatly and walked down the steps to the pavement, trying not to break into an undignified trot. Unreasonably, but with total conviction, she knew the man was evil. Diane must get away from there.

# Chapter Nineteen

The play took her mind off Diane, though it felt strange sitting in the theatre along with all the comfortable matrons with permed curls. As far as Jill could tell, they were all wearing the same sort of jersey two-pieces or shirtwaist dresses as they filed in from the coaches that had delivered them from the suburbs. In the interval they shared chocolates, devoured ice cream, queued for cups of lukewarm tea in the inadequate theatre bars, chattering excitedly like schoolgirls on an outing.

Jill couldn't recall ever having been to a matinée before and hurried round to Fiona's dressing room, feeling a stranger in unfamiliar territory.

'Hul-*lo*. So you used the tickets after all?' Fiona was lying on the floor with her legs and feet braced against the wall.

'One of them – I thought, if you don't mind, I'd give the other to the young chap who's producing a local drama. He's crazy about the theatre.'

'Sure. You can use it any time. Those seats are kept for me or the director until curtain-up. It's one of my few privileges. Who is this young man? Is he attractive? Send him round if he is. I'm fresh out of interesting men at the moment. The last bugger has upped and married some droopy deb – a pity. He was loaded *and* quite imaginative in bed.'

The dresser who had let Jill in, hung a costume on a rail, clicked her tongue in mock-disapproval, then turned to a corner where a kettle was steaming.

'Tea? Or something stronger?' Fiona's upside-down face asked Jill. 'Can't get up for the moment. Five minutes of this and I revive sufficiently for the second act. The blood's supposed to freshen up the brain. If you believe that you believe anything.'

'I'm enjoying the play. That young man John Selling is good.

So are you, of course. I thought the last bit when you took him to bed was delicately done.'

'Yeah – particularly when you know John is as gay as they come and goes heavy on the garlic; it's bloody difficult for either of us to pretend to be carried away by passion.'

'But why pick on you to play the older woman? You don't look more than twenty-five.'

'Thanks. I'm thirty-seven. I wanted the part. The character is meaty – a change for me. Love metamorphoses the hard-hearted rich bitch I play into a human being and then I lose him to someone his own age . . . not an original plot but the writing's good. You wait till you see the end; I go mad with jealous rage.' She smiled happily. 'Bookings stretch beyond Christmas – that's damn good for these times. But look here – how about you?'

'I'm fine.'

'You could fool me. Despite your immaculate hair – who does it for you? – you look what my mother used to call "peely-weely". Are you looking after yourself? Did you have to see the play alone?'

It was her warm, kind tone rather than her words that made Jill break into humiliating sobs. 'I'm sorry, so sorry,' she gasped, searching blindly for a handkerchief. A tissue was dropped into her hand by the dresser, who pressed her shoulder, indicated a cup of tea on the dressing table and melted away.

Jill was conscious of a scented arm round her shoulders. 'C'mon, buck up,' Fiona said softly.

'I'm sorry. I'm being pathetic.' She reached blindly for the tea, slopping some of it into the saucer, and bent her head over the cup. Fiona was silent whilst she recovered herself but stroked her back as if soothing a cat. Jill sniffed and bit her lip. 'It overwhelms me sometimes still. I can't believe it's all over for me and Douglas; sometimes I want to hit other people for being alive when he isn't. All sorts of ghastly, selfish people whom nobody would miss are walking around, and Douglas has gone.' Fiona exuded such a warm humanity that she felt she'd known her years.

'Well if I go out and garotte a few of the ghastlies, would that help?' Fiona put a finger under Jill's chin so that she could smile at her. 'No of course not. You have to go on living, make a life for yourself. You've had the gift of love, something few people find. Be grateful. So many women simply have memories of tedious affairs or boring, conventional marriages. Were you ever in love before?'

'No, not really. No-one who really meant anything.'

'Were you unhappy then?'

'No, I suppose not.' Before she'd known Douglas she would have described herself as happy, even fulfilled. 'You see I had an interesting job at Fred's, enough friends – of both sexes,' she emphasized to the amatory Fiona, 'to take care of my spare time.'

'Well, then.' Fiona turned her hands out. 'Count yourself lucky. All that and the added bonus of having known love. Not everyone can say that.'

Jill blew her nose. 'If you've never loved, you don't know how I feel.'

'I've never truly loved a man,' Fiona said quietly. There was a long silence. 'But I adored my daughter. She died when she was seven.'

Shock and sympathy hit Jill at the same time. 'I'm so sorry. I didn't know.'

'Of course you didn't. I was deranged when Sunny died. And bitter. But then I asked myself if the seven years of having her were worth the anguish . . . and of course they were. I couldn't wish I'd never had her. I behaved like a robot; made myself work, eat a little, drink a lot, and gradually I became human again. The hurt and emptiness are still here,' she put a fist on her chest, 'but I function. So will you.'

She kissed Jill on her wet cheek as the dresser came in again with rather more noise than necessary.

'I've got to go on again. That's got two meanings,' she smiled sweetly at Jill. 'Give me a ring when you next come to town and we'll have lunch or a late supper after the show. Now you go and watch the next bit where John is supposed to be torn between love and loyalty to me and his passion for another – he can hardly keep it up. And that's another double meaning,' she laughed.

Jill marvelled at her ability to switch from seriousness to gaiety in seconds. She herself tried to sound normal as she turned at the dressing-room door. 'Fred Rosomon would be happy to give you a discount by the way . . . I saw him yesterday. I told him you were a great advertisement for Fred's but he was more interested in knowing if you were short of a boyfriend.' She smiled. 'Don't worry. He's fairly harmless. They'll be sending you a card which you just produce when you want anything.' As Fiona changed swiftly into a clinging red silk dress, every inch a siren, Jill hurried back to her seat.

# Chapter Twenty

She would weep no more. There'd been moments alone when she'd let slip control, beating the wall with her fists out of a sense of futility. The violence of her raving had frightened her, leaving her weak and wrung out. Now the oddly comforting and noisy rocking of the train home sent her into a dreamy trance. Wasn't it much worse to lose a child you had created and nurtured, and cherished hopes for, than a husband? Why compare? she thought. Both are devastating. Yet Fiona had carried on, so had Tania. She wasn't a special case.

Seeing Fred's again had conjured up a ghost; that of the spirited, competitive woman she had been. She'd had an itch to make improvements – there were so many things obviously wrong. Rosomon had been right about all those disastrous sarong skirts in tomato red, and the display had no sharpness. Perhaps she should go back. She must try to think of Douglas and the cottage as a beautiful interlude, a dream, but a fairytale that had ended.

Pondering what she should do, even considering joining Carla and her accessories shop, Jill came back to Tom Feathers' unspoken nervousness on the subject of Douglas's book. Soon she was worrying about Diane again and found that it lightened the intensity of her own misery. She'd tried telephoning Diane several times; she'd sent the sweater by post in the end, but hadn't heard from her. It was a relief that the Drama Group was beginning to take up more of her time. Lizzie Boston, who was also on the production committee, had taken to ringing her frequently with queries. She had once worked as a fitter for Norman Hartnell and Jill found her a talented dressmaker. Together they'd gone through the jumble-sale garments and Lizzie had carried off some that needed cleaning or repair.

'I won't do anything much to them until you've decided who wears what,' she said. 'That suit you wanted for Lady

Montgomery-Fitch will need letting out – but there's enough room in the pleat at the back. She's hippy, Lady Fitch, but not a lot of bosom. I think there'll be enough in the seams to ease the jacket a little.'

The clothes that Jill had chosen at Fred's arrived beautifully packed in tissue inside the distinctive glossy mauve boxes. She asked Lizzie to help her unpack them in the hall before the rehearsal, and loved seeing her round face light up as she helped shake out the tissue paper and hang the clothes on a rail. They made the jumble-sale finds look pathetic, even though Lizzie had had the Alexon suit cleaned and mended the pocket.

'Ooh, they're too good for a play,' the dressmaker gasped. 'Why I haven't seen anything of this quality for years – not since Mr Hartnell's days – well, he was Sir Norman later but I'd left by then. Always Mr Hartnell to me. You can't change as you get older can you?'

Usually Lizzie said little, but the new clothes made her chatty with excitement. 'You'll have to keep them at your place,' she said firmly. 'Can't leave them hanging in that dusty dressing room. Besides, they'd be pinched. Must have cost a fortune this lot.'

'No, my old boss gave them to me,' Jill said. 'Store-room space is expensive. He'd have to have called in a dealer who'd only give him peanuts for out-of-date stock.'

'Out of date?' exclaimed Lizzie. 'I think these are the last word! You are going to let April have this dress aren't you? You know, for when she has to dress up in the evening?' She stroked the flimsy silk fabric lovingly. 'My, won't she look lovely? Doesn't do herself justice the way she dresses. All those bits and pieces. Course she doesn't have no mother. Died she did, a year ago. She has to look after her dad and he's wrapped up in his garage. Cancer it was. Left too late.'

'Oh poor girl,' Jill said distractedly. 'Yes, I thought that for April, and this,' she held one of the dreaded tomato-red sarong skirts against her, 'for Sandra. Could you shorten it about three inches? It's too smart like this.'

Lizzie half closed her eyes. 'Yes – we could put it with that thin yellow tee-shirt from the jumbly, cut the neck down a bit.'

Jill grinned. 'You've got the idea. And some kind of chunky plastic necklace. Yellow and violet.'

Sandra drifted up at that moment and seized on the silk dress. 'Ooh, can I wear this?'

'No, we're just doing yours now,' Jill took back the dress. 'We've earmarked this skirt for you. But there's lots more things to come.'

Sandra looked consideringly at the skirt. 'Mmm – nice, but I prefer the dress.'

'It's not in character,' said Jill firmly. Sandra looked suspicious. 'I'm not wearing any old rag. Miles said my part was glamorous.'

'If you go to London you'll see this skirt on major display in Fred's window *now*,' Jill returned, knowing that Sandra with her penchant for magazines would have heard of Fred's. 'Price, one hundred and fifty pounds.'

'Good grief, I'd want a whole outfit for that,' Sandra looked at the skirt with new respect.

The clothes also caused a buzz of excitement among the cast. 'I say,' Edward Posner said loudly. 'Are we men going to be spoilt like this? A nice suit from Henry Poole for me I think. Haw haw.'

Miles looked at the clothes and then at Jill. He winked. 'You have managed well on the proceeds of the jumble sale.'

It was becoming a habit for most of the cast to drift to the pub after rehearsal. Jill had declined at first, but she was so busy discussing alterations with Lizzie the second week after the clothes arrived, that she walked out of the hall with her and on to the pub without realizing.

'Let me get you a drink,' said Miles materializing at her elbow. Jill hesitated. 'You always vanish at the end of a session. I never get a chance to talk to you.'

He disappeared to the bar and returned with two glasses of white wine and plunged into discussion of the rehearsal. When he paused for breath and to take a long draught of wine as if it were beer, Jill asked him if he'd like to see *The Song is Sung*. 'Fiona Trentbridge gave me her two tickets – I met her recently at a friend's.'

'Fiona Trentbridge!' he looked impressed. 'She's such a good actress. I've admired her since I was a schoolkid. Do you mean it?' He was a little hesitant, uncomfortable.

'Of course. I went backstage to see her after the matinée.'

'You mean you've already seen it?' He looked baffled.

'Yes. She gave me two tickets. They keep back a few seats for the stars and the director until curtain-up. I thought it would be a bit of homework for you,' she smiled at him. 'See how the direction compares with *The Glass Ceiling*.'

'Thank you. Actually, I'm disappointed. I thought you were inviting me to go with you.'

He held her gaze so long that Jill felt unsettled. He had lovely eyes, a light hazel, heavily lashed, slanting attractively at the corners.

'Well, how do you think everything's going – are you satisfied?' she asked hurriedly.

His expression changed, became brisk, businesslike. 'There's a lot to do – but I'm delighted with April; she senses instantly what to do. And Arabella is surprisingly good, or she will be by the end.' His enthusiasm returned and Jill sat back, enjoying listening to him, making room for Molly Ferness when she drifted over with a brimming gin and tonic.

It was pleasant to feel part of a team again, to have a mutual interest. She was impressed by Molly's shrewd comments about timing, and the respect with which Miles listened to her. Sandra squeezed in next to Miles, crossing her legs ostentatiously, leaning one possessive hand on Miles's shoulder. April said little. She smiled briefly if Tom teased her, listened with apparent interest to Edward Posner when he explained in boring detail why he felt compelled to change his lines in the script, but she was remote, apart. Jill wondered what she was thinking.

'Are you into your part now?' she asked her, her question drowned in the chat and banter of the others.

'Not yet. I haven't met anyone like Margaret. Down here women don't seem to have careers, but I need someone to model her on.'

'Perhaps Arabella knows someone – she must know practically everyone in Dorset.'

April smiled faintly. 'She wouldn't lift a finger to help me.

You heard what she said at the reading. Something about me being skinny, insignificant and with a common voice. She's always correcting me. She'd like me to be so bad that Miles will have to replace me.'

So she had heard Arabella's tactless remarks after all.

'I think she just likes throwing her weight about,' Jill said comfortingly. 'And let's face it, there's quite a lot of weight to throw.'

# Chapter Twenty-one

'I must start on the sets. I've a lot of work on at the moment and not much spare time. There won't be any scenery at this rate.' Peter Smith stood, arms akimbo, in front of Miles.

'I'm sorry, mate. I haven't had time to think about it.' Miles looked up exasperatedly as he was scribbling on the script to make Sandra's part simpler. She constantly stumbled over the same passage, making it meaningless.

'Couldn't Jill do it?' another voice piped up. 'I mean, she went to art school and has done shop window displays. She must have some idea.'

'I heard that! Not on your nelly,' Jill called. 'You're far too fond of giving me jobs Miriam Mander.'

'Oh, that's an idea. Jill,' Miles caught her hand and gazed up at her from his perch on a battered piano stool. 'I'll help just as soon as I've got this to scan and made Sandra understand her movements. But you could rough out something simple so that we can give Pete an idea or two to work on.'

'You've nearly finished the costumes,' Miriam added. 'You keep on fiddling with them unnecessarily. Lizzie can cope now.'

'I've threatened to gag you before,' Jill frowned good-humouredly at Miriam. 'I'm not *fiddling*. I'm still hunting down accessories, and I have to dye some shoes for Sandra and April's last scene.'

Miles got up and put his arm round her shoulders. 'Ah . . . please Jill. I would like you to have a go. It would save me so much time and anxiety.' She was conscious of the masculine warmth of his arm, knew he was using the same flattering technique on her that had won over Sandra and Arabella, but she found herself giving an indulgent laugh and relenting. 'Oh, all right! But an art school course twenty years ago doesn't make me a set designer.'

'What does?' Miles widened his eyes and spread his hands,

and then caught sight of Sandra who appeared from the so-called dressing room where she'd been absorbed in fluffing her hair. His expression changed to one of brisk determination. 'At last Sandra. I've been waiting for you.' He caught her hand and pulled her on to the empty stage. 'Now here's the door and there's the desk, and out there is the audience. Let's just walk on and round so that you don't keep talking to the back of the stage. The audience want to see your pretty face my pet, not your back view.'

Simpering, Sandra allowed herself to be walked round the imaginary props, leaning coquettishly against Miles's guiding arm.

'That's how it's done,' Jill bit her lip, irritated with herself for succumbing so easily to his manipulative charm. 'Aesop was dead right.'

'Eh?'

'You know, that one about the wind and the sun having a bet over who could make a man take his coat off? The sun won of course.'

What the hell, Jill thought. She could put any amount of time into the play, she had little else of any significance to do and it helped her to ignore the fact that Diane hadn't bothered to telephone or drop a line to thank her for the sweater. When she'd bought that sweater, she'd built up a mental picture of Diane's pleasure and now she felt rebuffed. Subconsciously she yearned to find in Diane something of Douglas that would assuage the continuing ache. She'd begun to fantasize about their relationship, believing that they would become close, companionable, anything to keep a tenuous link with Douglas.

In the pub later Miles came across and thanked her. 'I don't know what I'd do without you,' he said in a low, intimate voice. 'You're so professional. Could you and I discuss the sets? I have a few ideas.'

'Now?'

'Could I come over tomorrow?'

'Miriam has only just wished this job on me. I haven't had time to think.'

'All the better if we have a discussion first. We mustn't spend a lot, but we need something flexible that could double for several scenes. Tomorrow then?' he pressed her knee as Arabella demanded his attention.

Arabella's antagonism towards April had not diminished. 'You must acquire more presence,' she boomed at her. 'People won't even notice you're on the stage the way you shuffle in.'

Jill smiled inwardly as April said, apparently humbly, 'I'm sure you're right. Perhaps you'd show me how to acquire this stage presence.' Her pale face, with the translucent skin stretched across wide cheekbones and a small pointed chin, tilted innocently.

Arabella tutted and took a large sip of her gin and tonic. '*I'm* not a drama coach, my dear girl. Just remember that if you don't carry your part you let down the whole cast. All of us.'

'I'll try not to do that,' April mumbled, but Jill caught her ghost of a grin as she looked down.

She always seemed to arrive with Tom and remembering that Diane had said what a flirt he was, Jill wondered if April was involved with him.

She was annoyed the next afternoon, when Miles walked in casually just as she was struggling with the doors of the wood-burning stove. 'I didn't hear you ring.' Jill was tart.

'I didn't. I came in round the back. I'm sorry, was that impertinent?' He tilted his head questioningly and smiled apologetically. 'No-one locks doors in Sherville. I guess I didn't think. Here, let me do that.' He knelt down in front of the stove and fiddled with the door and a poker. 'There – a cinder stuck in the groove that's all.' He sat back on his heels and looked at her. 'I can't tell you how glad I am you joined. You're such an enormous asset. The only one with any sophistication. You seem to grasp what I'm trying to do before anyone, except Molly.'

'You're a rogue. You think you can butter everyone up.' But her irritation melted away. He was so single-minded in his passionate desire to make a success of his play that she felt a bond. That was how she'd been when she had first started at Fred's, determined to turn the vulgar little shop into something

127

stylish. She couldn't blame this young man for the same qualities.

'I suppose you're expecting to see sketches of the sets already?' she teased.

'As a matter of fact, yes – you've had,' he looked ostentatiously at his watch, 'twenty-seven hours and forty minutes. That ought to be enough for anyone.'

'Well, we'd better not waste any more time.'

They spent the next hour or so discussing the sets, the cost, what could be achieved by one willing part-time carpenter, a bunch of press-ganged painters and a gaggle of amateur scene shifters.

'You're a slave driver,' Jill said at last. 'But I think that will work. I'll draw something out for Peter.'

He'd admired her quick facility with a pencil as she'd sketched ideas and diagrams while they talked.

'That's what they teach you at art school,' she retorted. 'It's basic training – nothing to be so fulsome about.' She got up abruptly, conscious of his nearness and his warm gaze. 'I think we deserve a drink – what would you like? There's a half-finished bottle of white wine in the fridge.'

'Lovely.'

When she returned with the bottle and two glasses he was browsing along the shelves of tapes and records. 'You promised to come and hear my jumble sale 78s – you've nothing as good as my golden oldies – make me cry they're so poignant.'

'I've done enough crying lately.'

'I'm sorry.' He looked contrite. Everyone knew by now that she'd lost her husband. 'Shall I put this on?' he held out an LP of Ella Fitzgerald.

Jill shrugged. 'If you like.' She didn't know whether to be charmed or annoyed at the way he'd made himself at home. Before she knew it, Ella's throaty singing throbbed into the low-ceilinged room, reinforcing a growing intimacy in the atmosphere. She sipped her drink, thinking of Douglas, longing for the sheer physical release of sex, the warm aftermath of contentment.

'I don't suppose you've got any biscuits or anything have you,

Jill? I didn't have any lunch. I've only just realized how hungry I am.'

Jill was jerked back to the present, and to this attractive young man sitting on the floor, leaning back against the sofa, a little too near for comfort. The last thing she wanted was someone to remind her of what she was missing. But looking at his young face, she collected herself. 'Of course. Would you like a sandwich?'

'Oh no, just something to nibble to take away the pangs. I'll forage when I get back to the cottage if the mice haven't got there first.'

Impulsively Jill asked if he'd like to stay to supper. 'It'll be scraps,' she warned. 'Something conjured up from tins. I don't do much shopping now.'

'Could I really? Thanks, if you're sure you don't mind.'

At first she wondered whether she'd been wise, but it turned out to be a surprisingly enjoyable evening. Miles had seen so many of the plays she had seen, seemed to have total recall of the casts, the directors, the reviews and always had something perceptive to say himself. He talked of his mother and her job – it was true *The Glass Ceiling* was based largely on her experience as a working woman up against the male establishment – and of his young sister just starting in the sixth form, and anxious to be a vet. 'But it's so competitive, she'll have a real struggle.'

'Worse than a playwright?'

'It's easier for me. I know I'll make it, but she doesn't even know if she'll get into veterinary college.'

Later, as he went to go, he stood in the doorway of the cottage looking at her for a moment, solemn and unsmiling.

'You're absolutely smashing,' he said softly, and quickly bent to kiss her cheek before wheeling his bicycle out of the shadows of the cottage wall where it was propped.

Next morning she found on her doorstep a tight posy of brilliant mahonia leaves with drooping scented yellow racemes, surrounded by a Victorian ruff of anonymous grey leaves. The accompanying note read, 'You deserve a dozen red roses but these are all I could find.' Her pleasure was mitigated by a slight disquiet as she put the posy in a yellow pottery mug on the kitchen table.

# Chapter Twenty-two

It was some days later that, returning from the village, Jill's heart leapt as she saw Diane's smart black car on the small drive. The girl was sitting with her head resting on the back of the seat, her eyes closed, smoking.

'Hi!' Jill tapped on the car window. 'How long have you been here? I went to pick up the laundry from the post office – can you imagine?' She laughed and opened the door. 'I can't get over the incongruity of pensions and stamps jostling with sheets and pillowcases. Come in. You must be frozen.'

'The car's warm. I had the heater on full blast. I've only been here a few minutes.'

'Can you stay?'

'If I'm not in the way.'

'Of course not. Bring your things. I'll make some tea.' Talking too much, too rapidly, to hide the rush of pleasure she felt at the surprise visit, Jill led the way to the cottage. Diane looked even thinner, she was concerned to notice, and somehow unkempt, but Jill was idiotically pleased to see her wearing the violet sweater. 'I'm glad you liked it,' she nodded at the sweater. 'I thought it would suit you.' She wished she was wearing it with something more appealing than black cord jeans in need of a wash.

'Yes. It's pretty. I suppose I should have thanked you.' Diane smiled faintly. 'I'm not good at that sort of thing.'

How much talent does it take to say thank you Jill thought, a burst of indignation clouding her delight at seeing Diane again, but she kept her expression and voice mild as she handed over a cup of tea. 'How are things?'

'Well, it's all quiet on the Peter front if that's what you mean.' Her voice was careless but she seemed jumpy, on edge. 'I phoned a friend of his. He said he'd hardly seen him but that he'd telephoned his office and spoken to him there. So Peter

130

must be going into work.' She leant back against the chair, and fumbled for a cigarette. 'It's all so tedious.'

'A bit of an understatement. You were very frightened before. Is his wife still phoning you?'

'What?' Diane looked surprised and then collected herself. 'Oh, his wife. No. Not lately.' She jumped up and walked about the room fidgeting. 'It's blown over. Forget it. It's not your problem anyway.'

Jill's eyes narrowed. Was that elaborate Peter story a total lie? There was something about Diane's replies that seemed disjointed, as if she'd forgotten all about the melodrama now. She seemed wound up, jerky, smoking in a series of rapid puffs, blowing the smoke out almost as if it irritated her.

'What have you done about your flat?' she changed the subject.

'Oh that! I've had a new security system put in, even the windows have bloody locks on the handles. They're so complicated I can never open them, so I guess I'm safe. Practically asphyxiated, but safe.'

'I meant about selling it.'

Diane frowned. 'Haven't you heard there's a recession on? Property isn't selling.'

'I think you should try.'

'What do you mean?' Diane got up again stiffly, like someone holding their breath.

'I called on you, when I was in London to see Rosomon and my solicitor. I was a bit surprised, in view of what you told me it cost, that it looked a bit scruffy, but I expect it's nicer inside. Your neighbour came to the door and said you were out, but he wouldn't let me in to leave a note. He was rather belligerent in fact. I must say he seemed an odd type to be a friend of yours.'

Diane's expression was guarded. 'Chris is all right.'

'He gave me the creeps.'

Involuntarily Diane shivered. 'Why were you spying on me? What did Chris say to you?' There was no mistaking her anxiety.

'I wasn't spying,' Jill said pleasantly. 'I was going to ask you to have lunch with me – to tell you about my meeting with the solicitor.' She deliberately didn't answer the second nervous question.

131

Diane paced about the room, hugging herself. 'Chris is all right, I tell you.'

'If you say so,' Jill spoke mildly.

'Well, when do I get Daddy's money then?' Diane's voice was truculent.

'Is that what you came down for?'

'Yes, of course. Why do you think?'

The reply was so brutal that Jill felt winded. With difficulty she explained that there was a minor tax problem, but the money should be through in two or three weeks.

'But I need it *now*.'

The tall thin body bent over Jill's seated figure; the eyes, with the pupils mere pinpoints, the whites a curdled yellow, seemed dead, yet they stared unnervingly into her own.

'You don't seem to understand. I need it now.'

With a sudden dreadful certainty, Jill knew. She grabbed Diane's arms above the elbow. 'Diane, are you taking drugs?'

For a moment they both looked at each other and then Diane flung away.

'Christ! You *have* been spying. What did Chris tell you? Did he ask *you* for the money?' Her expression was ugly, but she was clearly frightened.

Jill stood up, her face white, she was trembling but she went to Diane and put her arms about her.

'Look love, do you realize what you're doing? Drugs are dangerous. I knew there was something terribly wrong the moment I saw you. I thought you were ill. You look dreadful.'

'It would be no problem if I had that money. I need cash, now, I keep telling you and telling you.' Her voice was a moan and she pushed Jill away and slumped into a chair, clutching her arms about her body and rocking backwards and forwards. Jill put one arm about her and stroked her hair with the other hand. She was appalled to see it was dirty and uncombed, and as it parted at the back, the thin vulnerability of the nape of the neck was filmed with a grey grubbiness.

'We're going to get you out of this mess,' she said firmly. 'You're going to leave the flat, get away from that awful man, and stay here until you're better.'

'You're so bloody *reasonable*,' Diane burst out. 'Sitting there without a bloody care in the world, telling me bloody well what I should be doing. It's only money I need, I tell you. You could at least lend it to me.' The last words degenerated into a whine, and she sank her head on her knees.

'I think you're tired out,' Jill said gently. 'You don't look as if you've been taking care of yourself. Go and have a lie down whilst I put together some supper.'

'I don't want any supper.' She virtually spat the words out, but Jill wanted her out of earshot so that she could ring Roger, ask what she should do. Her mind was whirling, trying to conjure up all the half-digested facts and horror stories about drugs that she'd gleaned casually from detached glances at newspapers or television programmes. She felt frightened and impotent, but she tried to hide it as she held on to Diane.

'Well, go and have a nice warm bath,' Jill was firm, gently propelling her visitor to the staircase. 'You'll be able to relax afterwards.' She talked soothingly as if to a small child as she ran the water tipping in half a bottle of expensive scented oil.

Diane gazed at her, her mouth sagging, her eyes with the unnerving dead stare following Jill's movements, strangely quiet and obedient. Then when she'd pulled off the violet sweater, she jerked away, throwing the sweater into a corner of the bathroom, covering her pathetically small breasts and bony rib cage.

'I hate you, you know that,' she snarled. 'H – a – t – e you! Does that spell it out?'

Jill flinched. 'I'm sorry about that,' she said as calmly as possible. 'I was hoping we'd be friends, help each other.'

Diane looked as if she was going to scream at her again, she drew in her breath and then suddenly her mouth opened and she started to bawl like a child.

Jill knew that the best thing was to be as brisk as possible, to take charge, 'I'm going downstairs now. Go on, get in the bath and you'll feel better.' Why she was insisting on a bath she had no idea, but she felt a small triumph as, closing the door, she saw the painfully thin figure climb into the water.

Her stepdaughter had changed so much in the short time since she'd been before, but I probably just didn't recognize the symptoms last time Jill thought. Fortunately Roger himself answered her phone call and after a few questions said he'd be round. As far as Jill was concerned, it couldn't be too soon. She didn't approve of Diane's display of bad manners, but she felt responsible for her and wasn't going to see her go under.

When she returned to the bathroom Diane was sitting huddled in a towel on the wicker chair staring at the door. 'Why did you leave me,' she asked piteously. 'I can't stay in that bath alone.'

Clumsily, she threw off the towel and climbed back into the bath. 'Don't leave me?' she begged. A lump rose in Jill's throat. 'Of course I won't.'

The doorbell rang and Jill knew it would be Roger. 'I won't be a moment,' she promised but as she left the bathroom Diane, with wild scrabblings got out of the bath. 'You promised,' she wailed. 'You said you'd stay. I knew I couldn't trust you. I won't stay here alone,' she moaned.

'I'll be back, don't worry.' Jill raced out of the bathroom, terrified herself at the dread in the girls' voice.

What had happened since she'd last been here?

# Chapter Twenty-three

'Well, at least she hasn't been injecting,' Roger sat back in a chair in the kitchen. 'I checked her over and couldn't find any sign of that.'

There'd been a terrible scene with Diane when she'd realized who Roger was; she'd screamed insults at Jill, then wept and pounded the kitchen table with her fists. Roger had been stern, pushing Jill out of the room, and only emerging to usher Diane upstairs to bed some twenty minutes later.

'It's not going to be easy,' he went on. 'She's on quite a heavy dosage. She's discovered, as they all do, that you need more and more of the stuff to achieve the same effect.'

'What's she been taking, d'you know?'

'A bit of everything. Mostly heroin, but she's tried crack, Ecstasy, alcohol, cough mixture, you name it she's had it.'

'I suppose that's why she was so desperate for money.'

When Jill told Roger the amount, he whistled, 'That's going it, even at London prices. Was she supplying anyone?'

'I don't know. I only know what she told me and that may not be true,' she said wearily. 'How can we help her?'

He looked firm. 'We can't. I've seen this before. They suck the life out of the family. It's beyond anything you or I can do. They have to *want* to give up.'

'But she's ill. She has no-one. No father, no job, some kind of unhinged married man after her, an unsympathetic mother . . . and she's all I have left of Douglas.'

'Douglas has gone. You can't hang on to a remnant of him like this.' Roger softened his tone slightly. 'Jill, she's not yours.'

'I've got to help her all the same.'

'Even so, it's down to her. She has to want to give it up. That's the hardest part.'

'I'll make her want to give it up,' Jill's voice was steely.

'Where is her mother?'

135

'I don't know.' A jealous possessiveness made her reluctant to involve Frances. Guilt rose as she told herself she should have made more effort to befriend Diane when Douglas was alive, she ought to have realized the gap his remarriage must have left in his daughter's life. If she'd been less selfishly anxious to keep Douglas to herself, excluding the rest of the world whilst they revelled in their own happiness, Diane wouldn't have felt so rejected. She should have asked Diane to stay with her after the funeral. Instead, she'd accepted her cool competence then as proof that she didn't feel as deeply as Jill. Jill, huddled in her own grief, had ignored Diane's.

'I think the man I saw at her flat has something to do with it. I felt there was something wrong, something evil about him,' Jill said slowly. 'Diane seems terrified of him. She wanted to know if he'd asked me for money. If he's responsible, I could kill him.'

'More usefully, inform the police,' Roger said. 'It's better for him to be inside than you. As for Diane, perhaps now she knows you know, she may make more of an effort. She obviously trusts you.'

'Trusts me?' Jill looked up, sudden pleasure lightening her spirits.

'She wouldn't have come here if not.'

'She only wanted to borrow money.'

'Of course. But, subconsciously, she also wanted you to know she was in trouble, hoping you would help her.' He smiled slightly and Jill noticed how tired he looked. 'She must take the decision, but there are places that can help. In fact there's a very good one not far from here, where they have a very high success rate. Believe me, Jill, unless you know what you're doing she'll drag you down with her. It's a well-trodden path.'

'She is Douglas's daughter.'

He sighed and picked up his bag. 'I must go.'

She went up to the spare room. Diane appeared to be asleep. In the low light from the landing, her skin looked grey, her eyes sunk in dark sockets, the long dark hair spread lifelessly on the pillow.

Jill went softly to her own room. Expecting not to sleep, she tried to read, but anxiety and exhaustion made the words irrelevant and meaningless.

She awoke a couple of hours later, still clutching her book, surprised to find she'd dozed off.

She recognized the noise that had disturbed her as the sound of a motor engine. Fearful, she sprang out of bed and when she got to the window she saw the dark solidity of Diane's car against the softer dark of the night sky as it jerked out of the short drive, without lights. She could hear it travelling steadily up the hill, the engine thrumming as it was gunned to a higher speed.

Jill stood looking after it, long after it had gone. 'Damn, damn, damn,' she said to the empty night.

# Chapter Twenty-four

Several times the next morning she rang Diane's flat, un-surprised when there was no answer. She wondered whether to drive up after her and was irritated when Roger rang and flatly forbade it. 'You can't help her. She has to make her own decision. That's a vital part of the cure – how many times do I have to say that?'

Reluctantly she agreed to do nothing, but she couldn't settle to anything, not even the costumes for *The Glass Ceiling*. She eyed the folder of sketches and notes with dislike.

A faint wintry sun was struggling through the clouds, lighting up the frost in the hollows of the garden. She went outside, her bowl of bread at the ready for the elusive duck. Tiny spikes of green were spreading out from under the hedge – the first sign of the snowdrops that had been such a delightful surprise their first winter. She looked at Douglas's glade. The trees had been delivered and Pauline had helped Gus place them, firmly sticking in canes and squinting her eyes to visualize the shape and spacing. They looked dispiritedly spindly and immature, lacking promise, the large circles of bare earth round the roots crisped with frost. Jill spied the duck crouched under a bush on the further bank, trying to look invisible but eyeing her hopefully. Jill moved slowly so as to reassure it and threw the bread on to her side of the river. The duck did not emerge until she had walked away and hidden herself behind a large shrub. With satisfaction she watched it slide into the water, paddle the short distance to her bank and stretch its neck forward, its beak hoovering up the scraps of bread at lightning speed. When Jill came out from behind the bush, the duck squawked crossly, opening its wings to skim to a safe distance.

It was one of those days that could turn out either fair or foul. On impulse she took the car out of the garage and turned its nose down the hill, crossing the narrow bridge to the opposite side of the river. The weather had been so miserable lately that she willed the sun to win its battle with the clouds. She drove aimlessly, until she suddenly realized she was near the small house of her rescuers. She stopped the car and shyly walked up the narrow brick path. Mrs Morrish seemed surprised to see her, but asked her in.

'I didn't thank you properly for looking after me so well when I fell in the ditch,' Jill explained.

'Oh, it was nothing. Wet through you was. I must say you're looking better now. I was afraid you'd catch your death.'

It was what I was trying to do, thought Jill, ashamed now of her feebleness. 'I hope you got your clothes back all right?' She had had them cleaned and Mrs B had given them to her husband to take back since, being a milkman, he delivered all over the area.

'Would you like a cup of tea? I was just making George one – he comes in about now.' Mildred Morrish busied herself with cups, pouring milk from a glass jug, an unfamiliar inch of cream on top. It must come straight from the farm, unskimmed, a conjecture confirmed for Jill when George walked in with a small old-fashioned milk churn. 'I was telling Mrs Mortimer she was lucky not to have pneumonia after that wetting she had.'

'Ay. We had a wetting too with that wine she gave us, dint we Mildred? – wet our whistles all right with that dint we?' He chuckled at his own joke.

'You were very good to me,' Jill spoke warmly.

'Oh, it's no matter. When George here broke his leg and four ribs on the tractor, people ferried me everywhere. I don't drive see, and we're so cut off here. But they took the kids to school, me to hospital, did my shopping.'

Jill reflected as she drove away that in London she probably would have been left to 'catch her death'. In the block of flats where she'd lived before Douglas she barely saw her neighbours, all living secret lives behind double-locked doors and barred windows, their homes bristling with alarm systems.

Driving on, enjoying the increasing sunshine, she was amazed to see Arabella halfway up a winding lane frantically waving her arms.

'Oh, at last – I was wondering if anybody lived in this

godforsaken spot! Not a soul has been past for over half an hour.'
She was flustered and upset. 'I didn't know what to do – I
couldn't leave the car with the engine running and walk to get
help. Heaven knows where the nearest house with a telephone
is over here. I was afraid the engine might overheat and catch
fire with Peregrine inside.' She was almost babbling. Jill saw
that Arabella's car was backed into a tractor entrance to a field
and her obnoxious dog was barking hysterically through the
closed windows.

'What on earth has happened?'

'I stopped to pee behind the hedge,' Arabella said, recovering
some of her composure and speaking majestically. 'I was driving
back from a meeting in Sturminster Newton but needed an
urgent Nature stop. When I returned to the car Peregrine was
so glad to see me, he jumped up at the window and put his paw
on the central locking system. I can't get in and the engine's
still running and poor little Peregrine is frantic.'

There wasn't much Jill could do except offer to drive to a
garage and get help. 'But do be quick,' Arabella pleaded, 'the
windows aren't open and I'm afraid Peregrine will suffocate.'

Jill wished he would, he was yapping so wildly, but drove off
quickly. She'd no idea where there'd be a garage, but then
she saw a signpost at a minor crossroad with Frimpton a mile
and a half away. She smiled. Didn't April McIntosh live in
Frimpton? Her father had a garage. The irony of it pleased her
and she accelerated.

McIntosh Motors was much more than a garage; next to the
petrol station was a car wash, a workshop, and across the
forecourt, an opulent showroom shiny with new Saabs and
BMWs. April, sitting behind the cash desk reading, was surprised to see Jill but when she heard what had happened she
couldn't help giggling. 'They say if you're frightened of anyone,
you should just imagine them sitting on a lavatory. I'll think
of Arabella peeing behind a hedge next time she tries to bully
me.'

Jill left it to Mr McIntosh, a shy Scot with vivid blue eyes
and sandy hair, to rescue Arabella and headed back for the
cottage. The sun had disappeared now and the countryside had
reverted to its winter gloom. She wanted to get home to a fire

and a book, and to check out the forlorn hope that perhaps Diane had returned.

It was some hours later when an imperious ring on the doorbell disturbed her reading. It was Arabella. 'I came to thank you for helping me,' she said stepping inside without invitation. She swept a considering glance round the tiny hall and marched into the living room. 'I must say you've made it look very attractive,' she said graciously.

'Thank you.' Jill stood, waiting.

'I'm afraid I was rather, rather *distrait* earlier. I didn't let you know how much I appreciated your aid – I could have been stuck there all day. I couldn't open either the boot or bonnet, they both only open from catches inside the car. I tried breaking the window even though Harold would have been furious, but it's made of toughened glass. I must say I didn't realize modern cars were so like armoured personnel carriers.' She sat down unasked and picked up a bowl on the low table to scrutinize the marks on the base. 'Mr McIntosh was *so* efficient. I must say he had the matter under control in minutes. What a nice man.'

'For a petrol-pump attendant?'

Arabella looked up sharply but went on with only an imperceptible pause. 'He made me follow him to his garage to check over the plugs or points or whatever they are. The engine was red hot.' She hesitated. 'But that girl was there, April – such an unsuitable name – I'm sure she'll make fun of me at the Drama Group.'

'She's too nice for that. She's Mr McIntosh's daughter. I suppose she helps her father out. It was she I spoke to when I found the garage.'

'Oh well, I can't have her telling all the others. She could make me seem so foolish.'

'Hardly. It was an accident.'

'I know but it isn't very dignified to have everyone know one was caught short behind a hedge,' Arabella said with difficulty. She was fidgeting with the clasp of her handbag, opening and shutting the metal frame with a large click. 'I suppose I have been rather critical of her. She might be nursing some resentment. I thought perhaps you could have a word with her.'

'I think you're worrying about nothing. April seems to be really decent.'

'My dear, I know the type only too well. What you don't realize is how some people are only too glad of the opportunity to ridicule someone in my position. But I shall buy my petrol from McIntosh in future. You might tell his daughter that.'

'I'm sure he'll be grateful.' The sarcasm was lost.

'Isn't it strange? Harold said he plays golf with McIntosh. I was flabbergasted. I mean, the golf club people are quite fussy about who they have as members and they wouldn't take Arnold Nussbaum, even though he is very rich and has a small estate the other side of Warminster.'

'Why not?' Jill felt herself stiffen.

'He's Jewish I suppose,' she said vaguely, oblivious of Jill's tone. 'Anyway because McIntosh has a handicap of three, Harold says they all queue up to play with him. Curious isn't it? I suppose if you're good at sport it cuts across class barriers. I think I read somewhere that a boxing champion – and you know how *they* speak – was invited to send his son to Eton. *Imagine!* I think I might ask McIntosh to join one of my committees. That will please him, don't you think? Put him among the more influential people of the county. Judging by his set-up – *if* it's really his own – he must be quite affluent. I could fit him into my Days Out for the Blind Association. The blind, poor dears, like to get about, especially if the drivers describe the country they're passing through. McIntosh's Scottish accent might be a difficulty, and I wonder how articulate he is, but still, they're grateful for anything.'

Jill wondered how people put up with Arabella. She talked not only as if blind people were a race apart, some curious little tribe of impaired intelligence, but also as if it was a privilege to be on one of her damned committees. She felt her blood boiling and suppressed an urge to smack her caller in the face, wipe off her smug expression.

'What about you, are you doing anything for other people? You must have plenty of spare time now you haven't a husband to look after.' She cast a bright, considering look at Jill. 'How about some fund-raising? Once people know you were married to a well-known writer they'll be anxious to talk to you, and they'll shell out more.' Arabella cocked her head questioningly on one side.

That's supposedly my reward for helping her thought Jill grimly, but out loud she said in a pleasant, conversational tone: 'I must say you're not only one of the most tactless women I have ever met, but also one of the most snobbish. I'm beginning to wish I'd left you stranded.'

Arabella looked flabbergasted. 'What do you mean? Have I said anything wrong?'

'Oh, for heaven's sake!'

Arabella heaved herself to her feet, her brow creased in genuine puzzlement. 'I remember now Faith Cruze said something about your being a little, well odd.' She nodded kindly at Jill. 'You mustn't wallow in self-pity, you know. I know you've lost your husband but you must brace up. There are plenty of people worse off than you, you know. Do something for others, that's the ticket. Get involved with the deprived and forget yourself.' She nodded in a self-satisfied way as though she'd solved another little difficulty. 'Now I must go.'

Jill strode to the door, seething but silent in the face of such monumental insensitivity. As she furiously pulled it open she found Miles in the porch, arm lifted about to ring. 'I didn't want to make the same mistake twice,' he laughed. 'I was going to ring this time.'

'Miles! What are you doing here?' Arabella loomed behind Jill's shoulder. 'Have you come to fetch me? I'm in my own car. How did you know I was here? Have you heard about my drama this morning already? Mrs Mortimer was so kind. A real Samaritan.'

Miles looked embarrassed. 'Er no, I came to see Jill actually. What have you been up to Arabella?' he added jovially.

Arabella frowned her disapproval. 'I see,' she said in her Lady Bracknell voice. 'Don't forget Miles, that you were supposed to be giving me and the treasurer a report on the expenditure so far. Watching costs is vitally important you know.' She stalked to her car and reversed out of the gate with a spin of gravel.

'Not the blue-eyed boy at the moment are you?' Jill asked. 'What did you want?'

'Nothing. I just came to see you. I was lonely and wanted to talk to someone *simpatico*.' He smiled boyishly. 'Besides, my stove is belching smoke into the living room.'

'Come in then. I'll try to recover from that dreadful woman. Why hasn't she been strangled by now? But you can't stay long.'

# Chapter Twenty-five

Jill wondered afterwards if Miles was beginning to have a crush on her and then concluded she was flattering herself. He'd attempted to kiss her cheek again as he left, but she'd side-stepped it. Her preoccupation with Diane had come back and she didn't give it that much thought. She had telephoned her flat again after Miles had left, but there was still no answer.

She slept very little, listening hopefully for the return of Diane's car, turning over in her mind possible ways to wean her off the dope. In the morning, unrefreshed, she decided she would ignore Roger's advice and go to London. She was letting Douglas down if she failed to help his daughter. And then, as she was driving along the Bayswater Road, near the turn off to Diane's flat, she spotted a police car. Of course she should go to the police. She could tell them about her suspicions of Chris. But would they hassle Diane as well? She couldn't risk that. She wished she didn't feel so out of her depth.

Her heart was knocking almost audibly as she arrived at Diane's place and pressed the buzzer. There was no answer. She buzzed several times more and was about to turn away when someone came up the steps, a young girl who had a key at the ready.

'Oh good,' Jill said hurriedly. 'I've forgotten my main key. I was just trying to raise someone to let me in.'

The girl didn't seem suspicious. 'I'm terrified of doing that. I keep mine on a cord round my neck. But I don't suppose you'd have had to wait long in any case, there's so much coming and going here it's like Piccadilly Circus in the rush hour. What's your flat number?'

'Three.'

'I'm five, top floor. I moved in two weeks ago – only temporarily. It belongs to a friend who's just got a job in Brussels.' They climbed the stairs together and the girl bid

Diane a breathless goodbye as she prepared to puff her way up another two floors. 'See you around. What about your door key?'

'There's a spare hidden under the mat,' said Jill quickly.

'Oh that's all right then. Come and have a coffee some time. I'm in most evenings.'

'I will,' lied Jill. She leant against Diane's door. Now what?

There was a tall window at the end of the short corridor and she sat on the windowsill. She gazed idly outside, wishing she had a book with her. She had no plans. She was just hoping to see Diane, after that she would play it by ear. A car drove up and parked at the opposite kerb. She saw the man from the ground-floor flat, the repugnant Chris, crossing the road to the front door. She tiptoed to the stairwell and watched him enter, and then open his own door. There was a scrap of rock music before it closed. She went down again and paused outside his door. She was sure she heard Diane's laugh, or rather a distortion of her laugh. She couldn't hear words. She fled upstairs again as a figure loomed against the glass of the front door and she heard a buzzer in Chris's flat. Convinced Diane was in there, she crept upstairs again. Perched on the hard windowsill she watched, wondering what she'd do if Diane came up the stairs with Chris. The girl from the top flat was right. There was a lot of coming and going. Three people went out and two came in during the half hour she sat there. She was more than ever convinced that this Chris was a dealer.

Very shortly she heard the music again as the door opened downstairs, and Diane's voice said '*Ciao*'. Jill shrank into the corner of the window as slow steps dragged upstairs. Diane was fumbling clumsily with her lock, exclaiming 'Shit!' as she missed the keyhole. As the door opened, Jill made a sudden rush, slipping in behind Diane and pushing it shut with her back.

'What the bloody hell are *you* doing here?' Diane was staring at her, mouth open.

'I came to see you,' Jill said evenly. 'You left without saying goodbye. I thought we'd have some lunch, talk things over.'

'There's nothing I want to talk over with you. Just leave me alone.'

'I want you to see Tom, Douglas's agent. He's pushing the publisher to bring out a boxed set of your father's books. He wants you to submit a foreword. We could go and see him about it now.' She grabbed at the first idea that came into her head, anxious to get Diane away from that building. She saw she was holding a white packet and guessed it was heroin.

'Isn't that macabre? A dead man's books.'

Jill recoiled at Diane's brutal tone. For a moment she couldn't speak. She gulped and went on, 'I thought you needed money. *To Jericho and Back*'s among them, and of course you would be paid for the piece. And Tom might even be able to find you a job in publishing. That would interest you wouldn't it?' She was babbling, conscious of Diane's eyes on her, of the suspicion in her face, of her fingers twisting the small packet round and round.

'What about my probate money?'

'Yes, well I told you that's almost through. If you like we can go to my bank now, on the way to Tom Feathers, and I'll see what I can lend you. I have to make arrangements for a large sum.'

She held her breath as Diane thrust the packet into her jeans' pocket and straightened up. 'OK. I'll come.'

'You'll need a coat, it's cold.' Jill spoke almost mechanically, wondering whether they'd get past the ground floor without the dreaded Chris coming out; and then what would Tom Feathers say if the two of them turned up out of the blue?

Safely in the car, her legs turned to jelly in sheer relief. Diane sat slumped in the passenger seat and ignored Jill's arm reaching across her to fasten her safety belt. They passed a bank of three phone boxes, but Jill suppressed the impulse to stop and phone Tom; she couldn't risk Diane running away. Turning over her next move, she decided to take her home with her right now. It was much the best option.

She zigzagged through the maze of Notting Hill until she got on to the road to Heathrow and the M25, glad that Diane didn't notice the click as she activated the childproof doorlock.

After about twenty minutes Diane stirred slightly. 'I thought Tom Feathers's office was in Bloomsbury.'

'Oh, he moved. Offices are cheaper out here. He deals mostly on the phone these days.'

They got past the airport turn-off and were speeding along

the M3 when Diane roused herself again and looked at Jill. 'This isn't the way. Where are you taking me?' Her voice rose in a scream.

'I'm taking you home,' Jill said firmly. 'You're ill and I want you to get better.'

'Stop the car. I want to get out. I'm not going with you.'

'Diane,' Jill took one hand off the wheel and put it on Diane's knee. 'You're not happy leading this sort of life. Your father's heart would break if he could see you now. You're beautiful and intelligent, and you're wasting your life. You could die if you go on like this. I'm serious.'

'It's my life.' But she muttered rather than screamed, and slumped against the seat again, accepting defeat. 'I won't stay,' she threatened. 'You can't keep me against my will.'

'I know that. I want *you* to want to stay.' Jill turned her head to look at her, but Diane was staring out of the window. She appeared to sleep for the rest of the long drive, but her body kept giving convulsive twitches and she moaned and muttered incoherently. When they turned into the cottage she got out of the car without protest, and let Jill propel her inside. Jill hurriedly made tea, keeping a wary eye on the pacing figure.

'Was it true about the new edition of Daddy's books?'

'Yes.'

'And did Tom Feathers really say he wanted me to try doing a foreword?

'It was absolutely his own idea. He said he'd ring you about it, but you've been out rather a lot. I've been ringing you myself.'

'I go to Chris's flat when I'm lonely. There's always people there. People who don't criticize or interfere.' Her face crumpled suddenly. 'I want to go back to Chris.' She was shaking and hugging herself, pacing up and down the kitchen. 'He looks after me.'

'Is he the one who gets you drugs?'

'It's none of your business.'

'I'll get Tom Feathers on the phone now,' Jill ignored the outburst. 'Then you can talk to him yourself.' She picked up the kitchen phone, praying Tom wasn't in a meeting or out. She hoped he'd remember their conversation.

\* \* \*

148

She managed to convey enough to Tom to jog his memory and handed the receiver to Diane. It was a fairly one-sided conversation as Diane's responses were monosyllabic, except when she said, 'I can't write' and 'How much?' Followed almost immediately by an incredulous 'Is that all?' She put the phone down and patted her pocket for cigarettes. 'Shit. I've left my ciggies behind.' Her expression was sly as her fingers found the white packet. 'Well, you were telling the truth about the boxed set anyway. I don't know if I can do a foreword, but I suppose they have someone who can rewrite it. I'll go upstairs and think about it. Hardly worth it for the peanuts on offer though.'

Jill's instinct was to snatch the dope from her, but she restrained herself. She knew enough to know that it couldn't stop all at once and if Diane went to her room she could ring Roger.

'Roger, don't tell me off for trying to do all I can. Just give me the name of that place you mentioned; I want her to start treatment as soon as possible,' she said firmly when Roger Mander remonstrated with her. 'There's no-one else to help her.'

'Yes there is,' he said bluntly. '*Herself*.'

Jill's old skills of decisiveness and cajoling were deployed until Roger gave in and agreed to ring Hedera House. 'Give me ten minutes and then ring them yourself,' he said wearily, his patience worn out. 'But don't expect Diane to be grateful. If they accept her, she's in for a very tough time. She won't thank you.'

'I don't care about that. I want her better. I shall be letting Douglas down if I don't do everything I can for his daughter.'

There was a pause and then, 'Jill, are you sure you're not just trying to take over her mother's rôle?'

'If I am it's one she's already abandoned,' she retorted angrily.

She rang Hedera House next. A very authoritative voice belonging to someone who introduced herself as 'Clarissa' ('We don't use surnames here; many of us are recovering abusers') said that yes she had just been speaking to Dr Mander but unless it was desperately urgent they couldn't find a place for a week.

'It's not desperate but it is urgent,' Jill said. 'I'm afraid she'll run back to London any minute. I've virtually kidnapped her.'

There was an exclamation of disapproval. 'This isn't a jail,' Clarissa replied. 'She must come of her own free will. We don't keep people locked up. If she comes, she can leave at any time, and if she doesn't agree to going on the programme we shall ask her to leave. There's a two-month waiting list for National Health patients, so we can't have anyone wasting our time.'

'I see,' said Jill humbly.

'We ask that there is no outside contact for a week. If you want to know how she is you can ring a nurse, but she mustn't ring you or you her. Is that understood?'

'Yes.' Clarissa told her they followed a ten-day 'de-tox', 'because withdrawal symptoms can be frightening.'

'What do you mean, what happens?' Jill's mouth was dry with apprehension.

'It depends on what they've been taking and how much. They shake and sweat, sometimes hallucinate. They feel pretty dreadful,' Clarissa said cheerfully. 'We give them clonidine to help but only for ten days. After that they have to cope without.' Blithely she added, 'Don't worry, it's just like boarding school.'

Jill was dealt a further shock when Clarissa told her they charged £1,200 a week. 'We're a charity. Those who can afford to pay subsidize those who can't.'

When she finally put the phone down, she felt very much in need of a strong drink. She went up to Diane's room and knocked. Diane was smiling stupidly, and Jill saw a scrap of scorched kitchen foil and some spent matches in the lovely ceramic bowl she and Douglas had bought locally.

'Hi!' Diane said dully. Her eyes watched Jill apprehensively, though she seemed sleepy.

Jill bent and put an arm round the thin shoulders, her voice a persuasive whisper, 'Diane, I want you to stop this.' Her finger flicked at the foil. 'Or rather I want you to want to stop it.' She sat down on the bed. 'You realize, don't you, that if you're caught using this stuff you can go to jail? And if you go on using more and more, eventually you'll kill yourself. Plain statement of fact.' She folded her arms and gazed at Diane. 'You're ill and you've got to make yourself better. Roger's told me of a special clinic not far from here which has a very good reputation. They'll help you. If you won't go for your own sake, go for Douglas's.'

Diane shut her eyes and sighed noisily. 'Now you've made your little speech will you please leave me alone?'

Disappointed Jill left the room. She remembered she hadn't put the car away and went outside to garage it. She longed for Douglas with a deep intensity, frightened of the future for his only daughter.

'Hullo! I see you have a clutch of fieldfares in your garden.' The cheerful voice belonged to James Montgomery-Fitch, binculars round his neck.

'Have I?' she looked round mystified.

'Those birds there, bit like a large thrush. I startled them as I walked along your lane. After the windfalls I expect,' he nodded at some rotting apples. 'I was going to tuck in the thickets by your river and do a spot of bird-watching, but it's colder than I thought.' He was different from the demoralized youth who had been trailing behind his fearsome mother.

'Would you like a cup of tea to warm you up?' Jill offered. She was suddenly afraid of returning to the cottage, of being alone with Diane.

James blushed with pleasure. 'That's very nice of you, thanks.' He followed her in through the back door. Two teacups were still on the table.

'Diane's here,' she said as she saw him noticing them. 'We had a cup of tea when we drove back from London but I'm ready for another. Do you know a lot about birds? I started to take an interest in them about a year ago when I saw a very pretty one from the kitchen window. It was a goldfinch, I found out.'

'They're quite common,' said James. 'I suppose I know most of the birds around here because I've been watching them since I was small, but I'm not a serious twitcher.' He smiled. 'I can lend you a good book on birds – it's very clear on identification.'

'Thanks. I'd like that. My husband bought me a little pair of binoculars when I got excited about those that came to the garden – there's a tree outside the kitchen window that they seem to like. In London you only ever see pigeons and starlings. The pigeons always look so sharp – like street traders.'

'What about sparrows?'

'Of course, the sparrows, little urchins,' she echoed.

At that moment Diane came into the room and Jill caught James's quickly camouflaged look of surprise. The change from the slim girl at his mother's dreadful drinks party to this skeletal figure was obvious. He politely stood up as Diane came into the room.

'Hi,' she greeted him. 'D'you have a cigarette?'

' 'Fraid not – I don't smoke.'

'I might have guessed,' she said sourly.

'I'll go and get you some,' he offered. 'There's a pub about a mile away.'

'Oh, great. I'll come with you,' Diane glanced defiantly at Jill.

'I walked here,' James said apologetically. 'I haven't a car.'

'Oh shit!'

'It won't take me long,' James offered again. 'I'll jog.'

'We can take Jill's car,' Diane challenged Jill. 'I want to go out. *Mine* was left in London.'

Jill was afraid to let her out of her sight but she could hardly keep her prisoner. She clattered the teacups into the sink. 'As you wish,' she said. She was suddenly very tired. She pushed back her hair in a gesture of resignation, and walked into the sitting room to light the fire. The cottage was cold, and she felt as frozen as a block of ice. She fervently wished Douglas was there to hold her and comfort her. 'I am trying Douglas,' she said out loud, 'but it's so hard.'

Restless, unable to sit, she decided on impulse to ring the police about Chris whilst Diane was out. As long as Diane was staying with her, she couldn't be involved, could she? Feverishly she rang Directory Enquiries for the number of the Notting Hill Gate police station. She was taken aback when she got through to the number she was given surprisingly quickly and a friendly female voice asked if she could help her. She was put through to someone from the drug squad as if her call was routine. The woman police officer sounded so sympathetic that Jill told her about Diane, shared her fears that if Chris was a dealer, Diane would be implicated.

'Don't worry. If someone informs we give them protection. Your stepdaughter needn't be involved.' Jill, reassured, gave the details. 'Thank you, madam,' the officer said, taking her name and address. 'We'll put a watch on the flat. Ground floor you say? If there's unusual activity, an abnormal number of people coming in and out we'll get a search warrant. Then if we find the stuff, bingo.'

Jill had no qualms about them being successful, she just hoped they'd find enough evidence to pounce on Chris before Diane returned to London. It was clear she wasn't going to be able to keep her here.

# Chapter Twenty-six

When James had delivered Diane back from their pub jaunt and left, Jill produced some supper although she had no appetite herself and Diane only ever pushed food around her plate. She made some *spaghetti alla carbonara* with a crisp green salad. Conversation was difficult. Jill didn't want to revert to Hedera House, and searched for some neutral topic to try to keep a slight semblance of normality going.

'I was wondering if you know anything about word processors? Tom Feathers is convinced that Douglas's last book is somewhere inside the one upstairs. He was working on it before ... before our holiday,' she said with difficulty. 'I think he must have finished it because he seemed so carefree in France. I'm sure he'd have been preoccupied if he'd been in the middle of something.'

'What's it about?'

'I don't know. When I asked, he seemed as if he didn't want to talk about it.'

'Why are you so anxious to find it? You can't want *more* of his money.'

'Don't be cheap.'

'It can hardly be one of his usual action-packed thrillers if he was in Sherville when he wrote it,' Diane said contemptuously. 'I can't think why you gave up fashion to rot down here.'

'I didn't rot. I was very happy.'

'Well, there's nothing to keep you here now. Why don't you go back to your own world, then perhaps you wouldn't have time to poke your nose into my affairs. You don't belong here.'

'I don't belong anywhere.' The full force of her misery hit Jill. She abruptly switched on the television, grateful for the sudden cackle of the audience, the grinning face of a presenter as he milked the reaction to a mild witticism.

A slightly shamed expression crossed Diane's face as she

caught sight of the desolation in Jill's who leant back, drained, against the sofa.

'I'm going to bed.' She hovered, waiting for Jill to react, but she simply said, 'Good night' in an exhausted tone without opening her eyes. Diane walked uncertainly out of the room, the television laughter mocking her as she glanced back.

Jill was unable to sleep, disturbed by Diane's pacing. She heard her go downstairs and got up herself, crept to her door, fearful of what Diane would do. She had taken the precaution of keeping her car keys with her overnight, but perhaps Diane would try to walk to the main road and hitch a lift. Then she heard the comforting sound of the radio. She went back to bed, straining to listen for the noise of an outside door being opened, but eventually she heard her visitor come up to her room again.

About eleven the next morning Diane appeared, gaunt and jumpy. 'Cut my hair,' she said to Jill.

'What?'

'Cut my hair. Go on, cut it all off.' She grabbed the kitchen scissors and waved them. 'Cut it off or I'll do it myself,' and she pulled a thick strand of hair from the side of her head and sawed through it.

Jill hid her shock. 'All right. If that's what you want. Then perhaps you'll wash it. It's quite dirty.'

She trimmed the long lank hair to a short bob. 'There – you look like Louise Brooks. Quite an improvement!'

Diane glanced at herself in the kitchen mirror in silence, then left the room. Jill heard her going up the stairs. What was she going to do now?

In a short while she reappeared, shivering, her hair dripping wet, a towel round her naked body. 'I haven't any clothes,' she said piteously. 'You gave me no chance to pack anything.'

Jill shepherded her out of the room. 'Come on, you'll freeze. You can choose something of mine.' She opened her cupboards. She always kept her clothes beautifully arranged on proper hangers, trees in her shoes, part of her training to treat good garments with respect. After a minute Diane chose a red tweed skirt and a cream sweater; the last three times Jill had seen her she'd been dressed in black from head to foot, except when she'd arrived in the violet sweater. A slight hope began to well. Could she be trying to change? Unable to tell, she watched the scrawny vulnerable figure slide on the skirt which hung on her jutting hipbones like a rag.

'That looks nice. Let's dry your hair.' She blow-dried Diane's new look, trying to coax the hastily shorn ends to curve under. As she finished, James appeared knocking on the back door.

'Hullo,' he said a trifle sheepishly. 'I brought the bird book you wanted, Jill.' He turned to Diane. 'Hi. Like the new hairdo! Want to come with me? I'm going out with Peter Smith, he's going to cut and lay a hedge. Few people do it now, but it makes a much better finish. Nowadays they simply mutilate them with machines, or grub them out altogether.'

'Who the hell is Peter?'

'A friend. He's a tree surgeon. He wants to conserve a strip of hedge that he thinks is a relic of Saxon days.'

Diane stared at him. 'Is that your idea of fun?'

James blushed. 'It's interesting,' he said defensively. 'You can tell how old a hedge is by the mix of its tree and shrub species.'

'Riveting,' Diane said sarcastically, but to Jill's surprise she got up and put on her jacket. 'Might as well.'

They were back within an hour. 'I don't think Diane is quite well,' James told Jill awkwardly.

Diane was shaking and making peculiar whining noises, her eyes staring in that blind way that so frightened Jill. 'I saw them watching me in the bushes,' she said through chattering teeth. 'Lots of them, when I turned round they'd gone to the other side.'

Jill tried to hold her to stifle the shaking but she broke away.

'I'm going back to Chris. There aren't any of them there. You can't keep me here.'

She stormed up the stairs. Jill wondered if she had any of the heroin left.

'She's into drugs, isn't she?' James said quietly.

'Yes.' Jill nodded helplessly.

'I recognize the symptoms. She looked awful yesterday, that's really why I came today. I thought I might help. A good friend of mine died of an overdose.'

'Don't frighten me,' begged Jill. 'I'm trying to get her into Hedera House, but I can't force her.'

'Shall I talk to her?'

'I don't think she'll listen.'

'I could try.'

An hour later he came down. 'She's badly frightened herself. She thinks some "things" are after her. I told her about Jimmy, this friend of mine. She knows she's sick but she can't make the effort to get help.'

Diane followed him downstairs a few minutes later, gulping as if she couldn't breathe. She stood in the middle of the floor, her eyes swinging wildly from Jill to James. She clutched her ragged fringe with both hands, pulling at the hair. 'You've got to save me,' she cried to them both, her wail so piteous that both James and Jill rushed to her side.

Jill reached for, and found, her hand. 'We'll all go and see this clinic. Hedera House will know how to help you. I spoke to them, they sound very pleasant.' She threw Diane's coat over the bony shoulders and the three of them went out.

James sat in the back of the car holding Diane's hand and talking to her in a low, soothing voice. He seemed to have gained her confidence for she had turned her face towards him.

Well-kept lawns and shrubs surrounded Hedera House, a large Victorian mansion – with one or two hideous modern pre-fabricated annexes tacked on the sides. As she opened the car door, Jill was grateful for the unexpected ray of sunshine breaking through the wintry grey clouds and making everything seem more cheerful. She and James walked either side of Diane along the short distance to the front steps, but as they reached them Diane baulked like a racehorse at the starting gate.

'I can't,' she wailed, fright widening her eyes. 'I want to go home. I want my Daddy.'

The heart-rending, childish cry demoralized Jill but James held Diane tightly, smiling encouragingly at her. 'You're going to be fine,' he said. 'They're nice people here. Nothing awful is going to happen to you. You want to get better don't you?'

His words took the fight out of her and making incoherent mumbling noises, she allowed herself to be led up the steps.

157

The reception area was like a large, comfortable living room, cheerfully decorated with good rugs on polished floors and reproductions of the more familiar Impressionists framed on the walls. Jill had been dreading some kind of forbidding institutional atmosphere, and immediately felt relieved. As they stood uncertainly a businesslike young woman walked up smartly and raised an enquiring eyebrow. Jill stepped forward. 'I'm Jill Mortimer. I rang someone called Clarissa a day or two ago about my stepdaughter.'

'I'm Clarissa. Yes, I remember. Has she agreed to come in?'

'Yes. She suddenly seems to have got worse. It *is* desperate now and I'm at my wit's end.'

Clarissa went over to Diane and took her hand. 'Hullo dear. I'm Clarissa. I used to take drugs. I know what you're going through. You can stay with us for a while. You'll have a nice room and we'll help you to help yourself get better.' Diane stared at her. 'If you don't like us you can leave,' Clarissa smiled. 'This isn't a prison.'

Two attractive young men came in through the door, smiled and nodded at Clarissa as they walked to a swing door at the far end of the room. 'That's Simon and Anthony. They're guests here, too, for the time being.'

Clarissa looked at Jill. 'OK, leave her with me. I'll send June along in a minute.' Her arm across Diane's shoulders she guided her through the far door. As she went through Diane started to create a fuss again, but the swing door cut off her protests.

Jill felt her knees about to buckle, and looking at James she saw his eyes were glazed with tears.

'I don't think I can bear it,' Jill told him. 'It's like drowning kittens.' James squeezed her hand in reply.

A short plump woman came up then, announcing that she was June and that there were a few forms to complete. These turned out to consist mainly, it seemed to Jill, wincing inwardly at the total, of asking her to undersign the fees and to be willing to come and fetch Diane if she refused to co-operate with the treatment. She hesitated at the line asking for Diane's next of kin, but she stifled her misgivings and gave her own name. After all, she hadn't the faintest idea where Diane's mother was. Glad that at least she wasn't short of money, she signed.

Driving home, she was grateful for the silent presence of James beside her. Away from his mother, he seemed so mature, so understanding.

'Thanks for your help and moral support,' she said as she dropped him at the entrance to Stourbridge Court. 'I couldn't have coped without you. You seem to have some magic touch with Diane.'

He reddened, looking gratified. 'I'll keep in touch if I may.'

'Please.'

# Chapter Twenty-seven

Jill's sleep that night was again very disturbed, haunted by visions of the emaciated Diane. She also kept seeing an unfamiliar face that was meant to be Douglas, looking at her with an expression of hurt and betrayal.

Next day, despite feeling drained, she tried to garden but it looked so damp she lost enthusiasm. Unable to settle to anything in the cottage, she made an excuse to see Lizzie Boston. Lizzie's house opened straight off the narrow pavement as the road entered the village, one of a terrace of old-fashioned two-up-two-downs which Jill supposed had once been farm labourers' cottages or for the workers in the worsted factory that had dominated Sherville.

Lizzie had her back to the small window, bent over a sewing machine. Hanging from the picture rail that ran round the room was an assortment of garments in varying degrees of finish, with a lace wedding dress minus one sleeve in pride of place on a dressmaker's dummy.

'Oh, I'm so glad to see you!' Lizzie exclaimed, 'I've just thrown over Lady Fitch's dress in despair. You know the one she wears at the company's annual dinner when April accidentally on purpose spills wine on her. It's much too small and there's nothing to let out.' She showed Jill the dress.

'Is there anything here to salvage?' Jill asked, looking at the remains of the jumble-sale garments. The finished costumes were hanging in the village hall, behind a padlock fitted by Peter. She found something of a similar fabric but different colour. 'It looks as if we'll have to cannibalize two frocks in order to make *one* for Arabella.' She smiled at Lizzie's dubious face. 'We can put in a printed panel down the front and use the left-over bits to make a cape effect over the sleeves – then it will look meant.'

Cutting and tacking the garment for Lizzie to machine

was therapeutic, as was Lizzie's chatter. 'Do you do lots of dressmaking, Lizzie?'

'Well, there's always somebody wanting something. It all comes at once and I'm rushed off me feet, or else there's nothing to do and I'm wondering how we're going to manage for extra pennies. Got a wedding order on now,' she nodded at the half-finished lace gown. 'And the bride's mother's two-piece. I like weddings best. I've done nearly seventy this last five years, sometimes the bridesmaids and pages as well. Though as I see it, if they've been living with a chap it isn't right to have all that spectacle. It's hypocritical. And some of them have been seven months' gone.'

She rattled on, her machine keeping time with her tongue, except when she stopped to make a cup of tea for them both and urged Jill to a piece of sticky jam sponge. 'Go on m'dear, it's all homemade, even the jam. Jim has a row of raspberry canes out back and when they ripen I can't keep up with them. Freezer's full, course it's only a small one, there's no room in this place but you know before me and Jim were married the old lady who lived here brought up seven kiddies in this house. Wouldn't believe it would you? She went into an old people's home. Seven kids and not one of them would take her in when she was too old to look after herself. Disgrace I call it.'

Jill went back to the cottage inexplicably cheered. She had not been above relating some of her own stories of the fashion high life for Lizzie's goggling pleasure, and as she set about producing a meal for herself she felt a sharp nostalgia for Fred's and her very different existence of a few years ago.

She'd been at the top of the fashion buyer's tree then, a fact confirmed by the overtures from big stores in London and New York, and the commission to design the costumes for *White Meadows*. If she hadn't been asked to do that, her life now would be very different. She remembered the battles she'd had to get some of the famous designers to let her have first pick of their collections and exclusive use in London of those numbers she'd bought, the feeling of triumph when she'd beaten the fashion directors from Harrods or Harvey Nichols to a new designer.

She'd always chosen sales assistants who had a fashion eye, telling them, 'If you guide women into something that flatters them they'll come again. It's continuous sales we're interested in not the one-off.' And her policy had paid off. The cream of fashionable London trooped into Fred's, willing to clobber their credit cards in exchange for the confidence that Jill's chic taste would give them. She wished for her old life now, to escape from this alien country of dark muddy lanes, few shops, and lacking in decent cinema or professional theatre.

On impulse she picked up the telephone to ring Carla, anxious to hear her chirpy voice, to talk to someone who cared. 'About time too!' scolded Carla. 'I thought you'd gone native.'

'Not a chance. How are things in the wicked city?'

Carla, always sharp, must have caught the yearning hidden by the offhand tone for she said quickly, 'Why don't you come and find out? There's a good film I was planning to see, come with me.'

'I don't think I can.'

'Why ever not? You were boasting about your train service or how easy it was to drive up in a couple of hours. Stay the night, let's have dinner at the Belvedere, get drunk, have fun.'

'All right.' She was amazed at herself. 'I'll come by train tomorrow. What's your man scene? Am I interrupting anything?'

'I only wish you were. The ones I seem to fancy are married or gay, and I've decided married men are off the menu. Far too complicated.'

'Then I'll be with you by six.' She felt a secret twinge of excitement, like going to a ballet when she was small and in love with Margot Fonteyn. The next morning as she packed an over-night bag and pondered what to wear, she started to worry. Suppose Hedera House rang about Diane; suppose Peter Smith needed to speak to her about the sets or Lizzie found fresh problems with the costumes? But she pulled herself together and drove to the station, leaving the car in the yard. She felt a bit nervous, unlike the last time she'd gone up when there'd been more purpose to her visit; she'd crammed in Tom Feathers, Fred Rosomon, her solicitor, the hairdresser and dentist, Diane's flat and the theatre. Now she had no particular errand, she was simply gratifying a pang of longing.

# Chapter Twenty-eight

Before she realized it, engrossed in her book, Waterloo with its new Channel tunnel platforms under construction slid outside the train window. The busy terminus seemed to be in a state of dismal upheaval, the station road pitted with half-finished repairs and the usual exit closed, but she was shocked after she crossed Westminster Bridge to see lighted Christmas trees and decorations. She had to check her diary to assure herself that it actually was mid-December and Christmas was a mere few days away.

Jill gazed as the lights winked and magnified through a sudden mist of tears. Last Christmas Day she and Douglas had been alone together, waking up late to a brunch of smoked salmon and scrambled egg washed down with champagne. They'd filled a stocking for each other with silly jokey things, and then driven to Studland Bay to walk in the crisp, sunny morning air along the cliffs to the Old Harry Rocks, fascinated by the relentless swelling and crashing of the waves in a froth of spray on the boulders beneath. They'd been almost alone except for a couple of stoical surfers in wet suits and some excited small children eager to fly an elaborate new kite. They'd had a festive dinner by candlelight with a bottle of Douglas's hoarded Château Latour, and their special presents to each other, the antique garnet pendant for her and his books bound in black hide and tooled in gilt for him. Afterwards they'd played word games and watched television and went to bed, drenched in happiness, to make slow, gentle, and exquisite love.

This year she would be alone. Everyone else would be preoccupied with their own families. She was glad that the thick traffic, which the taxi driver cursed and muttered about, gave her time to compose herself before they reached the elegant black wrought iron-and-glass doors of Carla's block of flats in Holland Park.

It was comforting to tread the thick carpet of the reception hall, to gaze at the awe-inspiring bank of poinsettias (the building's only condescension to Christmas decorations) and to have the nodding hall porter call the lift for her. After the cottage it seemed like a foreign land, so luxurious, so contained, so safe. Wild emotions would have no place here.

She sped to the ninth floor, and as the lift slid open straight into Carla's hall she was met by her friend's smiling face. Carla held a frosted glass of champagne in each hand.

'How's that for timing?'

They laughed and kissed, and Jill followed Carla into the large living room, the windows on three sides giving views over Holland Park and Camden Hill. Carla had a sure hand with colour, and the room looked vivid and exotic with its carefully chaotic mix of patterns against soft yellow walls and a dark ochre carpet.

'So, how's the country bumpkin? Ready to park her pitchfork?' Carla eyed her sharply after she'd dropped her bag in the pretty spare bedroom. 'You've lost weight,' she accused. 'Much too thin.'

'Can't be too thin or too rich, you know that,' Jill returned as lightly as she could. 'Anyway I took your advice,' she teased. 'I've got involved in the local drama group. I'm their costume designer, wardrobe mistress, set designer, and probably when the first night dawns, make-up artist, scene shifter, and resident psychiatrist to boot. No wonder I've lost weight. How are your plans for opening this wonderful accessory shop?'

'Oh, they're gelling, I'll fill you in over dinner,' Carla said airily. 'Finish that glass, I'm ahead of you. We're going to see a film, apparently terrif, and then I've booked a table at The Belvedere. It's in the orangery in Holland Park, lovely setting of course but I chose it because it's only five minutes away, so if the buggers say they can't call us a taxi we can stagger home on foot. Not that I wish to do so,' she added hastily.

It was a good film and Jill enjoyed it but she had the uneasy feeling that she was abandoning Diane. When they got to the restaurant she went off to phone Hedera House.

'She's settling in,' a nurse said noncommittally.

'How is she feeling?' Jill persisted.

'As well as can be expected,' the cautious reply came. 'The first few days are difficult, you know.' Then she added succinctly, 'For everyone.'

Jill's heart sank.


Carla had already ordered drinks when she joined her at the table.

'OK, what's up?' she said firmly. 'Who have you been phoning and why are you looking like a wrung-out dish rag?'

'It's my stepdaughter. She's been drugging. I've put her into a clinic.' She didn't mean to tell Carla but the impulse to share the burden with someone so worldly, so unshockable, and so much her friend, was impossible to resist.

'Christ!' Carla reached across for Jill's hand. 'You poor kid. I know what that's like. My brother went through that whole mularky. Where is she?'

Carla nodded at the name. 'That's one of the best. Hilary went to somewhere in Somerset. I thought he was dying. In fact he *was* dying. They performed a miracle.' She blew cigarette smoke. 'He's fine now. Marketing director of the petfoods division of Yetterdens, married with twin boys. As square as they come. Even lives in Esher.'

Jill smiled weakly. 'It's partly my fault. I didn't realize when Douglas and I married that she felt left out. Her parents were newly divorced, she was only sixteen, she adored Douglas. I took her hostility as a threat, she always seemed so cool, so sophisticated even at that age. Whenever we took her out she barely spoke. She was uphill work and I suppose I gave up too soon. She would never come down to the cottage. It was only at the . . . at the funeral that she seemed a little more human. She was wonderfully supportive then.

'Your fault? Don't be an idiot. What about her mother; where is she?'

'I don't know exactly. I suppose she's in the phone book. She lives in London but Diane seems to see little of her. She thinks her mother regards her as a failure because she didn't get to university. Frances is into culture with a "K". She runs the

Pantheon Gallery now, advises Carl Bickerstaff on his art collection, has a monthly salon of the literati.'

'Christ, enough to drive anyone to drink or drugs.'

'Then Diane had some oddball after her, a married man; at least so she said. And she's in debt. Obviously she's been buying drugs, though she told me she'd lost money gambling. But she's been living beyond her means anyway, for someone working in an estate agents. She has an expensive flat in Notting Hill Gate, but I assumed she had some boyfriend who helped with the expenses. I didn't enquire. Neither did I notice the signs until her last visit . . .'

'She's in the best place. Leave it to her mother to sort out now,' Carla suggested. 'What's she doing letting her kid run around like that unsupervised, just because she didn't get enough A'levels? The woman's a criminal! Poncing about with arty-farties whilst her daughter's scoring . . .' She paused to puff indignantly at her cigarette. 'Get out of it. It's not your problem.'

'She's Douglas's only child. She's all I have left of him.'

Carla's eyes narrowed through the smoke. 'You can't cling to the dead by claiming a piece of the living. Not even if she were your own flesh and blood.' She stubbed out her cigarette. 'Which she isn't.'

'Oh, don't let's talk about it any more. There's nothing I can do for the moment – no-one's allowed to see her for at least a week.' She forced another smile, anxious to divert Carla from the subject. 'Tell me about your shop.'

'*Boutique*. In the old-fashioned French sense of the word, not the King's Road version,' Carla said loftily. 'In fact, I think I'm going to make it like a gallery – the handbags in frames on the wall and lit like works of art. Belts on metal sculptures, shoes on a gleaming spiral staircase, very modern jewellery; I want to get kids from the art colleges to bring me their work first, to build up a directory of artisans I can commission.' Her face was alight with enthusiasm as she described her plan. 'I've got a brilliant woman accountant who's been revising and revising a business plan; she has good ideas of how to raise the capital. It's going to happen.' She nodded her head emphatically. 'Why don't you come in with me as a partner?'

Jill was caught up in her enthusiasm. 'It sounds great.' She should join in, get back to the world she knew. If not at Fred's, then with Carla. It was stupid to hang on to the cottage like some sacred totem or rural shrine. She discussed the project as eagerly as Carla, injecting some of the ideas with her own experience at building up Fred's.

'You see,' Carla sat back in triumph. 'You've still got your magic touch. You look alive again. Will you think it over?'

Jill laughed ruefully. 'It's *your* concept. If I go back at all I should go to Fred's or somewhere like it.'

Carla was wise enough not to push. There was enough lambent ambition there to give her hope.

The next morning when Carla had said farewell and gone to work after a frantic breakfast of scalding coffee gulped through three telephone calls, Jill sat in the windowseat gazing out over the London she had lived in almost all her adult life. She could get a flat again in a block like this where there were no worries about the central heating working, light bulbs were replaced, things delivered. Life was so much easier with well-stocked shops that stayed open late, that never ran out of bread because it was early closing day, where if you were too tired to cook you could fall on a take-away or a neighbourhood bistro.

She hated inefficiency and what could be more inefficient than a cottage in a rural hideaway where she had hardly any friends or support system, and no function except to fuss over some amateur drama group? She had no knowledge or previous experience of country life. She was virtually ignorant of gardening and yet she was saddled with an acre and a quarter of land. It was ridiculous.

Exasperated with herself and her indecision, she strode to Kensington High Street and bought an armful of white tulips for Carla. She returned to the flat, put them in water, scribbled a warm 'thank you' note, called a taxi and left. How simple life was in town.

Gazing gloomily out of the taxi window at the grey damp mist clinging to the buildings and Christmas decorations, her eye was caught by a couple, walking erratically because of their entwinement, on the pavement in Sloane Street. The girl was wearing a fake fur coat so spotted that any self-respecting leopard would have disowned it immediately, high-heeled shoes, a bright red handbag and enough make-up to empty the beauty counters of Selfridges. One hand was clutching a large Harvey Nichols' carrier bag, and her other arm was wound round her man. Jill had little difficulty in recognizing Sandra but she experienced a shock when the man with the armlock turned out to be Tom Houlderton. She shrank back into the taxi, afraid they would see her, but Sandra was giggling and looking coyly up at her partner, oblivious of anything or anyone else. Jill felt a pang of disappointment in Tom.

It was none of her business, but she found herself dwelling on the couple. Presumably they'd stayed in a nearby hotel and the Harvey Nichols' bag contained Sandra's reward. Depression enveloped her at the passing shop windows filled with glittering lights and Christmas present ideas.

Later, on the train home, she closed her eyes and tried to shut out the whole idea of Christmas. When an enormous fat woman came round pushing a trolleyload of drinks and sandwiches, Jill ordered a large whisky. 'My, you're getting the Christmas spirit early luv, aren't you? It's only 11 o'clock. That'll be two pounds. No water, have to have that for me teas. Ice? Soda?'

'No thank you, nothing.'

'Neat eh?' She passed on down the empty carriage, chortling to herself.

In the station yard Jill was glad to see her familiar blue car waiting for her, looking dusty and somehow reproachful. She turned the ignition, suddenly anxious to get home. She'd left the central heating on, but the living room would be lifeless without the wood-burning stove sending out warmth and colour. Just as she was about to pull out of the station yard someone tapped on her window. It was Tom's wife Claudine Houlderton, smiling pinkly at her through the window.

'Hi – I ran along the platform to catch you up but you walked so fast,' she said breathlessly. 'Can you give me a lift? Tom's gone to see his aunt in Basingstoke. She's over eighty and not very well.'

At Jill's invitation, Claudine settled into the passenger seat, unusually animated. 'I can't wait for Tom to get home! I've been to the hospital. We've hardly told anyone yet, but I'm pregnant. I can't believe it! They've given me a special diet, and Dr Mander has to monitor me every week. I've had four miscarriages you know, and each time it took ages to get pregnant again. But this time they're more hopeful of it going to full term. I'm almost afraid to believe them.' She chattered on excitedly and Jill wondered if she'd ever find out that Tom's aunt was a nubile blonde of twenty-two with a large bosom and long legs.

She dropped Claudine at the barn, touched by the joy in the happy girl's face as she very carefully got out of the car.

She drove too fast the few miles to the cottage but as soon as she saw its fat stone shape rising out of the damp fog at the bottom of the hill, she relaxed and smiled with relief. It was still there. It seemed so solid, so serene and comforting, that she was instantly glad to be back despite how she had dwelt on the merits of life in a modern block of flats.

Once reinstalled, she glanced out of the kitchen window as she heated soup and cut some cheese for her lunch, and was entranced to see the duck waddling up the lawn to the kitchen door.

'Oh, you've missed your breakfast have you?' she said, throwing it some bread. The duck fluttered a few feet away and then stopped, dipping its head to look back at her with shrewd black eyes. Then, sensing she meant no harm, it turned, stretched its neck and gobbled the bread greedily. 'There, that's the last. Come again tomorrow.'

# Chapter Twenty-nine

Jill spent Christmas Day alone, despite being invited by Miriam Mander to join them. She would feel too much like the spectre at the feast she told her, and anyway had lots of things she wanted to do. She drove to the coast and walked to the Harry Rocks. There she sat on the cliff, huddled in her coat, knees to her chest, gazing out over the cold grey sea and trying to picture Douglas's face. Sometimes she could recall his mouth as he smiled, sometimes his eyes, but she still couldn't make a whole picture.

On the way back she made a detour to drop a small gift, just after midday, at the Morrishs' and was pressed to a glass of sweet sherry. George and Mildred's oldest daughter was there, her three small children engrossed in new toys on the floor of the tiny living room, and a strapping young man of about eighteen was introduced as 'their baby' which caused him to redden and kick the stove.

They pressed her to stay and have Christmas dinner with them. 'Sure m'dear, there's plenty. Twenty pound turkey I've got, been in since dawn. And the puddns. Made them last October. You're very welcome, int she Dad?'

A lump rose in her throat as she looked at their kindly faces beaming at her, George Morrish nodding vigorously to endorse his wife's invitation. 'How good of you, thanks, it's sweet of you but I have to get back.'

She'd bought some smoked salmon and a chicken. She set the low coffee table elaborately, eating her meal in front of the fire whilst watching an old Fred Astaire and Ginger Rogers film, and drinking most of a bottle of Sancerre. The wine made her sleepy, and she dozed, dreaming of Douglas in a curious muddled sequence where he was trying to reach her across the river at the bottom of the garden but was constantly frustrated by strange people cutting him off from her.

On Boxing Day she was allowed to see Diane. She went to Hedera House apprehensively, taking with her an assortment of books, chocolates, a white cashmere scarf and a tapestry kit.

Diane looked strained, but she was scrupulously clean and her room pin-neat and tidy. She thrust the books back ungraciously.

'We're not allowed those. You'll have to take them away.'

Jill was puzzled. 'That seems very strange.'

'Ask Clarissa if you don't believe me. What's this?' she asked blankly, when she opened the tapestry.

'It's just something soothing to do. I covered a footstool when I was ill last year and found it therapeutic. If you don't like it, give it to someone else. I thought the colours and the design were attractive.'

Diane tossed it aside indifferently.

'It's a pretty room,' Jill began.

Diane gave a short mirthless laugh. 'If I don't keep it clean and tidy, everybody else loses privileges. That's how it works here. We all have our chores.'

'What privileges?'

'Oh, television or videos, table tennis, shopping trips. I couldn't care less, but the others make it obvious that they do.'

'What are the others like?'

'People.' She shrugged. 'A mix. Some are quite nice, but they don't let you alone. There's a cabinet minister's son in here, and a woman about your age who drinks. They're OK. Could be worse, I suppose.' She looked pleadingly at Jill. 'Can I come back with you now?'

'You can. But you're not better yet. Give it a little longer. I know it's hard but . . .'

'You know nothing of the sort!' Diane snapped. 'You've no idea what I've been through. It's hell!' She stopped, suddenly biting her lips.

'Can't you hang on? You need to feel able to cope without that destructive stuff.'

'At least it made me feel good. Now I feel like jumping in the lake.' Her eyes were wide and frantic.

Jill was honest. 'You're not locked in here. You can leave at any time. But if you do, Clarissa told me, there's no second chance. You'd be on your own.'

They both sat in the thick silence of the small room. Eventually there was a knock and a shaved female head peered round the door.

'Coming?' it asked Diane. 'Dr Rayburn is going to talk to us.' Jill was treated to a suspicious stare.

Diane scrambled from the bed almost eagerly. 'My stepmother,' she said offhand. 'She's going now.'

Dismissed, Jill followed Diane out of the door. 'I'll come again soon,' she promised.

'Suit yourself,' Diane said indifferently as she drifted slowly behind the tall, loping figure of the other girl and disappeared down a corridor.

Later that afternoon Jill went into Douglas's study, anxious to find the unfinished novel. It was a treat she'd been saving for herself. But when she found the computer manual and sat down to study it, she was daunted and perplexed by its nearly 900 pages. Irritated with herself for failing to understand the jargon, she was grateful to be interrupted by the doorbell. It was James, looking shy and embarrassed.

'I just thought you might like to come for a walk,' he said diffidently.

'I'd subscribe to the whole set of the *Encyclopaedia Britannica* if that's what you were selling right now,' she said. 'Anything to get away from that ruddy machine.'

'What machine?' He looked bewildered.

'Oh, my husband's word processor. There's his last book in there somewhere and his agent asked me to find it. But it baffles me.'

'Well, I expect I could help. We used computers at school. There's no mystery.'

Jill widened the door. 'You could fool me. The instruction book is written in Chinese. Come in. You're the answer to a prayer. The walk can wait.'

Jill showed him to Douglas's study. 'There's the machine, and the manual. Both have given me a deep feeling of inferiority.'

She was astonished as James confidently switched on the machine, pressed a few buttons and brought up a list of files on the screen.' Here we are – is there anything recognizable?'

'You're brilliant!' *From Dark to Light*, the title of the new book was there, jumping out of the screen.

'Want to see it?'

'No. Not now.' She was suddenly shy, anxious for Douglas's words not to flash coldly on to the screen in front of a stranger.

James seemed to understand. 'There's bound to be a floppy disk of it somewhere, but in any case it can be printed out whilst we have a walk,' he said. 'You don't have to read it on screen. Look, this is a laser-printer – the last word. Your husband knew what he was buying. I'll just see it's loaded with enough paper.'

Reassured, and excited, Jill watched as Douglas's last words began to slip page by page through the printer. She had to tear herself away to leave the room with James.

It was already getting dark and the weather wasn't really conducive to walking, but Jill was in a state of anticipation and she trudged contentedly enough beside James as he pointed out various cottages and named the surrounding hills and woods.

'You're a genuine countryman,' she commented. 'Were you born here?'

'Yes. But Dad was a Londoner until he married. He gets bored by the country, though he likes hunting and he has a rough shoot.' His own distaste was obvious.

Jill liked this sweet-natured young man. He had a lot of charm once he was out of his mother's orbit. He explained that he wanted to do something with nature or the environment. 'But what? I'm not academic. I'll never get a worthwhile degree even if I get to university.'

'Plenty of people manage to live without a degree, you may be surprised to hear,' she grinned at him.

'I wouldn't mind doing something in Peter Smith's line. Conserving woodland, forestry, organic farming.' He gazed at her. 'But can you imagine what my mother would say!'

'Yes,' Jill said grimly. 'And I'd take absolutely no notice.' She laughed. 'Refer her to Prince Charles – that should shut her up.'

They turned back after about twenty minutes and walked in silence for a bit until he said diffidently, 'How's Diane?'

'Not too bad. I went to see her this morning.'

'She's only been there for a fortnight, hasn't she? That's when they have withdrawal symptoms. It's horrible. My friend couldn't take it. He went back twice, but then he left for good. He was found dead in a squat in Stockwell.'

'Don't,' Jill implored. 'I'm trying not to think that it might not work. It has to!'

She told him about Tom Feathers' idea for Diane to write a foreword. 'But I suppose she won't feel up to it for a while, and he wants the publisher to rush out a commemorative edition.'

'I think it's a good idea. Give her something to do. She might find it easier to use a tape recorder. I did that once when I was trying to write poetry,' he said shyly. 'I used to say it out loud in the dark. Of course it was no good. Just a phase I went through.' He looked sideways at her and gave a self-deprecating smile.

'Were you in love at the time, by any chance?'

'Yes.' He laughed suddenly. 'With a Norwegian domestic we had at school. I was sixteen and she was twenty-four, but she was so pretty. She always looked as fresh as snow.'

'What happened, did she go back to Norway?'

'No. She married the geography master.' They both laughed.

When they returned, James went to see that the manuscript was printed. Jill placed him under strict orders not to read any of it and made some tea. He came down with a neat pile of paper. 'There's about four hundred pages – I should think it's all here,' he smiled.

'You're an angel.'

'Er, do you think Diane would like a visit from me?' He reddened as he asked.

Jill looked at him, inwardly amused at the way he blushed so easily. 'I'll ask. I'll see her again shortly. I'm sure she can use all the friends she's got but don't expect to be greeted with open arms. I wasn't.' She hoped he had not fallen for Diane.

Obviously aware that Jill was dying to get on with her reading,

James didn't linger and as soon as he'd gone she settled down to *From Dark to Light*.

Wonder gripped her as she realized it was *their* story, hers and Douglas's, fictionalized of course, but clearly recognizable from their first meeting, from the funny incidents during the filming of *White Meadows*, and from their few rows – mostly over the move to the country. Everything was there! And Douglas had included the character of a wistful adolescent boy, who'd lost the power of speech. Could that be Diane, exasperatingly unable to communicate?

Jill grew cold, not only because she was so rapt that she'd let the fire die down, but also because it seemed that Douglas had known of his imminent death. There, in black and white, was a scene where his doctor in London told him his heart muscles had deteriorated beyond repair. She remembered now the check-up he'd had in London, when she was recovering from flu. He'd brushed aside her question about why he hadn't gone to Roger, saying the chap in town had all his records. It was nothing, he'd said, pure routine, although she remembered he had been unusually quiet afterwards. He'd known. And he hadn't told her. She thought back, begrudging any time she had wasted getting her hair done or shopping, when it could have been spent with Douglas. She realized at last why he'd insisted on a long holiday together. It hadn't been just for her recuperation as she'd supposed. And she knew now why he had not bothered to save himself the exertion of long walks up the hills, swimming and bicycling. He had known it wouldn't make any difference.

She read on, gripped and beginning to understand more with each page. Douglas had not wanted anything to cloud his last weeks or months with her. He'd wanted them to be intensely happy, carefree. If she had known the truth, she would have fussed, tried to cushion him, make him rest. And even if she had, it wouldn't have been any use.

His other books had been about escapades in exotic countries, journeys through unfamiliar terrain; this too, was about a journey but an impatient, irritable one until he'd found a surprising, unexpected happiness under his nose in London: meeting and marrying her. Through the book, at times

175

uncharacteristically poetic, ran his love for her. The cottage had come to mean a symbol for him of peace and contentment. She remembered how often he'd asked her if she missed London, breaking into a big grin and kissing her when she'd stood back to look at some antique shop find and answer, 'What do you think?' There was understanding for the adolescent character too, but frustration at being unable to cure his dumbness. The end of the book, which she reached by staying up into the early hours, was a sweet resignation, a gratitude for the experience of mutual love.

It could have been mawkish, but he'd woven into the love story a believable plot. She wept when she'd finished, but the lump of misery in her chest was no longer there. Sadness and longing still, but above all a deep pride that she had made him so happy.

After a short and sleepless night, she rang Tom Feathers and told him the manuscript had been found and was on its way. She stuffed the pages into a large padded envelope and drove to the little post office in Sherville to register it.

Tom had asked about Diane's foreword, but she told him not to count on it. Diane had not written before and was apprehensive about it. 'Well, try to encourage her. The publishers are keen on the idea. If they like *From Dark to Light*, they want to go for simultaneous publication – the new book and a reissue of Douglas's backlist.'

Half-heartedly, she promised to talk to Diane. She felt a bit reluctant for Diane to do her piece now: as if it would be an intrusion on 'their' book. Then she was contrite. She had squeezed Diane out of Douglas's life, not deliberately but through her lack of imagination; surely she could be generous enough to share his last book with her. Douglas had shown how upset he was that the 'dumb adolescent boy' had not been drawn into their life. She could at least do this for him, see that Diane was made well again, and made to feel wanted and loved.

# Chapter Thirty

After her first unsatisfactory visit Jill had telephoned Hedera House but hadn't spoken to Diane again. 'She has a lot to do,' Clarissa explained. 'She's writing all day.'

'Writing!'

'Part of the treatment. They have to describe themselves, their childhood, their family, the people they've harmed. It all has to come out. It can be very painful. And she's had to get up at five this week.'

'What on earth for?'

'Punishment. Drugs make them lose all sense of time, night or day. We have to force them back into a routine. If they're late for breakfast, they have to get up earlier and lay the tables, prepare the drinks for everyone else. Diane was late for breakfast two days ago.'

'That sounds rather harsh.'

'It is. Like schooling a horse.'

The opening night of the play was less than four weeks away, forcing Jill to push her own worries to the back of her mind. There was a rehearsal on Wednesday in the village hall and, for the first time, it became clear that Miles was beginning to get worked up. He had lost his easy charm and the flattery that he used to coax the best out of everybody. Now he shouted in exasperation when a twitchy woman called Anne Knapp, who had a very minor part, kept missing her cue.

His nervousness infected the others and people were fussing, ready to blame each other for not chasing up the printers, ordering more paint, arranging press tickets.

Jill was used to hectic schedules and the excitable temperament of fashion designers, and took in her stride the sudden eruption of self-importance and apprehension. Besides, she and Lizzie felt complacent about the costumes, which were virtually finished, and each was looking forward to the dress rehearsals. The female rôles had all been fitted. Arabella had been inordinately pleased with her dress that had been compiled from two others.

'So flattering, this cape effect. I must get you, Lizzie, to copy it for me in navy blue.' She primped in front of the inadequate cloakroom mirror, straining to see the bottom half of the costume cut off by the washbasins.

Sandra, too, was pleased with her outfit, at least until she saw April in the dress she had coveted. The rainbow silk clung to April's slim, shapely figure and floated out from the hips in a flutter of crystal pleats that changed colour with every movement. Her arms and shoulders were bare, and her slender neck was revealed as Jill had roughly piled the ragged mass of her light brown hair on top of her head.

'I thought Miles said *I* was to be glamorous,' Sandra railed. 'I haven't anything like that. I should wear it – Miles said April's part was meant to be mousey.'

'It's too small for you,' Jill cut in swiftly. 'Besides your hair wouldn't look anything against these soft colours. Wait until you see your other frock – Lizzie's been sewing some sequins on the bodice. You'll overpower April.' She winked at April as the girl quickly slipped away.

To prove her point, she produced the electric blue dress they'd finally decided on for Sandra, cut from a kimono they'd snaffled from the jumble sale. Lizzie had giggled as she'd tacked boxfuls of multicoloured sequins all over the low-cut bodice, and then added layered net frills over the too-short skirt. 'Sandra will love this,' she'd said gleefully. And Sandra did indeed, her mutinous expression mollifying as she seized the vulgar garment and held it against herself in the mirror.

'You look like a starlet at a film première,' Jill said lightly. 'All the men will fall for you.'

'They do anyway,' Sandra said intent on her image. 'Can I show this to Miles?'

'Not yet, it's not finished. The zip's only tacked in,' Jill said hastily. 'It'll be done by the dress rehearsal next Wednesday.'

She'd seen no meaningful looks between Tom and Sandra, or any behaviour indicating a close relationship. Indeed Sandra seemed to ignore him, whilst her possessiveness with Miles was becoming so marked that Arabella had been provoked into saying in a loud voice to Miles: 'Really Miles, how can you let that little hairdresser keep pawing you! You're much too friendly with the cast. After all, you are the director.' She took to frowning at Sandra who simply tossed her head and provocatively crossed her legs, revealing even more thigh than usual.

In the pub that evening Tom happened to be next to Jill, the two of them, owing to the arrangement of the pub furniture, slightly apart from the rest of the cast. He sat forward, holding his drink between his knees and looked at Jill.

'Are you coping better now?' His expression was guileless, kind and concerned. 'You must've been very busy with the costumes; has it helped?'

She nodded, without speaking.

'I'm very glad,' he said gently. 'Claudine is pregnant,' he told her, smiling. 'She's so happy. The doctor thinks it will work this time.'

'I know. She told me at the station. She got on my train at Salisbury. She'd just been to the hospital.'

'Too excited to keep it to herself. I suppose the whole village knows by now. What were you doing in Salisbury?'

'Nothing. I was coming down from town. I'd spent the night in Kensington with a friend.'

'Oh.' His eyes searched her face.

'How was your aunt?' She hadn't meant to make such a remark or put such emphasis on the 'aunt'.

His expression cooled slightly but he didn't look away. 'You saw us?'

Jill nodded.

'And are you going to tell Claudine?' he asked scornfully.

'Don't be insulting,' Jill said coldly.

'I'm sorry. Of course you wouldn't.' He ducked his head and sipped his drink. 'She's on such a high now, doing precisely as the doctor ordered, I'd hate her to be hurt. We've been trying for a child for such a long time. I'd given up, but she became obsessive. I'm terrified for her mental state if this one ends in disappointment again.'

'It won't,' Jill spoke warmly, deeply ashamed of her ill-considered remark. His flirtations and affairs were nothing to do with her. 'Let me get you a drink to celebrate.' She walked hurriedly to the bar, anxious to get over the tactless moment. She felt at home in this pub, even if it did have memories of when she and Douglas had stayed there. It was such a friendly little place, escaping the lurid carpets and mock tudorization of so many others. She joined the men propping up the bar, jesting with John the landlord about the darts game he'd lost to one of them.

Miles came to stand gloomily next to her, a pint in his hand. 'It was grim tonight, wasn't it? How can I get Edward to drop that booming voice? You'd think he was on the quarter deck.'

'It wasn't too bad. There's still time.'

'And Sandra. She *will* turn her head when she's speaking, so that her voice is lost at the back of the stage. She won't listen to a word I say.'

Jill paid for her drinks and patted his hand. 'Think of how good Molly and April are. And Arabella, surprisingly enough. It'll be all right on the night.' She went back to Tom, who was leaning back against the wall, gazing at the ceiling.

'I'm a bloody fool.'

'Aren't we all,' Jill said cheerfully. 'Here, drink up.'

'It was just a one-off. I know Sandra is the local tart. I just got so fed up with Claudine's timetables and temperature charts. Sex wasn't fun any more. She was virtually having a countdown to the very second when it's supposed to be the most propitious time to conceive, and then dragging me off to bed. I'm just a means to a baby, not a husband. It didn't do much for my masculine appeal.'

Jill lifted her glass, ignoring his words. 'Here's to little Tom.'

'Little Tom? Is Claudine pregnant at last?' It was Peter Smith beaming at Tom. 'How wonderful! Give her my love.'

Jill didn't want Tom's confidences. She turned with relief to Peter. She had come to admire him as she'd worked with him on the sets. He had a sturdy character and wasn't afraid to argue, suggesting adaptations to her designs to make them more practical. They had three sets to create, an office, the factory interior and the hotel where the company dinner-dance, which was the climax of the action, was held. Peter had bags of imagination and was currently hugely enjoying directing the press-ganged volunteers to paint the flats. A lot of paint had been sloshed around and excitement was building up as the cast began to see the play taking physical shape.

Outside it was raining again. Jill hurried to her car, head down and then felt a hand preventing the door closing. 'Can you give me a lift?' Miles peered in, his jacket over his head. 'My bike had a puncture. I got a lift part of the way here, but now I'm stuck and I don't fancy walking in this.' He grimaced.

'Of course. Get in. You'll have to tell me where it is.'

'I forgot, you haven't been, have you? I said I'd play you my 78s. It's by the back entrance of Stourbridge Court, about a mile further on.'

He gloomed all the way to the cottage, depressed at the way some of the cast still weren't word perfect, still made the same mistakes he'd pointed out in the early days; in particular some of them declaimed instead of talking naturally.

'Isn't it any better than *Rosencrantz*?'

'I suppose so,' he admitted reluctantly. 'But that was total disaster. I can't bear even to think of it. I don't think we should ask the press again, it would be too awful to have more rotten notices.'

She reached the tiny cottage, a redundant lodge, black and uninviting in the heavy rain. 'Come in for a coffee,' he said. 'Do, please. I can't bear my own company right now.' He overrode Jill's objections and propelled her forwards, holding the side of his jacket over her head and pushing open the unlocked front door with his foot.

He lit an oil lamp inside the door. 'I'll get the fire going in a jiffy,' and he threw a pile of sticks on to the ash in the open grate. 'At least I'm never short of fuel, the woods come right up to the back.' The fire was quickly blazing and he filled a kettle from a sink in the corner and set it on a bottled gas ring standing on a battered table over a piece of asbestos. 'Not many mod cons, are there?' he grinned. 'But I don't pay any rent. It's been empty for years.' He spooned some instant coffee into two mugs from a shelf over the sink. 'My larder,' he gestured to two more shelves which contained some sugar still in its paper bag, a glass jar of spaghetti and a few tins, a wrapped loaf of bread and some butter on a saucer. 'I don't give many dinner parties.'

Jill laughed. 'It's cosy enough.'

'When the fire doesn't smoke. It does when the wind is in the wrong direction. There's a bedroom and what is laughingly called a bathroom with a fierce copper boiler that hisses alarmingly, but the water comes out in a trickle. It takes me half an hour to fill the bath.'

Jill sat on a lumpy sofa covered with a cheap cotton bedspread. He opened his hands. 'One day when I'm a famous director at the National, I shall reminisce about my lowly beginnings as a penniless but ambitious playwright working from a hut in the woods with only mice and marauding deer for company. And I shall say the only thing that kept me going was a beautiful woman designer.'

He dropped on to the sofa beside her and leaned towards her, touching her cheek with his forefinger.

Jill leaned away. 'You haven't any doubts about your future?'

'No. I'll be there some day.' He slid his arm along the back of the sofa and smiled at her. 'You've been a marvellous support. It gives me confidence just to know you're there at rehearsals, putting in a quiet word when things get tense, tactfully defusing a situation. I've watched you. You can handle people. I haven't said much but I draw strength from you.' His arm tightened across her shoulders. 'In fact, I suppose you've already realized it, I'm in love with you.'

'Don't be silly.' Jill moved sharply.

'I'm not. I think I fell for you as soon as the first rehearsal got under way.'

Jill banged her cup down on the small table. 'This is ridiculous. I'm not the slightest bit interested in a boy half my age. I'm going.' She marched to the door but he swiftly cut off her exit.

'I mean it. I do love you. Age difference is immaterial. I like the fact that you're mature and experienced. You must believe me. Come to bed with me now and I'll show you how much I love you.'

Jill looked up at him, her face frozen. 'I can only assume that you had too much to drink at the pub. Now if you'll get away from the door, we'll forget this ever happened.'

He dropped his arm, and said dejectedly, 'You don't care for me, do you? I thought you did – a little. You've always been so sweet to me.'

He opened the door for her, but as she passed through he pulled her to him and crushed her in a fierce kiss. 'Doesn't that tell you anything?' he demanded. 'Are you going to remain pining for a dead man for the rest of your life?'

Jill gave him a look of icy disdain and said a flat, dismissive 'Good night'.

In the car she found she was shaking not only from anger, but also from the fierce sexual yearnings stirred by a man's arms and warm lips. She banged her clenched fist on the steering wheel, angry with herself, with Miles, and with Douglas for leaving her.

# Chapter Thirty-one

Jill had been twice more to Hedera House, but each time she came away depressed and disappointed. Diane mostly sat gazing silently into space as if Jill wasn't there, ignored any presents she took her, and gave no reaction when Jill chatted about the village and the Drama Group. Only when Jill mentioned that Tom Feathers had asked again about the foreword did her gaze flicker.

'Is that true?' she asked.

Jill nodded. 'Time's getting short. I brought you a little tape recorder. It might be easier to talk into that as your thoughts occur to you, rather than writing them all out.' She laid the small machine on the bed.

Diane ignored it, looking out of the window. 'I don't know why you come. I don't want you here. You're nothing to do with me. I don't have to do what you say.'

'I know that,' Jill's voice was steady. 'I like to see you, hear how you're getting on.'

'Well I'm not. Don't come any more.' She shifted her chair so that her back was to Jill.

Jill gazed at it for a minute or two in silence. Then she got up. 'All right, I'll go now. If you don't want me to, I won't come again. But I'd like to know how you are.'

There was no response from Diane and she quietly left the room. There was no-one in the hall when she left, so she let herself out.

At home she telephoned Clarissa.

'It's normal,' Clarissa reassured her. 'She's going through group therapy now, with a psychiatrist. They have to face up to themselves, search their souls, admit their faults. It's hard to take. I know; I've done it. But it's necessary to get rid of all the old emotional furniture, find out why you've been trying to escape. She's doing rather well actually. She's fitted in, seems to have made a couple of friends.'

Jill explained about the lack of success of her visits.

'Don't worry. Knock off the visits for a while. Wait until she asks you to come. She will. Ring me any time, I'll let you know how she's getting on.'

A little relieved, but not altogether convinced, Jill put the phone down. Diane's recovery was obviously going to be a long haul; maybe she'd hoped for too much too soon.

On the kitchen table were the broken pieces of the ceramic bowl she and Douglas had bought. 'Sorry about the pot,' Mrs B had written. 'I caught it with my apron as I was hoovering. I'll pay for the damage if you'll let me know how much.'

Jill looked sadly at the pieces, remembering the day they'd discovered Yvonne Staidler. Her young dog had bounded out of the gate and Douglas, unable to stop in time, had caught it with the car wing. The dog skittered away on three legs, yelping with fright. Douglas, white with shock, had captured it and carried it up to the house, where its distraught owner had appeared. But as soon as he set the animal down again it lolloped away, clearly unhurt. When Douglas returned to the car he found Jill being sick at the side of the road. Yvonne had insisted they sit down and have a cup of tea. They'd ended up buying the bowl and some gaily decorated plates, firm friends with the puppy who rushed after their car as they drove away.

Jill drove over to Yvonne's. There was very little chance of finding the same thing, but she didn't want to lose this reminder of Douglas. Yvonne's face fell when she saw the pieces. 'Oh dear, what a shame! I was proud of that. It was one that had really come off. I don't know if there's anything like it. I've just emptied the kiln as a matter of fact.' She worked in a large chilly barn attached to her modern bungalow and now led the way, telling Jill to keep her coat on. Another young woman was there, dusting some of the pieces of pottery; Yvonne introduced her to Jill as a friend from art school days who engraved glass. 'Well, she blows it as well really but she hasn't got her own furnace.'

'Are you near?' Jill asked, partly to deflect her disappointment with the pottery on the table.

'Not really. I'm from outside Blandford.' She fished in her

Third World woven sisal basket and gave Jill a card. 'If you're passing, call in. I can do with some customers.' She gave a short laugh.

'Anything here you like?' Yvonne asked anxiously.

Jill looked at the variety of bowls and jugs – nothing was as attractive as the broken one. 'I suppose that was such a favourite that it's difficult to find anything as nice,' she said carefully. The colours of this new stuff were not appealing, although the shapes were good. Some of the glazes were uneven. 'I'd like that one in a clearer yellow,' she pointed. 'Perhaps with that mulberry and not quite so much green.'

Yvonne's face clouded. 'I could try,' she was dubious. 'They never work out quite the same. Frankly, I've got to sell this lot before I buy more materials.' She looked embarrassed.

'Well, I'll take this,' Jill said hastily. 'It's nearly the same.' The pots weren't expensive, this one could go in the kitchen somewhere.

As Yvonne wrapped it she asked casually, 'How's your husband? Has he run over any more dogs?'

'He died,' Jill said quietly. 'Early October.'

'Oh I'm so sorry . . . I didn't know . . . I wouldn't have asked.' Yvonne was distressed. 'He was so sweet with Bounder. I *am* sorry.' She looked away as Jill turned blindly to the barn door.

'I must go. Thanks for the pot. Let me know if you manage that yellow again.'

She headed for home, telling herself she was a fool to be thrown by such questions. Evidently not everyone knew about Douglas. She made herself think about Yvonne's pots. There was so much good stuff there, yet it just missed being first class. She needed to refine her colours. It was clear she wasn't selling much, but who was going to trek to a small out-of-the-way village like that? And Yvonne couldn't hope to make a living out of the craft fairs in the county; some were so poor anyway, hardly to be dignified by the word 'craft'. She really needed help with marketing, introductions to a few influential journalists on the fashion magazines. She sighed – so many craftsmen and women had no commercial training or instincts.

★　　★　　★

'Hullo.' She didn't recognize the low throaty voice on the telephone at first. 'You've saved me three hundred pounds. I owe you a lunch at least.' It was Fiona Trentbridge. 'My dear I've spent a fortune at Fred's – even I was wincing and then they lopped off a huge twenty per cent. I was so pleased I nearly spent it all on something else. Your Mr Rosomon was darling. Insisted on taking me to lunch.'

'*Did* he! Watch out,' Jill laughed, her spirits lifting. 'He hardly ever buys anyone lunch. He worries about the mark-up on a pound of brussels sprouts. He'll be after you with the persistence of a double-glazing salesman.'

'Oh, I can handle him – I liked him though. He seemed lost somehow and that always gets to me. But about this lunch? When are you coming up again?'

'I haven't any plans.'

'Then make one. How about Friday week? No matinée, I shan't have to rush back. In any case the play's coming off on the Saturday. Has to make way for a musical that's been booked in, and there's nowhere in the West End for a transfer at the moment.'

'So soon? I thought you were in for a long run.'

'So did I. Producer's fault. It was announced two weeks ago, so we're over the shock. Bloody rotten luck for the cast, but that's showbiz as they say. Anyway, lunch. Let's go to the Ivy, it always makes me feel as if Noel Coward and Gertie Lawrence will come in any minute.'

'That'll be lovely,' Jill said sincerely. 'One o'clock?'

'Dear me, no!' Fiona was shocked. 'I never arrive until all the other tables are full. One-fifteen at the earliest. I'll book, and I'll wear the suit I bought from Fred's. It's to die for.'

When she rang off, Jill was still smiling. She had to dye some men's shirts for the play, and she pottered in the kitchen boiling saucepans of dye, dipping the fabric until she'd got the colours sufficiently strong. It was fun trying to delineate the play's characters by their clothes, and she decided the flirtatious company boss, played by Edward Posner, should have three or four flamboyant bow ties.

\* \* \*

Later that day, when the bell rang she opened the door to a white-faced Miles.

'I'm sorry. I came to apologize,' he said, making no attempt to come in. 'Will you forgive me?' His eyes were serious and he looked tired.

Jill nodded, unsmiling. 'I've forgotten all about it.'

'Well, I haven't. You may think I'm crazy but I do love you. I can't think of anything else.'

Jill looked cross. 'Now don't start again. I'm old enough to be your mother.'

'That makes no difference,' he protested. And as Jill began to close the door, he jammed his foot in it. 'But I promise I won't say another word until you've recovered from the loss of your husband. I was too precipitate, but you looked so lovely and were so sympathetic.'

'Miles this has gone far enough.' Jill's voice was cold. 'If you go on like this, I'm withdrawing from the Drama Group. Immediately.'

'I promise, promise, promise,' he said beseechingly, supporting himself on the door jambs and leaning towards her. 'But please let me see you. You don't know how much I *need* you.'

Jill felt her lips twitch. He was playing a part, Octavian to her Marschallin. She had forgotten how theatrical he was. 'Miles, you and I have a lot to do before the first night. I suggest we both concentrate on the jobs in hand. Now if you don't take your foot out of the door, I'll do it a serious injury.'

He gave a deep sigh and removed his foot, shaking his head sorrowfully as he turned to walk up the path. Jill shut the door and giggled. She supposed she ought to be flattered really. She shouldn't take him so seriously. He had obviously cast himself as some romantic hero determined to sigh for an unattainable love.

# Chapter Thirty-two

The tickets were printed, suddenly making the play seem more of a reality, and Edward Posner gave everyone an allocation, sternly telling them they had to sell them. Jill was in despair as she knew so few people. She posted a couple of complimentaries to the Morrishes, gave two each to Gus and Mrs B and asked Clement and Frank, stressing to Frank that she wouldn't be offended if he hated the idea of an amateur production. Her membership of the Drama Group was proving to be quite an expensive item. She wondered about Diane, but she'd decided to abide by Clarissa's instruction to wait until Diane herself asked to see her. She also wrote to ask Carla if she'd like to come down for the weekend of the play, telling her she was responsible for her involvement in the Drama Group and had a moral obligation to provide support. But she had no idea if any of them would turn up.

The posters had been designed by an art student and were due to be delivered from the printers any minute, and local shopkeepers were being browbeaten into displaying them.

Then they had the first dress rehearsal. It was chaos backstage; Lizzie, Jill and Miriam, together with a schoolteacher called Frances Miniver who was also part of the production committee, fought to keep the costume changes going in the small space. There was a dress rail and a rather spotty mirror, poor lighting and two rickety wooden chairs, with which Jill had to manage make-up and the costume changes. She put Frances, a rather serious woman, in charge of the accessories. She had a list for each character and she was under instructions not to let anyone on stage without the complete outfit. She took her job so seriously that she prevented Sandra from answering her cue until she had laden her with several ropes of beads and some huge plastic earrings, while Edward desperately repeated 'Miss Loxton' louder and louder.

At the end the cast stood expectantly on stage, looking enquiringly at Miles, preening a little in their costumes and make-up, not a little pleased with themselves. He sat on the floor, his head in his hands. 'It was terrible,' he moaned. 'Terrible.' There was consternation all round.

Miles got up. 'OK, break.'

He took Arabella by the shoulder and walked her up and down the hall earnestly gesticulating. She was listening and nodding with unaccustomed deference. Next, he brought April and Tom together to show how the last scene had been played too quickly, losing the romance. He went through each part individually, whilst the rest of the cast sat silent, despondent.

Jill could understand his despair as the play did seem to have lost shape and momentum. But when he tackled each problem area, as would become a Peter Hall or a Trevor Nunn, Jill had a sudden thrill of insight. He really was going to be good one day; whether as a playwright or director she couldn't tell, but in her bones she knew his self-confidence was absolutely justified.

The last week saw them all bursting with expectancy. They'd had another dress rehearsal, this time with the scenery, which had worked like a dream. Jill congratulated Peter Smith who smiled in acknowledgement, as if he took it for granted that anything he had made would work well.

They had another full rehearsal on the Wednesday before the play opened. It was even smoother and, as far as Jill could tell backstage, the action had more drama. As they broke for coffee during the interval, Miles looked happy. He put his arms round April and kissed her on the mouth. 'You were splendid in that scene. Real sparkle.' He hugged her for a long moment, looking into her eyes. She held his gaze, and then broke away, thanking him coolly, apparently unfazed by his unusual praise, except for a faint blush.

Sandra, watching the little scene, scowled and stalked up to Miles. 'I want to talk to you in private,' she said, jerking her head at the small cupboard of a room that housed the photo-copier.

Arabella's intake of breath was expelled with a loud hiss as she said, 'Well really, that girl!'

Miles followed Sandra with an amused shrug of his shoulders.

Tania Fellowes was talking to Jill when shouts and bangs were heard from the photocopying room. 'Who's murdering whom?' Tania whispered just as Sandra rushed out, tearing off her costume as she did so.

'And you can find someone else for this bloody part. I've had it!' She stopped as she saw everyone staring at her, smiled mockingly at them, and then provocatively stripped off the rest of her clothes, swinging a rope of beads and swaying her hips like a striptease dancer as she disappeared, in her underwear, to the dressing room.

Everybody was thunderstruck. Edward Posner cleared his throat in embarrassment and said 'I *say*' in a strangled way to Tania.

Miles stood in the doorway of the small room, hands on hips, his face white and set. 'OK, everybody. We can't do any more tonight.'

Arabella walked over to him. 'Miles what *is* going on? What was all that shouting about? I've a right to know. I'm President of the Drama Group.'

'Yes, well, I'm sorry Arabella. As you could hardly help hearing, Sandra has walked out. She seemed to think that I was going to take her to some disco tonight. She's a bloody menace. Good riddance!' He sighed in exasperation.

'Well, the first night is only a week away, you'd better make it up,' said Molly Ferness pragmatically. 'There's no-one to take her place. Celia was supposed to be the understudy, but as you know she's broken her leg. She's still in hospital, poor thing – I went to see her a few days ago and she's sick at missing out on all the so-called fun.'

'*Fun!*' boomed Arabella. 'But Molly's right, Miles. That girl must be made to behave. I shall go and give her a good talking to right now for letting everybody down like this.' She sailed across the floor to the dressing room before anyone could stop her.

Tania followed, turning to grimace over her shoulder and gesture helplessly.

Miriam looked at Molly. 'Bit too much drama and not enough group if you ask me.'

More shouting emanated from the dressing room. Arabella emerged, face red and bosom heaving, as 'Don't talk to me like that, you old trout!' came through the door in a last riposte from Sandra. Tania was shaking her head.

Miles leaned dejectedly against the stage. 'Now what?' he asked. 'Her rôle is crucial. Is there a chance Celia will be out in time? She could hobble about – even characters in plays break their legs.'

Molly shook her head decidedly. 'She's in no fit state. Besides, she's missed all the rehearsals. Pauline – you could learn the lines, or Jill?'

Miles looked up hopefully.

'I can't,' Pauline said emphatically. 'A woman of fifty-odd is not going to look right as a tarty secretary having it off with the boss, however good the make-up.'

Jill shook her head. 'Don't look at me. I'm no actress. Can't you rewrite the part?'

'If I did it would mean rewriting lots of the others too – there's too much interaction. No, we'll have to think of someone else – April do you know of anyone?' But his query was greeted with a blank look.

'Well, let's pack up now,' Tania said decisively. 'And *all* have a good think. We can't do anything at this moment. The best chance, Miles, is for you to get round Sandra somehow, make her change her mind.'

'I don't think I could bear to be on stage with that young woman after what she just said to me,' Arabella said heatedly.

As they all began to put their things together, Jill went to the dressing room to hang up the costumes. Sandra was sitting on one of the rickety chairs, still only clad in her red bra and minute pants trimmed in black lace, smoking negligently.

'Please don't smoke in here,' Jill asked her quietly. 'It's too small and the costumes could easily catch fire.'

'I couldn't care less. Good thing if the whole place went up in smoke,' Sandra said contemptuously, but she slowly moved to put out her cigarette after another rebellious puff or two and began to dress.

'Pity you're leaving us,' Jill said as she began to pick up some of the costumes. 'You looked great in your outfits – you'd probably have had your picture in the paper.'

Sandra turned to stare. 'You think so?' She considered the prospect. 'Yeah, I fancied myself in that blue dress.' But her scowl returned. 'He'd have to come on bended knees to me first,' she said. 'I saw him kissing April McIntosh – and it's not the first time. He's supposed to be *my* boyfriend.'

Jill was startled that anyone could take Miles's flirtations seriously; they were so obviously part of his stock-in-trade, just as he buttered up Arabella outrageously, and played the lovesick swain with Jill herself. Jill suddenly felt sorry for Sandra. Her pride was obviously very bruised. Evidently her fling with Tom Houlderton wasn't enough for her.

Later, Jill locked the empty dressing room after her and went outside where only Pauline, Molly and Miles were left. 'If anyone has any influence with the *Wessex Weekly* and could persuade them to take a picture of our glamour girl in her last act costume, I think she might change her mind,' she said.

'Good idea,' Molly nodded. 'We could ask them to send a photographer and get Sandra to give another Page Three display like the one we've just been treated to.'

Miles looked surly. 'She's not even very good; she just looks the part,' he said knowingly.

'Well, Miles, it's up to you,' Molly said lighting a cigarette. 'It's your play, your production; it would be a bloody shame to let that girl wreck it.'

They went their several ways, Miles gloomily pushing his bike uphill, devoid of energy to pedal.

# Chapter Thirty-three

The Ivy was as crowded as Fiona could wish, but she still arrived late, swooping up to kiss Jill in the tiny bar, leaving a trail of bemused waiters and a cloakroom attendant anxious to take her fluffy red coat. She was wearing a very fitted black tweed suit with a short skirt, the scoop necked jacket outlined in silk braid, with large gilt buttons down the front. Her long legs were in fine black tights, well displayed by the short skirt, and her blonde hair was straight and shining, caught at the temples with two gilt combs.

'You look great,' Jill appraised her laughing. 'Is that the suit? Montana?'

'In one! I love it.' She unbuttoned the jacket to reveal a low-necked white silk tee-shirt. 'And I bought a heap of Jil Sanders, plus *five* silk shirts because I couldn't make up my mind between the colours. Your Mr Rosomon stood by, his eyes on stalks. So *cheap* with that discount!'

Jill laughed again. 'Accountancy isn't your forte is it? You save twenty per cent and buy three times as much. No wonder Fred took you to lunch. The mark-up on his stuff is well over two hundred per cent.'

They went into the restaurant, two attractive, well-turned-out women causing heads to turn; and there were some nudges as Fiona was recognized.

'I'm sorry about your play,' commiserated Jill.

'So am I, but it's not too bad in my case. My agent had sent me the script of a TV serial, very gritty, which starts filming shortly. I *could* have done the two but it would have been a push. The play's very demanding.

'But it's not so great for the others. John Selling has cabled a boyfriend in Los Angeles hoping he'll invite him out there, and Claudia is back on the books. She'll get something soon; television commercials are very profitable even if they don't do a lot for one's career. I'm sure the play will be revived but that's not the same thing when you're counting on a steady income for once. Bloody producer – he was supposed to check the dates.'

They ordered and Fiona said, 'What's your news? You're looking a little better. Less drawn and pathetic.'

'Thanks!'

'Well, you had that lost, large-eyed look the waifs have in those begging ads from orphanages. What are you up to?'

Jill told her about the Drama Group, and about cajoling the costumes out of Rosomon. 'With a few decent things from Fred's, and a clever local dressmaker who's ex-Hartnell, we've managed to dress a cast of ten.'

'Oh, of course. I remember now. The young chap you gave the ticket to. He came backstage. He told me a bit about the play. He wrote it, didn't he? Good-looking, very confident. I'd have taken him out to dinner if I hadn't already been fixed up. Dishy, *very* dishy.'

'Yes. Miles Lambert. But it's all a disaster. The first night is a week today and a silly girl who fancied he was in love with her – he's a consummate flirt, very sure of his charm and uses it to get his way – found out he wasn't serious, so there was a row and she walked out on Wednesday. She wasn't very good, but the understudy, who's even worse and hasn't rehearsed, has broken a leg.'

'An everyday story of showbusiness. And I suppose our heroine, the elegant Jill Mortimer, is to step in and save the day?'

'Impossible! I'd be hopeless. In any case I'm in charge of the costumes and make-up. I hope we'll find *someone* willing to mug up the lines. It's not a big part but it's an important one.' She tackled her smoked trout. 'I've asked Frank and Clement to the performance, but I don't expect them to come. Would you like to? Your play's finished, a weekend in the country would do you good. I could put you up. It might be amusing for you.'

'I was just thinking that,' Fiona said unexpectedly. 'There are always withdrawal symptoms when a play finishes. I get terribly restless and depressed.'

'It would be lovely if you'd stay for a few days. A friend of mine, Carla, may come for the weekend; I haven't heard yet because she's in Milan, but there's still room. And I could ask Frank and Clement to Sunday lunch if they can't face the play. Frank said he runs a mile from amateur dramatics.'

'I mean, I was thinking I could take over the part. That is if you don't find anyone else.'

She made the offer almost diffidently so that for a moment Jill didn't take it in. Then she put down her fork and sat back with a gasp. 'You can't be serious!'

'I am.' Fiona said it calmly, delicately forking a piece of tagliatelle into her mouth without ruining her lipstick. 'Good for me. Besides it would be fun. Especially,' she paused, looking up grinning, 'especially if Clement came. Worth it just to see his face!'

'But, but Fiona Trentbridge in a village amateur drama . . .' Jill was still stunned by the suggestion. 'You'd scare the rest of the cast to death.'

'There you underestimate me,' she went on eating, spearing bits of mushroom with her fork. 'I get on very well with people backstage. In any case, you said it was only a small part. How long is the script?'

'There's about six or seven speeches, not long ones. But it's her affair with the boss, and her betrayals, that are crucial to the action. Are you truly serious?'

Fiona nodded.

'Then I must tell Miles. Right now! He won't believe me, but I must put him out of his misery. Excuse me.' She left the table.

'This is no time to joke, Jill,' he said on the telephone. 'I'm desperate. I've been psyching myself up to go and placate that Sandra bitch, but I'm too enraged still.'

'I'm *not* joking, Miles. I'm having lunch this minute with Fiona Trentbridge in the Ivy. I was telling her about our little drama and she *offered* to take Sandra's part. It would never have crossed my mind to suggest it.'

She was deafened by an Indian whoop the other end of the line. 'Fiona Trentbridge in *my* play.' He whooped again. 'Let me speak to her, please, I won't believe it until I do.'

'We're in the middle of lunch, but I'll see if she'll come to the phone.' Jill went back to the table beaming. 'Miles can't credit it either. He can't take it in. You'll have to talk to him.'

Fiona dabbed her lips and sighed. 'And I thought this was going to be a nice quiet girls' gossipy lunch. All right.' She smiled intimately at a waiter about to clear their plates so that he fell back a step. 'It's no big deal,' she said carelessly. 'And that young man was extremely sexy.'

Miles was waiting at the station for Jill when she got back that evening, pacing up and down. As soon as he saw her, he darted up and hugged her. 'I've met every possible train. I'm not dreaming am I? Fiona Trentbridge, *the* Fiona Trentbridge of West End and television fame, is actually going to appear in a play by Miles Lambert?'

She nodded, laughing at his shining eyes and the way he prowled at her side, stooping to look into her face, searching for confirmation.

He leapt into the air and punched it like a footballer scoring a goal. 'Now everybody will flock to see it. Or rather her.'

When he finally left her at the cottage, he was full of how he was going to get the first train to London in the morning to drop the script in on Fiona Trentbridge personally.

But next morning all Jill's preoccupation with the play was banished by Diane's telephone call. 'I've got to see you,' she said urgently. 'Will you come over?'

'Of course.' She wanted to ask if everything was all right, her mind slipping through the possibilities that Diane had discharged herself or had been asked to leave. But she tried to sound calm. 'When shall I come?'

'Now, of course.' Diane's voice was fretful.

Half an hour later Jill arrived at Hedera House to find Diane prowling about the large, pleasant reception lounge. She was wearing Jill's red skirt and an unattractive patterned sweater, faded and felted from poor washing. 'You sent me in here without any clothes,' she accused as her first greeting. 'I want to go to London and get my things. And there's my car. And what about my mail? You didn't think of any of that did you? I've probably had the telephone and electricity cut off.'

'I'm sorry. No, I hadn't thought of that.'

'I want my own clothes, not yours.'

'Why don't you just give me your flat keys and I'll go and sort things out? I'll go by train and drive your car back if you tell me where you keep it.' She felt that if Diane went to town she wouldn't come back, and there was still the threat of her getting into the hands of Chris again. Jill had no idea if the police had done anything in that department.

'You told me I could come and go as I like,' Diane pointed out mulishly. 'You said I wasn't a prisoner. But it's not true, is it? You're a liar. You want me to be locked up in here.' Her voice started to rise. 'Well, I'm going home. And you've got to give me the money to get there.' She was shouting and kicking the furniture.

'Diane, please! We can go together if you like.' Her heart sank as she realized the girl was no better.

Probably drawn by all the noise, Clarissa came into the room. 'Oh hullo. I didn't know you were here, Mrs Mortimer.' She looked at Diane's tight face and clenched hands, and carefully straightened a small table that Diane had kicked aside.

'Aren't you going with Astrid and the others to the group meeting, Diane? It starts at noon doesn't it?' Diane scuffed a toe into the carpet and said nothing. 'Gerald always feels able to speak more freely when you're there. You're really helping him.'

This time, Diane looked up with a quick flash of pleasure before resuming her sulky expression.

'I want to sort out my flat. I haven't any decent clothes. I don't know what's happening there.'

'Ah, Diane, come on. You know we arranged about your flat and the services on the phone. And Mrs Mortimer brought some clothes in for you.'

'I *want* to go,' Diane insisted. 'You can't keep me here.'

'Of course not. If you really do want to go, there's the door, it's not locked. But you know the rules. If you go, you can't come back. And if you have made your mind up, I think it would be nice if you went to say goodbye to the others first. They'll miss you. They won't know you're not going to the meeting and they'll be waiting. They won't start without you.'

To Jill's surprise Diane went out of the room without further protest.

'She'll calm down,' said Clarissa. 'The others'll help her over this patch. They build up a tremendous mutual support through these group sessions and when one of them's going through a bad time they all rally round.'

Jill shivered. 'Is she making *any* progress?'

'Yes. We all had a hard time with her during the de-tox, but she's out of that now. It's just that she's been very volatile since her mother came down.'

'Her mother!'

'Yes. Her mother featured a lot in the written exercises she has to do – as you know, they all have to write out their feelings and reactions, describe their life, their early memories. She wrote so much about her mother that our Dr Rayburn contacted her, asked her to come down. Actually I didn't even know her mother was still alive: you put yourself down as her next of kin.'

Jill bowed her head. 'I didn't know where her mother lived. I didn't think they had any contact now,' she said in a muffled voice.

'Well, we've sorted that out. Truth is essential if we're to know how to help.' Clarissa's voice was mild but Jill felt reproved.

She forced herself to ask, 'What was her mother's reaction?'

Clarissa folded her lips. 'Obviously I can't tell you what happened, but the visit did upset Diane. Actually that's helpful. You see, they have to confront things, even painful things. Addicts rely on drugs to dodge unpleasantnesses, failed relationships, their own inability to set goals for themselves. Drugs, if you like, switch off a light in their minds. They cease to grow mentally. All this digging around, writing every day about themselves and their relationships, helps them to come to terms with things as they are.'

'Is her mother going to look after her now?' Jill spoke half-heartedly, ashamed of her jealousy.

'Diane has to look after herself,' Clarissa said decidedly. 'That's the whole point of Hedera House. We enable them to face up to reality, to accept responsibility; to have a spiritual, though not necessarily religious, awakening. Dr Rayburn tries to get to the root of whatever's alienated them in the first place, starting with family relationships. Diane seems singularly without family; she says she only has a grandmother living in an old people's home . . . apart from her mother, of course. Is that true?'

'I don't know,' Jill answered slowly. 'Her father's brother was killed in the war and his sister died about six or seven years ago. Her father and I were only married for a little over three years. I don't know anything about her mother's family.'

She wanted to ask *Did she mention me? Has she written about me?* But she couldn't find the courage. Then Diane came slowly back into the room.

'Here are my keys,' she handed a small bunch to Jill without looking at her. 'I'm going to stay for a bit longer. My car is garaged under the house two doors away, number sixty-three; I'd like my clothes and,' she paused and scowled at them both, 'and there's a clown on my windowsill, I'd like Joey.'

Jill felt a small rise of hope. 'I'll take the next train,' she nodded, 'and bring your things straight back.' She went to kiss Diane, but she turned away and quickly left the room again.

'Depressing, isn't it?' Clarissa said briskly. 'They always seem to turn on the ones who love them best. Diane will be all right but you mustn't expect too much too soon.' She touched Jill's arm. 'For a wicked stepmother you're not doing too badly.'

Jill answered her grin with a smile and walked to the door. 'I expect I'll be back about six or seven. Is that OK?'

'Just drop her things in – don't try to see her again. Write to her, though. They like getting letters. I told you before, it's just like boarding school.' She gave a friendly goodbye wave.

# Chapter Thirty-four

It was curious to be in Diane's flat again. In the good-sized bedroom with its cushioned window-seat, lolled a white-faced clown doll, a teardrop drawn under one eye, presumably Joey. Feeling an intruder, Jill scooped him up and then opened drawers and a large fitted wardrobe to select a collection of skirts and sweaters, trousers and a big topcoat, and a couple of pairs of shoes. She didn't linger, but on the way out she scanned the bookshelves in the huge living room. There was a touching collection of children's books, the *Golden Treasury* next to battered Enid Blytons and *The Secret Garden, Children of the New Forest*, and several Angela Brazils. But there were also many modern novels from Martin Amis to Anne Tyler, Margaret Drabble to John Updike, plus the accepted classics such as a full set of Jane Austen, George Eliot, Charles Dickens, and the Brontës. There was none of Douglas's work. Jill didn't pack any books, accepting but not understanding the ban at Hedera House.

The phone rang as she was leaving, giving her a shock. Her first instinct was not to answer it, and then she thought it might be Diane with instructions to collect other things. 'Yes?' She answered cautiously.

'Di, is that you? Where've you bin? I missed you luvvie.' And then as Jill didn't answer, more threateningly, 'Who is this? I'm trying to find Diane Mortimer. She owes me a lot of money.'

Jill felt sick with fright. She drew a deep breath. 'I am from Miss Mortimer's lawyers,' she said as firmly as she could. 'If she owes you money perhaps you would let us have an itemized bill. We're looking after her affairs for the time being. You can send it to Farrer and Co. We're in the phone book.'

She put the phone down and let out a breath, listening to a door opening two floors down, wondering what to do if someone challenged her. There was no further sound, and she stole into the corridor, double-locking the door. She waited a few moments, preparing to run up to the fifth floor and ring the bell of the young girl she'd met last time she was here, if the awful Chris came upstairs.

After a few more moments she crept silently down to the hall and let herself out of the block. Once in Diane's car, she was brave enough to look at the dark windows of the ground-floor flat, but there was no sign of life.

She broke the speed limit most of the way home, and dropped Diane's suitcase at Hedera House at about seven o'clock. Back at the cottage, she tucked Diane's car at the side of the garage. It wasn't big enough for two. Then she telephoned Roger Mander.

Miriam answered. 'Oh, Roger's not in yet. Why don't you come over? I want to talk about what we can do about Sandra. I took it upon myself to try to persuade her to change her mind – even had an unnecessary hairdo in the interests of "Us All" as Arabella would say, but there's nothing doing. Roger thinks the schoolkid daughter of one of his patients might help out.'

Jill was dead tired, but the thought of joining the two comforting, commonsense Manders was enticing. She wanted to talk to Roger about Diane, hoping he would assuage her own sense of failure, and it would be more exciting to break the news about Fiona Trentbridge in person. She wondered if Miles had told anyone. If so, unusually, the tidings hadn't reached Miriam.

Jill enjoyed Roger and Miriam's open-mouthed amazement when she told them, with a carefully contrived nonchalance, that Fiona Trentbridge was going to be a temporary member of Sherville Drama Group.

'But does she realize it's only a small part?' Miriam asked incredulously. 'I can't imagine someone like her in a minor rôle. And the village hall!'

Jill went on repeating that it was true, Miles had spoken to her himself on the telephone.

Miriam shook her head in amazement. 'Pauline must be told at once. As press officer, she must tell the papers and the local radio stations immediately. It'll be a sell-out.'

202

'I left that to Miles. I had to go to London today. Diane wanted her stuff collecting.'

She told them all about her depressing visits to Hedera House, and her fears about the man living below Diane's flat. 'I thought the police would have got him by now but I think he's still there.'

'They have to have sufficient grounds before they can get a warrant. Don't worry, they'll get him in the end.' Roger was calm. 'But I'm much more worried about you taking it so to heart that she's rejecting you. That's normal behaviour in this situation. And you mustn't get so involved. She's a grown woman, spoilt and immature, but an adult. She is not your daughter.'

'But she's Douglas's,' Jill shot out.

'I know. But he was wise enough to let her go.'

'Yes, and that's the whole point. It was my fault! I was so happy with him that I didn't realize how rebuffed she must have felt. We were both selfish; we should have understood that she was more upset than she showed. An over-critical mother, a father wrapped up in another woman, no really interesting work and, as far as I can tell, few friends. She was only sixteen when they were divorced.'

'Poor kid,' Miriam sympathized. 'A very vulnerable age. I'd feel just the same as Jill, Roger.'

Roger made an exasperated noise. 'Jill isn't thinking straight. She's built up some emotional entanglement with Diane that's unhelpful to them both. However, I'll say no more. I'm outnumbered. Besides, I want to see the ten o'clock news.' He smiled at Jill to take any sting out of his words, and went into a small television room off the main living room whilst Jill helped Miriam clear the table and stack the dishwasher. Both women were too involved in the dramas on their own doorstep to have more than a passing interest in the troubles of the rest of the world.

The next morning, a Sunday, Jill lay in bed gazing at the unseasonable blue sky. It was after eight and already light. She'd slept soundly, for once untroubled by dreams, and she was feeling lazy, unwilling to get up, wishing there was someone to bring her coffee and croissants in bed as they did in the hotels she used to stay in on her buying trips.

She began to think seriously, again, of going back to London. She had to do something; she couldn't let her brain atrophy. Why was she dissipating her energies playing around with costumes for an amateur dramatic society? In any case, that would all be over in another week. And yet she felt a reluctance to take a decision. She had to wait to see how Diane got on, be on hand if she needed her. And there was still lots to do in the garden if it was to look as Douglas had envisaged. She smiled sadly at the thought of a summerhouse on the riverbank where they were to have watched the sunsets, yet she felt she'd still rather like to design one, and Tania had talked enthusiastically of the stream.

'You could have all sorts of water plants down there, a bog garden,' she suggested eagerly. She'd called one day to give Jill a seedling of a paeony called *mlokosewitschii*. 'I have the mother in a tub and somehow this little infant started life in a crack in the paving. Imagine – it's as difficult to grow as it is to pronounce – yet look at this! Nature never ceases to amaze me. You can call it "Molly the witch" if you can't get your tongue round its real name.'

Jill had shown her the garden: the planting that Douglas and she had tentatively started and the saplings that were the beginnings of the glade they'd hoped to create.

Tania had been enthused, itching to help. 'You're so lucky,' she'd said. 'It has shelter, aspect *and* a lovely shape. I envy you! You'll have such fun bringing it all to life.'

Her enthusiasm had rekindled Jill's own interest. She'd begun to read the gardening books, surprised at the range of garden styles there were, just like fashion in the play of shape and contrasts, or monotones. She remembered the breathless enchantment of Frank's garden when he'd switched the lights on. She could do something like that with this patch if she stayed.

The telephone interrupted these pleasantly idle thoughts. 'Your young playwright stayed the night in my flat,' Fiona's low voice said with a chuckle. 'He was hanging about the theatre when I arrived for the Saturday matinée looking as if he hadn't slept or eaten for days. I've just sent him out for the Sunday papers, but this is just to warn you he's dragging me down today for a rehearsal.' She laughed more openly. 'I've never met anyone so single-minded. I find him quite fascinating! God knows what my telephone bill will be – he spent hours ringing the rest of your Sherville Players or whatever they're called, and haranguing them to turn up.'

'What a cheek! You should have been firmer.'

'No, he's right. He's very professional. It's necessary if the first night is next week. There was a lot of spluttering the other end of the line, but he insisted on everyone putting off their mother-in-law visits, or whatever else people do on Sunday in the country. He kept sayng "This is an emergency, you've got to come". Quite terrifying.'

'And is it on?'

'Apparently – somewhere called Stourbridge Court. He couldn't get the village hall.' She laughed again, clearly enjoying the situation. 'I wondered if you could give me supper and put me up? I can catch a train back on Monday morning.'

'Of course! Stay the week if you can. You are marvellous to do this.'

'It's a hoot. Besides I have definite designs on that young man. He'd make a smashing toyboy.'

Jill wanted to ask if she'd slept with him already and bit her lip as Fiona went on, 'If I hadn't been so tired after two shows and he hadn't been uninterested in anything but *The Glass Ceiling*, I'd have dragged him into bed last night. By the way, what does this Bella character wear?'

'Horrid tarty clothes too short in the skirt and too low in the bodice.' She wondered if Lizzie Boston would have enough time to alter the costumes to fit Fiona; she was so much slimmer than Sandra.

'Sounds just my style. That's Wonder Boy ringing the bell now, I'll have to let him in. See you later.'

When Jill arrived at Stourbridge Court it was to find Arabella in her element, ordering people about, getting part of her large room cleared of furniture, telling her cook that she would have to make sandwiches for 'the cast'.

'Miss Trentbridge will be lunching with Sir Harold and

myself in the breakfast room. The cast can have wine and sandwiches in the dining room. Now, please let's get on, Mrs Dalbridge. She'll be here any minute.'

Arabella spotted Jill. 'Oh, good! I've called the caretaker to go along to the village hall and let you in for the costumes. If you go now, pick up Lizzie Boston on the way, you'll be back in time for the first rehearsal. The train arrives just after eleven – I've sent James to pick up Miles and Miss Trentbridge. How clever of him to secure her for the part of Bella! I'd really like to see Sandra's face when she hears about this.' She looked impatiently at her watch.

'If the caretaker can let me into the hall why can't we rehearse *there*, with all the props and scenery?' asked Jill, not moving.

'Oh, it's too difficult to explain – something about furnaces and insurance. In any case, I'm sure Fiona Trentbridge would rather be in the comfort of Stourbridge Court. Now do hurry.'

Irritated, but impressed by Arabella's energy, Jill drove to the village, stopping at Lizzie Boston's on the way.

'Well, what excitement, eh?' Lizzie said. 'My husband's ever so fed up. He likes his dinner on the table at one on Sundays, always the same: roast beef and roast potatoes, then apple pie and cream, week in, week out. And here am I having to tell him how to heat up a shepherd's pie I've taken out of the freezer. Like a thundercloud his face is. Stumped out the back to dig the garden.' She twittered away, her tape measure already round her neck and a pincushion on her wrist. 'Pauline rang me about an hour ago to tell me the news. Fiona Trentbridge – she was on that Terry Wogan show, wasn't she? Ever so lovely.'

The caretaker who looked after the village hall looked as grumpy as Lizzie's husband must have done. 'I don't expect to be called out on a Sunday, I don't.' He grumbled away about Lady Arabella this and Lady Arabella that whilst Jill and Lizzie loaded the car with the costumes. 'No good wanting to bring 'em back later, either. You'll have to keep 'em till Monday now,' he growled as he re-locked the hall after them.

Back at Arabella's house, Fiona was already holding court, smiling and chatting to the cast gathered shyly about her. She caught sight of Jill and went up to kiss her. 'All these lovely people working on a Sunday, aren't they marvellous?' she said in a voice loud enough for everyone to hear.

Arabella took Fiona's arm possessively. 'I've put aside my little study for you to change in,' she said. 'I'll show you where it is.'

'Oh, how kind of you. But, thanks, I'd rather be with the others. They're going to have to help me so much.'

Miles, who was both elated and nervous, seized Jill. 'She's wonderful! She let me show the play to her last night, even after she'd been to a farewell party on stage at the theatre. She'd done two performances, too. She took the script to bed with her to learn her lines, and she's been mugging them up all the way here on the train.'

They had a read-through, just so that Fiona could see the moves on stage, and then they all changed into their costumes. The scenery was lacking, but they were all riveted by Fiona's interpretation of the part, totally different from Sandra's, still a tart but with a sense of humour and self-mockery.

By seven o'clock, after three run-throughs, they were all exhausted but exhilarated. Fiona had fitted in without any fuss, and after their initial nervousness and stiffness, the actors forgot who she was as her laugh rang out whenever she forgot her lines. She sashayed in during the last scene wearing the dreadful electric blue dress that Lizzie had pinned at the back to fit her, with a magazine stuck under the sequinned belt to take up the slack at the waist. Sandra was quite a generously built young woman. Then, just as Arabella's character was about to make her speech at the company dinner, Fiona deliberately turned to reveal the pins and tucks in the back of the dress, making April giggle and Molly break into one of her schoolgirl peals of laughter.

She'd also gained Brownie points by sweetly telling Arabella that as she needed to get to know everybody, she thought it more fun if they all lunched together. Arabella could do nothing but give in graciously, and join the rest round the dining-room table. Sir Harold had hovered, looking hopefully at the chattering crowd, but Arabella had waved him away with, 'Your meal's in the breakfast room, Harold. We're talking shop.'

Jill had looked for James, but apparently he'd taken himself off into the countryside for the rest of the day.

She and Miriam had nudged each other during the third run-through as Edward Posner, playing the chauvinist who was supposed to be having an affair with Bella, threw himself into the flirtation with greater enthusiasm that he'd ever shown with Sandra, grabbing Fiona more often than was strictly called for.

Finally, Pauline whispered something to Miles, who nodded. 'Right ladies and gentlemen, that's enough. You've been splendid. I'm sorry if I spoilt some of your Sunday arrangements.'

Though tired, they all seemed reluctant to leave the glamorous aura of Fiona.

'Do wait a moment,' Arabella called imperiously. 'On behalf of us all, I would just like to say how pleased and proud we are to have Miss Fiona Trentbridge in our midst. I'm sure Sherville Drama Group will never look back. Now if you stay a little longer, I've asked Mrs Dalbridge to serve some champagne.'

There was a general buzz of conversation and Edward was heard to say, 'Er ha, er speaking for myself, I haven't enjoyed a Sunday so much for a long time.' His words were uttered whilst leering at Fiona who smiled warmly up at him.

Jill saw Fiona draw April a little apart from the others. She was talking to her seriously and April's face lit up at something she said.

Jill offered to drive Lizzie Boston home again, but she said she'd asked Tania to give her a lift as it was more on her way. 'I'll get started on the alterations tomorrow. What a good job we'd finished the costumes. Always pays to get ahead if you can, I say.'

Fiona went up to thank Arabella for being so kind in lending the house. 'I hope we haven't wrecked your lovely room,' she said pleasantly. 'And I must say you play a very realistic trade union leader. I'm sure in real life you'd have me out on strike in no time.'

Arabella looked gratified. 'Harold and I would love you to stay to dinner.'

'I'm sorry, I'm dead beat. Sunday is the one day I rest usually, and last night was late as my play came off and we had a

208

wake. I'm going home with Jill, to have a hot bath and fall into bed.'

'I didn't know you knew Mrs Mortimer.'

'Arabella, it was through Jill that we're lucky enough to have Fiona,' Miles broke in.

'Indeed! I am surprised. I thought you, Miles, had persuaded her.' Miles looked irritated and embarrassed.

Tom and April came up to him. 'We're just going. Do you want a lift or have you got your bike?'

Miles cast an appealing glance at Jill and, getting no response, sighed, 'OK. I'll come. Feel like a pint?'

The three of them went off.

In the car Fiona leant her head back. 'I really am shattered. It's been quite an emotional week, with people weeping all over the place.'

'Well, you can go straight to bed and I'll bring you something on a tray. You were terrific. Everybody loved you.'

'Of course. It's what's known as my personal charm, only exceeded by my lack of conceit.' She gurgled a low laugh. 'I quite liked the old battle-axe. She's not at all bad in the part. Pity she's married to that creep of a husband. Did you see him prowling outside the window of that little room where we changed? A congenital lech if you ask me.'

# Chapter Thirty-five

Molly rang on Monday to suggest that the Drama Group clubbed together to give Miles a present at the end of the first night.

'Of course we must,' agreed Jill. 'What do you suggest?'

'I was going to ask you, you're the arty one. He's too young for a piece of engraved silver, even if we could afford it.' At the word 'engraved' Jill remembered the girl she'd met at Yvonne Staidler's, the craftswoman who worked in glass.

She suggested her and then said, 'I don't know whether she could do a commission in the time, but I'm ready to drive over to see what she's got in stock,' she said. She thought, ruefully, that she had become more involved in this group than she'd ever intended.

'And Pauline says we ought to have a party afterwards,' Molly went on. 'Eldridge Pope do a sale or return on wine, and they loan the glasses, but I suppose Arabella will want to do her Lady of the Manor act and have the élite among us up there.'

'A party in the village hall will have so much more atmosphere,' Jill said firmly. 'Redolent of wet wool, mothballs and Women's Institute jam.'

'Not to mention armpits and make-up,' Molly hooted. 'I'll tell Pauline to organize it and contact the others, then we won't have to do any pulling of forelocks.'

Fiona drifted down in a white wool dressing gown piped in white satin. She looked younger without make-up and with her hair tousled. 'I slept like a log. It was wonderful. A dear little bedroom, so pretty! And I love the cute bathroom, except the ceiling slopes so sharply one side that I'd develop a list to port if I used it often.'

Jill was pleased, neither Carla nor Diane had said anything nice about the little guest suite. It had taken a lot of bullying to persuade the builders that it was possible to fit in a bathroom, and Jill had hunted everywhere to find the curious half-bath, half-shower unit that had defeated their objections.

'What's that lovely smell?'

'Fresh air?'

'Could be. I was hoping it was eggs and bacon.'

'Eggs and bacon!'

'Mushrooms? A teeny sausage?'

Jill laughed. 'With your figure? Sorry, there's nothing like that; but you can have fruit, some health-giving muesli and I could poach you an egg on toast.'

'Then I'll have to settle for that,' she said genially. 'But we can have lots and lots of tea, can't we? I go on squeezing the pot.'

Jill took out a wire basket of large brown eggs. 'These are from Mrs B, my daily. Her husband keeps chickens. If you're lucky you might get one with a double yolk.' She told Fiona of her errand to track down a gift for Miles, but Fiona declined to go with her.

'I'd rather stay here and cosy up to that log fire. I'm feeling a little washed out, and I need to memorize Bella's immortal words a little better.'

With difficulty, Jill eventually found Laura Harding's tiny thatched cottage tucked beside a redundant railway station, the front hedge almost touching the windows. Laura was visible and wearing a voluminous tracksuit over an assortment of sweaters, her hands in mittens.

She came out and said she remembered Jill. 'Don't take your coat off,' she warned, as she led the way indoors. 'There's no heating on. Can't afford it.' She switched on the oven to give a little temporary warmth. 'Did you want to see my work?' she asked eagerly.

Jill nodded. 'I've only come to look,' she said carefully. If it was no good, she would have to buy something cheap as a token gesture and leave.

But in a very light shed opening off the kitchen door was a wide white counter full of beautiful glass. Propped against the shed windows was an assortment of coloured glass plates exquisitely engraved with imaginative birds and animals, leaves and flowers, fine flowing lines curving round the plates as the light streamed through them to make coloured patterns on the counter.

At Jill's exclamation of pleasure, Laura's anxious expression changed to relief. 'You like them?'

'They're beautiful. I'd no idea.' She handled a faintly tinted wine glass with spiralling lines of slightly stronger colour emphasizing the stem, feeling the satisfying weight. There were two large bowls and some pretty scent bottles as well as more plates on the counter.

'I made the wine glasses hoping people would buy them for Christmas presents,' Laura explained. 'But I only sold three sets. Didn't cover my hire of a furnace for a day. The bowls are left over from the work I did at art school.' She looked dispirited again.

'Where do you sell?'

'There was a craft fair in Blandford, which wasn't bad, but people really wanted small, cheap things. The scent bottles went quite well, but I warned the customers the stoppers wouldn't prevent evaporation and that put them off. My boyfriend said I was crazy and I should have let them find out for themselves but it didn't seem fair. I took some samples to a Blandford gift shop, and another in Sturminster Newton, but they don't have a steady trade. The odd wedding or anniversary present. Otherwise I just rely on word of mouth. I put an ad in the local paper but the response was zilch.'

'But you have such talent.' Jill was indignant. She spoke about Miles's present and Laura picked a goblet from a box of straw. 'How about this? It's my favourite and I don't really want to sell it, but needs must.' She shrugged. 'I could engrave that for you in time. I haven't much else to do except look for a job. I've decided this,' she made a sweeping gesture, 'will have to be a hobby not a career. It wasn't too bad when my boyfriend lived here and we shared expenses, but we just broke up.' She gave a little self-conscious laugh.

Jill felt pity and irritation; like Yvonne, this girl had no commercial sense. It wasn't enough to drift about hoping people would seek out talent. Couldn't they see they had to push their work? She was tempted to be candid but it was none of her business. Instead, she told Laura that as the play was called *The Glass Ceiling* a piece of glass to commemorate its performance would be rather apt, and she decided on the goblet. They discussed the engraving and then, before she left, Jill bought a set of the wine glasses. She felt rather guilty because she had no need of them but the recklessness was worth it to see Laura look much more cheerful when she left.

When she got back to the cottage, she found Fiona curled up in a big armchair reading her lines.

'Hi,' she stretched langorously like a cat. 'I've had a deliciously lazy time. Our clever playwright telephoned, wanting to know what I thought of yesterday's rehearsal, and how soon could we have another. I think he was angling to come round, but I said you were out and I was very adamantly resting.'

'Good.'

'Oh and a strange young woman, thin and dark but rather beautiful, called and left you that.' She pointed to an envelope. 'She wouldn't leave her name, or come in. There was a car waiting at the gate with a couple of other people in it. She seemed thrown to see me and asked if you still lived here. Who was she? Not, I hope, another nervy member of your Drama Group?'

'My stepdaughter,' Jill said tensely, her stomach knotting at the sight of the envelope. What was Diane up to now? She picked up the envelope and took out several sheets of sprawling handwriting with a yellow Post-it sticker attached to them.

'Jill – if this is any use would you please have it typed and sent to Tom Feathers, though I don't suppose he'll use it. Diane.'

No love, or personal message. She looked at the pages with foreboding, wondering how Diane would react if Tom did reject it.

'I'll make a cup of tea.' Fiona got up swiftly after glancing at Jill's face. 'I've learned my way around your kitchen. I've been nibbling non-stop since you left. Bella's costumes had better not be taken in *too* much.'

Jill sank to the sofa and began to read. Fiona took her time over the tea, and when she returned to the room tears were streaming down Jill's face.

'Oh God, I can't bear it.' She held out the sheets to Fiona.

'She's written about her father so poignantly it's breaking my heart.'

Fiona took the sheets, raising her eyebrows questioningly to make sure Jill meant her to read them. Jill nodded and sipped the hot tea, her eyes still welling with tears. Fiona read in silence and when she looked up she too had glistening eyes. 'It's the most moving thing I've read in a long time. Her words are so simple, yet passionate. She can certainly write. Tell me about her.'

Later that evening Jill called James, thankful that he answered and not Arabella. 'Guess what? Diane has written the foreword to her father's last book. It's perfect! This is a real cheek, I know, but as you know your way around that infernal machine upstairs would you come over and show me how to type it out? I need to get it to the agent as soon as possible.'

He agreed at once, glad to be asked.

'Stay to lunch and meet Fiona,' she added, when they'd arranged he would come over in the morning.

She'd stopped off to shop in Blandford on the way back and laid out her purchases on the kitchen table. 'Bacon, sausages, mushrooms, tomatoes, I jibbed at kidneys but would you like some? I could pop to the village.'

Fiona laughed. 'No, I don't eat breakfast usually, but when I stop working it seems to give me a labourer's appetite. Creamy mashed potatoes, blackberry and apple pie, comfort food.'

They spent the rest of the day pottering, and Fiona picked a bunch of snowdrops from the garden. 'Aren't they lovely, so brave to flower at this time of the year.'

Carla had dropped a postcard to say she would come down for the play. She had a new man in tow. 'He's divine. Not married, certainly not gay, what can be wrong do you think? Anyway, a weekend away from me might concentrate his mind a little.'

And that evening Frank telephoned, and in a long-suffering voice said that of course he and Clement would come 'as long as no-one knows I'm a theatre critic.'

'Now I'll *have* to be word perfect,' Fiona commented when she heard the news. 'Come on, hear my lines.'

# Chapter Thirty-six

Jill telephoned Diane after James had gone home.

'Diane, you've written a beautiful piece. I wish Douglas could have read it. He would have been so thrilled. I've sent off a typed version to Tom Feathers this afternoon.' There was a long silence, and Jill was wondering what to do when a voice came in almost a whisper.

'Is it really any good?'

'It's wonderful.'

Then came a sob. 'I want Daddy to be pleased with me.'

Jill's throat closed. 'He would be. If you can write like this, you could be as good as he was. It moved me to tears.' There was another long silence.

'I can come out for visits, you know.'

'Would you like to come here?' Jill closed her eyes, praying she wouldn't put her foot in it, fracture this tiny beginning.

'Not to stay.' The voice was hurried, breathy. 'Just for lunch, perhaps.' Jill, straining to read her mood, heard a catch in her voice. 'But there was a strange blonde there in a dressing gown.'

'Fiona Trentbridge. Remember you told me you'd seen her in *The Song is Sung*? It's ended its run early and she's set the village by the ears because she's going to take over a tiny part in the Drama Group's production of Miles Lambert's play. You remember that young man who took you to lunch?'

'Yes.' She was uninterested. 'Will you come to fetch me then?'

'Of course.'

'Tomorrow?'

'Whenever you like.'

'Tomorrow.' She sounded like a child, uncertain, apprehensive.

Jill put the phone down and turned to Fiona beaming. 'That's the first time she hasn't bitten my head off. She asked, actually *asked* to come to lunch . . .'

'I'll take myself off to the pub – that young Lothario can afford a pub lunch can't he?'

'Perhaps that would be tactful,' Jill was hesitant. 'I've no idea what she'll be like. But a third person might be too much for her.'

'Yes, she'll be feeling strange. She might want to talk. Besides, I want to discuss some things with Miles about the production, one or two little suggestions he might find helpful.'

Jill had a sudden thought that perhaps Diane wouldn't be allowed out, but when she rang Clarissa she was reassured. 'She can go but alcohol is strictly not allowed.'

Jill felt apprehensive when she went to collect Diane. She took her a bunch of snowdrops from the garden; they seemed to have multiplied this year, spreading like a ragged white carpet under the hedge, in isolated patches in the grass, through small gaps in the low stone wall. Diane took them and sniffed them, putting them carefully in a tumbler of water by her bed. 'They look so delicate.'

She wore no make-up, and her hair had been properly cut since Jill's amateur hack job. She was pale, but seemed more relaxed, and she was wearing the violet sweater Jill had given her with a grey flannel skirt. Jill felt an optimism rising. Surely the fact she'd chosen that particular sweater had some kind of significance, a desire to please?

Diane's eyes widened as they went through the front door, and she seemed to hang back, fearful of getting into the car, but three inmates came round the corner from one of the annexes and waved to her. She then got in quickly, waving back and calling 'See you after lunch', as though to reassure herself she was going to return.

It was strange how Diane seemed to have gone from fearing Hedera House to regarding it as a safe haven. Jill remembered how her own father had been reluctant to come home from hospital after his first heart attack, afraid of leaving the expert, confident custody of the nurses. In the enclosed confines of the hospital he had been cheerful, interested only in ward life, indifferent to her and her mother's chat about the outside world. When he'd returned home, for a pathetically short time as it turned out, he was querulous, impatient, constantly reminding his wife to give him his medicine. Perhaps Diane was the same, feeling unsure, a little frightened of her first tentative steps towards convalescence?

'Who are they?' Jill asked as she let out the clutch. 'They're very young.'

'Charlie's only fifteen. He's been glue sniffing. He was smoking fifty cigarettes a day. His dad's in prison. The girl, Karen, is an undergraduate at Cambridge. She was tripping on LSD. The other one, the taller man, is Alex our counsellor.' She answered flatly, like a tour guide repeating the same script over and over. 'Everyone has to confess. We all know about each other.'

'Does that help?'

'Yes.' She was silent for a long time gazing straight ahead, taking little interest in the scenery. 'Karen's not going back to Cambridge. Her parents won't make her. They've been to see Dr Rayburn several times and they say she can decide for herself. Her father's very clever, and wanted her to be a scientist like him. She wants to learn to be a carpenter. Alec says you can be anything you want to be, you just have to have a goal.'

When they got to the cottage Diane hovered close to Jill as she put a fish pie into the oven, whipped some cream for a chocolate soufflé.

'Shall I lay the table?'

'Thanks, yes. Would you like to eat here in the kitchen or in the dining room?'

'Here. It's so cheerful. The dining room is dark.'

'I know but I don't eat in there on my own. At night, when we used it, the candles and the lamps made a big difference.'

'Are you . . . are you all right now? I mean on your own.' The last words were said in a rush as Diane clattered the knives and forks on to the table. Jill was absurdly pleased. It was the first time she had asked how she was.

'I get along. There's an unfillable gap, but I'm not quite such a ninny as I was at first.' She kept her back turned at the sink as she washed the salad. 'And you?'

'I miss Daddy more than ever but . . .' she controlled the tears in her voice, 'writing about him made me feel so much better. Before I copied it out, I talked into the tape recorder as you suggested. I began to feel as if he was really there, in that little room, listening carefully. He didn't always listen. He pretended to but I could tell his mind was elsewhere.' She finished laying the table in silence and then she said, 'Do you think he could have been there? Is there life after death?'

Jill felt a twinge of fear. Was it essential to her peace of mind, to her recovery, to believe that? She didn't want to destroy any vital shred of hope or confidence in Diane.

'How can we tell?' she said lightly. 'Some people firmly believe in the spirit world, others in reincarnation; who are we to say they're wrong? I'm not religious, and frankly I don't believe in an after-life, but sometimes I sense a feeling of warmth and comfort, particularly here in this cottage, that seems to have nothing to do with the temperature.'

'I'm glad you didn't pretend. Dr Rayburn says when you're dead, you're dead; but that the way you have lived your life, the love you have given, stays on.'

'What a lovely way to put it. I'm sure he's right. Your father loved you very much.'

'And you.'

'I hope so. Both of us.' She smiled tenderly at Diane. 'He was generous with his love.' Anxious not to let the conversation become mawkish, she served the fish pie. 'James typed out your piece. I hope you don't mind? I can't understand that machine upstairs and asked him to help me, in the end he did it himself. He even found Douglas's last book in it, and printed that out.'

'It gives me an odd feeling that Daddy's book should be here, going through the processes as normal, when he's not. For a long time I hated his writing. It always took him away. I wouldn't read any of his books when they came out.'

'I found it difficult to read this last one. I kept breaking down again.'

'You always seemed so competent.'

'So did you. If it hadn't been for you at the funeral I wouldn't have got through the day. I felt so despairing.'

'Is . . . is Daddy's book . . . I mean, what's it about?'

'It's a love story,' Jill said simply. 'I can't describe it any more than that. You must read it.'

In the silence that followed there was a palpable closeness between them.

'Did James say anything about my piece?'

'James? No, of course not. He has a sensitive nature and he'd have considered that to be intrusive. He has real character that young man, if only his dreadful mother doesn't sap him. He's interested in conservation but is afraid he won't get anywhere without a degree.'

'Like me.'

'Darling, if you can write like that without any training or experience, you'll be a writer.'

'I might not be able to do it again.'

'You might not. But it's worth a try isn't it?'

'I'd like to see James again,' she said. 'He was nice to me.'

'He likes you. But don't hurt him,' Jill said quickly. 'He hasn't much self-confidence. Don't lead him on.'

'I meant I want to see him as a friend,' Diane said with dignity. 'Later, when I come out. We aren't allowed any new relationships now.'

After lunch Diane offered to help clear up and when she caught Jill's quizzical stare of disbelief, she smiled faintly. 'We all have to do chores at Hedera House. It's compulsory.'

Jill drove Diane back at about four o'clock, greatly cheered by the obvious change in her. 'Would you like to come and see *The Glass Ceiling* on Friday?' she asked. 'With Fiona in it, it'll be a hit.'

'No,' Diane shivered. 'I don't want to be in a crowd of strangers.'

'All right. But you'll come again soon?'

'Yes.' She ran up the steps of the house, and turned at the top to wave. 'Tell James thank you,' she called.

Jill drove herself home, more cheerful than she'd been since Douglas had died.

# Chapter Thirty-seven

Fiona made an appearance at the pub with Miles that did not go unnoticed. A few people had seen her television plays, even fewer had seen her in a stage play, but most seemed to have seen her on the *Terry Wogan Show* when she'd turned the tables on the genial Irishman by asking him about his own sex life. When the news spread that she was to act with the Sherville Drama Group in *The Glass Ceiling* there was a sudden run on the tickets, just as Jill had predicted.

Feeling a lot happier about Diane, she could concentrate on her preparations for the first night. She drove all the way to Bath to buy food for her guests, ringing Carla to bring some delicacies from Harrods. Since Fiona had been staying with her, she had begun to enjoy cooking again, taking pleasure in the actress's surprisingly robust appetite. But her more exotic ideas were frustrated by the village shops which, apart from the delicatessen with its good French cheeses and various German and Italian sausages, limited themselves to very basic ingredients.

She planned to put Carla up in the tiny room that Douglas had used as a dressing room, and they could both share the bathroom sandwiched between that and Jill's room. She had thought guiltily that she ought to offer Carla her own, more comfortable room but she couldn't bear the idea of anyone else sleeping in the bed she had shared with Douglas.

Looking at the large empty bed, she was consumed with a physical yearning for Douglas and a terrible sense of waste. How was she to live without sex? Even before Douglas, she had always enjoyed it. But the love she had shared with him underlined how shallow her previous relationships had been. Their love-making had sometimes been exotic, sometimes gentle; it hadn't always ended in climax but they'd experienced such a mutual pleasure and contentment that the thought of bodily intimacy with anyone else repelled her. And yet, at forty-four, the bleak thought that there was nothing ahead but celibacy depressed her.

Impatient with her morbid thoughts, she caught up the pretty sheets and duvet for Carla and walked decisively into the makeshift bedroom, determined to keep her mind on the weekend ahead.

Fiona had been bombarded with insistent invitations from Arabella but so far had evaded them by saying firmly that she never went out when she was working. This was a statement Arabella clearly didn't accept, for Sir Harold was then despatched to try his dubious charms. Obviously believing he cut an impressive figure on horseback, he rode his hunter round to the back door of Jill's cottage, rapping on the kitchen window with his crop, and bellowing, 'Hullo there!'

Jill was out, but Fiona had already spotted him through the window and had deliberately opened the front door, stalking round to the back where he was leaning sideways in the saddle and attempting to peer through the windows.

'I beg your pardon,' she said in a loud, icy voice. 'Did you want something?' Her blonde hair was piled loosely on top of her head and she was wearing a green chenille sweater and tight green velvet pants.

'Aha, our celebrity,' Sir Harold said ogling her, trying to turn his horse round. 'What an improvement on the scenery. A lovely young woman like you can't be stuck in this tinpot cottage day in, day out. You're to come to dine at Stourbridge Court. Bella's very anxious for you to meet some people, a little upscale from the villagers of course, hah hah.'

'Your horse is trampling on my friend's snowdrops,' Fiona replied. 'I have already said no to your wife. Please don't force me to be rude.' She turned her back, leaving him shouting out attempts to change her mind.

Pauline telephoned, her voice bright with the excitement of being a press officer, a rôle she had volunteered for originally believing it would simply entail mailing details to the local newspapers, only one of which, the *Wessex Weekly*, had any circulation to speak of. Now, urged on by her sister Molly, she had phoned the news desks and the radio and television stations listed in the Yellow Pages for both Dorset and Wiltshire, and was amazed at the lively response to the news that a well-known West End actress was to join Sherville Drama Group for a rôle written by a local playwright.

'*Local* playwright?' she'd queried Molly dubiously. 'Miles only moved here last year. He wasn't born here and he'll move on when he finds a job. It's Sir Harold's rent-free cottage that keeps him here.'

'He's local at the moment,' Molly pointed out. 'That's all that matters.' Unlike her sister, she knew the value of publicity. Now Pauline wanted Fiona to come to the village hall for a photo call. 'Well, that's what the papers called it,' she said importantly. 'I've asked the cast to be there at eleven o'clock, but it's really you they want. It wouldn't surprise me if a few noses are put out of joint.'

Fiona wasn't normally averse to publicity, but she sounded doubtful. 'Oh dear, I don't know what my agent will say. I haven't told her about this little lark. She thinks I'm resting.'

'I'm sorry. I didn't know. I thought it would be a good idea.' Pauline sounded deflated. 'Everybody's turning up for it. I said you'd come.'

'Well, I will, but you'll have to make it clear I can't be photographed without the rest of the cast.'

When she arrived, late, everyone was in a flutter at the idea of their picture in the paper. Of course Arabella had turned up and was busy telling the photographer from the *Wessex Weekly*, a tired seen-it-all-before middle-aged man in seedy clothes, how to get the best shots. Two other photographers were asking for Fiona Trentbridge, indifferent to Pauline's attempts to introduce Tom and April.

Fiona adamantly refused to appear alone in any shot. 'Mine is the smallest part imaginable,' she purred. 'These are the stars,' and linked her arms through Tom's and April's, collecting Molly, Edward and Arabella, and urging the others to group about them. The photographers did their best to separate them but, against a determined woman who knew how to get her own way, they finally gave in, variously muttering about the dire fate that awaited them back at the picture desks.

Miles arrived on his bicycle and grinned when Pauline awkwardly explained that the photographers didn't need the playwright. 'They'll have to mention the play and that's all that matters,' he said cheerfully. A spotty girl reporter from the local BBC station, lugging a Uher, a professional tape recorder, introduced herself and asked to interview him and Fiona. Fiona was still occupied with the photographers and Pauline watched Miles smile captivatingly at the girl, relieve her of her burden, and shepherd her in the direction of the little coffee shop – where Pauline had no doubt she would be subjected to the full battery of his charm. That young man would indeed go far.

That night, the cast, newly energized by the excitement, turned up for another rehearsal, thrilled to hear from Edward that all the seats had been taken. 'We could do a matinée on Saturday as well,' he suggested hopefully. 'That would be all profit.'

'I don't think I could cope with that,' Tania shivered. 'Two evening performances is as much as I can stand. I'm a nervous wreck.'

'Once you've got an audience out there the adrenaline flows,' Molly reassured her. 'The rot sets in when it's all over.'

Jill found her chief rôle was calming everyone down. It reminded her of the hysteria that surrounded the press shows at Collection time in Paris. Suddenly no-one could remember their lines, they grew frantic over their costume changes and hysterical when Miles made some last-minute alterations to their positions on stage. Only Miles and Jill knew that the improvements emanated from the glamorous Fiona, or her popularity might have sunk a little.

They had three more rehearsals, the last, on Thursday, so disastrous that the overbearing Arabella left the stage in tears, whimpering to Jill in the dressing room, oblivious of Lizzie ironing in the corner, that Miles had been beastly to her. After the break Edward returned for the second half distinctly inebriated, unable to keep his hands off Fiona alias Bella, and for the first time even the silent April raised her voice to argue with Tom about the emphases in her speech.

Only Molly, her hair redder than usual, seemed her usual matter-of-fact self, although a slightly heightened colour stained her raddled cheeks, and a sudden tendency to tell risqué stories gave away that even she, a professional, was excited. She told Jill and Miriam in the confines of the little dressing room that she had been to have her hair tinted at Solange, and had enjoyed describing the recent excitement to Julian, alias the eponymous Solange. She had watched Sandra's face in the mirror as she shampooed another client. 'I held my hands this far apart,' Molly chuckled, indicating about ten inches, 'to show Julian how much Lizzie has had to take off the waist of Bella's costumes. That Sandra looked as if she would murder me!'

# Chapter Thirty-eight

And then it was Friday. When they'd first gathered for the play reading in November, the opening night was comfortingly away into another year. Now the hall was full, the expectation palpable, and behind the dusty curtains even the calm, careful Peter was keyed up as he eyed his scenery, anxiously reassuring himself that all was in order.

Jill worked at speed, directing the wardrobe assistants, doing the make-up, and trying to keep the small space organized. Miles paced backstage, his eyes blazing with excitement, his tall, slim body tense, futilely attempting last-minute directions until Fiona told him to leave them all alone, have a drink in the pub and watch from the back of the hall. 'We don't need you darling, get lost.'

Carla had arrived in the early afternoon and Jill had asked her to look out for Frank and Clement, who'd be sitting with her. 'But I've never met them. I don't know what they look like.'

'They're pretty unmistakeable,' Fiona drawled. 'They'll be wearing something outrageous. Frank goes in for capes and fedoras, and Clement's wardrobe is usually rich, colourful and a size too small. Last time I saw him in town he was wearing a mustard yellow overcoat with a brown velvet collar and what looked like a fur tea cosy on his head.'

Apart from one slip, when Edward caught his foot in something left carelessly in the wings and erupted on stage rather than walked on with his usual careful, rather rigid stance, the first half went swimmingly. Fiona peered through the curtains at Frank, sitting between Carla and Clement, with arms folded and an inscrutable expression on his face. As she looked, the three of them got up and picked their way out, no doubt to the nearby pub which had set up a special wine bar for the audience in the interval. After last night's episode with Edward the cast were discouraged from drinking, but Pauline had organized tea and coffee for them backstage.

The second half started well, until Pauline, with a serious face, came to tell Tom Houlderton that Claudine had started bleeding and that Roger had been winkled out of the audience and was on his way to her. Tom went white. 'Oh no! Not again. I'll have to go home.'

'But you can't,' boomed Arabella. 'This is your big scene. You can't leave us all in the lurch. Dr Mander will look after her perfectly well.'

'But Claudine'll be in a terrible state. She's been so worked up about this baby. You don't know what it means to her. This time she was so confident. She's done everything the hospital told her.'

Jill looked at his stricken face. 'You're on now Tom, finish this scene and we'll ring and find out how things are. April is cueing you *now*.'

He was pushed on to the stage by Molly who said firmly, 'The show must go on, remember that.'

Pauline undertook to telephone Claudine's home and Molly frantically signalled to John, the understudy, currently helping Peter with the scenery, to come over. He slid behind the painted curtain at the back of the stage, causing it to bulge and move, and looked petrified when told he might have to go on. He had conscientiously attended all the rehearsals, and had stood in for Tom once or twice, but was no romantic hero. Fiona smiled her full wattage at him. 'All understudies dream of taking over the lead, now's your chance.'

He looked dazed. 'But the audience will have seen Tom in the part so far. They won't understand.'

'Someone will have to go and explain,' Lizzie Boston said.

'But I can't remember a single line,' he pleaded. 'I can't go on cold.' He began to sweat, trembling visibly.

'Don't worry,' Fiona reassured him. 'I've dried up many times. You'd better get some make-up on and get changed.'

Ignoring the fuss, Arabella sailed on stage, demanding to know why the blue collar workers hadn't been invited to the firm's dinner dance, and threatening a mandatory union meeting just as April's character was trying to meet a deadline for a prestigious contract.

Just before the scene ended, Pauline returned. 'Claudine's already gone to hospital. Dr Mander says there's nothing Tom can do but he can go straight there if it will make him feel better.'

'He must finish this first. There's not long to go,' Molly said decidedly.

Miles came in. 'What's up? What's happened?'

'Tom's wife has been taken to hospital. He says he'll have to drop out.'

'Christ!' Miles hit his brow. 'John's not much good.'

John twisted his hands miserably. 'I know.'

'Oh John, sorry, sorry. It's just that you haven't rehearsed enough. I didn't mean to hurt your feelings. Tom will just *have* to finish,' Miles said grimly.

'That's what I say,' Arabella came off stage, her face running with sweat. 'He would be letting us all down after all the work we've put in.'

'Tom's wife must come first,' Jill ventured quietly.

Miles turned on her. 'Well, *he* hasn't always thought so,' he spat. 'There are plenty of women in this village who can testify to that. Why should he suddenly start playing the devoted husband now!'

Jill turned her back on him as Tom came off stage.

'Did you get through? Is she all right?' he asked breathlessly.

'Dr Mander's had her taken into hospital just to be on the safe side,' Pauline soothed. 'He said there's nothing you can do but if you want to, you can go to see her.'

'Only you're going to finish this bloody play first,' Miles broke in.

Tom gave him a withering look. 'Don't tell me what I can or can't do, Lambert. Not when my wife's in hospital.'

The atmosphere was charged. April stepped up to Tom. 'I'm sorry about Claudine. I'm sure she'll be all right, but if you want to go, John and I can manage . . .' She broke off and gazed into the corner of the wings where John was vomiting into a red fire bucket.

He looked up and weakly wiped his ashen, damp face. 'I can't do it.' He shook his head miserably and threw up again.

'Neither can I,' Tom said with finality. 'Claudine needs me. Even if there's no risk, she'll be hysterical. I've got to go.' He pushed past Molly, shrugging off her attempts to hold him, darting between the scene shifters as they moved the set for the last act.

'Christ almighty! What a wimp.' Miles kicked the wall.

'Don't just stand there,' Fiona said with authority. 'Get into that dinner jacket and go on yourself. You wrote the play. You must know the lines.'

Miles looked surprised and then was electrified into action and sprang into the dressing room tearing off his clothes. 'Someone must announce a change of cast to the audience just before curtain-up,' he yelled.

'I will, of course,' Arabella took charge and in due course marched on stage, garbed in evening dress for the last scene.

'Ladies and gentlemen. We have had a slight emergency among the cast. Mr Tom Houlderton's part in the last scene will now be played by the play's author, Mr Miles Lambert. Mr Lambert is stepping in at short notice and we ask you to bear with us for the slight delay.'

There was a murmuring of surprise from the audience and a little sporadic applause. The curtain went up scarcely more than three minutes later on the scene of the firm's annual dinner dance. All the cast were in evening dress, strolling about chatting to each other at the reception before the principals took their place at the dinner table which moved noiselessly forward thanks to Peter's clever arrangement of pulleys. Miles slipped into the group. His hair needed smoothing but otherwise he seemed apparently unruffled.

April looked absolutely ravishing. But it was Fiona, resplendent in her electric blue silk and taffeta, glittering with sequins, who set the cast alight – mincing and swaggering, making ambiguously saucy remarks to Ed Posner's character. She milked the scene for all it was worth, raising laughs that had never been obvious in the script before, firing Molly to compete in her own rôle as a disapproving office manager. The two professionals ad-libbed here and there, confident, revelling in the skill they had to take the play to new heights.

The curtain came down to rapturous applause and cheers,

and the cast had to take call after call. April and Edward pushed Fiona to the front to take a solo bow, and she, with a dazzling smile, held out her hand for Miles to take his. Under the spotlight his fury with Tom and his nervous tension might never have been. His step was hesitant, his smile shy as he shook his head in gentle self-deprecation as the audience clapped and stamped their feet. He kissed April's hand and bowed deeply to Fiona.

'That man's not a playwright, he's a born actor,' chuckled Pauline. 'Look how the audience are reacting.'

'Who would guess there isn't a shy or diffident bone in his body,' Jill, clapping and smiling, agreed.

The atmosphere backstage was euphoric. And as they were all chattering and laughing, Peter and John, now recovered but shame-faced, were bringing in crates of glasses and bottles.

'Well, well, well,' Frank Huxtable appeared and loomed up to Fiona. 'Darling perhaps you should go on the stage professionally. I've never seen a better scheming little tart.'

Fiona flicked the net frills of her ghastly dress and simpered. 'Oh sir. What a shame my mother's Mrs Worthington. She's been told never to let her daughter on the stage.' She laughed. 'Come on, what did you couple of old queens really think?'

'Who was the office supervisor?' Frank squinted at his programme. 'Molly Furness. She was very good. Pity her part wasn't bigger. And the double-barrelled lady who played the terrifying union boss with the penetrating voice? She was all too believable.' He sipped his drink. 'But you know better than to ask me such questions here. I thought Jill had asked us to supper. This isn't it, is it?' he said in mock dismay.

Jill helped Lizzie and the others hang costumes in the right order for the next day's two performances and then joined the others. She watched Miles, in a corner, holding both April's hands to his chest, looking down at her as he talked. Then he bent and kissed her, not just a congratulatory peck but a long, passionate smooch. When he broke away, they both stood looking at each other. April's lovely face was tilted up to his.

When he kissed her again, Fiona nudged Jill. 'I was wasting my time there,' she said ruefully, indicating Miles. 'No fool like an old fool. Oh well, back to the Rosomons of this world. Win some, lose some.'

Miles took April's hand and drew her into the centre of the room. Grabbing a glass of wine he called for silence, and then thanked them all for putting on a wonderful performance and, most of all, for putting up with him. He reached under a table for two bouquets of flowers and gave one to April – 'The prettiest engineer in the world.' And, pulling Fiona over, he gave the other to her for 'adding West End lustre to Sherville's Drama Group.'

It was Arabella's turn, and she came coyly up to him, wreathed in smiles, hands behind her back. 'As President of Sherville Drama Group it is my pleasure to present you with this little memento of the production. It was a huge success tonight,' and she kissed him rather clumsily on the cheek as she handed over the beautiful engraved goblet.

It was after midnight when Jill rounded up her guests. They'd stayed longer than intended, carried along by the relief and exuberance of the cast.

Tania had surprised everyone by doing a very uninhibited tango with Frank. And Molly, drunk in a jolly way, had intercepted a grim Mr McIntosh bent on breaking up the intense tête-à-tête Miles was having with his daughter, and insisted on him joining her on the floor. Edward Posner was sitting dazedly on a chair drinking solidly.

Jill hoped their collective hangovers wouldn't ruin the extra matinée performance tomorrow.

# Chapter Thirty-nine

Roger's car was parked in the cottage's short drive and he was inside, asleep.

'Poor dear, he's had a bad week of long days and short nights,' Miriam said, knocking gently on the car window to wake him up. They all trooped inside the little cottage and fell on the buffet Jill had left ready. Frank and Roger opened the wine whilst Clement stood at the table sampling each dish thoughtfully in turn.

'How's Claudine?' Jill whispered to Roger. 'Will the baby survive?'

He shrugged. 'Who knows? If she's going to lose it there's nothing much we can do. It might be Nature's way of aborting a damaged child. The hospital may well keep her sedated; it's important she lies flat, relaxes.'

Jill was struck by the pragmatic way Roger talked. She supposed that doctors had to be emotionally immune, distanced from their patients, or they would go under.

'Well I must say, as amateur productions go, that was streets ahead,' Frank said loudly, breaking in on the various conversations. 'The play has its faults but it was extremely well written. Who exactly is Miles Lambert?'

Miriam told him about Miles's background.

'Has he done anything else? No? He should. And the girl, the lead, Margaret. She was really out of the ordinary. Is she a professional?'

'I'm glad you asked that,' Fiona interrupted. 'I've told April how good she is. Apparently she always had the lead in school plays. I asked her if she'd ever considered acting as a career. She's a quiet, self-effacing little thing off the stage.'

'Not one of your faults, dear heart,' Frank murmured. 'And *does* she want to act?'

'I'm sure she does. It's just that her mother died not very

long ago and her father hasn't got over it yet. She thinks she can't leave him.'

'Her father'll never stand on his own whilst he leans on her,' Roger interjected.

'People need people,' murmured Carla, lying back against the sofa, legs outstretched, drink in hand, the picture of lazy contentment.

'Of course. But as companions not crutches.'

'Jill what is the secret of this delicious chocolate mousse? It has a hint of ginger and about a pint of brandy, but there's another *je ne sais quoi*.'

'Refer to Harrods,' Jill said dreamily, half-asleep. 'I cheated.'

They all sat around gossiping until the small hours. Then Roger, openly yawning, pulled himself to his feet, pointing to Fiona, curled up on the floor against Frank's legs, fast asleep.

'Yes, it's time I took the Doc home,' said Miriam levering her solid body reluctantly from an armchair. 'Are you sorry now, Jill, that I browbeat you into joining? Where would we have been without you?'

'It has been therapeutic,' Jill admitted, helping her on with her coat. 'You're quite a hustler. Almost as bad as Arabella.'

The two Saturday performances went without a hitch, with Tom playing his own rôle again. The relations between him and Miles were strained. They nodded coldly to each other without speaking. Several people asked after Claudine, but Tom had no news beyond that the doctors were keeping her under observation for the time being. The cast didn't reach the peak of the opening performance, although it was still very creditable. Molly was in her element, keeping everyone in fits backstage and becoming more and more out of control on stage. 'She's pure joy,' Fiona said to Miles. 'Let her rip. She won't miss a cue.'

The anticlimax, after so many weeks of preparation, was severe, especially when Jill said goodbye to Carla and Fiona. They drove back to London together on Sunday afternoon, laughing and joking with each other as they slung their cases into the back of Carla's car. Watching them settle into it, Jill felt a wistful envy as she waved them goodbye and turned dejectedly back into the cottage, emptied again of life.

The next day was cold and grey with lowering clouds and sudden eruptions of driving rain. She gazed out of the sitting-room window at the sodden and uninviting garden, wondering how she had ever agreed to live here. Gloomily she contemplated the days stretching ahead. She had little to do now except help Lizzie pack the costumes in plastic bags, dump them on Tania Fellowes for storage, and see that any borrowed accessories and garments were returned.

'Shame to see all these lovely clothes doing nothing,' Lizzie commented as they folded the costumes. 'I don't suppose they'll be used again next year.'

'We should give them away,' Jill said irritably. 'They'll probably do a period drama next year.' In a way she wished she'd never become involved. She felt lonelier, if anything more bereft, than when she'd joined the group.

'April ought to have this one, it suited her so well.' Lizzie held up the silk dress admiringly, loth to pack it away. 'But I don't suppose she goes anywhere where she could wear it.'

'Give it to her anyway.' Jill was short.

'I suppose Edward would have to decide that. It's the Group's property, he's treasurer.'

'Well I donated it.' She was conscious of Lizzie's surprise at her brusque tone, and wanted to be deliberately cantankerous, to lash out and hurt somebody. But then she caught Lizzie's puzzled expression and felt ashamed. 'Ask Tania,' she said more gently. 'She'll know how to handle it.'

# Chapter Forty

Not only had the local papers done the Sherville Drama Group proud, but the *Mail on Sunday* had also carried a full, over-egged story, no doubt tipped off by a stringer on one of the locals. Fiona was shown surrounded by the cast and there was also a studio picture of her which they must have got from her agent.

When Jill went into the village she heard a discussion of the play in every shop, and people were asking each other if they'd seen the papers. Lots of them, some she didn't even know by sight, nodded at her, somehow knowing that not only was she associated with the play, but also that she was responsible for Fiona Trentbridge's appearance in it. A diffident Faith Cruze blocked her path as she came out of the greengrocer's. 'Jill, can't we be friends again? I'm sure you were just not yourself last time we met. Still upset over poor Douglas, I suppose. Come and have a coffee now and tell me all about *The Glass Ceiling*. I hear it was you who brought Miss Trentbridge down.' She smiled her brittle social smile. 'Unfortunately we were away at the weekend and couldn't come.'

'Good,' said Jill. 'I'm afraid you're in my way.' She stepped off the narrow pavement to pass Faith.

'Jill!' Faith called after her, a red weal staining her neck, 'Don't be silly. Come to dinner. Bring Fiona if she's still here.'

Jill walked on.

She prowled around the cottage feeling flat, at a loss. She was determined not to sink back into the useless lethargy that had gripped her after the funeral, but she had no idea what to do with herself.

She telephoned Tom to ask after Claudine. 'They've stopped the bleeding. They're doing another scan this afternoon. She'll be there for at least a couple of weeks. She still has to lie flat, as still as possible.'

'Oh, how boring. Does she want a visitor?'

'She'd love one. She's too uncomfortable to read for long and lies there imagining all sorts of dire things. She cries every evening when I leave.' He sounded very low.

The weather next day was cool, but the sun just occasionally pierced the heavy cloud blanket as Jill pottered in the garden, pulling up weeds which were more obvious now that the shrubs were bare of leaves. She dug up clumps of fading snowdrops and transferred them to the river bank, hoping they'd spread under the birch tree. She'd read in one of the Sunday papers that snowdrops should be transplanted 'in the green'. She invariably read the gardening columns now, trying to make sense of the writers' confident assumption that all their readers were knowledgeable experts.

After lunch she went to see Claudine, but was shocked by her pallor and the darkened skin around her eyes. She had a drip in her arm and a heartbeat monitor. 'It's the baby's. Sometimes the rhythm changes and I get frightened. The nurses are cross with me because I keep ringing for them to check everything is normal.'

She listened to Jill's stories about the play and how good Tom was.

'I thought I'd ruined it, but I was so frightened I wanted him with me.'

'Miles stepped in, but Tom was brilliant the next day.'

'I'm so afraid he'll go off with some other woman who can have babies. I know I bore him, going on about getting pregnant, but I can't think of anything else. It's become an obsession.' Her eyes rolled suddenly. 'Jill you crossed your legs. You mustn't sit by the bed of a pregnant woman with crossed legs – it impedes birth.'

Jill laughed. 'What superstitious nonsense,' but she uncrossed her legs when she saw Claudine was serious. She didn't stay long but when she got up to go she squeezed Claudine's hand. 'I'll come again if I may.'

'Please.'

*      *      *

On Thursday she was sitting in the kitchen having a desultory breakfast whilst listening to the *Today* programme when the phone rang.

'Have you seen *The World*?' Miles demanded as soon as she answered.

'Not yet. I'm listening to the radio,' Jill said, turning the volume down.

'The theatre critic has written about me, about *The Glass Ceiling*. He was in the audience on Friday.'

'I know. I asked him. He had supper with us afterwards.'

'But why didn't you *tell* me?'

'I thought it would make you and everybody else more nervous than you already were.'

'That's true! But *afterwards*?'

'Afterwards, if I remember rightly, you were deeply engaged discussing matters of technical interest with April,' she teased, laughing.

'Oh.' There was a moment's embarrassed silence but then excitement got the better of him. 'Listen, I quote:

"This play shows a contemporary grasp of the sex war in the work place. Miles Lambert, a young playwright fresh from Cambridge, has managed to capture the frustration and conflicting emotions of women who have been educated to believe in sexual equality only to find no-one has bothered to tell the men. Miles Lambert hasn't the maturity – yet – to handle the sexual longings and passions of the young protagonists, but he has a deep understanding of career-motivated young women up against the glass ceiling – a glass ceiling put invisibly but firmly in place by frightened, insecure males with outdated attitudes.

"I was very surprised to learn that the engaging young female lead was a complete amateur. She conveyed a bruised and battered dignity as she suffered not only the machinations of her jealous boss, but also the old-fashioned implacable attitude of a female shop steward played as a terrifying old battle-axe by Lady Arabella Montgomery-Fitch, wife of the MP. In the last scene April McIntosh's

236

tender and forgiving love for the man who tried to thwart her career was very moving.

"This was an amateur production acted by a village drama group, except for the baffling appearance of the delectable Miss Fiona Trentbridge as a hussy of a secretary, but it was as enjoyable as anything I have seen this season in the West End." '

Miles drew a deep breath. 'I can't believe it!'

'Yes, it's marvellous! Has April seen it?'

'I don't know. I'm not sure her father takes *The World*. He seems more of a *Daily Express* man. I'm going to ring her right now.'

Several other people rang, having seen the newspaper. Jill tried to telephone Frank to tell him what pleasure and excitement his review had generated, but he had left for Manchester. She telephoned Fiona, too, but got her answering machine. Everybody seemed to have something to occupy them but her. She decided to visit the mother-to-be again that afternoon.

She took with her some spring flowers and glossy magazines, and was glad to see Claudine had a little more colour. She had been moved to a ward with three other young women and was having a giggling chat with them when Jill arrived. She listened to Jill's account of how the villagers were delighted with all the publicity, and read the cutting of Frank's review. 'But he doesn't even mention Tom,' she said peevishly, 'He was in all but the last act that first night.' With that she lost interest in the play, and returned to the baby, saying she was enjoying hospital life. She then launched into a description of the various nurses, what the doctor had said and all too many gynaecological details for Jill.

'Have you had children?' she asked suddenly.

'No.'

'Oh? Couldn't you have any?'

'I don't know. I didn't try. I didn't have a man I loved enough to have his children, and when I did, it was too late.'

'But don't you feel unfulfilled, cheated?'

'My career filled my life until I met Douglas.'

'And now you've lost Douglas and you haven't any children either.'

Really she was a tactless little thing. Jill pretended to pick something off the floor to hide her face, regretting her visit. She left soon after, conscious of Claudine's pitying eyes following her out of the ward.

Her duck had not shown itself in the last few days though the bread had disappeared. She asked Gus if he'd seen it. He shook his head disapprovingly. 'It's them rats that eat the bread,' he said, repeating his earlier warning. 'You'll have them in the house if you throw bread out there. You don't want to encourage 'em. Or ducks,' he added under his breath, stumping off with a spade to turn over the vegetable plot.

# Chapter Forty-one

It was a couple of weeks later when Jill came in from the garden to hear the telephone ringing.

'That you Jilly? Look 'ere you've got to 'elp me out. That Christine is leaving. We 'ad a row over her orders this season – you should've seen what's been delivered. It won't sell.'

'You used to say that to me Fred.'

'Ah girl, you always throw that up at me. It was only at first, you know that. I left you alone after a couple of seasons dint I? I've had three bad seasons in a row thanks to her. Nearly bankrupt I am! Anyway I told her she dint know a Moschino from a Marks and Spencer and she flounced out. Good riddance I say, but it's left me without a buyer. You've gotta come back. I can't manage without you.'

'I'm sorry about Christine, Fred. But two years is a long time to be out of the fashion business – I'm out of touch.'

'Oh, you'll soon get back into the swing of it, Jilly. You've got flair. Come up, and I'll buy you lunch. We can talk about it then.'

Jill laughed. 'Now I know you're serious if you're buying me lunch. I'll come up, but no promises, mind. Perhaps I can suggest someone. Who's doing a good trade these days? Have you looked at their buyers?'

'No-one, it seems to me. I'm in the wrong business, love. It's time I retired, found meself a nice young lady to look after me.'

She grinned into the phone. Fred had been talking about a nice young lady ever since she'd known him, but the women he chased always tended to be good-time females on the make. When she put the phone down she found herself thinking why not? It was time she made up her mind. It was more than six months since Douglas had died, she couldn't go on vacillating. She was just a spare part down here. Fred's, at least, really needed her.

The following day after a visit to Diane at Hedera House, Clarissa took Jill aside. She told Jill that Dr Rayburn thought she was ready to leave soon. 'But he suggests she goes to *Nuages*. It's a halfway house, a sort of convalescent home if you like. She'll have more independence than at Hedera though there's still a counselling and support system.'

'That must mean she's nearly better?'

'Yes. But not cured,' Clarissa said warningly. 'Dr Rayburn would like to see you, to explain things. Can you manage Friday at three p.m? Diane will be on her shopping trip with some of her group then.'

'Of course.'

She was curious to meet Dr Rayburn, and at the same time a little embarrassed since she had put herself down as Diane's next-of-kin. She wondered if he'd refer to her lie, and squirmed mentally. Everything at Hedera House seemed so strict.

Diane had written to Jill, a week or so after her visit to the cottage: a cool letter but less self-centred than usual. She'd even asked polite questions about the garden and *The Glass Ceiling* performances. It was clear that she was more in control. Jill was genuinely glad of that but was afraid that now, as a result, their relationship would end before they had a chance to be friends in a normal way. Probably Diane and her mother had mended their fences since this crisis, the counselling had no doubt helped them to understand each other's shortcomings.

She begrudged Frances Mortimer any new rapport with her only daughter, and was unable to prevent herself picturing them together. It made her wish she hadn't given way to Douglas over having a child. It would have been possible to get pregnant, plenty of women these days had a first baby in their forties; and she would have had a child of her own to assuage her sense of loss.

On the train to London the next day she tried to be businesslike about her future, knowing that what she needed to fill the gap was hard work. She wondered what sort of contract Rosomon might offer her. And before she realized it, she was idly considering where she'd look for a flat, what new changes she could make to entice customers back to Fred's . . . a budget-conscious department perhaps? People weren't so able to pay high prices for designer labels these days. She could develop the own label range, keeping to a price limit without sacrificing style; it would mean trawling for cheap manufacturers, perhaps through Thailand and Korea. It could be interesting.

It was time to look ahead, turn the lock on the three halcyon years with Douglas and try to start life anew. Ambition and hard work would have to substitute for love and closeness.

As she entered the restaurant she was immediately greeted by Rosomon. 'Hullo, hullo Jilly girl. Sit you down, I've ordered some champagne.'

His face seemed to twist in pain as he thought of the cost of such a gesture, and seeing his expression Jill was able to let her breath out in a small shaky laugh. She knew him so well! Treating her to lunch at The Four Seasons in the Inn on the Park must be agony for him. The familiarity of his moans made her feel at home.

Despite an offer of a generous contract reinstating her as a director of Fred's, she refused to make a cut-and-dried arrangement over lunch. 'It's very tempting Fred, but I want to think about it some more. I'd have to find somewhere to live, consider what to do about the cottage . . .'

'Cottage! Whaddaya want a cottage for? You're not a country girl. Always was a mistake you going down there.' He'd never forgiven Douglas for weaning Jill away from Fred's. 'You can rent somewhere until you find the place you're looking for. Or,' he screwed up his eyes and mouth as though trying to stop his next words escaping, 'you could stay in a hotel on expenses.'

Jill laughed out loud at his expression. 'The Ritz is a couple of hundred a night, Fred. Be careful . . . I might say "Done".'

When she said goodbye to him, firmly resisting all his urging to make a commitment there and then, she rang Carla. 'Can you slip out for half an hour for some tea?' she asked her. 'I want to talk to you.'

They met in a little Italian café near Fingles, the small, very successful department store where Carla was the accessories buyer.

'Sounds ideal,' Carla said when Jill had told her of Rosomon's offer. 'You have him over a barrel. You could make what terms you like.'

'Yes, but—'

'Look, I know I mentioned my project,' Carla was uncharacteristically awkward. 'And there's still no-one I'd rather have with me on *that*, but I don't think it's going to come off after all. Don't turn Rosomon down on that hope.'

'I wasn't thinking of that. But *why* isn't it going to happen? You seemed so confident last time.'

'Money. It'd cost a bomb to do it the way I want; the return on capital is too unpredictable for the backers, and I won't compromise.' Her mouth set mulishly. 'I haven't sufficient cash to do it by myself. My accountant has stood on her head to make the figures work but the climate isn't right. People are drawing their horns in. But I'm so bloody bored with Fingles!' She shrugged and smiled. 'Crazy isn't it? Good salary, security, travel . . . perhaps I'm getting menopausal, wanting to do something different.'

'What's happened to that new man you were telling me about?'

'He's still around. He has pots of money but refuses to put it into my boutique, so I'm a bit off him at the moment. He's in Japan right now. I like him but . . . I suppose I'm not the marrying kind. Look, I have to get back, someone is coming to see me at four. You can stay with me whilst you look round for a flat. In fact, check out the porter at my block. There may be something there – you could do worse. Of course, there's one drawback. I'd be on your doorstep!'

They strolled back to Fingles together. 'Take Fred's offer,' Carla said as they parted. 'I'd jump at it. What's the countryside got to offer? Hyde Park is thick with crocuses right now and there's enough green grass to last any sane person a lifetime. *Ciao!*'

At Waterloo Jill bought *Vogue* and *Harpers, Marie Claire* and *Elle*, and several popular but less stylish magazines. It was a long time since she'd bothered to look at them, whereas at Fred's she'd considered it part of her job to keep tabs on not only the British but also the European and American magazines. It had been two-way traffic: Jill, with her recognized style sense, was a sounding board for the less sure editors. She could sometimes subtly steer them away from garments that might make a great picture but which were not going to walk out of the shop, and they, in their turn, were happy to credit Fred's as stockist for many of the clothes they featured, which was good publicity.

Not much had changed, she reflected, as she looked at the pages. Some of the fashion editors had swapped places, there were one or two new photographers given prominence, but the pages were still full of cropped pictures of clothes looking remarkably similar to the ones of two or three years ago. Then the models had leapt aerobically about the pages, their healthy-looking faces seemingly nude of make-up; now they were more languorous and sultry, heavily lipsticked with thin plucked eyebrows, but there was no fundamental change in the clothes. She felt a deep boredom as she flicked over the pages, a weary déjà vu. And how many times had she read that navy was the basic colour for spring? Did she really want to re-enter this world? And yet, what else could she do?

The rocking of the train on top of the champagne at lunch sent her to sleep, and it was lucky the engine stopped with a jerk and a loud hiss at Gillingham or she would have dozed all the way to Exeter. She got out stiffly, deliberately leaving the magazines behind, her mind foggy with sleep, and climbed into her car.

She passed the barn where Tom and Claudine lived and thought regretfully that when she went back to London she wouldn't be there to see the baby when it arrived. The days were a little longer now and in the remains of the thin daylight she noticed the hedges had a faint green opacity, as if green veils had got caught in their black twiggy outlines. Nature was gearing up for spring. Who would look after Douglas's glade? Tania had said she would have to feed the saplings bone meal, and hoof and horn, and to make sure the ground around their roots was kept free of grass and weeds. Gus wouldn't bother, unless she stood over him; he was only really interested in his vegetables.

Besides she and Tania had planned to potter round gardens open to the public, notebooks at the ready, for inspiration on

243

new plantings. She had become intrigued with the idea of the bog garden. And there was the summerhouse. Perhaps she could keep the cottage for weekends? But she was pragmatic enough to know that wasn't feasible. Fred's would be hard work again, haphazard hours, trips abroad, sudden crises demanding instant attention. She and Douglas had tried to combine their two lives before and they'd ended up exhausted and irritable by the weekend, sometimes having to cancel going to the cottage at all.

As she turned into the lane that led down the hill to the cottage, her eyes strained for its long grey shape to loom out of the twilight. It always looked so fat and comfortable tucked behind the low stone wall, as if it had simply grown out of the hillside. She switched the engine off and sat in the silence, looking at her home, remembering the joy when they'd found it, both she and Douglas instantly sure that though it looked so uncared-for and neglected, it was what they wanted.

# Chapter Forty-two

Dr Rayburn was a small man in his late forties or early fifties, with thick dark hair falling untidily over one eyebrow, rather beautiful brown eyes and a casual manner reflected in his tweedy, crumpled clothes. He shook hands with Jill, indicated a chintz-covered armchair and sat in its twin on the other side of an empty fireplace. There was a long silence whilst he stared down at his clasped hands as if they would suggest an opening gambit. Then he looked up suddenly and said, 'Does Diane mean anything to you?'

'Why, yes, of course,' Jill stumbled over the words in surprise at his question.

'How much?'

'She's my late husband's only child. I wish she was mine.' She felt embarrassed. 'I mean, we didn't have any children.'

He made no comment. There was another silence and Jill's eyes flicked nervously round the room settling on various objects without focusing.

'I assume you know her background?' He ran his hand through the flopping lock of hair, temporarily slicking it into place. Jill nodded but he went on. 'Apparently her parents were estranged through most of her childhood. She wasn't academic which disappointed her mother. Her father was indulgent, but away a lot, researching his books.'

'I know. She's had a bad time,' Jill said in a low voice, feeling partly responsible.

'Here, we've been able to help and support her. When she's depressed there is always someone with her . . . it's all part of the treatment. A firm routine, but a strong support system.'

Jill nodded again.

'Normally, after six or eight weeks here, if the patients get over the worst – and they don't all, I regret to say – we like them to go to a halfway house for about six months, sometimes less. There they have more freedom to look after themselves, but they're still with other people who've been through what they've been through, who understand if they freak out and feel desperate for a fix or a drink again. It's a commune of fellow-sufferers who help each other through the bad patches.'

'Clarissa told me that you think Diane's ready to go to a halfway house.'

'Yes. She's afraid of course. She feels safe here, but on the other hand she's impatient to stand on her own feet which is a very healthy sign.'

He got up and walked to the window, gazed out and then turned back to her, standing over her. 'I was wondering if you would still support her financially at *Nuages*. It isn't as expensive as this place, but it's still a lot and you're not her mother.' He sat down again and when he smiled a sweet smile, the lock of hair fell once more over his brow.

'I gather her mother has been to see her,' Jill said carefully. 'Won't she want to take care of her now she knows about Diane's condition?'

Dr Rayburn shook his head decisively. 'No. That's out of the question.' He pressed his lips together as if to prevent himself saying more, but added after a minute or two, 'I'm afraid we didn't have much success with Mrs Mortimer. She was deeply ashamed to find Diane here and she refused to co-operate. She felt Diane should "pull herself together" and that we were simply indulging her desire to be the centre of attention.'

'I find that incomprehensible,' Jill said quietly. 'Did she realize how dangerously ill Diane has been?'

'I told her. But she refused to accept the message. It's some people's defence mechanism.' He sounded weary. 'If I recommend Diane for *Nuages*, will you support her still? Not simply financially, but by giving her the feeling that there's someone who cares about whether she gets better?'

'Naturally. We haven't really had a chance to get to know each other well in normal circumstances. But I am fond of her and I loved her father very deeply.' Her voice broke and she bent her head. 'For that reason alone I would want to care for her.'

'I'm glad.' He smiled.

'Will she be able to stay with me for weekends, once she gets to *Nuages*?'

'If she wants to. She must make her own decisions. But if she does stay with you, you must be very careful. Temptation can be lethal at this stage. You mustn't, for instance, keep alcohol or even relatively harmless drugs like tranquillizers around. Is that difficult for you?'

Jill thought of the recent months of misery when she'd often fled to the bottle; and of the enjoyment she and Douglas had shared in taking wine with a meal, tasting and trying bottles from unexpected regions like New Zealand or Chile.

'Yes.' She smiled wryly. 'I have to say it *will* be a sacrifice in some ways but . . .' she shrugged, 'if it's necessary, of course.'

'When they're into drugs, or any kind of dependence for that matter, they cease to grow mentally. Here she does her share of the chores, keeps to a routine. If she stays with you she must do the same. And you,' he smiled the sweet, melting smile again, 'you must live your own life. It's so easy to let them take over.'

He stood up and shook hands. 'Thanks for coming to see me. I'm sure Diane will be fine in time.'

Driving home she felt a black rage with Frances. She had obviously damaged Diane with her absurd expectations, her lack of emotional warmth and now she'd rejected the girl when she most needed help. Their reunion must have been a grim moment for Diane.

Back at the cottage Jill poured herself a drink to calm down, and stopped as she was about to sip it, realizing how easy it was to lean on alcohol or, presumably, drugs. She drank the wine anyway, wincing slightly at the idea of ridding the house of the bottles Douglas had so carefully chosen.

The phone rang and she reluctantly picked it up, expecting more pleadings and blandishments from Rosomon, but it was Carla.

'Hi! Look, I took it upon myself to talk to our porter on the off chance about a flat, and there's a lovely two-bedroom corner one going two floors above mine. The couple who have it have been posted to Washington – he's a journalist, Joe tells me. Why don't you come and have a look? Stay the night. We can go to another film. You should get it at a good price because they're in a hurry to leave, and his paper is paying all his expenses.'

'Thanks, that's good of you to bother,' Jill said slowly, trying to think. It was going too fast. 'I haven't talked to Rosomon again.' She gazed idly at a stroke of sunlight coming through the open kitchen to bounce off a copper jug on the oak chest in the hall. The jug was filled with fluffy yellow catkins. She remembered Douglas bringing in an armful of catkins last year, the sleeve of his jacket smeared with pollen.

'I'm not sure I want the job,' she said slowly. And as she spoke she knew that was the truth. She couldn't leave this place, this home she had made with Douglas. It was too dear, too precious. Her voice became firmer. 'I know I've been thinking about returning on and off for some time, but it wouldn't seem like fun any more. I've done all that.'

'I don't believe it.' Carla sounded scandalized. 'I thought you'd virtually made up your mind. You must be mad. An offer like that won't come your way again.'

'I know,' Jill sounded apologetic.

'What you mean is that you've planted your feet in the mud of Dorset and taken root. You've forgotten how to run any more! Don't be silly. You don't see yourself bottling jam with the Women's Institute and running up frocks for the next amateur dramatic production, do you?'

'That's the city view of country life. It's not really like that but, well, to be honest, I've had a germ of an idea for something else at the back of my mind. Diane's leaving Hedera House,' she said inconsequentially.

'Ah, I see! You want to play Mother, relieve your frustrated maternal instincts. You're making a big mistake, Jill. That girl has her own life to lead and so have you. You mustn't become possessive for sentimental reasons.'

'I know. And I won't.' She wondered if she was being honest. 'But she needs a bit of propping up right now. After all I have been partly responsible for her problems, marrying her father.'

There was silence at the end of the phone. Then Carla said in a new careful voice, 'If you're really sure you're going to turn down Rosomon's offer, do you mind if *I* contact him? I'm so bored with Fingles and, who knows, he might eventually be persuaded to open a specialist accessory boutique.' She gave a half laugh.

'He'd be so relieved,' Jill said warmly. 'I can phone him and pave the way for you. He's quite nice to work with providing you're firm and the sales graph is on the up.' She laughed.

'Thanks. Of course, I still think you're out of your tiny mind,' Carla said. 'But what *will* you do? I can't see you drifting round arranging flowers or going to coffee mornings.'

'I haven't thought it through yet, but there are one or two talented craftspeople around here. You remember those pottery plates in my kitchen? And there's a clever glassblower who engraves. Then there's Tom Houlderton, the painter. There must be others. None of them has any idea about marketing or selling their work except by taking a cheap stall at a local craft fair. I thought I could act as a kind of agent for them. Open a permanent exhibition in a big town, show their work to selected stores like Liberty's, for instance. Perhaps produce a glamorous catalogue for overseas.' As she spoke she could see the idea taking shape and her enthusiasm rising.

'Not much money in it,' commented Carla tersely.

'I know. But I don't need it. I'm quite well off. I think it would be something useful to do.'

'You've really made up your mind then? You don't even want to see the flat, take the weekend to think it over?'

'No. I'll ring Rosomon now. He's always liked you but I'll remind him how brilliant you are.' She laughed. 'And you are! Best of luck.'

# Chapter Forty-three

Rosomon took it badly. 'But Jilly you can't do this to me. I need you! Look I'll give you a bigger percentage of the profits . . .'

'No. My mind is firmly made up. I'm sorry. I have to be here to keep in touch with my stepdaughter for a bit. She's been ill and she needs me and, to be honest, I don't feel the same enthusiasm for fashion I once did. Without that vital ingredient I know I wouldn't be very good any more. Fred's needs someone dynamic and single-minded to give it momentum and I know *just* the person for you.'

She told him about Carla's good taste and skill.

'But I thought she bought accessories.'

'She does, for Fingles. But we both had the same basic training at Bostons. When you first knew *me* I'd only been buying separates. She goes to all the fashion shows, you know that. You often meet her there.'

Grumbling, disappointed, clearly regretting his investment in Jill's lunch, he finally accepted that nothing would make her change her mind, and agreed to see Carla.

'Fingles will be devastated if they lose her,' Jill added slyly, knowing he would like the idea of capturing someone valuable to someone else. 'She's done wonders for the sales of their accessory department. It's a big money-spinner for them.'

Her conversation with Rosomon had given Jill an idea. She brought in the empty cardboard wine boxes she kept stored in the garage ready to take to the recycling depot in Gillingham, and filled one with bottles of Douglas's best wine. She telephoned a carrier to deliver it to Rosomon. She filled a couple more and left them with a brief note at Roger's house, and she decided to insist that Mrs B and Gus took some. She reckoned she might as well get organized now. Who knows, Diane might suddenly ask to visit.

She hadn't articulated her own plans until she'd talked to Carla on the telephone. The concept of establishing a centre from which to market local crafts had crystallized as she'd spoken, but she realized that she had been subconsciously thinking about something along those lines ever since she'd visited Laura Harding's chilly cottage.

Impulsively she called some estate agents in Bath, Blandford, Frome and Dorchester, telling them she was on the look-out for premises that could be used as an exhibition gallery, with good parking, lots of light, easy access from main road and rail connections.

She was in the delicatessen when Pauline came in behind her. 'Isn't it all flat now the play's finished!' Pauline grumbled. 'I enjoyed all those reporters and photographers buzzing around. Talk about fifteen minutes of fame, it felt more like five. Still, we hit the news didn't we?'

Jill nodded and turned to choose some cheese as the long-suffering assistant stood waiting for them to finish their chat.

'Have you heard about April?' Pauline asked abruptly as Jill was turning to go. 'Her father's going to miss her.'

'Why? Where's she going?'

'She's come all over stage-struck. Your Fiona Trentbridge told her she had talent apparently, and now she can't think of anything but getting into drama school or repertory. She's such a wee slip of a girl, I shouldn't think she'd be tough enough for that life.'

'There's more to her than there seems on the surface.'

'Yes well. Alex McIntosh dotes on her, especially since his wife died. Molly saw April in the village and had a coffee with her and heard all about it – April's been coming into the village a lot since the play. Can't think why, Bruton's shops are a lot nearer and they have a better butcher. Of course, it might have something to do with our local playwright,' she said archly.

'Thank you Jenny, and some cottage cheese please,' she interrupted herself.

'I hope April realizes what a difficult life it is, even for good actors,' Jill said worriedly.

'She says she does. She phoned Fiona Trentbridge to ask her

advice. Amazing isn't it? You wouldn't think April would have the temerity to telephone such a well-known actress would you? Molly, of course, reinforced Fiona's warnings. After all, she's had plenty of experience of the stage too. But April just said it was what she wanted to do. Oh help, we're causing a queue. Sorry Dorothy,' she apologized to a plump matron who was tapping impatiently on the glass counter. 'Three pounds, you said Jenny? There, the right money.'

Jill plonked her shopping in the front seat of the car and walked up the street to the tiny shop selling vacuum cleaners, food processors, radios and personal stereos. It would be an idea to get a little portable television set for the spare room, make it more comfortable for Diane when she came to stay. She found Miles was in the shop.

'Jill! How are you?' His tone was over-hearty and he blushed.

'I'm looking for a little TV. What about you?'

'Oh, just buying torch batteries. Something to read by, there's no electricity in the cottage as you know.' His blush deepened. 'I'm going next door for a coffee,' he said hurriedly. 'Come and join me when you've finished here?'

Jill nodded, and turned to consider the two or three television sets on show. They were so ugly she realized she would have to trail into Bath for more choice, but she bought some light bulbs in a cowardly effort to appease the attentive sales assistant.

Miles was sitting facing the street, his eyes alert to passers-by. 'I've ordered you a black, no sugar, is that right?'

'Thanks. What have you been up to since the production ended? I had withdrawal symptoms at first. It must have been so much worse for you.'

'For a day or two. But I pored over the press cuttings and they cheered me up.' He smiled a self-deprecatory smile. 'Conceited aren't I? I was so chuffed about *The World* piece that I wrote to your friend Frank Huxtable to thank him, and he invited me to lunch – at The Garrick!' His eyes widened. 'All those pictures of actors and playwrights. I was knocked out. And I saw Donald Sinden there. It was wonderful. Anyway, Mr Huxtable suggested I try for a Young Playwrights bursary; if I get it, I'd have enough money to live on whilst I finish my next play.'

'Whoa! You're going too fast for me. What next play?'

'The one I started last summer. It's very different from *The Glass Ceiling*. More emotional, I think. Mr Huxtable thought it sounded interesting, but also,' he drew in his breath and paused, gazing at Jill as if willing her to guess his news. 'He thought the Royal Court or the Almeida might be interested in putting on *The Glass Ceiling* if I could somehow reduce the number of characters. That wouldn't be too difficult. I think there are too many anyway. Of course, he stressed it was only a suggestion, it'll be up to the artistic directors. They must have tons of stuff sent to them. But I suppose if I sent them a script, with a cutting of his review, they would at least read it.' He looked hopefully at Jill.

'They sure would! Frank is very influential. If a critic of his stature thinks your work has merit, that will count for a lot. And what will happen to the Sherville Drama Group?'

'Oh, I suppose it will go on,' Miles gave a disinterested shrug. 'They'll go back to Oscar Wilde.'

'So that makes two of you. Pauline told me that April is going to try her luck on the stage.'

Miles looked extremely self-conscious. Away from the Drama Group he was much less self assured. 'I know. April's dad is very upset; he can't bear the thought of her going away, and thinks it's all my fault. Every time I call for her he won't speak to me, just stumps out to his garage.'

Jill sipped her coffee to hide her smile, but he looked up suddenly and caught her eyes crinkling.

'Well OK, I have been seeing a lot of her. We've got so much to discuss. April thinks an aunt of hers in London would let her stay, and she might know of someone else who wants a lodger. I couldn't afford to rent a flat.' He started drawing patterns in the sugar bowl with his spoon. 'I was an ass about you, wasn't I? You must have laughed at me.'

'No. I was very cross, but I suppose rather flattered.'

'You looked so sad and vulnerable, yet you kept going with the play. You were an ally. I had a crush on you. I suppose I got carried away.'

'You revel in drama, that's all,' she said lightly. 'I do hope everything works out for you. You and April must come to say goodbye before you go.'

253

'I thought you'd be going back to London now.'

'So did I. But I've changed my mind.' She got up to go. 'I shall hope to see both your names in lights before too long.'

As Jill walked back to her car she saw April park a little Ford Fiesta and hurry towards the coffee shop. Her cheeks were pink, for once, and her hair was piled on top of her head as Jill had done it for the play. She had abandoned her drab layers for a slim green skirt and a fitted plaid jacket. She looked enchanting. Envy of their love triggered a strong yearning in Jill. She wondered how long it would be before she got over this constant need for Douglas's arms around her, the warmth of another body closely linked with hers.

# Chapter Forty-four

Jill spent the next few days working on her plans. She had quite a solid bit of capital: her own savings and the proceeds of her flat which she'd sold when she'd married Douglas, and he had left her everything. The cottage was unencumbered. His books had made a lot of money in the last twenty years and, un-interested in money for its own sake, he had turned over his affairs to a reputable firm of financial advisers who had invested prudently. She could afford to lose some money in a risky venture, if the worst came to the worst. She was confident that she could find enough producers of quality crafts who would be glad to let her show their wares. Yvonne and Laura would jump at the idea for a start.

It took her a surprisingly short time to find near-perfect premises in Frome. She'd been showered with estate agents' details of derelict barns and warehouses, garages and empty offices. Once she had made up her mind to start a business, she worked with her old efficiency and speed. One of the last properties on her short list was a long, low build-ing that had once been a boat builder's yard. It had plenty of space for parking where the boats used to be, a pretty frontage to the River Frome which Jill instantly saw as a perfect site to show off good, modern garden sculpture and pots.

The boat builder had gone bankrupt and a bank had re-possessed the property. Jill insisted to the agent that she was only interested if her offer was accepted immediately, with contracts exchanged within a month. The young assistant handling the property had tended to treat her as a casual time-waster. Now his jaw dropped at her crispness and he promptly rang the bank, eyeing her as he dialled as if she were some strange species. He reported that the bank had given a qualified yes, providing she could produce some good financial references. 'Tell them they're my bankers,' she said crisply. 'They can look me up on their computer.'

During the weeks whilst the contract was going through she rang Tania, Pauline, Ed Posner, Clement, everyone she could think of, in an effort to discover an architect who would understand the kind of space and light she needed to show off the products. But in the event she found Alistair Brunton herself. He was gazing at the boatyard as she locked the door behind her after looking at it again once it was really hers.

'Do you own this place?' he asked.

'I do now.'

'You mean you've just bought it?'

Jill nodded, smiling. 'More or less yesterday.'

'Oh.' He looked disconsolate. 'I was just thinking what a marvellous studio it would make.'

Her interest quickened. 'Studio? Are you an artist?'

'No. An architect. We need more space. Business, I'm glad to say, is surprisingly good.' He smiled showing very white teeth in a tanned face. 'One of the virtues of designing for foreign countries. They don't seem to be as bothered by a diving economy as we are.'

'What sort of work do you do?'

'Mostly commercial. Schools, offices, theatres, shopping malls; a few houses if they're interesting.'

'May I look at samples of your work?' Jill asked. 'I want to convert this place into a gallery.'

He piloted her back to the centre of Frome and a small private car park behind an old building. 'We're on the first and second floors,' he smiled, guiding her to the door. 'Unfortunately there isn't a third or we needn't move.'

'Just like architects to have nice old buildings for themselves and build nasty modern ones for other people. Why can't you add a floor?'

'Planning permission. It wouldn't be in keeping with the rest of the street, and I agree with that restriction. But come and have a look at pictures of my nasty modern buildings,' he smiled.

As soon as Jill saw pictures of Alistair's buildings and conversions she knew he would be right for the boatyard.

'Tell me all about it over lunch,' he suggested. 'I can't concentrate when I'm hungry.'

He took her to an attractive little pub with a small first-floor dining room where a dumb waiter sent steaming food into the restaurant.

'I haven't broached the subject to the first two craftspeople I have in mind,' Jill said when she'd explained her ideas. 'But it struck me that they need an outlet and proper marketing. There must be others. I want the display area to be flexible, and the walls to accommodate pictures.'

It was pleasant to discuss her ideas with him. He seemed to grasp what she wanted immediately. 'How soon would I be able to see drawings?' she asked at the end of the lunch.

'I don't know . . . let's see, I'm going to Ghana for a week. There's a job out there I have to check on – I could sketch some ideas on the plane. It's a long flight. I can get one of the chaps to do some measuring, look at the services. I don't suppose there'll be any trouble over planning permission . . . I'll give you a call soon after I'm back.'

Jill drove home, her head buzzing. It was too premature to talk to Yvonne or Laura yet. When she had the plans, something concrete to show them, so that they could visualize what she had in mind, would be soon enough. The conversion would take weeks, probably months. It wouldn't do to raise their hopes. But she needed to find out if her hunch was right.

Over the next days, she combed local papers and county magazines for news of craft fairs and exhibitions, driving all over Wiltshire, Dorset and Somerset, making copious notes and collecting business cards. Tucked away in small villages and towns, she found local artists and potters, creative people who were not on the commercial map. She found a basket maker who worked in natural-coloured reeds and osiers; another discovery was a tall, slender girl who, paradoxically, forged iron, creating elegant modern fire irons and fire baskets. And a young man who sculpted in chicken wire, moulding graceful life-size animals. Some had the skill but not the style, like the wood-worker who made bowls which showed the fascinating grain of the wood but in heavy unaesthetic shapes. She itched to ask him to make them thinner, lighter, so that on a table they would look poised, as if ready for flight. She wanted to encourage them to create wares that were both attractive and saleable. She was becoming very excited about her venture.

Alistair Brunton telephoned on his return and asked her to come over and see his plans. 'They're at the first draft stage, but it looks as if it will work. Can you manage Wednesday? I have to go to the Midlands on Thursday and I'd like to present the ideas to you myself.'

On the long inside wall of the boathouse, facing the road, Alistair had blocked out the windows and suggested a wall of movable screens on sunken tracks which could slide to open or close, revealing well-lit alcoves for pottery or other artefacts; the screens themselves would be of cream, hessian-covered board. When they all slid together they could be used to exhibit pictures. At the narrow end was a video screen 'For your rich customers who can sit in comfort and see a whole range of an artist's work, or you might want to hire out the gallery sometimes to local societies, make it earn its keep.'

She nodded, feeling panicky at the thought that she had not allowed for such a lavish design in her business plan.

'We can cut corners,' Alistair suggested as if reading her mind. 'The screens aren't essential but I thought they'd make an adaptable display area.'

'No, no. I particularly like that idea. And I won't have to spend any money on stock. The idea is that the artists and artisans will supply their work on a sale or return basis.'

'You haven't asked how much all this will cost yet,' Alistair prompted.

'I bet I have a rough idea. I used to spend a lot of money on display once.' She gave him her estimate and he whistled admiringly.

'About five hundred out my way.'

They spent over an hour discussing the details. Jill liked his concentration and attention to the minutiae. She was leaning on one elbow, looking at his hands as they sifted through brochures of door handles and light fittings; thin and brown, with well-kept nails, they were capable, sensitive hands. She stole a look at his face, in profile next to hers, a straight brow, strong nose and then ridiculously long dark lashes making a deep shadow on his cheek. Alistair was very attractive but seemed unaware of it. He had made no attempt to use his charm, as some men would, to win her commission. Instead he'd relied on total confidence in his work.

When she left, having agreed the plans and signed an agreement for the work to be put in hand, subject to planning permission, she felt unaccountably forlorn. She wished he'd asked her to lunch again, it was nearly one o'clock. She liked talking to him and the prospect of a lonely return to the cottage wasn't appealing. She thought how much more enjoyable the project would be if she had someone to share it with. Douglas wouldn't have liked her striking out on her own. Once they'd moved to Dorset, he'd wanted her to be around all the time, blundering out of his study to call her and give her a hug, entering the kitchen to ask hopefully if it was time for coffee or tea. She realized, now, that that had been because he knew he had limited time.

Jill cheered up as she looked ahead to when the gallery would be opened. She would have a grand launch, ask the press down from London, invite the local art patrons. Then she'd need a brochure and a mailing list, particularly for overseas. She had business friends in several countries, she could ask for advice on whom to leaflet.

It was time to start approaching the artists. She spent the afternoon on the telephone. Some of the people she cold-called sounded suspicious, but Yvonne and Laura both grasped her plan immediately and were wildly enthusiastic. 'The standard has to be kept high,' Jill warned. 'Sometimes you'll be disappointed if I don't take something. But that'll be in your interests, too.'

'You mean it's a bit like the Craft Council in London,' the wire sculptor sneered.

'Roughly, but more commercial, less precious. A user-friendly gallery,' she laughed. 'I want anyone to be able to come in and wander round, get their eye in, perhaps save up for one beautiful thing even if they're hard up.'

'In that case I'm on,' he said promptly. 'I hate the hallowed hall atmosphere of the Craft Council. I always feel I have to talk in whispers. When will you come and look at my new stuff?'

Diane rang from *Nuages* and asked Jill if she would meet her for tea in the nearby small town. The days were longer now, but even so there was a violet mist wrapping the buildings; an elusive sun, which had made few appearances during the morning, had packed up for the day. When Jill arrived at the tea shop Diane had suggested, she was already there, sitting at a small round table, hugging a large brown envelope to her chest.

'Am I late?' Jill asked, kissing her without being rebuffed for once.

'No. I came early with some friends. They've gone to a cinema. I'm meeting them later.' She looked so much better. She was still slim, but she'd lost the painful bone-jutting angularity of the first weeks at Hedera House. Her skin looked clearer and her hair shinier.

'How are you?' Diane asked. Jill was surprised. She had so rarely asked after her.

'I'm fine.' She told her about the gallery project. She was fascinated when Diane ordered toast and honey and an assortment of cakes, and tucked into them unselfconsciously.

Diane looked up, catching Jill's amused gaze as she sunk her teeth into a piece of toast oozing butter, warmed honey dripping over her fingers. She laughed, licking her fingers. Jill had rarely heard her laugh, except for a sarcastic 'huh'.

'I seem to be hungry all the time! We cook for ourselves. I'm not much good yet. I've never learned, but I've bought a cookery book. This tea is on me,' she announced, helping herself to more toast. 'Daddy's money came through. I – I didn't have to pay out so much after all.' She looked down at her plate and dabbed up some crumbs with a licked finger. 'Chris has been arrested. He's in jail,' she shivered. 'It might have been me. Most of the money I owed was to him, I suppose you guessed?'

Jill nodded.

'Did you read about a drugs haul in Notting Hill Gate? It was in all the papers.'

It was news to Jill, and she said so.

'No names were mentioned, because it still has to go for trial.'

'I'm not the slightest bit sorry,' Jill said firmly. 'He was totally corrupt. I smelt evil as soon as I saw him.' She felt a bit peeved the police hadn't bothered to come back to her, but she supposed it was safer that way. Someone might get to hear she'd informed on Chris. She shivered in her turn.

'I don't want to go back to the flat. I've asked a local agent to sell it.'

Jill was amazed at the difference in her. Diane would never have been able to cope with the job of disposing of her flat before, or to talk so comparatively calmly about the repellent Chris.

'I'm glad,' Jill said quietly. 'Is there anything I can do to help? What about your furniture? You'll want another flat some day. I suppose you'll need to store it. Would you like me to deal with that?'

'Would you?' Diane asked shyly. 'I've been such a cow I'd understand if you didn't want anything to do with me.'

'You weren't yourself. I knew that. Of course I'll help, ninny.'

'You *can* mention the word "drugs" if you like,' Diane said calmly. 'We're taught to face up to the truth. We can't use euphemisms. *I was a drug addict.*' She said it slowly and then corrected herself. '*Am.*' Jill looked startled. 'No, don't be alarmed. I have to recognize that I'm vulnerable, that I mustn't take drugs ever again. Or alcohol.'

She was so matter of fact that Jill asked her if she was ready to leave the halfway house.

'Soon, I hope. There are times when I still feel wobbly and anxious, and I want to blot everything out. When I'm there I can call on anyone in the group, day or night, and they'll rally round.' She smiled. 'It's a wonderful feeling to know that.'

'I see.' Jill felt humble. She should have been there like that for this girl when she'd married her father. How insensitive she had been. 'And when you come out,' she asked carefully. 'Do you have any plans?'

Diane gulped her tea and helped herself to another cake. 'I was hoping I might come and stay with you for a while.'

'I'd love that,' Jill said looking at the bent head. 'I can't imagine anything nicer.'

'D'you mean it?' Diane looked up, hazel eyes, Douglas's eyes, boring into Jill's.

Jill nodded, unable to speak for pleasure.

There was a silence between them for a long moment and then Diane picked up the brown envelope. 'I'd like you to read this. It's a short story I've written. If it's any good I thought I might try to write for a living – like Daddy. Tom Feathers came back to me on the foreword I wrote, and was very flattering. But that was different. That didn't need any imagination. No, not *now*,' she cried as Jill attempted to take the manuscript out of the envelope. 'When you get home.'

'All right, and if I like it, what then? Send it to Tom?'

'Only if you think it's good enough. I'll have to go in a minute.' She glanced out of the café window and Jill followed her gaze. A tall, vaguely familiar figure went by and then came back again, peered in, and entered the shop. It was Alistair Brunton.

'So it *was* you,' he smiled. 'I caught a glimpse and then did a double take. I'm sorry, I'm not barging in – I'll sit over there. I'm dying for a cup of tea.'

'Diane, this is Alistair Brunton, the architect who's converting the boatyard I was telling you about. Diane is my stepdaughter.'

Diane said hullo cautiously, as if she wasn't sure whether she welcomed the interruption.

'We've virtually finished our tea. I can recommend the cream cakes!' Jill said mischievously, looking at Diane.

But Diane was gazing out of the window again. 'I must go. The gang's over there waiting for me.' She stood up and went to the cash desk to pay the bill.

Jill followed her. 'Let me have it.'

'No, no I want to.' She kissed Jill's cheek. 'Thank you for coming and don't lose that envelope.'

Jill stared after her as she hurried through the door and across a small green to a group of people standing round a parked car. She was definitely a different girl.

'Your stepdaughter?' Alistair queried. He'd sat at a different table and Jill joined him there. 'Then you're married?'

'Widowed.'

'I'm sorry.' There was a pause. 'Beautiful girl. Does she live here?'

'Nearby.'

A plump waitress who had been skulking behind a lace-curtained door came to the table Jill and Diane had been sitting at and started to clatter the cups and plates together in a meaningful way.

'I'd like some tea please,' Alistair called across to her pleasantly.

She scowled at him. 'We close at five.'

'Then you have twenty minutes, I think.' He watched her affronted back waddle into the kitchen and laughed as he turned back to Jill. 'Isn't this a crazy country? Sometimes you get the feeling that everyone hates to do business . . . Talking of which, we're starting on your place on Monday. I got a couple of estimates from some reliable builders I use in Frome. The plans were passed at the planning committee last week: one of my chaps phoned a pal of his on the Council and got a verbal OK. The written approval came yesterday.'

He sat back as the waitress barged up to the table; she plonked a teapot and cup and saucer heavily on the table. 'That was very quick.' Alistair smiled up at her sullen face. 'Nice and hot too.'

Her expression looked slightly less thunderous. 'Do you want any cakes?'

'Will my life be worth living if I say yes?'

This time she broke into an unwilling smile. 'I can get you some if you like.'

'Please. And another cup and saucer for my guest.'

'I've already had some.' Jill shook her head. 'So if they start on Monday, how long before it'll be ready?'

'I don't know. If my builder can put all his men on it, then three to four weeks. Depends on whether the special materials are delivered on time. It's all in hand though.' He sipped his tea and grimaced. 'Perhaps I shouldn't have insisted.'

When they left the tea shop it was almost dark. 'Where's your car?' he asked. 'I'll walk you to it.'

A few seconds later she fumbled clumsily with her keys and he took them from her.

263

'Here, let me,' Alistair opened the car door.

'Thanks.'

'Don't forget your lights.'

'No.' She felt unaccustomedly gauche.

He bent down as she switched on the engine. 'How long since your husband died?' he asked quietly.

'Nearly seven months.' She put the car in gear and lowered the window. 'Goodbye.'

He raised his hand in salute and stood watching as she drove away.

# Chapter Forty-five

Tania called for her so that they could go together to Pauline's nursery to pick some plants and vegetable seeds. 'I used to grow just those that the veg shops only seem to sell when they're large and old,' Tania observed. 'I don't bother with cabbage and brussels sprouts. Broad beans – they're so sweet and tender if you pick them really small, and baby courgettes. The shops don't seem to sell them until they're the size of cucumbers. I like them when they're thumb size. And tomatoes, of course – then you avoid those production-line tomatoes from Holland that are tasteless and watery. Oh dear, I do miss my vegetable garden.'

'Well I'm sure I'll have plenty of gluts; Gus is bound to produce enough for a small army.'

'Thanks. But you'll entertain more now, won't you?' Tania asked. 'Friends are important.'

'I know. But I haven't much enthusiasm for all that without Douglas. It doesn't get better does it?'

'Yes, it does. It becomes a chronic ache, you're aware of it all the time but it's not so debilitating that you can't carry on a normal life, enjoy things. You enjoyed the play, didn't you? And you're getting interested in gardening, and the summerhouse. Did you find an architect for that by the way?

'Oh, that wasn't why I wanted an architect. It won't be that grand. No, I'm playing round with a new project.' She told Tania about the gallery, on the river.

Tania was openly envious. 'If only I had had the courage to do something like that! I didn't have a career, just one of those useless jobs as a stop-gap before marriage. I know someone who makes beautiful outdoor pots, huge ones, so satisfyingly tactile that you want to stroke and pat them. They're weatherproof too – I'll take you to see her when you're ready.'

They arrived at the nursery to find Molly writing out an invoice for someone with a truck-load of plants. 'Pauline's in one of the greenhouses,' she said selfconsciously as Tania and Jill looked at her in frank amazement. The badly dyed rust-coloured hair that always seemed to have been nibbled by rats was replaced with a nimbus of silvery grey hair brushed smoothly up round her face. She was wearing pearl stud earrings and a plain navy sweater, with an expensive silk scarf round the neck, over navy pants. She had lost half a stone at least and it showed. They couldn't comment in front of the customer and merely exchanged looks and went off to find Pauline.

'I know. She's a changed woman,' she chuckled, when they said how attractive Molly looked. 'She had it dyed to match the roots, so that it grows out gracefully. And she's given up smoking too. Irritable as a dog with fleas. Don't say anything, but I think she's setting her cap at Alex McIntosh. She made him dance with her at that first night party – she was tight of course, she's always outrageous when she's had a drink or two.' She laughed good-humouredly. 'He drove her home, which was just as well with PC Heller in the audience, and he's been coming here once a week to play bridge ever since. Took her for a drive to Weymouth on Sunday. Now, come and see some special camellias and daphnes I've been hoarding for you. You'll go mad!'

When they got back to the cash desk Molly was writing out labels. 'I see my sister's about to relieve you of a small fortune again,' she nodded to their low trolley loaded with container-grown plants.

'Molly, you look wonderful!' Jill said warmly. 'I do like the new hairstyle, you look as though you're wearing a silver halo.'

'Halo!' snorted Pauline. 'Should be horns and a tail. She's brought the wrath of Arabella down on us.'

Molly gave her familiar schoolgirl hoot of laughter. 'I only offered Jamesie a job in the nursery for the summer.' She drew herself up and puffed out her cheeks in an imitation of Arabella. ' "My son's not a hireling, Molly. He's going to Oxford or Sandhurst, I haven't made up my mind which yet." ' Her mimicry was perfect. 'I have to hand it to Jamesie, though. He looked embarrassed – this, as usual, was taking place in Watson's, which was fairly full at the time – but he said quite firmly that he'd like to talk to me about it and when could he come over. She dumped her shopping in his arms and pushed him out of the shop.'

'But James telephoned shortly afterwards and he's going to start here next week,' Pauline added with satisfaction.

Tania drove with Jill to the cottage to pick up her own car.

'Stay to supper,' Jill suggested. 'You told me to entertain more, didn't you? I've bought a small loin of lamb, too much for one. Anyway, I've an idea I want to put to you.'

'Thanks, that would be nice. But let's find places for the loot first.'

Jill looked in vain for the duck as they worked out where the sweet-smelling daphnes were to go. She was disappointed at its non-appearance. Tania urged her to keep the camellias in big pots on the paved area outside the kitchen door. 'You can move them to the deck of the summerhouse when you've built it.'

Over supper, in the small dining room alight with candles, and with a bowl of primroses from the garden in the centre of the table, Jill asked Tania if she'd like a job in the gallery.

'I've got to have someone to mind the shop while I'm dashing around looking for new acquisitions. It can't be just anyone. I want someone who has taste and style, who'd be able to handle customers sympathetically, who'd make an effort to be clued up on the various artists and their work. It needn't be full time to start with. What do you say?'

'Me?'

'I said someone with taste and style.'

'Yes!' Tania said promptly. 'No second thoughts. I've been thinking what a good idea it is ever since you told me about it this afternoon. I was longing to be involved. But I told you I've never had a serious job before.'

'I'll take a chance.' Jill smiled.

When Tania left at about ten o'clock they had it all cut and dried, the opening discussed and the hours Tania would work. Jill discovered Tania knew quite a few cultivated people in the area who would be prospective customers and useful to invite to the launch.

'My husband's job,' she explained. 'We used to get around a lot. He was chairman of a group of West Country newspapers.'

Next morning Jill telephoned Tom Feathers about Diane's short story. '*I* like it; it's curious and offbeat, but the characters are very well observed. I don't know enough about publishing to know whether it's saleable, say in a magazine, but it's worth your seeing.'

'Of course. And whilst you're on, the publishers want to launch *From Dark to Light* in May. Will you and Diane feel up to press interviews? There'll be a great deal of media interest but it might be painful for you to talk about Douglas.'

'I'm not keen. But it would depend on the journalist. Some can be crass, but I know they'll need to promote the book.'

'You can be selective.'

She told him about the gallery.

'I'm glad you're picking up the threads again. Why don't you insist on being interviewed there? They'll do it if they want you enough. It doesn't hurt to be a little hard to get sometimes.'

Ten days later Diane asked to spend the weekend with her.

'May I bring a friend? Well, she's my minder really. They don't like us to go anywhere alone. She's the one who mostly holds my hand when I'm in a state. I think you'll like her. She's called Jo.'

Mrs B and Jill moved the divan from the dressing room into the spare room and made up the beds. Jill was torn between looking forward to the weekend, glad of this further proof that Diane was better, and apprehensive in case she put her foot in it.

When Alistair Brunton rang to ask her to come to Frome on Saturday, to see how the work was progressing, she had to decline.

'I can't,' she said regretfully. 'My stepdaughter's coming for the weekend.'

'Wouldn't she like to come too?'

'Not this time.'

He sounded disappointed, and explained, 'It's coming on well but I want to make a small alteration to the plans and I need your approval.' They arranged a Monday afternoon meeting instead.

Jill drove to *Nuages* early on Saturday morning. It was a lovely day and unseasonably warm; primroses were studding the banks, so prolific in places they looked like large plates of scrambled egg, and the bluebells were in bud in the woods, not yet in their full-flowering intensity but giving a faint blue smudge under the trees. Jill felt her spirits rise.

Diane was waiting for her clutching a small suitcase on her lap and looking tensely at the door. Next to her was a woman a few years older, with sharp, watchful eyes set in a plain, pale face. Her hair was mousy, cropped short, and she wore rimless glasses. Diane got up eagerly and brought her companion forward by her hand.

'This is Jo Robinson. My stepmother, Jill.'

'Pleased to meet you,' Jo said in a nasally cockney voice, without smiling.

'It's a beautiful day,' Jill said conversationally, shepherding them out of the house and into the car. 'Such a lovely drive here. I'm beginning to believe summer is just around the corner at last. Is Jo short for Josephine?'

'No Joan. I hate it. I hate Josephine too.'

That seemed to end all conversation for a bit, but once in the cottage things warmed up.

'It's lovely!' exclaimed Jo. 'I've never been in a real cottage before. It's like those pictures in story books.' She wandered around, touching things, peering into the inglenook, stroking the bare stone above it. 'I live in a council flat in Stepney,' she announced. 'It's ugly and dirty. Kids spraycan the walls. I used to meself,' she said candidly. 'There's nothing else to do except frighten people. I used to do that too, specially old people.'

'Jo was a drug addict too,' said Diane matter of factly. 'We all are at *Nuages*. But she used to inject. Show her your arms Jo.'

Jo willingly pushed up her sleeves and held out scarred arms. 'And me feet,' she added. 'I got hepatitis. That's when I went to rehab, after hospital,' she said bluntly.

Appalled, Jill struggled to appear as calm and casual as her guests. 'I have a letter for you,' she turned to Diane. 'It came yesterday morning.' She knew it was from Tom Feathers and prayed that it was encouraging.

Diane went white as she read it and her hands shook. Jill noticed that Jo moved protectively near her.

'He likes it,' she said in a whisper. 'He likes my short story. He thinks he can sell it to *Granta*. Read it.' She thrust the stiff white letter at Jill.

Dear Diane,

Jill has sent me your short story, and I must say I read it with real enjoyment. I don't know if you know the magazine *Granta* but it has a good reputation for producing new writing and I feel pretty sure they will take it.

I don't know whether you intend to write any more, but on the evidence of your foreword to *From Dark to Light*, and now this, I think you should go on. If you do want to write for a living I would be happy to talk to you, and if you feel like coming to London to have some lunch and discuss whether you would like me to represent you, as I did your father for nearly thirty years, please give my secretary a ring to fix a date.

    Kindest regards,
      Yours sincerely,
      Tom Feathers

'Well well well,' Jill said smiling. 'Who else would have an agent of Tom Feathers' reputation *asking* to represent them. He must be impressed! Congratulations.'

'You don't think he's just being kind because of Daddy?' Diane asked anxiously.

'He couldn't sell a story to *Granta* on that basis,' Jill said decisively. 'Nor would he want to sign you up.'

Diane smiled widely and looked at Jo, waiting for her approval.

Jill realized she had rarely seen the girl smile so happily. It made her look about fourteen. She was moved when Jo went over and put her arms round Diane and kissed her.

'Let's go for a walk whilst the sun's out,' Jill suggested. 'Jo hasn't seen how lovely the countryside is around here. And then we'll have some lunch.'

She couldn't believe how docile Diane was. There was no

trace of the mood swings she'd experienced the previous time she'd stayed.

'I'm going home next week,' Jo volunteered. 'At least, I'm going home until I can find a job and somewhere to live on my own.'

'That'll be lovely,' Jill said warmly. 'I expect your parents will be pleased to see you.'

'Only me Mum. Me Dad's in clink. Breaking and entering. About his tenth conviction. He won't care. Me Mum will,' she added. 'She was worried sick about me before. She's a dinner lady,' she added inconsequentially.

'Jo wants to train to be a nurse,' Diane put in. 'Only she hasn't any O'levels.'

'I can be an auxiliary though,' Jo added. 'And at least I can live in a nurses' home. Mr Wright is going to see what he can do.'

'Mr Wright is the administrator at *Nuages*,' Diane added. 'He tries to help people resettle outside. I think I can leave soon, too. Will that be all right?' she turned to Jill. 'You did say I could come and stay, but I wasn't sure you really meant it.'

'I'm longing for you to come home,' Jill put her arm across Diane's shoulders. She was surprised to see Diane turn her head away to dash tears from her eyes. The drops twinkled in the sun as she sent them flying with the back of her hand.

Next morning, Jill was up early, woken by the sun streaming through the east-facing window of the bedroom. As she looked out of the window she saw the duck waddling up towards her, and behind her, self-importantly following, were ten or eleven little brown and yellow powder puffs. She couldn't believe her eyes. So that's where the duck had been all this time, sitting on a well-hidden nest somewhere.

She went quietly into the garden with a handful of bread and gently threw it towards the mother duck. Then she sat down on the old wooden bench and waited. The fluffy ducklings scurried about, heeding the mother's warning clucks, pecking at the ground in a businesslike way. Jill marvelled at their self-sufficiency already. She wished for Douglas so intensely, wanting to show him this little family, that she couldn't believe

271

he wouldn't come out behind her, laughing delightedly and crowing that he had always known there would be ducks.

She went inside to make some coffee, her eyes damp. Diane came into the kitchen. Her hair was nearly shoulder length now, thick and straight and shining again.

Jill gave her a clear-eyed smile.

'You're up early! Come with me, I want to show you something.'

Diane followed her outside and gave a cry of delight.

'Oh, the darlings!'

'I've just thrown them some bread, but I expect they prefer worms and beetles and things we don't want to think about before breakfast.'

'I'll hurry Jo up. I bet she hasn't seen ducks this small before.'

Jill drove both girls back in the early afternoon. Jo had picked primroses and budding bluebells on their walk the day before, though Jill had tried to restrain her. 'But there's so many,' she'd protested, bewildered. 'You can't want them all. I shall think of this when I'm in London.'

Jill gave up. Obviously she had had so few pleasures in her grimy life and wasn't used to wild flowers. 'You must come to stay again,' she had said.

Jill had baked cakes and scones for tea, and she packed the leftovers in a plastic box for them to take back.

'At this rate, when I see you again I'll be as fat as a pig,' Diane told her.

In the evening Jill sat outside again, wrapped in Douglas's old coat, as though by wearing it she could share with him the pleasure of watching the ducks bobbing along the river until they were out of sight. She hoped they would tuck themselves in somewhere where a fox couldn't get them.

As she stared into the fading twilight, thinking of Douglas, she realized that for the first time since he had died, she could recall him in total; his smile, his large comfortable body, his strong voice. The angry hurt she had felt at not being able to visualize his features seemed to seep away, and she felt a calm, peaceful acceptance of his death, a gratitude that she had known such love.

# Chapter Forty-six

The road to Frome was blocked by a serious accident on Monday and Jill was held up and then diverted through another route, so that she was late arriving at the boatyard. Alistair Brunton was pacing up and down outside, looking impatiently along the road she should have come in by, so that she surprised him by arriving from another direction. She gave a little toot on the horn and his relief was obvious as he saw her. He rushed to open the car door.

'I thought you weren't coming,' he said. 'I've been so anxious to hear what you think. We're ahead of schedule.' He led the way into the boatyard. 'I thought I'd better sneak some more space for the cloakrooms, which means the reception area is smaller, so I want your approval on that.' He switched on the lights. 'Do you like it?'

Jill stood entranced. The floor wasn't finished and there were workmen all over the place, but the screens were up. The blocked-up windows in the wall had been replaced by skylights in the roof, like glittering dormer windows. 'It can make a row when it rains, but you get every ray of light there is,' he explained, racing ahead of her like a small boy, opening and shutting screens and windows, pulling out the storage trays. 'There are dimmer switches on every light so that you can change the atmosphere – these are the special low-voltage lights which they use in the top art galleries. You can get a pool of brightness on a pot, and soft light around it to throw it into relief.'

He showed her a sample of a low table. 'Several of these, I suggest, down the centre to display the goods. It's made by a young furniture designer from that Makepeace place in Beaminster; are you going in for small pieces of furniture? I'm sure he'd let you have these at a low price in return for getting a credit in your catalogue.'

'I don't see why not. I hadn't thought of furniture yet, but small pieces would fit in. I don't want the place cluttered. That's why I'm going to have a glossy, loose-leaf catalogue to show each artist's full range. Sometimes of course I'll give an entire exhibition to one artist if he or she merits it.'

'You really believe in this, don't you?' he asked looking into her face.

'Of course. I couldn't do it otherwise.'

'We'll be through in about ten days, I think. Eddy, my builder, has another job on and he's hurried these guys through so that he can switch them to the new site.'

Alistair shuffled his papers together and stuffed them into a bulging folder, tucking it under his arm as he guided her to the door. 'That's it then. I'm glad you're pleased.'

'Absolutely delighted.'

He looked at his watch. 'Nearly a quarter to six. If you can wait whilst I check on things back at the office, I'll buy you a drink. Unless of course you have an engagement and want to rush off?'

'No, no engagement. I'd like a drink after that journey. It was very trying.' She didn't like to say that as she no longer had drink in the house, the idea was particularly appealing.

'Leave your car here then, and I'll bring you back for it afterwards.' She lowered herself into the bucket-shaped seat of his Porsche.

'I thought only advertising men had Porsches,' Jill challenged him.

'I know. I'm slightly embarrassed by it really, but it *is* so beautiful. I find myself stroking it sometimes! Hopeless for passengers in the back, but then that doesn't bother me now.'

'Now?'

'I used to have a wife and son. Sam had to go in the back then. I still have a son,' he said hastily as he saw her sympathetic expression. 'But Sue and I are divorced, so Sam sits in the front now. He's nine.'

'Is he with you?'

'On and off. Weekends, holidays. Not enough.'

'I'm sorry.'

'Don't be. Except for Sam, I'm much happier now on my

own. Here we are.' He parked behind his office. 'Come up and meet the chaps. Cyril has done a lot of work on your plans.'

When Alistair was eventually through with his messages and letters to sign, they drove to an old house outside Frome that had been converted into a small country hotel. The bar was furnished with deep armchairs and sofas, and copies of *Country Life* and *Horse and Hound* were strewn around. It was totally empty. 'It's a bit early. I hope they'll serve us.'

As he spoke a young woman came into the room to take their order.

'White wine, please,' said Jill.

'Make that a bottle.'

'No, please. You forget I have to drive home. I don't want to be breathalysed.'

It was very quiet and pleasant. Jill told him again how pleased she was with the conversion and he said she was an ideal client, decisive but open to suggestions.

'What was your job? You mentioned display,' he asked.

She explained about Fred's and its lowly beginnings. 'It was fun at the time but I didn't really want to go back after my husband died. It no longer seemed a challenge.'

'I saw your face when you told me you were a widow. You haven't accepted it yet, have you?'

'I have now. It was strange. Until yesterday I'd been unable to visualize Douglas properly. I felt cheated and upset, as if I hadn't loved him enough. I was angry that he was taken away when we'd had so little time together. But yesterday, sitting in the twilight after my stepdaughter had gone, I had total recall. His voice, his smile, his body, and suddenly this sense of peace. I knew I'd stopped being angry at the waste, that I'd come to terms with his loss. I think it was the ducklings.'

'The ducklings?' He looked blank and she wondered why she was talking like this to someone she hardly knew.

'There's a narrow river at the bottom of the garden. It was choked and neglected when we moved in, but Douglas and the gardener cleared it. He wanted to build a summerhouse there and watch the sunsets. He used to insist there were ducks on the river. I'd pull his leg about it because it's not much more than a stream really. But then there really was a duck some weeks ago. I tried to encourage it, but when it disappeared I was very upset. And then, yesterday, she appeared on the lawn, heading a family of eleven ducklings. Somehow it made Douglas real again, as if something he believed in was true. I can't explain it,' she broke off, feeling embarrassed. 'I'm sorry, it must be the wine.'

'Then you must have another glass.'

She was grateful for his tact. 'I don't think I ought to.'

'You said you had nothing on, would you like to have dinner with me? We could have it here, the restaurant is one of the best around.'

'I must get back.'

'Why? If you don't have dinner with me I shall be forced back to my little Frome flat to eat by myself. And I can assure you when you've had defrosted quiche varied with defrosted pizza, eating in a restaurant with a companion is a real treat.'

She laughed. 'All right. That diet sounds disgusting!'

Over the meal, Alistair talked about his jobs in foreign countries. He had designed a new university in Ghana; he was working on plans for a hotel in Bali. 'Bali is so beautiful that I almost resent making it more comfortable for tourists, but the Balinese need their money.' And he was signed up to convert a Victorian monstrosity in the Midlands into flats.

She liked the different expressions that chased across his tanned face. He had the same enthusiasm for his work as Miles, but there was little sign of a large ego. She watched his hands. He used them a lot to explain a point, to describe a shape. She wanted to hold one, to feel the warmth of a man's hand in hers, and was alarmed at the feeling.

'Why are you divorced?' she asked suddenly. 'Sorry, that's rude. It's no business of mine.'

'It was one of those hideous mistakes, nobody's fault. Just youth. We were both twenty-two, wet behind the ears, with totally different perceptions of what we wanted to do with our lives. Unfortunately when we realized that, Sam was already on the way. We stuck it out for five more years, then Sue met someone else, so we "rationalized" our relationship as they say. No hard feelings. I just wish I could see more of Sam.'

\* \* \*

He drove her back to her car, lonely in its dark, empty parking space in front of the gallery.

'Thanks so much for taking pity on me,' he said as he opened the car door for her.

'It wasn't pity, it was a pleasure,' Jill said, and meant it. She had enjoyed the evening. It was so nice after all this time to be with a man, though she felt there was more to it than that; she acknowledged a disquieting undertow of attraction on her part, and of that she felt ashamed.

# Chapter Forty-seven

Although the builders had finished on time, the gallery opening was going to have to be delayed because of the non-delivery of the reception area furniture. Alistair telephoned Jill with the news, furious with the laconic manufacturer.

'That's what's wrong with this country. There's no sense of urgency, of being businesslike and efficient. I've tried for alternatives but that won't save time now; this was being specially made.'

Jill was fed up but philosophical. She was used to delivery delays at Fred's. 'Don't worry,' she reassured him. 'I need all the time I can get to be ready myself.' She didn't explain to him that Diane was coming home. Mr Wright, the administrator at *Nuages*, had telephoned suggesting the end of the following week. She wanted to be around for her arrival, not dashing off preoccupied with the gallery.

Jill had rearranged the spare bedroom to make it more like a sitting room, and had eventually tracked down a television for the dressing room. She'd also added a small writing table from her own room. She collected Diane on a rainy Saturday, feeling nervous. She refused to look ahead to the time when Diane would be ready to take off again on her own. She wanted to make her life so pleasant and comfortable that she would be happy to stay in the cottage. Roger Mander would tell her that she was being dangerously possessive and, subconsciously, she knew it herself but she felt compelled to hang on to this last physical link with Douglas.

Once she moved in, Diane had a touching desire to be with Jill. She followed her about the cottage and garden, accompanied her into the village, hung around her when Jill was working. Jill assumed it was because she still wasn't totally ready to be alone.

*Nuages* had given Diane the address of Narcotics Anonymous.

'I can call them for help if I feel I'm sinking,' she said simply. 'I have to realize I'm more vulnerable than other people.'

In some ways Jill felt Diane's new self-knowledge made her seem the more mature of the two of them, and yet in other ways she was childish. She had Joey the white-faced clown on her bed, and often tucked it under her arm as she trotted about the house after Jill.

Anxious to take up Tom Feathers' offer of lunch, yet afraid to go to London alone, Diane rang and fixed a date and then diffidently asked Jill to go with her. 'I have a panicky feeling I'll meet Chris,' she explained. 'I know he's in jail but I'm terrified he'll get me for not paying up.'

Jill went with her on the train, worrying whether she should alert Tom to the dangers of alcohol for Diane, but in the end decided it wasn't fair to her. She had to have faith in Diane's own ability to cope. She'd arranged to have lunch with Carla whilst Diane met with Tom.

Fingles had insisted on Carla working out her notice. Despite the inconvenience Fred Rosomon was delighted by this re-assurance that Carla was so valuable.

'Of course I'm buying for Fred's anyway. I just give Rosomon the list of the stuff I've seen at the shows and he puts in the orders. I'm working like stink doing two jobs at once and it's cost me Paul.'

'I thought he was so perfect.'

'He was, as long as he came first. He says he won't play second fiddle to a dress shop. So much for equality. Made me mad, calling Fred's a dress shop.'

'What else is it?'

'A way of life,' Carla said grandly, and giggled. She relished the prospect of her new job and repeated that Jill was mad to have turned it down. 'You wait, I shall get Rosomon to add my accessories boutique sooner or later. It'll be a natural expansion.'

When Jill met Diane at Waterloo for the return journey, she was beaming and couldn't stop talking. 'Tom was so stimulating. He told me it was important to have a routine,' she said solemnly. 'Graham Greene wrote every day, sometimes only

279

two hundred and fifty words, but he produced a book a year. He said if you keep at it, writing and rewriting, you have to improve.'

'As you know Douglas was disciplined, too,' Jill said. 'Every morning, sometimes as early as six o'clock, he'd work in his study. He didn't like being interrupted but sometimes he'd wander out, sniffing the air as a hint I should make him some coffee.'

Diane had told Tom she had an idea for a novel and now she reported, 'He was very pleased. I have to write a synopsis and three or four sample chapters. Then he can sell it to a publisher and I get an advance.'

'*If* they like it,' Jill said warningly. 'Don't raise your hopes too high just because you've had a little early success. Remember Douglas had loads of rejections in the beginning.'

Diane put Tom's advice into operation immediately. When she wasn't writing in her little room she was reading copiously. She helped Jill, and she kept her own quarters clean and tidy rather than let Mrs B touch them. 'It's a bit degrading to have other women do your dirty work don't you think?' she said to Jill.

'I don't know. She's unskilled and she needs the money. I don't think that's exploitive if one doesn't treat her like some inferior being. It frees me to do the work I do best.'

They had several such discussions. Diane's social conscience seemed to have been awakened at Hedera House and *Nuages*. Jill enjoyed their conversations. She wondered what it would have been like with Douglas there. It was sad that he had been an intermittent father, indulgent one minute, absent the next. Diane hadn't mentioned her mother once. Jill wondered how she felt about Frances now. Her own anger against the unknown woman had risen again like a black bile. Diane was hers now by default.

Shortly after their trip to town the Boathouse Gallery opened. Tania had sent invitations to all her friends; Jill had urged hers to come down from London, including some of the fashion press who she thought might like the idea of the gallery, the river, and parts of the old town as locations for a shoot. It wouldn't hurt the gallery's artefacts to be featured in the glossies as background.

The local press were all lined up, and all the exhibiting artists were present, their CVs neatly printed below colour pictures of their work. It was as crowded as a private view. Caterers were there to pour champagne and offer refreshments: pastry shaped like miniature ceramic pots stuffed with crabmeat, smoked salmon and chicken.

Jill darted among the throng, spots of hectic colour in her cheeks, her dark curly hair springing round her head as Douglas had liked. She watched Diane stolidly refusing all offers of champagne, carefully sticking to mineral water, and was proud of her. Who would recognize the bony wretch who had been so maladjusted?

Only when it was all over did they sink on to the new furniture, exhausted.

'I think that went very well,' Tania said decidedly. 'Laura could have sold that large blue bowl over and over, and I heard someone ask that young man who made the tables if he accepted commissions.'

'Well, it's not volume business, that's for sure,' Jill yawned. 'In any case I didn't expect many people to buy at the opening. Let's go home now, I'm whacked.' She wanted the quiet solitude of the cottage. Since the duck had reappeared she felt Douglas's presence constantly. She could understand why some people went to mediums after they'd lost someone they loved. But she needed to find her own mode of living without Douglas now, and perhaps the gallery was the answer. She locked up and followed Tania and Diane to the car.

She saw Alistair getting into his own car at the other end of the car park, behind Laura and a new boyfriend who was having a job to get Laura in his car. She was giggling and distinctly tight, wanting to dance round the car park.

On impulse Jill went across to Alistair. 'Thank you once more for making such a splendid job of the boatyard – and for coming today. I really appreciate it.'

He looked up at her unsmiling. 'I suppose I won't see you again now?'

'Why not? I'll be in Frome often. It's my turn to invite you to supper.' She spoke brightly, conscious of an unspoken sub-text.

He looked at her a minute longer, and then nodded coolly. 'I see. Well I'm glad it went well.' He gave another nod and got into his car.

Jill returned glumly to the others. He had misunderstood.

# Chapter Forty-eight

In September, Jill went to Paris. She had received a request for ceramic samples and decided it was more useful to go in person, to establish contact with the shop in question. She now had three potters on the gallery list, and she hoped to launch them on the international market. Tania, as she had suspected, was immensely capable and thoroughly enjoying her new rôle. She could safely be left in charge.

Diane was writing seriously, sending each chapter to the long-suffering Tom for comment before she would tackle another. He had got her an advance from a small publisher for her proposed novel, and she was scrupulous in keeping to the routine he had suggested. When not writing, she had made friends with Claudine and was besotted by the underweight scrap of humanity that was Claudine's and Tom's child, born nine weeks prematurely.

Jill had taken Diane to see Claudine once the baby had come home, and Diane had taken one look at the screwed-up, mewling face, the tiny waving hands on red stick-like arms, and fallen in love with her. Now, whenever she could, she would act as unpaid nursemaid to Serena. 'It must be lovely to have a baby,' she had said to Jill. 'Wouldn't you have liked a daughter?'

'Yes. But I have one now.'

Diane had looked startled for a moment. 'I can't think of you as my mother,' she said seriously. 'More as my friend. Is that hurtful?'

Disappointed at her reply, Jill had shaken her head un-truthfully. 'It's just that you're all I have left of Douglas, I suppose I'm in danger of becoming possessive.'

'Friends are better than mothers. You can't choose your mother.' Diane's expression was desolate just for a moment.

It was then that Jill had screwed up her courage to suggest that Diane should have Douglas's study and learn how to use his word processor. It was something she had considered when she saw Diane writing laboriously by hand, crumpling sheets of paper, throwing them away, and painstakingly rewriting. Then the sheets had to go to a freelance typist in the village. But at first Jill had not been able to bear the idea of anyone but Douglas sitting at that desk.

Diane's eyes had widened. 'Do you really mean it?'

'Yes. It seems wicked to keep that room empty, a useless monument. All that expensive equipment going to waste. I should have let you have it ages ago. He was very proud of it.'

Diane did move into Douglas's study and Jill found, after the initial twinge of regret, that it didn't hurt. She would go up there after she came home from the gallery and sit in the armchair to chat with Diane, to hear how the day's work had gone. The room was full of Douglas's presence but now it was a comforting presence not a distressing one.

She had no qualms now about leaving Diane for a few days whilst she looked around Paris for other possible outlets. She spent a lot of time with Claudine and the baby, and James was often about in the evenings, taking her on walks or challenging her to a game of tennis which, according to a rueful James, she played rather well. And Miriam had offered to have her to stay at night if she was nervous of being alone.

On the way back Jill's plane was delayed. She telephoned Diane from Paris to explain that she would be late, and sat resigned to a long wait in the airport lounge, combing through some French art magazines she had bought. Delays and re-scheduled flights had happened to her so often on her buying trips that she'd long ago given up indulging in futile fuming and fretting.

'What is it that's so riveting in there?' a voice said. Looking up coldly to freeze the pick-up, she stared straight into Alistair's blue eyes. 'You haven't lifted your eyes from that magazine for ten minutes.' He was smiling at her, a touch tentatively, as if not sure of his welcome.

'I don't believe it!' she exclaimed. 'Are you on this plane?'

'Yes. I've just checked at the desk. We're in danger of being sent to Manchester. There seems to be fog at Heathrow. Shall we go and have a drink? You can tell me how well the gallery is doing. I've popped in once or twice, but I always see your assistant.'

She followed him to the bar.

'Champagne?'

'Goodness. How lovely!'

'Why didn't you phone me? You said you were going to ask me to supper.'

'I did,' she said carefully. 'I was always told you were away. I thought it was a tactful brush-off.'

'Is that the truth?'

'Yes.'

'Then I'm glad I ordered champagne.'

They sat there, gazing at each other. Then he smiled, and picked up her hand. 'Are you still in love with your husband?'

She looked down at his brown hand clasping hers and felt its dry warmth.

'I always will be,' she looked at him candidly.

'And there's no room for anyone else?'

She was saved from answering by the booming announcement that their flight was being called, and there was a rush of impatient passengers to the boarding gate. They gulped the last of their drinks and collected their hand luggage. Their seats were in different parts of the plane but Alistair whispered to the stewardess who tactfully asked the man next to Jill if he would swap.

'You haven't answered my question,' he said after they'd fastened their seat belts and listened to the mechanical recording of the safety instructions. 'I'll put it another way. If I call at the gallery tomorrow, would you be able to face having dinner with me?'

Jill felt a churning in her stomach. 'I'd like that very much,' she said quietly.

The plane thundered along the runway and soared effortlessly into the sky. Jill leant back and closed her eyes. She could see Douglas smiling.

**THE END**

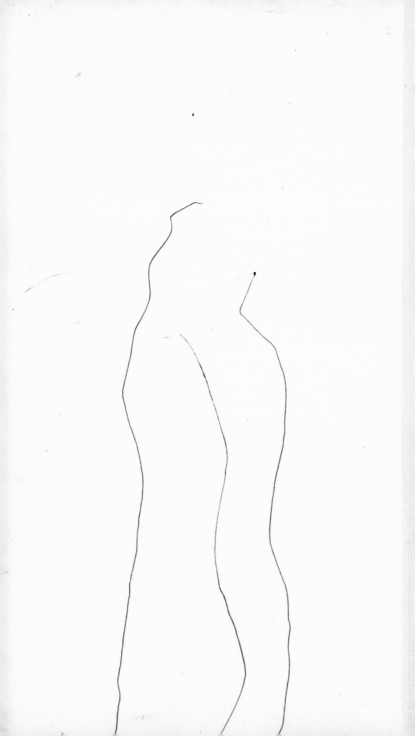